A Tale of a Ring

Ilan Sheinfeld

Translated from the Hebrew by Anthony Berris

The Jew always wanders to his homeland.
And in his homeland too.
The essence of Judaism is yearning.

Esperanza Gantz

One

Many years ago in Sedlec there lived a couple, Naphtali Breine and his wife Bruria, and their life was wretched in the extreme. Six times Mrs. Breine conceived, and six times she gave birth to a boy or girl. At first the infants appeared to be healthy, but after three or four months they began to convulse and a cherry-red stain appeared in the white of their eyes. Not two years elapsed from the appearance of the stain until they departed this world.

This happened six times and the Breines almost made up their minds not to bring any more children into the world. How much anguish can a person suffer? To carry an unborn soul for nine months, deliver a boy or girl, nurse the infant with its mother's milk and its father's hopes, sustain it for a few months, pray to God, give charity for the little one's soul, and finally to wake up one morning and find it convulsing and its eyes gaping at the world around it with the same malignant stain in them. This infant, too, would restore its soul to the Creator and be buried beside its brothers and sisters in the row of small graves in the Sedlec cemetery.

In the end Mrs. Breine was with child for the seventh time. This time she gave birth to a girl named Reine-Chaya. This daughter neither convulsed nor did her eye bear the stain. For three years she grew undisturbed and filled her parents' hearts with joy.

But there are people who attract the torments of the world, and of all the world's dwellers these malaises choose to settle in their hearts. This is what happened to the Breines and their daughter, Reine-Chaya, whose given name was not enough to cleanse her of suffering. The illness, falling sickness, was first discovered at the termination of Yom Kippur. The cantor in the Great Synagogue of Sedlec concluded the recitation of the *Kaddish* mourner's prayer and his lips were already murmuring the supplication, "Next Year in Jerusalem", and the verse "He who maketh peace in his high places" stood ready on his parched lips, lips that longed for food and drink like those of every Jew at the end of a day of fasting. After the *shofar* was blown for the last time, precisely at the end of the concluding prayer, little Reine-Chaya collapsed in the women's section of the synagogue.

She stopped breathing, the veins in her little neck began bulging, and white, blood-flecked froth began oozing from her mouth. Her mother saw this and started screaming '*Shema Yisrael*', Hear, O Israel. The Jews, weak from fasting and prayer, hurried to her side.

The child lay on the floor, convulsing like an animal whose time has come. The rabbi and the beadle pressed on the corners of her mouth, trying to prize it open so she would not, Heaven forbid, swallow her tongue and die of suffocation. As they did this her mother could hear the women of Sedlec chattering among themselves saying that one of the local demons had entered the child's body. And if it had done so just at the end of Yom Kippur, then it was surely a sign that Mrs. Breine had committed a transgression of modesty.

She was beside herself with grief and could not answer them. The moment her daughter opened her eyes she hugged her amid the sweat and froth, blessed the living God, and hastened to carry her home. But the memory of the words uttered behind her back did not leave her. Even then she realized that when her daughter reached marriageable age she would have difficulty in finding her a husband, and so she would have to do everything in her power to find a cure for her.

Throughout her youth Reine-Chaya was tortured by all the cures that were tried on her. When she was a girl her mother would mix oil with her own milk and drop it onto the back of a silver spoon, and then drip five drops onto the top of the little one's head and with both her hands rub it into the fontanel. Even when the child suffered an attack of falling sickness her mother would do this, but to no avail. It was a wonder she survived those days.

Mrs. Breine went to consult Shlomo-Yitzhak, the epicene miracle worker who lived in Sedlec.

Shlomo-Yitzhak was renowned in the region for his wisdom and magic. Jews and gentiles alike from the villages and big towns would come to him seeking his advice. If gentiles asked him where his powers came from, he would tell them that many years ago, before he reached bar-mitzvah age, he awoke in the middle of the night and saw before him a slender angel with two pairs of wings. The angel extended a hand of light and touched his forehead – and since then he had been a seer. To other gentiles, particularly those richer than the others and who did not believe in angels, he would say that once he awoke in the middle of the night and before him stood a dead woman's spirit. The spirit entered him, and since then he had been a seer.

Only the graybeards of Sedlec knew that the spirit that had entered him was the spirit of his mother, Chaya-Esther the witch, and by virtue of this he began wearing his mother's clothes and growing breasts.

Shlomo-Yitzhak gave Mrs. Breine nine pieces of iron to put under the infant's pillow. But to no avail. He therefore counseled her to wait until she grew a bit and then give her nine mustard seeds to swallow every morning.

Reine-Chaya would remember the taste of that mustard for a long time. It had the taste of bile, but the taste of a cure it did not have at all. Her attacks continued and worsened as she grew up.

Then her mother decided to seek the advice of a gentile healer. Since he was not a Jew, the terrors of the marsh did not assail him and so he went with her to the big marsh outside Sedlec, picked for her several species of herbs and roots, and adjured her to swear to cook the herbal mixture in four cups of water and give her daughter three glasses of the brew a day before she ate a morsel. This concoction had been tried and tested, and had even helped the falling sickness of the wife of the wealthy landowner of Sedlec, whose name had been Crochety Chava-Leah until her convulsions ceased and her irascibility vanished. But Reine-Chaya was not cured by it. Then her mother traveled to consult with the sages of Pshiskhe from whence she returned with a particularly revolting medicine.

The sages of Pshiskhe told her that in order to drive out the sickness from the patient, it must be made abhorrent to her by feeding her the most disgusting food. So she went to the market, bought a donkey and slaughtered it, and then roasted the beast's liver and gave it to her daughter to eat. The child filled her belly with the donkey's roasted liver – and vomited her heart out. But a cure did not come of it.

Her mother did not give up and cooked the most repulsive dish the sages of Pshiskhe had taught her. On the edge of the marketplace she sought a cat that had just had kittens, took the afterbirth and dried it on a storehouse roof. Once the afterbirth had hardened she ground it into a powder, went to the flourmill with nine grains of wheat, made flour and mixed it with the cat flour. Then she baked a cake and fed Reine-Chaya with the cat cake and with milk mixed with the cat's afterbirth powder, and saw how her daughter paled and convulsed and white froth came from her mouth with her nausea, but she was not cured.

Mrs. Breine did not know what else she could do, and so she decided to take her life in her hands and with her daughter went to the big marsh.

It was a forbidden place since it was the home of demons and evil spirits. But because her desire to cure her daughter was so great, daring and courage overcame the proscription.

The mother went over to a tree, made a small hole in it into which she put her daughter's finger- and toenail clippings, and also hair from her head and body. She stuffed it all into the tree and said to the demons, "This is your portion." And as she closed up the hole she said to them, "As this hair and these nails will never return to the sick girl, Reine-Chaya will never again suffer from falling sickness, forever and ever Amen, Selah." And all this while Reine-Chaya was blindfolded so she could not see the tree.

But this, too, did not work, due either to the hunger of the Sedlec demons or the severity of her daughter's illness.

One day a wise man came to Sedlec, and what he instructed her mother to do greatly affrighted Reine-Chaya. Because Mrs. Breine had to wait until she saw a corpse.

And so, on the day the beadle of the Old Synagogue in Sedlec died, Mrs. Breine went to his house with her daughter and asked his wife's permission to view the deceased.

Mother and daughter went into the deceased beadle's room where he lay cold and gray-faced. The mother closed the door behind them so as not to cause the widow further grief. She took the dead man's hand, placed her daughter's hand in it, and told her to repeat after her: "*Ich beit eich nemt bei mir zu die schlafkeit fon der nichpeh, ich vat ess nicht shatten on mir vat ir ton a toiveh.*" (I ask you to have mercy on me and take with you my sleep, the sleep of falling sickness, it will not harm you, and you will be doing me a good deed). Then she told her daughter to lay her hand on the dead man's chest and ask him for forgiveness – and sent her home in tears.

But even the plea to the dead man was of no avail. And so Reine-Chaya had to undergo fumigation with a cockscomb immediately after the bird's slaughter, and then fumigation with the heart of a fresh fish, and she was given a special amulet and started walking around with salt in her pocket so she could swallow it with the onset of a convulsion. All this was of no help. Meanwhile her life became troubled and bitter because of all the prohibitions imposed upon her in the hope she would be cleansed of the falling sickness, including being forbidden to be angry, and she was also forbidden to listen to musical instruments or the sound of millstones at the old flourmill, and she must be careful not to eat warm bread, or black bread, or cheese or beef, she must never eat the head of a fish, a fowl or an animal, she must never drink tea but only cold boiled water, she must never fast, not on the Fast of Esther or on the Four Fasts, not even on Yom Kippur. And with these proscriptions they compounded her suffering and she was ostracized.

Two

Reine-Chaya grew up to be a beautiful girl, but lean and flawed as a Torah scroll cast into the archive for disused scrolls. She did not find a bridegroom because she had been born with a sickness, and from time to time she would be found rolling on the ground in a fit, white froth spraying from her mouth and her eyes rolled back into her head. This sight was frightening and horrifying and it kept the young men of the village away from her. Some feared that if they married her they would have to be on their guard throughout their life together, lest she fall and die, Heaven forbid, in some ravine, and there were those who feared that she would swallow her tongue in her sleep and die without giving them sons.

Had her mother not decided to seek the advice of a learned rabbi who lived in Kosnitz, the girl was destined to live out her life in loneliness. The mother's journey to the rabbi, who was renowned throughout the region as a man versed in the arcane, took several days. But when she arrived and told him her story he shook his head and said, "Go to the Rabbi of Kotsk, only he knows which is the right way for your daughter."

The mother did not despair and a few days later mounted the wagon of a Jew who took her a long way, through Krice and Amshinov and Gombin and Gostynin, through Mezerich and Lukba and Radzin, to the Rabbi of Kotsk. Mrs. Breine was on the road for many days, sleeping here at an inn and there in the house of a farmer the carter she had hired knew. As she had relatives in Radzin, she decided that she would break her journey only with them, refresh herself in their house and then reach the Rabbi of Kotsk safe and sound.

Mrs. Breine's relatives in Radzin were the Vrubels, the family of the ritual slaughterer who over the years had become a butcher and meat merchant. He had sons and grandsons and great-grandsons, each of whom was a meat merchant and well versed in the butchering of animals, and each of them knew how to separate the thigh muscle from the good cuts and how to salt and how to dry and how to separate a piece of meat for one dish, and a piece for another.

Mrs. Breine was warmly welcomed into the Vrubel home with a dish of flanken soup. When she told them where she was going the youngest son, Yossl, jumped up and said, "I will take you along the road to Kotsk."

For it is well known that out of respect for the Rabbi of Kotsk, who in his youth walked to Lublin to seek a teacher, and because of the song sung by the Kotsk Hasidim which says that one should not ride to Kotsk but walk, the road to the Rabbi of Kotsk passes through fields and dark forests.

Thus he said and thus he did. The boy accompanied his relative all the way from Radzin to Kotsk, and before taking his leave of her gave her a knife and a small butcher's cleaver as sharp as a razor for protection against robbers.

Mrs. Breine walked alone through the forest, between tall, ancient trees, and imagined that she was taking the same path as the Rabbi of Kotsk before her, a sharp-witted boy with his knife in his hand on the way to the Seer of Lublin to seek a teacher, who carved his teacher's words on a tree trunk. Thus she allayed her fears of robbers and brought protection on herself to walk to Kotsk in peace.

As she stood before the gates of Kotsk, Mrs. Breine said to herself, Here I am, a Jewish woman from Sedlec, standing at the gates of Kotsk as if at the gates of a temple that has one great and strong pillar, which is the Rabbi of Kotsk, and around him all his disciples, each of whom is a pillar in himself. And with her eyes she could see the terrible splendor of Kotsk that the learned rabbi projected onto his surroundings. But as she drew closer to the court of the Rabbi of Kotsk she became dispirited because she remembered for whom and for what she had come to the Rabbi of Kotsk, and a kind of sadness fell upon her so that her face, which earlier had been illuminated by thoughts of great sanctity, turned gray with suffering,

A Jewish woman passed her and saw a mother and wife who resembled a bottle of sadness on two legs. She was greatly alarmed and immediately took her to the rabbi's court. On the way Mrs. Breine told her of all her troubles with her daughter, ill with falling sickness, and with all the rabbis that had given her advice.

"With his teaching the Rabbi of Kosnitz breaks the hub of the universe," said her companion, Rachel daughter of Shmaya the Cobbler of Kotsk. "But he sent you to Rabbi

Mendel of Kotsk because he knows, as we all do, that with his teaching Rabbi Mendel of Kotsk touches upon the hub of Man."

Mrs. Breine heard this and was in awe of the Rabbi's power. Her legs almost betrayed her.

"Do not be afraid," Rachel told her. "Every rabbi gives according to his stature. These things are not given equally to many. But the Rabbi of Kotsk will give to you, with God's help, for you and the healing of your daughter."

Mrs. Breine reached the door of the Rabbi of Kotsk and saw many Jews standing there. One came with a note asking to be given greater fear of God and another came with a note asking to heal the soul. One came to ask for a livelihood and another came to ask for sustenance. Because of the many good deeds crowding around his door, she was afraid she would not manage to enter into the Rabbi's presence, and she started to cry.

The Rabbi of Kotsk heard a woman weeping, came out of his room, and made his way to her through the crowd. He stood next to Mrs. Breine and without a word beckoned her to come inside and close the door behind them.

Mrs. Breine began telling him the story of her daughter, Reine-Chaya, in its every detail, from the nine mustard seeds to the cat's afterbirth. As she told her story, the Rabbi saw how she existed, Heaven help us, like a vessel filled with sadness.

"With such a degree of sadness, Mrs. Breine," he said, "it is small wonder that you are unable to bring down mercy upon yourself and your daughter."

Mrs. Breine raised her head and wanted to reply.

"*Sha, sha,*" he said. "A person is like a clay vessel whose contents are the fundament. Your words came from the heart and entered the heart. Do not be afraid. Go now and rest at the house of Rachel Bat Shmaya, and while you rest I will think on what to do for your daughter, may she live in good health."

Mrs. Breine left his room with a somewhat lighter heart. Rabbi Mendel stood and began to pray. As he prayed he saw before him the suffering of the maiden, Reine-Chaya, and her sickness and her sadness, that she had no bridegroom, and of all her brothers and sisters only she remained, and without a husband at that, and he began to see before him a ring.

Rabbi Mendel looked deep into his soul and saw a gold ring, and with it its sister, another gold ring, both of which fastened the shoulder straps of the breastplate of the High Priest's garment, and on the breastplate twelve stones with the names of the twelve tribes of the Children of Israel. And he told himself that those two gold breastplate rings are as the rings of bride and groom, and from their conjoining are born the souls of the Children of Israel in every generation. And then he thought that if one puts on a ring, care must be taken against worship of material and greed and against pride and the enjoyment of the vanities of this world. And then he decided that the ring that would be placed on the finger of Reine-Chaya would also be engraved with the seal of her absence, as it is written, "In that day the Lord will take away the bravery of their anklets, and the fillets, and the crescents, and so forth. And it shall come to pass, that instead of sweet spices there shall be rottenness; and instead of a girdle rags; instead of curled hair baldness; and instead of a stomacher a girding of sackcloth; branding instead of beauty."

This, thought Rabbi Mendel of Kotsk, will ensure that the ring placed on the finger of Reine-Chaya would not be an object of pride but one of sanctity, an object that mentions the names of the Children of Israel, that joins the Deity and the Divine Presence and not, Heaven forbid, an object of beauty that heightens avarice.

Next day he summoned Mrs. Breine to his house, told her what he told her, and sent her on her way. He instructed her to continue on her long road to the port city of Danzig, where no one knows her, and where there was a synagogue of wealthy Jews.

"Go there and go up onto the pulpit and say thus and thus," the Rabbi told her, "and salvation will come to you."

Back in Sedlec they thought that Mrs. Breine had died from the travails of the journey or fallen into a ravine. There were some who suggested sitting *shiva*, the seven days of mourning, for her. But in her heart her sick daughter knew that her mother would return, she had to return, and convinced her old father not to do it.

All this while her mother continued her grueling journey along the roads until she came to the Mattenbuden Synagogue in Danzig. It was God's will that she reached the synagogue just as the congregation was breaking the fast, with all the congregants sitting in the synagogue and singing the praises of Queen Esther.

Mrs. Breine made her way through the congregation, which stood astounded at the sight of the strange, travel-weary woman. Bruised and beaten, she ascended the synagogue's magnificent pulpit and begged their help.

"Hear me, dear Jews," Mrs. Breine began, "I have come to you all the way from Sedlec. My daughter Reine-Chaya suffers from falling sickness. That is why no one in Sedlec wishes to take her to wife. I have sought the counsel of the Rabbi of Kosnitz, who sent me to the Rabbi of Kotsk, who sent me to you. And this is what he said: Take ten pieces of gold in the form of a coin, signifying the Ten Lost Tribes of Israel, a broken gold nail, an earring or a chain, a gold vase and even a gold buckle, collect them from ten young men who have reached manhood, in a strange city where they do not know who you are and who your daughter is. Then go to the Jewish goldsmith in that city and ask him to cast from those ten pieces of gold a protective ring for your daughter. Go back to your home and put the ring, the ring cast from the donations of ten Torah students, on the middle finger of your daughter's right hand. The ring will protect her from further fits and will even bring her a bridegroom, a goodhearted handsome bridegroom, the best of the Children of Israel."

The Torah students in the synagogue of Danzig and their fathers heard her plea and the words of the Rabbi of Kotsk, and talked among themselves. They were very excited, because they had no doubt which goldsmith was the subject of the Rabbi's words.

After a few moments the synagogue emptied, as if previously there had been no quorums of Jews in it who had fasted all day long in honor of Queen Esther.

Until all the men returned to the synagogue, their compassionate wives took her, gave her food and drink and even a change of clothing after the tribulations of the journey. Some time later they began returning, student and father, student and father. The synagogue treasurer stood beside her, a bag in his hand, and into it he put everything they had brought. One brought a gold vase with a cracked base, another a gold nail whose point had been blunted, this one brought a fragment of a ring that had cracked and broken with the years, and another a buckle that had become worn, until she had ten pieces of gold.

Mrs. Breine thought that now she had the ten pieces of gold, as she had been instructed by the Rabbi of Kotsk, she could go to the house of one of the women who had invited her to stay with her. But then the congregation split into two, like the parting of the Red Sea, and from it emerged a Torah student, a handsome, blue-eyed boy with a young beard already on his chin.

"I am Shmuel, son of Zerachia the goldsmith," he said, "and I will take you to my father who will make all these pieces into a ring for you."

It was said of Zerachia Bergman the goldsmith that he could turn iron into gold, and mix gold with silver and make all kinds of unions and meanings in the holy artifacts he fashioned. At first he made artifacts for the five synagogues of Danzig, but once the stories of wonders began to be associated with the artifacts he made in his workshop began to spread, Jews started sending messengers from all parts of the empire, and even from Poland and Russia, to purchase one of his sacred objects.

Numerous stories were linked with his work, among them one about a Torah scroll crown that would flower in the air of the world at the moment the cantor touched the scroll it adorned, and a story about a Prophet Elijah's goblet, which on every Passover Eve in the home of the wealthy man who had purchased it, would replenish itself with kosher wine, and would continue refilling itself throughout the year after the Passover Seder, as if it were waiting for the Prophet Elijah to come and drink from it, and all kinds of stories about a remedial ring and a healing ornament and a Torah pointer from which light emanated to illuminate the scroll for the reader as he read the Portion of the Week, but only once a year.

Shmuel took her in hand and led her through the streets of Danzig, beautiful Danzig through whose streets a cold sea wind blew, to his father's house.

When his father heard who had sent this good woman to him he needed nothing more. He listened to her story and immediately began thinking about what he could do for her.

For seven days Zerachia Bergman the goldsmith labored over Reine-Chaya's healing ring, and throughout that time Mrs. Breine told the goldsmith and his son of her daughter's merits. She talked and talked, understating the description of her daughter's illness and relating expansively about her piety, her beauty, her modesty and all her other virtues. She did the job so well that by the time the goldsmith completed his work on the ring he had made up his mind to send his son with her along with the ring. It was then that Mrs. Breine knew that Shmuel, the goldsmith's son, would place that ring on Reine-Chaya's finger when he took her to wife.

Hence the rumors that circulated in Sedlec about Reine-Chaya's ring. Jews who saw on a woman's finger a ring whose surface is not smooth and is inexpensive, but which bore a special dispensation from Rabbi Mendel of Kotsk, began discussing among themselves why the Rabbi of Kotsk had seen fit to permit a marriage with such a heavy ring.

They began telling about ten pieces of gold signifying the Ten Lost Tribes of Israel, to the point that apparently Shmuel Bergman's learned father, Reb Zerachia Bergman ben Shmaya of Danzig, had inserted a magical verse at the bottom of the ring, in accordance with the order of Rabbi Mendel of Kotsk. This verse endows the ring with special attributes that an ordinary wedding ring does not possess. In any event, just as she had left Sedlec along the highways and byways, sitting on the wagon of a goodhearted Jew from this town and that one, and her heart, a mother's heart bitter in her breast, so Mrs. Breine returned joyful and satisfied. And the Jews of Sedlec, who had witnessed many miracles throughout the years, had never seen such great rejoicing as that witnessed at the wedding of Reine-Chaya and Shmuel, son of the goldsmith of Danzig. For not only was Reine-Chaya cured of her falling sickness and had gained a sage and handsome husband, but nine and a half months after her wedding she gave birth to her firstborn son, who was later followed by three more.

Three

Shmuel Bergman had learned his craft from his father, and he settled in Sedlec and became a goldsmith. He was an erudite man. Every free hour he had was devoted to Torah study, and between his periods of study he would sit in his little shop fashioning silver ornaments. He received the precious metal from his father, but the words he engraved on the base of the goblets for Kiddush and at the bottom of the candlesticks he made, he was given by no man. He would engrave entire stories on the silver embellishments of his work. And so as not to give them a human semblance, lest he commit a transgression and fashion an idol, he would make the ornamentations of gold and silver, all worked into words and letters from the Portion of the Week and the Book of Psalms. His father, who was a master craftsman, taught him to write an entire verse of psalms in tiny silver and gold letters even on the bottom of a ring.

A short time after the bar-mitzvah of Gershon, their firstborn son, a rider came to Sedlec to inform Shmuel Bergman that his father's days were numbered. The Bergman family packed up their home, their belongings and their four children, and made haste from Sedlec to Danzig. But while they were still on the road the father passed away and they were only able to accompany him on his final journey.

It was there in Danzig of the time that it all began. It was there that this story had its roots. It was there that the ring began its terrifying dance.

For the time being the ring did not reveal its sinister nature. On the contrary, it turned Reine-Chaya into a happy married woman and mother, and when Shmuel and Reine-Chaya and their four children came to Danzig the ring was on Reine-Chaya's finger, protecting her from her falling sickness and enabling her to live like anyone else.

In those years the Jews of the city were split into five different congregations. In each one the Jews were of the same social status, and each had its own synagogue in which they had their own form of prayer, and around which they led their lives.

Shmuel Bergman would pray in the synagogue on Mattenbuden Street together with Jews who had come to Danzig from Russia. The synagogue's rabbi was Rabbi Israel Lifshitz, author of the *Tiferet Yisrael* commentary to the Mishnah. On the other hand, the rabbi of the Altschottland Synagogue at the time was Rabbi Dr. Abraham Stein, who had different, progressive ideas on the form of prayer, and who, as a result of his great erudition and his desire to move closer to the gentiles, delivered sermons in German in his synagogue, which even had a women's choir.

The more talk there was of emancipation, and the more the Enlightenment Movement spread through the Jewish street, so the congregations went into decline. Some of the Jews' children, whose parents sought to give them an education and bring them closer to positions of power, attended Imperial schools, and it was patently clear that they were gradually forgetting the values of their fathers' house. Even Shmuel Bergman's sons mixed with the children of *Maskilim*, and they slowly began avoiding going to the synagogue with Shmuel, and would spend more and more time with their friends on walks to the Old Port, to the river to catch leeches, or horseback riding in various parts of the city.

The split in the congregations affected not only Danzig but was evident throughout the Empire. The congregations' weakness was exposed again and again as they came up against manifestations of anti-Semitism, and so Dr. Kossman Werner and Martin Lazarus established the General Association of German Citizens of the Jewish Faith. The Association took upon itself religious instruction in schools in all the small towns and dealt with the Jewish émigrés from Poland and Russia so they would not be a burden on the congregations, continue on their way to America and not heighten anti-Semitism wherever they went.

The leaders of the Danzig congregations witnessed the establishment of the Association and decided to seriously discuss the possibility of uniting the five congregations in their city. They formed and convened a fifteen-man committee whose members included community dignitaries, among them Shmuel Bergman whose customers, and those of his father before him, in all the city's synagogues held him in high esteem.

For three years the members of the committee put their heads together. They faced many thorny problems, including disagreement over the degree of liberalism in prayer, whether all our brethren would agree to attend a synagogue where there was an organ and cantorial melodies of the new form of prayer, and who would collect taxes for the committee, and whether there would be a single community fund or five, and whether it

16

would be possible to overcome the gentiles' prejudices through information and persuasion, and so on and so forth.

One July day in 1881, Reine-Chaya went to the market as was her custom, but as she approached it she realized that something was going on. The people were talking among themselves crestfallen, and the sounds of haggling and the stallholders' cries had been replaced by a deathly gloom.

She walked among the stalls, surprised by the sudden change that had overtaken the market atmosphere, and asked one of the traders what had happened.

"Haven't you heard?" he whispered, "the *goyim* have plundered thirteen Jewish towns. They burnt synagogues, prayer books and Torah scrolls. The pogroms are so terrible that the Empire has dispatched the army there!"

Reine-Chaya suddenly felt her knees shaking, as if she were about to collapse. The trader hurried from behind his stall and dragged out a rickety wooden chair. She thanked him and sat down to rest.

After a few long moments he looked at her and asked if she was feeling better.

"No," she replied, "I must go home. But I haven't the strength to carry all these baskets," and pointed at the baskets at her feet.

The trader, who had known her for a long time, called his eldest son and despite her feeble protests sent him to escort the lady home. When she tried to pay him, the boy ignored her outstretched hand saying he had done this good deed on his father's behalf.

Reine-Chaya thanked him and as soon as he left she hurried to the wooden sideboard where she kept the ring in a drawer. And sure enough, the ring lay there on the piece of velvet on which she had placed it as she did each morning. But its stones, that were always dull as if their luster had been taken from them, were now gleaming strangely.

She brought the ring closer to her eyes, peered at it, sighed and put it on her finger. An irritating sting shot from the inside of the ring onto her skin. Reine-Chaya looked at the ring and said aloud, as if to herself, "Calamity is looming." Then she twisted the ring on her finger, sighed again, and left the room.

At that very moment, earlier than usual, Shmuel came home in alarm. He opened the door and rushed inside as if beset by great misfortune.

"Where are the children?" he asked.

Reine-Chaya was about to reply but he suddenly noticed the ring glittering like a huge eye on her finger.

"You already know," he said.

"Yes," she replied, "somebody in the market told me."

"The Community Association has sent out a letter about anti-Semitism," he said, and with a shaking hand took from his pocket a folded sheet of paper. "The messenger who brought it to me told me what happened."

"Words, Shmuel," Reine-Chaya said, "words can no longer help us."

"God have mercy on the victims," Shmuel murmured, "on the burned Torah scrolls."

"This is not the time for mercy," Reine-Chaya said in a hoarse voice, "now is the time to do something before this evil comes to us as well."

"What's to be done?" Shmuel asked, wringing his hands, "The blood has already been spilled."

"Call an urgent meeting of the committee today," Reine-Chaya directed. "You must complete the unification of the congregations. We must be strong now."

Shmuel left his house without eating lunch and went from one committee member to the next to convene them urgently.

The committee members who met in Shmuel's house that evening were of one mind that due to the pogroms they must urgently conclude their discussions on uniting the congregations. But then Gustav Davidson rose and fanned the flames afresh.

Davidson was a great philanthropist who owned numerous factories. He knew the ways of wealth and the paths of power, and thus he was also a member of the Freedom Party which he represented on the city council.

"We must build a synagogue," he said with characteristic fervor, "so long as there are five synagogues in Danzig there will never be a unified community."

"One synagogue for everybody?" the advocate asked in astonishment.

"Yes, a big synagogue, a unique temple that will strike awe in the hearts of all who see it. So that they won't think of burning it down too."

"Have you ever seen a *goy* who's frightened of a synagogue?' the advocate asked derisively. "They have no fear of the monarchy, so why should they fear God?"

"They're very quick with small synagogues in the small towns," Davidson replied, "but they would never dare attack a temple of stone taller than its surroundings!"

"Stone?" another member of the committee wondered, "a temple such as that would flaunt our wealth and then the attacks will be even worse."

"If we need a synagogue then we need a synagogue," the advocate added, "but why a temple?"

"Where were you thinking of putting a congregation made up of all five synagogues?" Davidson replied angrily. "In a *cholent* pot?"

Shmuel listened and felt that his heart was being torn apart, until he finally opened his mouth. The Mattenbuden Synagogue was where he had been circumcised and become bar-mitzvah. It was the synagogue he had attended every day with his father, Reb Zerachia, who had made all the small prayer house's ritual artifacts, including the copper menorah hanging above the Holy Ark, and the crowns adorning the Torah scrolls. Even the crimson curtain with its two embroidered gold lions, and on both sides of them the Tables of the Covenant embroidered in gold, had been donated by him in memory of his late mother. How could he agree to something that would ultimately lead to the closing of this synagogue? Heaven forbid that this synagogue should close its doors while he himself gave the closure his seal of approval.

Gustav Davidson listened to him. His pain touched him deeply.

"I can understand you," he said, softening his voice, "but if we do not act in accord to build a big central synagogue, even at the cost of the old ones' decline until they close completely, the rioters will do it for us."

Shmuel bowed his head to the table, studying the cracks in its heavy wood. At that moment he would have been happy for the wood to open up and swallow him. The others present were also sunk in thought, recalling, like Shmuel, Friday evenings and festival eves they had spent in their seats, facing the Holy Ark, and how they had come to the synagogue in their best clothes on festival eves to meet relatives, friends and neighbors there. Now they must do with their own hands what the vandals had done to the synagogues in the small outlying communities throughout Germany.

Gustav Davidson waited, studying the faces of his friends who were sitting, each one of them, immersed in his memories, his pain. "Building the new temple will take a good few years," he said after a long while, "but in the meantime each of the synagogues will continue to stand in its place and will stay open so long as it has at least two quorums of worshippers."

"And what then?" Shmuel asked, "What will happen to the synagogues afterwards?"

"Afterwards," Gustav Davidson said, "we will transfer the Torah scrolls from all the synagogues to the great temple, and we will open religious schools in the synagogues."

When Shmuel heard this his eyes lit up. This was an idea he could live with. The Torah scrolls, the curtain and the ritual artifacts would be transferred to the new synagogue for all the city's Jews, and a religious school would be established in the old Mattenbuden Synagogue that would strengthen Jewish education in the city. Perhaps he himself would be able to establish it.

Thus Shmuel Bergman consoled himself, without knowing that with his agreement to establishing the holy temple he was unwittingly bringing down a calamity upon himself and his family.

Four

For six years ships brought red-gray sandstone and dark brown granite columns from across the sea to the Old Port of Danzig; six years during which construction continued until the temple dome rose above the city. During this period the Bergman couple found themselves between the Russian and Danziger Jews, their hearts with Mattenbuden but their future in Altschottland, the more enlightened quarter of Danzig. This feeling was bound up with the influx of Jews to the city.

During those years Jews came to Danzig from Poland and Russia, Galicia and Romania, and endeavored to remain there with the help of their relatives in order to join up with their timber and leather merchant brethren, who were among the city's wealthiest men. Among these migrants were artisans, especially carpenters, women searching for their husbands or awaiting a "call" to take passage to them on a vessel sailing from Danzig, and many impoverished Torah scholars who knocked on doors begging and in so doing brought down upon themselves both the compassion and anger of the city's Jews.

The pressure of these poverty-stricken Jews on the Empire in general and on Danzig in particular reached a point at which in 1884 Chancellor Bismarck ordered the expulsion of Russian Jews from the Empire.

The situation of the Jewish refugees and their expulsion from Danzig depressed Shmuel greatly, and his wife took note of this. But at that time she was troubled not by the fate of the Jews but that of their eldest son, Gershon. For he had been almost a young man when they moved to Danzig from Sedlec, and if in his childhood he had absorbed the unique air of Sedlec and grown up on its stories and had become bar-mitzvah there, since their arrival in Danzig she had seen how he had moved away from his playmates in the Mattenbuden Synagogue yard and replaced them with new friends from the *Maskil* families of Altschottland.

Not only that, Gershon had grown tall and there were even the first signs of a beard on his chin, like the down of a day-old chick. And their neighbors in Mattenbuden, as people do, started bothering Reine-Chaya with questions about what he was doing, what was he studying and when would he find himself a bride. This troubled her so much that one day she swore that she would only give her eldest son to the daughter of a distinguished and

Maskil family from Altschottland. Shmuel understood that if his wife Reine-Chaya, a Sedlecer through and through, says something like that, then perhaps the time had come to distance themselves from the Yiddish-speaking peddlers and mendicants and the gloomy atmosphere of Mattenbuden, for even the most magnanimous of hearts can sometimes tire. Not only that, Shmuel, too, was moved to admiration of the good taste of his new friends, the members of the Community Committee, and began wondering whether he should give his sons, Gershon and Meir and David and Nathan, not only a Jewish education but also some of the spirit of the new *Haskalah*.

Thus the die was cast and Shmuel Bergman went to his friend Gustav Davidson and asked him to find a suitable house for him and his family in Altschottland. Davidson willingly responded and searched until he found them a large and particularly handsome house in the street where Walter Abramson, editor of the liberal Jewish newspaper, lived.

The Bergman family moved their belongings into their new, spacious, ten-roomed home that fronted the street and at the back had a fine, large and well-tended garden. The walls of the house, whose previous owner was a wealthy timber merchant, were paneled with fine wood and its floor was covered with dark wood that was pleasing to the touch. The previous owner had also left behind several fine pieces of furniture, including a splendid long sideboard that stood on its carved legs in the living room, and with a glass-covered cabinet for displaying ornaments, antique chests, a big escritoire with numerous drawers and compartments that seemed to be designed for holding secrets, and a thick and very wide rough wooden table that stood in the kitchen and was used both for cooking and meals.

The children were happy when they first entered the house and immediately began running through the numerous rooms, shouting and laughing joyfully, learning its spaces with their little feet.

When the carters finished unloading everything the Bergman family had brought with them from their old house, Shmuel asked his wife to come and stand with him at the front of the house. She followed him, stood facing the door, and then, with great ceremony, Shmuel again threw open the door for her.

"Welcome to your new home, lady of the house," he announced solemnly.

"Stop your clowning," Reine-Chaya laughed, walked inside, looked around and heaved a sigh of relief. "It really is delightful."

"Now give me your hand again," Shmuel said.

"You took my hand a long time ago," Reine-Chaya laughed at her husband's whimsy but ceremoniously held out her hand to him.

Shmuel fumbled in the inside pocket of his coat and from it took a square, carved wooden box. Reine-Chaya looked at it in surprise. He carefully opened the box and took out their wedding ring, his beloved wife's healing ring.

"Since when have you had it?" Reine-Chaya asked.

"Since the carters came to load the dresser from our bedroom," he replied. "With all the commotion you forgot it there."

"Impossible," said Reine-Chaya, "I've never forgotten it."

"Well, you did," Shmuel laughed, "and now give me your hand and I'll put it on a second time. But this time promise me you will never take it off again."

He took the ring from its box, buffed it on his lapel and slid it onto her finger.

"But how can I?" Reine-Chaya asked. "Look how big this house is. There's a lot of work to do."

"I've got you a good but needy Jewish woman, her name is Hinda, and from now on she will do all the hard work for you," said Shmuel Bergman. "From now on you are the lady of the house. You don't cook, you don't clean."

"Rubbish!" Reine-Chaya replied.

"She's a poor woman, it's a good deed."

"*Nu, schoin*," she said, "haven't you got a better excuse than that, Shmuel?"

"Here in Altschottland you can't live as simply as you did there," Shmuel said, softening his voice. "There is a different spirit here and we must become part of it socially. It's not a matter of stubbornness, it's a matter of status."

Reine-Chaya looked at her husband with her big brown eyes.

"It will be as you wish, Shmuel," she said, taking his hand in hers, "but the cooking in this house will be done by me alone."

"The main thing is that you take care of yourself," he said. "Don't take the ring off. Don't forget that it's your wedding ring too."

Reine-Chaya laughed, kissed her husband's cheek, straightened her fine dress, and went off to collect her children from all over the house.

That evening they ate a makeshift meal of a loaf of bread and sausage and fruit that she had prepared beforehand, and a good jar of *shmaltz* she had kept from the old kitchen in Mattenbuden, until her new kitchen would be stocked and ready.

Their new house was close to the port and towards evening the ships' sirens could be heard as they left and entered the bay, unloading crates of goods from over the sea and loading grain and timber and leather, or boxes of amber from the factories. The young children began attending the Altschottland Talmud Torah school, while Gershon was enrolled at a general school and began meeting with the neighbors' children, the majority of whom were the sons of affluent Jewish merchants, lawyers and physicians, who held liberal views and were disciples of the *Haskalah* movement.

In the way of youngsters who make new friends more easily than their parents, from the first days following their arrival Gershon became friendly with the son of their neighbors, Frank Abramson, the son of Herr Walter Abramson, editor of the *Allgemeine Zeitung das Judentums*, the newspaper of the German liberal Jews.

Frank was Gershon's age but shorter. His hair was golden-brown and honey toned, and his green eyes sparkled with mischief that would quickly be transformed into an expression of vulnerability and anguish. He was very intelligent, but introverted. Only with Gershon, who was taller than him, his features strong and sunken like those of a young, deep-thinking man, but with a constant smile, did he allow himself to open up. He shared with him his secret hiding places on the Abramson family's extensive estate, and particularly the house he had built in a big tree in the yard. There he would shut himself off for hours on end, and it was there that he kept his small collection of souvenirs – a button from a soldier's uniform he found in the street, a horseshoe for luck, a big rusty padlock into which was stuck a worked key bearing the initials of an unknown family, and a few old coins that he liked to put in the roadway to be crushed under the wheels of passing carriages. Gershon did not share Frank's love of metal objects, but was happy to have a close friend who went to school with him, with whom he could read the textbooks and talk to about matters of paramount importance, and now and then get up to mischief with him.

They would play with the glass fruit bowls in the Abramson family drawing room as if they were soldiers' helmets, and once even imagined themselves in the Danzig Fire Brigade by putting the glass bowls on their heads, going out onto the Abramson terrace – and urinating on the heads of passersby.

One day, when they were alone in the Bergman house, they erected a big tent of blankets from some of the rooms. They went inside. Gershon was sure that they would continue with their usual game, that they were soldiers about to go into battle. But then Frank asked him if he knew how to make bread.

Gershon looked at him, puzzled.

"What kind of a question is that?" he asked. "Make bread? What am I, a baker?"

Frank laughed.

"No, not that kind of bread. Come on, I'll show you something I learned from a soldier. How soldiers make bread."

"What do you mean, 'make bread'?" Gershon asked.

"Come along and I'll show you," Frank said, and ran to lock the door with the key, and then lay down on the blanket – and took down his trousers.

Gershon looked at him in amazement.

Frank didn't say a word. He was panting eagerly, he took off his underpants and revealed his hardening member to his best friend.

"Bring a cushion," he said.

In silence Gershon picked up a cushion and handed it to Frank. Frank lay on it and began rubbing his distended member against it.

"This is bread," he said, groaning with pleasure.

"I see," Gershon said, feeling his own small member becoming erect inside his trousers. "It's spilling your seed, but without touching."

"Yes, something like that," Frank giggled nervously and eagerly. "Get undressed. Let's see you do it."

Gershon complied and took off his trousers and underpants.

Then Frank asked him to lie on his back.

"I'll show you how soldiers really make bread," he told him, moving over and gently laying himself on top of him.

Gershon could feel the warmth of Frank's body enveloping him with a sensation he had never felt before. Their members rubbed against each other and his heart was pounding wildly. He was worried that what they were doing was unacceptable, but he could feel the pleasure of the act. Instead of pushing Frank off, who was smaller than him, he clasped him to his body with both arms. Frank started moving back and forth, rubbing his genitals against Gershon's warm, smooth body. He groaned and rubbed, rubbed and groaned, until they simultaneously ejaculated their adolescent semen onto each other's bodies.

They never spoke of this incident again, but only hinted at the degree of their willingness for the act. Averting their eyes was sufficient. They did not know what to call it but felt it was a private act, worthy of being kept secret, and that not a word should ever be spoken of it to anyone.

They met almost every day, went to the tree house, rubbed against one another until they climaxed, and immediately cleaned themselves up with a piece of white cotton cloth, that with time became stained and which Frank kept stuffed in crack in their hidey-hole high in the tree.

One day they were playing not in their usual hiding place, but inside the Bergman home. That day Reine-Chaya had gone out shopping for the Sabbath with Hinda the housekeeper. But unfortunately Reine-Chaya became tired from walking through the markets, left the housekeeper on her own and returned home earlier than expected. As always she went from room to room to see which of her children were already home from school, and since the rooms in their house were never locked she flung open the door to Gershon's room, surprising the two boys in the midst of their coition.

Reine-Chaya saw what she saw, and from her lips, from the depths of her chest, a great and bitter cry burst out.

Frank, as naked as the day he was born, leapt from Gershon's body, grabbed his trousers in panic, covered his nakedness with them, and fled. The naked Gershon rolled onto his side and quickly covered himself with the blanket on which he lay.

Reine-Chaya neither shouted again nor said another word. Stunned and horrified she left the room, went into her own room and for a long time only the stifled sounds of weeping were heard coming from inside.

Gershon heard his mother in her pain and fled the house. He returned only late that night, his hair disheveled and his eyes darting hither and thither, after his younger brothers were safely asleep in their beds.

As he stepped fearfully into the vestibule, his father lit the reading lamp that stood on the sideboard by which he sat waiting for his son to come home.

Gershon froze like an animal caught in the beam of a hunter's lamp.

Shmuel beckoned him closer.

Gershon stumbled towards him. As he drew closer he saw his father's face as he sat half in the light and half in darkness, and it seemed it had aged all at once.

"Your mother is asleep at last," the father said painfully, and with a finger to his lips signaled that he should be quiet. "Only God knows how she will get over what she saw."

Gershon opened his mouth to speak, but again his father cut him short with a gesture.

"I will not beat you," his father said quietly, the pain clearly evident in his voice. "You're a big boy already. I shall say just one thing. This is unacceptable. It is an act of gentiles. It is a great blasphemy."

The father fell silent, waited for a moment, took a deep breath and then continued.

"We have already been to see Frank's parents. In a few days time each of you will go off to a different university. You will never see one another again."

Next morning, when the Bergmans awakened from their troubled sleep, their big, new house was filled with the gloom of desolation. It was as if the Angel of Death had visited the house in person. Reine-Chaya went from here to there and from there to here in silence, mumbling intelligibly. Mr. Bergman requested Hinda to take her place getting the little children ready and sending them off to school, and she did not dare to ask what had happened. She could see that a calamity had befallen the household, even without knowing exactly what it was.

Reine-Chaya maintained her silence for weeks on end. She shut herself up in her room for most of the day as she did not want to come face to face with her eldest son so she should not see the sin in his eyes. Meanwhile Shmuel made all the necessary arrangements to send Gershon to the University of Hamburg, as had Walter Abramson who sent his son Frank, at the very same time, to the University of Berlin.

It was during those days of silence that Reine-Chaya made a vow. If God willed it she would find a bride for her eldest son, just as her own mother had found her a husband. And with her own hands she would put on the finger of his bride, her daughter-in-law, her own ring that had been fashioned from the gold of ten virgin Torah scholars in Danzig, the ring of her healing and sorrow.

Five

During the first few weeks that elapsed since Gershon left for university, Reine-Chaya would not see anyone except for her nearest and dearest, her husband and her three sons. She was incapable of performing any of the household chores. She wandered around the house aimlessly, her heart heavy with thought, mumbling to herself like a woman stricken by life, immersed in her grief like a bereaved mother. What she had seen had hit her like the stroke of an axe. The first beloved fruit of her womb involved in an act so abhorrent and which was unknown to and inconceivable for any Jewish mother, an act of gentiles, or of the sons of liberal assimilationists for whom the fear of God meant nothing.

After many days of mourning, one day she found herself dragging from under one of the beds the small wooden box in which she kept the old books from her girlhood in Sedlec. She sat down on the edge of the bed, carefully opened the box and from among the dry and dusty volumes that lay in it she took out the old book of supplications, on whose flyleaf her mother had written the *jahrzeit*, the anniversary of her grandfather's and grandmother's deaths. From the book's yellowing pages she slowly began reading a supplication for a woman arising from her childbearing bed, "*A neyeh techina far a froy, ven zi shteit oif fon kinderbet*", followed by one for a mother whose son is attending *heder* for the first time, "*Du bist der herr fon rachmones on fon der zindfargebung. Ich dank dir far der retung, vos du host mich geretet fon di bitere schmertzen un host mir gelozt leiben un du host mir gegeben naye kreften ich zol kenen oifshtein for der bet*" (You, Lord of mercy and forgiveness for our sins, I thank you for saving me from terrible pain and keeping me alive, and for giving me renewed strength to rise from my bed), praying silently, conjuring the image of her mother sitting reading the very same supplication, from the same book, at her bedside, and she was a little girl, and she began weeping for her mother and father, for her husband and her children and for herself, and for what had happened to suddenly ruin and shatter her world. But more than the words it was the warm rough feel of the book, its threadbare black binding and old pages, that was balm to her soul, as if it held within it the touch of her mother's hand, and into which she, too, had buried her grief and sorrow and from which she drew the profundity and greatness of her soul.

At the same time Shmuel Bergman also changed completely. He ate only sparingly and lost weight, and he looked like a man being drawn into himself. But unlike his wife who shut herself up at home, he increased his public activities and even took upon himself the overseeing of the construction of the big temple.

Each day he walked to where the workers labored over the construction of the synagogue, following the building's progress at first hand: the laying of the foundations, the building of the main hall with its three vaulted entrances, and the two rooms to its left and right, the casting of the ceiling, and the building of the wide balcony at the front, and later the slow construction of the women's section on the second floor, and above the temple a spire, and on it a huge dome topped by a turret, and two smaller spires at its sides, and in the temple's windows stained glass that shone in the sunlight, and on them depictions of the Twelve Tribes.

It was therefore hardly surprising that before the temple's completion all the committee members asked Shmuel Bergman, the son of the first Jewish goldsmith in Danzig, to cast in his workshop an inscription in gold letters that would stand in all its glory on the façade of the temple, welcoming all who entered.

Since the consecration of the synagogue, Shmuel and Reine-Chaya immersed themselves in visiting the temple. Shmuel became one of the pillars of the synagogue. He knew its every hall and every arch and every passage, and every one of the big brass lamps that adorned its ceiling. And if at first he found it hard to change from the form of prayer to which he was accustomed, to the liberal form introduced into the Great Synagogue by Rabbi Max Freund, he slowly adjusted to the innovations in the prayers, if only because of the beauty of the choir's singing.

The choir, conducted by Moritz Friedlander, stood on its dais on the eastern side and sang from there. Its hallowed singing was so beautiful that not only human beings but also angels would come from all over heaven to listen to it. It became particularly heightened and heartrending when Ya'akov Meisel was appointed the synagogue's chief cantor, and every Friday evening he would stand and thunder in his rich voice, "Come, my friend, to meet the bride."

The worshippers, all in their black Sabbath clothes and black hats, their shoulders wrapped in prayer shawls decorated with strips of gold and silver thread, would stand as one man facing east. Their good wives, in all their finery, would stand on the second floor, in the women's section, a long handsome balcony carved in warm, dark wood, and sing from their hearts too.

Reine-Chaya, who at the time was attracted to anything that smacked of religion, became most observant of the religious precepts and did not miss a single service. Every Friday evening she would bathe in the three-legged bath in the new house, massage into her skin an oil that heightened circulation and which had a deep and intoxicating fragrance of dark forests that attracted people from afar who wondered from where they had been suddenly assailed by forest verdancy and the gold of the sun and the twittering of birds. Over all this she wore tight-fitting undergarments that lifted her bosom and showed off her proud figure, and over them a fine dress of thin, blue or pink material. Around her neck she wore a string of pearls her husband bought her to mark the consecration of the synagogue, and on her head the tower of her hair in the shape of a rounded dome, and on her finger, her ring.

Handsome and excited she would sit among the women of Danzig in the women's section, her heart filled with joy and tranquility before the Sabbath came in, looking from her place at her husband, at Shmuel, standing there splendid and dignified among the other men bowed under the weight of their faith, him stealing a look at her now and again to see that she was all right and that she, too, was keeping an eye on him. Now and then Shmuel could hear Reine-Chaya's clear deep voice singing, together with the large, festive congregation in a feeling of joy and thanksgiving to the Creator, "Come, my friend, to meet the bride; let us welcome the presence of the Sabbath," in the melody especially composed to the words of Rabbi Shlomo Elkabetz in the Great Synagogue of Danzig. And every Sabbath when they came to the lines, "O sanctuary of our King, O regal city, arise, go forth from thy overthrow; long enough hast thou dwelt in the valley of weeping; verily He will have compassion upon thee," Shmuel would look up at her as if the words of the psalm were directed at her and all the worshippers were singing to her, and to her he sang in his heart, "Arouse thyself, arouse thyself, for thy light is come; arise, shine; awake, awake; give forth a song; the glory of the Lord is revealed upon thee."

And when she saw Shmuel's radiant face looking at her as he sang, Reine-Chaya's heart was filled with great love for him. And then the ring, her wedding and deliverance ring, would start to burn and glow on her finger. And when the worshippers sang, "Come, my friend, to meet the bride; let us welcome the presence of the Sabbath," the light emanating from her magical ring was so strong that it would pour down from the women's section and envelop the entire hall, shining with a great light from within the synagogue into the void of the world.

It is therefore hardly surprising that the worshippers began whispering among themselves about the nature of the ring, its lineage and uniqueness. The women that surrounded her in the women's section every Friday evening would look at the ring and the brightness emanating from it, and ask her to tell them of its properties and look at it from close up. And Reine-Chaya, who was a good woman with an aching heart, allowed them to examine her ring and would tell them about how the ring had actually been fashioned in this city, and how Shmuel, the son of the goldsmith of Danzig, had come to Sedlec with her mother and become engaged to her with the ring.

In every community in which there are Jews, the men and women relate all kinds of stories to each other, and these stories pass from one to another, from one synagogue to the next, and from congregation to congregation. That is what happened in this instance. The story started in Altschottland, wended its way to Mattenbuden and Weinberg and Langfuhr and Breitgasse, and in each congregation fragments of stories and partial memories were added to it, until it became extremely beautiful and splendid. And everywhere it was told it piqued people's imagination and gave them some hope. For rumor had it that the bride-to-be who would become engaged to Reine-Chaya's son would also inherit her ring.

Six

At this time the Litvinovsky family was living in Danzig. They were a wealthy family and although they were horse traders, in the view of all the city's Jews their daughter Bella was a worthy match. They owned large stables housing at least fifty horses. The father and son raised the horses for the Danzig police and the German army across the border. They sold the old, tired horses lacking in splendor to a Danish merchant who made sausages from them.

The horse traders did not count for much among the city's residents. Since they bought their horses from farmers in Kashubia they had become used to speaking farmers' language and would only seal a bargain over a glass of schnapps and after an exchange of graphic curses. The majority of the horse traders were also known for their untrustworthiness. They could take an old or sick horse whose days were numbered, tout it as a superior animal and sell it for the price of a noble steed. The horse traders and their sons also took their leisure in places inappropriate for Jews, like the inns and brothels near the port.

Asher Litvinovsky and his wife Berta were different. Asher was stocky and hirsute with sharp eyes that darted here and there beneath thick brows, a shrewd, quick-thinking man as one had to be with the farmers, the military and the police. But since he was a scion of a Hasidic family from Poland and had learned the Jewish precepts in his father's house, he observed the commandments and distanced himself from any form of deceit. Not only that, when he and his wife married and had a family in Danzig they decided to bring up their children both as Jews and on the principles of the *Haskalah* alike so that they would belong to high society without forgetting their Jewishness.

The Litvinovskys had two children, Shlomo-Heinrich and Bella. Their lack of success with Shlomo-Heinrich was more than made up by their daughter. Shlomo-Heinrich adopted the licentious behavior of a young horse trader and became a hotheaded womanizer, whereas Bella grew up into a good looking and reserved young woman, as she should. And the more her brother, whom she loved heart and soul, raised hell in the city, the more introverted she became.

Bella was very beautiful. Her eyes were green and her body was as slim and firm as a silver spoon. She had been attached to her father's horses since her childhood, and she particularly loved a gelding called Wallach and would brush his gleaming brown coat and long mane for hours on end. Now and again her brother, Shlomo-Heinrich, would lift her up onto the horse and lead her along the boulevards.

Heinrich was a mischievous child who would climb lampposts and trees in the street. He became so used to riding horses as a child that in his adolescence he had a bowlegged gait, as if a horse was missing from between his thighs.

Heinrich was not only a horseman but also a cocksman. From time to time he would bring women to his "office", the stable tack room, and enjoy mutual fondling with them on the old armchair that stood among the saddles and harness strewn over the floor. In the company of his friends he also frequented the brothels near the port. He was a well-built, quick-tempered man, always spoiling for a fight. Time after time the Danzig police arrested him after a drunken brawl in one or other of the brothels, but as he was the son of the family that raised horses for them, they would always release him without charge.

Heinrich had an excessive love of schnapps and this led him into some embarrassing acts. One night he took down his trousers and urinated into the Neptune Fountain in the city center. On another he fondled his privates outside the synagogue. On a third night he taught a young Jewish boy how to make bread.

The Litvinovsky family, that is, father, mother and daughter, conscientiously attended the Friday evening service at the Great Synagogue of Danzig. Asher Litvinsky went to a tailor to have well-cut black suits made especially for himself and his son, and even bought them very beautiful prayer shawls, embroidered with gold and silver, so that they would be accepted among the affluent of the city. His wife, Berta, took a great deal of trouble over her dresses and those of her young daughter, whose reputation preceded her, so as not to shame her husband when they attended the temple. So it happened that on Friday evenings and the Sabbath, Berta Litvinovsky and her daughter Bella would sit together with Reine-Chaya in the big women's section of the temple.

Berta knew full well who this woman was, the wife of a wealthy goldsmith and a well-known and respected member of the Community Committee. She knew, and sought her company.

One Sabbath morning, as Reine-Chaya took her usual place in the front row of the women's section, an unknown woman and her daughter pushed themselves forward to occupy seats next to her.

"Good Sabbath," the strange woman greeted her.

"A good and blessed Sabbath," Reine-Chaya answered the woman and her daughter, and immediately shifted her eyes from them to seek the figure of Shmuel who was speaking to the synagogue's treasurer on the lower floor.

The cantor banged on the reader's desk once, and then again, with his heavy hand and silence fell in the synagogue, which until that moment was filled with the talk of many people coming together in the ambiance of the Sabbath. The cantor began singing Sabbath songs in a voice that became ever more powerful, and the congregation followed suit. Then he began reading aloud the introductory verses to the *Amidah* prayer. As he did so the synagogue's treasurer turned towards the Holy Ark, murmuring the verses of the prayer and signaling with a hand that the time had come to rise.

The temple was filled with the sound of chairs being moved and the scraping of lecterns as the entire congregation rose, the men in the hall below and the women on the floor above, Reine-Chaya among them, who suddenly sensed that the strange woman and her daughter were stealing glances at her, but out of respect for the Sabbath service she made out that she saw and heard nothing.

As they reached the last verse of the Eighteen Benedictions, "Holy, holy, holy is the Lord of hosts; the whole earth is full of his glory", their eyes met again. When they sat down, side by side, Reine-Chaya took the initiative and held out her hand.

"Reine-Chaya Bergman. I'm pleased to meet you."

"Yes, I know," the strange woman replied, surprising her, "and I'm Berta Litvinovsky. And this is Bella, my young daughter," she said, nodding at her daughter who lowered her eyes as befitted such an occasion, but while her forehead was lowered, her green eyes were raised, endowing her with an impish look.

"The cantor sang beautifully today," Reine-Chaya said, ignoring the daughter's look.

"He always sings like that," Berta replied, "like a bird."

"Sometimes it's a raven, sometimes a songbird," Reine-Chaya laughed, "today he sang like a nightingale."

Berta shot her a cautious glance.

"If you like we can go outside for a while and get some fresh air," she said after a moment.

"I need it," said Reine-Chaya happily, "and in any case they're reading the Portion of the Week now and I must get home to lay the table for the men."

"Yes," Berta responded as she got her daughter up from her seat, "for those men who come home from synagogue on the Sabbath."

Reine-Chaya took note of her words but did not respond as she made her way after them between the balcony rail and the rows of seats, the three of them subject to the grumbling of the women they were disturbing at prayer and their diligent gossiping.

It was a warm day as the three women exited through the synagogue's wide door into the front courtyard. They sat themselves down on a stone bench that was half in the light and half in the shade.

"Ah, what a beautiful Sabbath day," Reine-Chaya sighed, arranging her handbag on her lap.

"It certainly is," Berta replied, smiling at her for the first time since first speaking to her that morning. "I wish everyone in this city would observe the Sabbath."

"Enough, Mama," the young woman suddenly interjected, "he goes his own way, and it is all right too."

"What do you know," Berta muttered, stroking her daughter's sleek black hair. "See what a beauty she is," she said to Reine-Chaya.

"Indeed she is," smiled Reine-Chaya, "but who were you talking about?"

"I'm ashamed to admit it," Berta said, wringing her hands in despair. "My son, Shlomo-Heinrich goes riding on the Sabbath instead of coming to the synagogue with his father and mother."

"Heaven help us," Reine-Chaya said.

"He's become a real *goy*, "Berta said, reaching for her daughter's hand. "Thank the Lord I've got a daughter, and such a pretty one too."

"This city is a bad influence on everyone, especially the youngsters," said Reine-Chaya, "that's why I sent my son to the University of Hamburg to acquire an education instead of roaming the streets and marketplaces."

"Is he already an advocate?" Berta inquired, a new tone suddenly stealing into her voice.

"Neither an advocate nor a doctor," Reine-Chaya laughed in response. "In his last letter he told us he'd decided to become a teacher."

"A teacher? What kind of a living is that?" Berta asked somewhat dubiously.

"It's a living," Reine-Chaya smiled, "the main thing is that he's a good person."

"The main thing is that he's a good person," Berta repeated, "not like my son who at his age is still getting into fights with *goyim* in inns."

"After he's helped Papa at work. Don't forget that, Mama," said Bella, again sharply interrupting their conversation, her flashing green eyes meeting Reine-Chaya's once again.

"I can see that you love your brother very much," Reine-Chaya said to her, "that's a good quality," she added, as with her left hand she gently stroked the girl's cheek, who quickly moved her face out of reach.

As she did so Reine-Chaya noticed that the ring, her ring, suddenly glowed as if an inner ray of light had sparked in it.

"That's a beautiful ring," said Berta, who had also noted the ring's change of color before their very eyes, "who is the master craftsman that made it?"

"My father-in-law, of blessed memory," Reine-Chaya replied, "this ring cured me of my illness and brought me my husband, may he enjoy a long life."

"What do you mean?" Berta asked as if astonished, and squeezed her daughter's hand to keep quiet.

Reine-Chaya held out her hand so they could see the ring, which now glowed as if its stones had just been extracted from the depths of the earth.

"Strange," Reine-Chaya said, "it hasn't glowed like this since the pogroms in the small towns."

That is what she said, and brought her hand to her eyes to ascertain that they were not deceiving her.

Then she began telling them her story.

Ever since they had told one another about their sons they had grown closer. Reine-Chaya felt a great affection for Berta Litvinovsky. Like herself, she had come from a small town in Poland and married a native of Danzig. Like her, she too was troubled by her son. But Berta possessed an additional quality. She did not have four sons like Reine-Chaya, but a son and a daughter. A young and beautiful daughter, who seemed not only to possess a strong character, but also came from a good Jewish family.

While his mother was planning his future, Gershon was doing well in his studies. He was studying education, reading theoretical works and literature and philosophy, and had even become aware of the new Zionist convictions and had met with Zionist leaders. From them he learned terms like "rejection of assimilation" and "the nurturing of enlightenment" together with "the preservation and renewal of Jewish culture", and gradually became immersed in thoughts on the history of the Jewish people and its future. At the same time he began writing learned articles that he published in the Jewish press of the time.

Had it been up to him he would have remained in Hamburg or moved to Vienna, which he longed to do since that city was the domicile of Theodor Herzl, Sigmund Freud and others, whom he perceived as inspirational interlocutors. But fate decreed otherwise. One day his young brother, Meir, came from Danzig bearing a letter from his father. He must hurry home, for a burglar had broken into the home of his parents, Shmuel and Reine-Chaya, stolen his mother's ring, and brought down calamity upon them.

Seven

The burglar who broke into the home of Reine-Chaya and Shmuel Bergman was not a thief at all, but a Jew from Romania, a simple man called Leizer Kochmann who lived near the Bergman family's old house in Mattenbuden, and had a small workshop near the port. His head was round and flat like a clock pendulum weight, in which two small, beady eyes constantly darted. He was a practical, watchful, shrewd Jew with a good pair of hands. It was said that when he was asked to build a wooden wardrobe for a family with many children, or a marriage bed for a wealthy man's daughter, a chest of drawers for a lady's chamber or a glass-fronted cabinet for a sitting room, he would immediately see a precise image of the piece he had been asked to extract from the timber in his workshop. It was as if he had been born with this tree trunk from time immemorial, and now all he had to do was give birth to the desired piece. Now and then he was summoned to the homes of Jews in Danzig to measure by eye the place of a piece he had been asked to make, or to repair an old piece of furniture. Thus he sometimes came to the Bergman family home and he knew the house well, its doors and locks and the stories that adhered to it like tree resin.

Despite his integrity and craftsmanship Leizer Kochmann entered the spacious Bergman family home to steal a ring, for like all the Jews of Danzig he too had heard of its reputation. He did not want the ring for himself but for a woman, for his beloved, Leah, who also lived on the edge of the Mattenbuden Quarter, and like Reine-Chaya, she too suffered from falling sickness.

Leah had lost both her parents and had no brothers, sisters or other relatives. She came from a poor family in Lodz. Her mother had died giving birth to her, and her father worked as a drawer of water and did his best to support his baby daughter. One day he drowned in the river, leaving behind a little orphan who was shunted from family to family and house to house until she grew up, reached Danzig along highways and byways, and found herself selling her body for a living.

Nobody knew how and why she had come to this profession, how she managed to rent the room where she lived and in which she received her visitors, from where she got this idea. But where the Holy One, blessed be He, does not succeed in saving a Jewish soul, necessity does. The sick, but good-looking Leah became a whore.

By and large she took care not to provide her services to men living close by, and they avoided her house. But Danzig was a commercial and port city, a big city, and numerous merchants came to do business there and send goods across the sea. They found their way to Leah's house, a foreign woman in a foreign city, a wanton woman.

To her misfortune, one day the bed in which she slept and in which she received her visitors, collapsed, and she found herself in need of the services of a carpenter. Thus she came to Leizer Kochmann's workshop.

When she came to his workshop Leizer was alone there, his upper body bared to the sunlight, bending perspiring over his workbench, energetically sawing a stripped and fragrant tree trunk. Suddenly the door opened and Leizer saw a young woman whose body was bursting from her dress like a honeycomb, her eyes a blend of warmth and sorrow, their pupils two dark balls of resin.

He left his bench and quickly pulled on his work shirt, which was hanging, full of dust and sawdust, on the back of the chair beside him.

"Don't bother, don't bother," Leah said in Yiddish, "I apologize for interrupting you at your work."

"Heaven forbid," Leizer replied quickly, buttoning his shirt as he banged the dust from it. "How may I help the lady?"

"I need to have a bed repaired urgently," Leah said without going into details.

"Can it wait for a day or two?" Leizer Kochmann asked. "Does madam have another bed?"

"No," Leah replied, shaking her head in embarrassment, "I can't afford it. If you don't come right away I'll have nowhere to sleep."

"If that's the case," Leizer said, stealing another glance at her, "I'll get my tools and come right away."

A few minutes later Leizer Kochmann and Leah left his small workshop by the port and started walking towards Leah's house in Mattenbuden. They walked in silence, only exchanging a few words. As they came closer to where she lived, Leizer noticed something odd. More and more people were looking at them in puzzlement and wonderment, and immediately averting their eyes. Even people who knew him, who had occasion to come to his workshop or meet him in the synagogue, moved out of his path as if they sought to avoid meeting him. One even stared at the woman and spat on the ground. This puzzled him greatly.

The room where Leah lived was small, too small for her and her visitors. It was on the bottom floor of a big building in Mattenbuden. The toilet and kitchen were shared by all the building's tenants. Because her room was so small, Leah had a signal for her visitors so they knew when they could come: when she was busy her window was darkened, and when she was free and waiting for a visitor, a thick tallow candle burned in it.

The candle was only extinguished when she had a visitor. It was only when Leizer Kochmann began visiting her, first on various pretexts like checking the bed, and later without saying another word, she would draw the curtain over the narrow window. Then the stark secret language would dissipate to be replaced by a different language, the language of lovers.

From the very first time he visited her, Leizer Kochmann felt that she was no ordinary woman. Her illness made her a saint in his eyes, and after he learned her history he realized that her illness had caused no one to want her, and that after the death of her parents she had been left penniless and forced to trade her body for a living.

She was not a regular whore of the kind that received sailors in the portside brothels, nor was Leizer one of her regular visitors. Leizer Kochmann went to Leah not to seek an outlet for his sexual drives, and Leah did not go with him to lead him into committing a transgression. On the contrary, she paid him good money for the new bed he built her, and each time he went to her they would do nothing, Heaven forbid, but sit and talk. Leizer, who lived alone, was happy that he had a woman he could sit and talk to, and she was happy she had finally met a decent man who demanded nothing of her but her laughter and warm heart, a good glass of tea and a slice of the cake she had begun baking each week especially for him.

But a man is a man and a woman is a woman and as time passed they came closer to one another, until Leizer, too, enjoyed the taste of the nectar of her body. But he did not pay her for it, and certainly not before their intercourse, but he kept her instead. It was important to him to differentiate between the act and the payment because he viewed their friendship as a link to love.

Leah became the love of his life. He was ready to sell his soul to make her his wife, provide for her and take her away from her profession. He wished nothing for himself, only that she should be healthy and that he should have enough money to provide for them both without her having to sell her body.

Most days Leah was just like any other person. But one day misfortune befell her and she suffered a convulsion while beneath a respected Jew, a bank treasurer. The Jew was lying between her breasts and performing his work when she suddenly started to convulse, and her sexual moaning was replaced by white froth bubbling from her lips.

The banker was very frightened, he dressed hastily and fled the house, convinced he had heard her death rattle and that her rolled-back eyes would haunt him forever. But Leah, who knew how to control the force of the attack, turned her face downward so as not to swallow her tongue and waited until the attack abated.

That is how Leizer, who was passing the house, found her. He saw it was darkened but the door was wide open. He knew right away that something was wrong. She was lucky that he rushed inside and went into her room, found her, and saved her from death.

The more he cherished her, the angrier Leizer became when she told him about the clients that visited her. So long as she did not tell him anything, and so long as when he came to her she removed herself from her occupation, tidy her house for him so it would look like the home of a single woman, he did not ask her about what she was going through, and she did not enlighten him. They would sit and talk about his past, his life, his memories, and imagine their future together. But one day she was unable to restrain herself and told him, with impish laughter, that Herr Mendel Grunem, one of the wealthy men of Altschottland, had brought his youngest son, Duvkeh, to her to savor his first taste of a woman. Perhaps then he would enter the marriage he had arranged for him with Tirzah, the daughter of the wealthy Schindler family that owned one of Danzig's banks.

At that time the custom of fathers talking between themselves about their children without their knowledge was in decline. But Mendel Grunem's business situation had worsened and Mendel, an active corn merchant, knew that only his son's marriage to

Tirzah Schindler would bring salvation both to him and his business. But one must think ahead, and to lure the fox into the vineyard he must first be given a taste of wine. So he took his son to Leah's room, whispered whatever he whispered to her, gave her a generous sum, and left them alone.

"The poor boy," Leah told her Leizerleh – which is what she called him in moments of great affection – "was standing shamefaced and helpless. With my own hands I took off his beret and his spectacles, and having no choice, his shirt and trousers too."

"Why are you telling me all this?" Leizer asked, feeling his anger awaken inside him.

"So you know what you're getting into," Leah replied, placing her hand over his. Leizer fell silent and let her go on with her story.

"He stood there pale and shivering, the son of a wealthy man, with two white sticks instead of legs peeping from his underpants, and a long white *leibeleh* covering his thin chest, that already had a few hairs sprouting on it. I could see he was so frightened, so I took him to my bosom like a child, I stroked his head to calm him, and at the same time let him feel the heat of the flesh."

"Enough," Leizer said, getting up. "I don't want to hear any more."

"It's enough for me too, Leizer," said Leah, soothing him. "It's enough for me that you know."

She did not tell him how the boy had sweated between her thighs, how she had knelt before him and made him groan, how she had guided him over her body and taught him the ways of a woman.

Leizer stayed with Leah for a short while longer and then fled the house, feeling his anger overflowing and carrying him forward, walking quickly, against his will, through the streets of Mattenbuden, and from there to Altschottland, running like a man pursued by a beast of prey.

He was angry with the father who had used his son to cure the ills of his business, with the use of Leah as a learners' mattress, and enraged with the boy whose helplessness had been replaced by the ability to pour his young manliness into Leah. All of Leah's whispered remonstrances on his way out, and her promises that when he had enough money and she had saved enough from her work, they would get married and then she would never give her body to another, did not help.

That night, as he roamed the streets of Danzig, embittered, talking to himself, feeling that he was sharing his property with another, he no longer remembered everything she had promised, but only the scenes that had risen before him on hearing her words.

It was a dark and freezing winter's night. As he wandered dispiritedly through the streets of Danzig that were already covered with a layer of thick snow, Leizer recalled the story of Reine-Chaya's ring, the magical healing ring of which he had heard so much. It was his desperation that reminded him of the ring's existence, and it was his anger that led him from street to street until he was standing in front of the Bergman house, which that night was shrouded in darkness like all its fellows in the street.

Leizer made his way to a side wicket into the yard that was the tradesmen's entrance. Despite the cold and darkness he remembered where the back door to the house was. Without much hesitation he took a length of wire he found in the yard and began picking the padlock until it yielded to his efforts and opened the door into the sleeping house.

Nothing of what happened next can be related here. It is the way of the burglar that his work is done in darkness. The interior of the house was so dark that we cannot know how he found the ring, how he hid it in his clothing and managed to make his escape without waking a soul, bent low and carrying off his loot.

A short time afterwards Leah was cured of her falling sickness and she and Leizer were married in a modest ceremony.

Reine-Chaya, meanwhile, began suffering particularly severe attacks of falling sickness that gripped her and assailed her and threatened to lay her low completely, as is the way of an old illness lurking in a patient's body until it steals in and wreaks havoc.

Eight

More than anything else done by the physicians, the healers, the miracle workers and the charlatans to help Reine-Chaya and ease her suffering, Shmuel was horrified by the bleeding with leeches.

After several days of incessant attacks, her husband and three children were at her bedside, hurting and weeping at the sight of their mother convulsing between life and death, as if an unseen hand was gripping her innards and hurling her unceasingly from side to side, Hinda grasped Shmuel's hand.

"Reb Shmuel, my heart breaks to see Madam like this," she said. "I will go to the *goy* who lives on the riverbank and bring him here with a jarful of leeches."

"Even the best physicians have given up hope," Shmuel replied, "so why leeches?"

"To cleanse the blood," Hinda said, "that's how many illnesses are cured. It's what they used to do in Russia every time there was an epidemic."

Weakened by his grief at the sight of his wife fading before his eyes, Shmuel gave his consent.

While Hinda went to the river to seek out the *goy* who lived there, Shmuel, bowed and downcast, plagued with remorse, went to look through the old papers his father had left, which were written on parchment in cursive handwriting, and among them all kinds of oaths and talismans against all ills and all harm. When he became bar-mitzvah, his father sat him down and taught him what was good for this and what for that, and the right way of etching words and spells at the base of a goblet or on the edge of a pot. But many years had passed since then, and the more he immersed himself in quotidian committee and community matters, and later the synagogue, all his father's secrets had been forgotten. For it is well known that miracles happen in a man's heart when it is void of any other thought, and his entire being is filled with tranquility of the soul and the fear of God. And miracles also depend on the air of the world, which must be good and suitable for their occurrence, not like the dry air of Danzig that had been permeated with worship of the Enlightenment, which broadens the mind but destroys the heart.

Shmuel sat going through his father's papers, but now, after so many years, they seemed like a congeries of separate letters hovering in the air, a secret code whose cipher he had forgotten.

Some time later Hinda returned to the house with a yellow-haired *goy* who looked homeless. He was filthy and dressed in rags, and held in his hand a jar in which swam dozens of small leeches, wriggling here and there, wondering why they found themselves where they were.

Shmuel did not know the *goy*'s name and title, but his reputation had preceded him as a man who had cured numerous children with milk they had suckled with their tiny mouths directly from the udders of his goats, skinny goats that grazed on the grass by the river.

Hinda sent the children out of the room, and once they had left she drew down the blanket, exposing Reine-Chaya's legs to the *goy*.

The *goy* drew close to Reine-Chaya, who was lying and convulsing on her bed, and with his fingers took one leech after another from the jar and stuck them to her legs.

The leeches smelt the woman's flesh and through it the pulsing of her blood, and immediately extended their minuscule suckers and began eagerly sucking her blood, smacking their lips and telling one another in their leech language how tasty her blood is. And Reine-Chaya, as if hearing the leeches chatting about the feast they were enjoying on her body, stopped convulsing and turned her head aside, her eyes agape and her mouth mumbling unheard words.

Hinda raised her eyes to Reb Shmuel as if reproving him and saying, look, look at my medicine at work.

The leeches drank from Reine-Chaya's body for a long time, until her face paled as if she were dead. Then they rolled their swollen bellies from her body and sang a paean to the Creator who brings forth blood.

Shmuel watched and did not know whether she had been calmed by the cleansing of her blood, or that she no longer had the strength to move in her bed from the loss of it. But he allowed the *goy* healer to complete his work, collect his flock of bloodsuckers, receive his payment and go, leaving him and Hinda beside his sick wife who lay in her bed mumbling meaningless words, like a woman upon whom the twilight along the road to the next world had fallen.

Next day Gershon arrived from Hamburg. Even before he changed out of his traveling clothes Hinda led him into the room and he stood at his mother's bedside. He saw her lying in the magnificent canopied bed that had been made by the master carpenter who had worked for them, and her face was at rest, pale, her head lying on an embroidered crimson pillow.

When she saw him, Reine-Chaya beckoned him closer. Gershon moved to her bed, knelt, and kissed her on the forehead. The kiss had the taste of pain, of sorrow, of an imminent parting.

His mother took her hand from under the blanket and put it into his. For a moment he lowered his eyes, seeing the blotches of age that had spread over her pale skin.

Her hand was weak and bloated, as if filled with water.

"Welcome, Gershon my son," she said. "You have come in time."

"In time for what, Mama?"

"You will know soon enough," his mother replied. "Shmuel! Shmuel!" she strained to call her husband.

"I'm here, I'm here," her husband quickly replied and stood leaning on his cane at her bedside.

"Send Nathan or Meir to bring the Litvinovsky family here."

"Litvinovsky?" Gershon asked. "Who are the Litvinovskys?"

"You will soon find out," she replied, "go and bathe and change out of your traveling clothes."

Gershon did his mother's bidding. He went up to his room with his luggage, which included a clothes trunk and boxes of books and journals and newspapers he had brought with him from Hamburg, and then followed the servant who had drawn him a hot bath, bathed and dressed. Then he heard the doorbell from the ground floor and thought to himself that the Litvinovsky family had probably arrived. He examined his appearance in the mirror and hurried downstairs, back to his mother's room.

As he entered the room he heard his mother exchanging a few words with a strange woman standing by the head of her bed.

"Berta," Reine-Chaya whispered, and blurted out a kind of strange laugh. "I'm not dead yet. Why are you both wearing black?"

"No, no, Heaven forbid," Berta wailed into her handkerchief.

"*Sha, sha,*" his mother soothed her friend, "there's nothing to cry about. I'm still here, Berta."

Berta continued to sob, her weeping growing louder until she had to move away from the bed lest she wet the sick woman with her tears.

For before they came they had spoken with Shmuel Bergman and agreed that they would not tell Reine-Chaya the bitter truth. A great calamity had befallen them that same week: their wayward son, Shlomo-Heinrich, had been killed when the horse he was riding in the main street of Danzig had thrown him. He had wanted to show one of his father's customers how healthy the horse was, but the rebellious beast had not only thrown him, but stood over him, kicking him in the head and sending him to the world on high.

The Litvinovsky family had only just risen from the weeklong *shiva* mourning period, but Berta did not say a word of this to her good friend Reine-Chaya so as not to add to her pain.

From the looks of astonishment directed towards him by the visitors, Gershon's mother realized that he had come back into the room, and called him to her.

Gershon was already a tall, well-built man. A thin mustache adorned his upper lip, and from his long hours of reading at the university he wore spectacles. He was wearing a solemn suit jacket over a waistcoat from whose pocket peeped a gold watch that had been in the family since his grandfather's day. His appearance spoke of nobility and well-being and aroused admiration in the hearts of those who saw him.

"Come, Gershon, come," his mother called with difficulty from her deathbed.

Gershon moved to his mother's side. She again extended a feeble hand and he quickly took it.

"Come, Bella," his mother murmured to the young woman, who walked towards her with the help of a surreptitious push to her backside from her mother.

Bella moved closer to the mother and gave her her hand.

"Gershon," his mother whispered, "if we had time I would tell you everything. But this is Bella, the woman I have chosen to be your wife."

Gershon's hand was slightly withdrawn from hers almost involuntarily, but she clasped it with her last remaining strength, brought it to Bella's and joined them.

"How I wish I had the ring here to give to you, Bella," the old woman said slowly, having ever-increasing difficulty speaking, "but it has gone. Gershon, swear to me now that you will restore that ring to the family and put it on the finger of your bride. Swear it."

"I promise you, Mama," Gershon hastened to reply, "the main thing is that you rest."

"And you, Bella," whispered the old woman said with difficulty, "swear to me that you will give it to your daughter or your daughter-in-law after you."

And Bella, who was beside herself with grief, for only recently she had encountered the utter dominion of death for the first time in her life, and now she was standing by the deathbed of her future mother-in-law, also swore the oath.

"I love you," Reine-Chaya told Gershon, barely forming the words, "I always loved you. Take care of your brothers and your father."

"I know, Mama," Gershon whispered painfully close to her face, his eyes glistening with tears.

"Don't cry, Gershon. Marry," his mother blurted, and immediately began quivering, bitter white froth spurting from her mouth.

Gershon and Bella, as if in unison, quickly rearranged the crimson cushion under her head, and Asher Litvinovsky, who also rushed to help, grasped both of Reine-Chaya's arms to raise her to a sitting position and prevent her from swallowing her tongue, Heaven forbid. But her small, thin body convulsed for another few moments, she emitted several gurgles, and then her head fell back and she restored her soul to her Maker.

Nine

One woman's nine months of anguish became another's nine months of carrying a child in her womb. Whereas Reine-Chaya tasted a soupçon of her death every day until she was finally consumed by it, Leah sailed on a sea of love. Not only had Leizer brought her a ring, he had stood under the wedding canopy with it and blessed her, and with it made her his wife. At the time, Leah and Leizer were unaware that the precipitate seed of Mendel Grunem's son had taken hold in her womb.

A short time after their wedding Leah felt that something was not quite right with her. Her menstrual period was late and she was assailed by ravenous hunger, she began eating more than usual and became tired from nothing. But people tend to put things off, and until her belly swelled in a way that could only mean one thing, she did not say a word, even to herself.

Leizer was somewhat puzzled by her sudden weight gain in such a short time, but he was happy that married life agreed with her. And apart from that, a woman should have something to get hold of, as they say, for if she doesn't then she is like a scrawny chicken that has no flavor.

Leah, on the other hand, took great care with her visitors and either practiced coitus interruptus or rubbed their members between her thighs, and she would only take Leizer inside her if his member was protected with a length of cow's intestine. They had, after all, said that they would only have a child when their financial situation improved. But she had allowed that same virgin, whom she had imagined was only a boy, to taste the depths of her body, and she had no doubt – the fetus in her womb was from the seed of Mendel Grunem's son, Heaven help us.

She did not dare to say anything about this to Leizer. The same night on which she had inducted the boy into adulthood from boyhood, Leizer had come to her, surprised her with a spectacular ring, knelt, and asked for her hand in marriage. She said yes, betrothed herself to him with the ring, and most surprisingly, had also been cured of her illness. How could she now shame him, break his heart?

One evening Leizer came home from his workshop, and after he had washed his body and eaten he sought, like any man seeking comfort from the travails of the world, to rest his head on his wife's belly. Leah tried to dissuade him, but he was insistent and laid his weary head on her soft abdomen, sighed, and even thought about taking a short nap in the warmth of her body, when he suddenly felt something moving and kicking him.

He leapt up from her swollen belly in alarm.

"What was that?" he asked her.

"The Sabbath *cholent*," Leah blurted.

"Beans don't kick like that," Leizer said, surprised, and extended his hand to her stomach.

Leah turned onto her side, trying to evade his touch, but he caught her and laid his wide, solid hand over her belly. Then he felt something unmistakable – the movement of a fetus swimming and laughing and suckling from all the goodness of his wife's body.

Leizer removed his hand in fright, holding it in the air in awe and looking into Leah's eyes.

"How long have you known?" he asked, his voice shaking, his eyes questioning hers.

"Don't be angry, Leizerleh," she replied gently, "only a month and a half."

"But that was when we were standing under the wedding canopy. When in God's name did it happen?"

Leah closed her mouth and remained silent. She knew full well that some things become evident through silence.

"No," he whispered after a moment, his voice breaking, "just not that."

"I'm sorry, Leizer," she said quietly, "I didn't know when I stood under the canopy with you."

"How is it possible," he mumbled like a man struck by a hammer blow, "how is it possible."

"I was a pawn in the hands of others," Leah replied, "and you took me with all my faults, Leizer."

"We must do something," he said with a look as sharp as a chisel.

"I'm a sick woman," she replied, and involuntarily, protectively, spread both hands over her belly. "Do you want to kill me?"

"Heaven forbid," he told her, "we must go to a specialist. Not one of those women who kill mother and child with their knives."

"I've been to the hospital," Leah prevaricated, "the doctors said that if I have another abortion I'll be as good as dead."

"But why?" Leizer demanded, unable to let go.

"Why? Because of everything I've suffered in my life!"

Leizer got up and began pacing the room restlessly. Leah said no more. At that moment she was unable to tell him how much she wanted to have her baby. But seeing him pacing from one end of the room to the other, not speaking, just kicking the floor, she could bear it no longer.

In the end she mustered the courage to ask, "Do you want to look for another wife instead of me?"

"What? What are you thinking?" he shouted.

"I don't know, Leizer," she whispered, "perhaps you really deserve another woman, not a castoff like me."

"Leah, Leahleh," Leizer knelt before his wife and with his hand wiped away her tears. "Heaven forbid that you should think that."

"Do you still love me?" A wail burst from her lips as she felt the ground shaking beneath her feet, which in a moment would swallow her.

"I love you, of course I love you," Leizer said, and laid his hand on his breast.

But as he spread his hand on his breast he felt how a deep pain gripped and bound him, the news was so hard to take. His wife was carrying another man's child in her womb, a child not his.

He got up and went to the window, staring at the stars sown over the firmament, illuminating the blessed darkness with their malignant, destructive light.

"Whose child is it?" he asked without turning round.

"The boy's."

A deep shout erupted from his throat, as if his heart had been ripped apart. Without thinking he grabbed his beret and coat and fled the house, agitatedly walking the streets, walking and thinking, until dawn broke through the belly of the night.

But morning came, and after it another night and morning, and no solution shone in its sky. Leah's belly continued to thicken and she ate for two, feeding the fruit of the seed of that pale-faced youngster with what he earned from his labor and rage. And Leizer, who felt his ire rising inside him and turning into hatred, tried to keep his distance from her, finding it hard to touch or caress her.

He loved her with all his heart and with all the rage in him, but as her pregnancy became more apparent she became defiled in his eyes, not in herself, but by virtue of what she carried in her womb. A memory of sin. A bastard. An accident.

He could no longer bear the thought that his beloved wife would give birth to a bastard by a stripling, and the more he began imagining how their life together would be, he saw how this baby would poison their life and put an end to their love. From these imagined scenes that horrified him came an idea, and the more he thought about it, it seemed that come what may it was the right thing to do.

Ten

A wedding usually possesses the flavor of happiness and joy, and all the more so a Jewish wedding at which the Divine Presence unites with the Deity, and the Jewish people brings sons and daughters together to magnify and glorify and exalt the name of its God and make them more in number than there are grains of sand. But a wedding that takes place, Heaven forfend, after two *shivas*, one on the side of the bride and the other on that of the groom, is a joyless occasion. And all the more so a wedding in which the bride has been forced upon the groom without him knowing her beforehand, while completely different thoughts are filling his mind. Here neither the delicacies, the wine, and not even the wandering musicians will help. A wedding such as this does not have even a grain of love in it.

Upright and frozen-faced, Gershon stood beneath the wedding canopy with Bella Litvinovsky, the woman of his mother's choice. The pain he had caused his parents in his youth and the deathbed promise he had made to his mother were what bound him like shackles around his ankles. It was enough for him to look at his father to evoke the memory of his departed mother as if she were standing there, radiant in her bright light, in order to utter the words of the blessing, place a ring on his bride's finger, stamp on the ceremonial wineglass, kiss the woman hidden beneath the veil, and suddenly find himself a married man without any means of escape.

Throughout his time at the university he had corresponded with his childhood friend Frank Abramson, who was studying in Berlin. In his letters he would argue with him over their differing views on liberalism, emancipation and Zionism, and while they disputed matters of paramount importance they did not mention a word about that fleeting youthful episode that at the time had forced them apart, sending them to different ends of the country. They would only talk to each other in their correspondence, all the while maintaining intellectual restraint that had nothing at all to do with the tumult of the heart.

Despite making no mention of what had happened between them in those far off days, from time to time Gershon felt that quite involuntarily and completely irrationally, that strange emotion that had first burst forth from him with Frank continued to emerge, and had become like a demon that since then had settled inside him. The demon lurked within him waiting to seize its opportunity, and when it was sure that Gershon wasn't looking, when he was totally immersed in thought and writing polemics and theorizing, it would raise its head, appear inside him and be revealed in all its force. Gershon did not know how to deal with it. Then he would feel a kind of strange hunger, a deep wave of an unnamed desire that followed every man that passed him, whether he were a long-limbed, black-haired student looking for rare books on the academic library's shelves, or a blond young man hurrying down the street.

The more he tried to suppress it as something that was forbidden to express or vent, so the power of the demon to swallow him whole increased. He would sink and drown in a deep sadness that threatened to sweep him away and close its dark abyss over him. Then he would shake off the pain that engulfed him, take his coat, seek to escape something that was completely inside him, go out and walk the streets of Hamburg, roam between its houses and along its streets like a man with nowhere to hide.

One night his feet led him by chance to the big park in the center of the city. From a distance he saw a few men crossing the wide road, looking around to make sure that nobody could see them, and then go through the big iron gates to be swallowed up in the shrubbery. He went over and stood by the iron fence, strained his eyes and saw dark silhouettes flitting among the trees and shrubs, coming together and parting, blending and vanishing in the darkness.

Gershon moved away from the fence and went into the park, walking hesitantly along its paths, trying to distinguish between the trees' shadows and those of the people concealed among them. They were men. Troubled men like him, walking around as if moonstruck, seeking one another in the heart of the vast darkness.

He would have been satisfied with what he had discovered had not he suddenly been accosted by a well-built, broad-shouldered man wearing a dark, elegant coat, who stood before him and looked deep into his eyes, his look saying what his lips did not utter.

The man beckoned him with his eyes to follow him into the darkness and Gershon obeyed wordlessly, following him through the dense, thick shrubbery, and letting the man have his way with him until he climaxed. The stranger let go of him and immediately disappeared into the darkness without even asking his name.

Since then Gershon found himself returning to that park in Hamburg now and again, grieving and ashamed, submissively surrendering himself to his demon if only to slake its thirst and let him study in peace for another day or two, read and write, without this lust that had claimed him, that continued to trouble him.

Eleven

When Leizer Kochmann stole Reine-Chaya's magic ring on that reckless night, he did not know that with one ring he was involving numerous stories and families across the sea, and bringing down troubles on his head from every direction. The first was his wife falling pregnant to the son of Mendel Grunem and giving birth to a baby daughter. The second was not only a family mourning the untimely death of a mother, but a bride with the memory of a hawk, who had seen the ring that should have been hers, but did not possess it.

Had everything gone smoothly since their wedding day, perhaps Bella Bergman would have been filled with joy and forgotten about the ring. But her marriage with that ring was for her and her mother a kind of mark of their acceptance, the family of horse traders with a wanton, dead son, into the Altschottland *maskilim* circle. But she was married to the son of a goldsmith, and even if she was not wearing his late mother's wedding ring, that heavy, deep-hued ring, that would look upon its surroundings like a big eye on Sabbath and festival eves in the synagogue, her father and Shmuel her father-in-law and Gershon had chosen another ring from among the antique ones fashioned by her father-in-law when his hands were still steady. A gold ring, nine carats in weight they had chosen for her, with twelve small diamonds set in it, symbolizing the twelve months of the year.

But that night, which her mother had said was to be the happiest of her life, was awful, a night of shame and affront.

After the last of the guests had departed, her mother and father and the groom's father and his three brothers escorted Bella and Gershon to the carriage to which four pure white horses were harnessed. Gershon mounted the carriage first, held out his hand and helped her up with her high-heeled shoes, while Meir, his young brother, quickly gathered up the train of her bridal gown and bundled it into the carriage after her.

They drove off along the main street of the city, the horses at a coordinated, ceremonious canter, their hooves striking the roadway and their bells tinkling as passersby turned to look at them, seeing that this was a wedding carriage taking the couple to their marriage bed.

Bella and Gershon sat in the carriage, looking through its small windows at the city as it passed them. They rode in silence, only the voice of the coachman spurring his horses on in German and whipping them up was heard, until the carriage drew up at the entrance to the Hotel Imperial in the center of Danzig.

The hotel servants hurried towards the couple, opening the carriage door and helping the beautiful bride down first. Her tall groom, clumsy in his movements and choked in his cravat, followed her slowly.

The servants led them through the doors of the hotel into a lobby flooded with bright light from big chandeliers. Thousands of sparks of light descended upon them from the ceiling.

The owner of the hotel hurried towards them. Not every day did he have the chance to host for their wedding night the eldest son of one of the most respected men of Danzig's Jewish community and the daughter of one of the army's suppliers of horses. He led them in person to the suite that had been readied for them.

They went into the spacious and luxurious suite, which was usually reserved for the nobility and princes, and inspected it in amazement. In the big room stood a canopied bed, its velvet curtains gathered, and on the bed a blue velvet counterpane with their names embroidered on it in crimson letters, and on it were strewn rose petals. On both sides of the bed there were small nightstands on which big tallow candles were burning. Fragrant bouquets, bowls of fruit and a silver salver with tiny wafers and pastries had been laid out all around.

They thanked the owner for his trouble, and after the servants had brought their baggage in and closed the door behind them, they were left on their own, finally alone together after a long evening.

Bella went over to the big dressing table that stood in the middle of the room, put her purse down on it and took off her tiara. She looked at herself in the big mirror over the dressing table and saw the fatigue in her face. She immediately took a handkerchief from her purse to repair her appearance.

Gershon slumped into an armchair on the other side of the room and finally took off the top hat he had worn all evening.

"Thank God," he said, loosening the cravat binding his neck.

"It was dignified and beautiful," said Bella, peeping at him through the big mirror.

"I feel as if I haven't slept for a fortnight," Gershon groaned.

"It all happened very fast," Bella smiled at him, "and now here we are."

"Yes," Gershon said, averting his eyes from her look.

She continued to sit, expectant and silent. He groaned again, but did not move.

Her mother had whispered to her not to fear this night. It is the nature of men that they know exactly what to do when the time comes. And there he was, sitting frozen, mummified in his clothes and his eyes downcast.

"It's warm in here," she said and removed the colored silk mantle covering the neckline of her dress, and now the swell of her breasts was revealed, reveling in the resplendence of the world.

Gershon shifted restively in his chair, his eyes lingering on an insipid landscape hanging on the wall facing him. Then he got up and went to the balcony door to open it.

"Could you help me with my gown?" he heard her asking from behind him.

He turned round. Bella turned her back to him, pointing at the fasteners on her gown. He hesitated momentarily, stumbled over to her, and then reached out and began unfastening her gown with incredible slowness and indescribable excitement. He stopped in the middle of the long line of fasteners so that she was unable to take the gown from her body.

"A bit more," Bella laughed, "otherwise I won't be able to take it off."

Gershon uttered a giggling sound and went back to work on the fasteners. This time he took his fingers the whole length of the line, unfastening it to her waistline, revealing her smooth, gleaming white back, and he was beside himself with embarrassment.

With both hands Bella pulled the gown from the front, and all at once turned her bare, abundant bosom to him, let him see it for a moment, and then moved close to him, laying her head on his chest.

Gershon's hands remained in the air for a moment and then he embraced her.

She could hear his heart pounding and fluttered her face over his elegant waistcoat, inhaling the smell of his body. As she did, she began undoing the buttons of the waistcoat with her small, nimble fingers, and then his shirt buttons, revealing his white chest with a thin line of fine black hair descending from it to the line of his trousers.

Gershon grasped her head with both hands and kissed her hair, her forehead, her eyes, and then planted a mischievous, childish kiss on the tip of her nose.

"There's too much light in here," he said, and moved her away from him. "let's turn out the lights first."

They each moved around a different side of the room, blowing out the candles and removing the light bulbs from their sockets. Within a few seconds the room was plunged into total, calming darkness. Now they were illuminated only by the light of a slender moon that could be seen through the big glass balcony door, casting its pale light onto the roofs of Danzig.

Bella stood in the darkness, observing the enchanted scene. Gershon came over and stood behind her, his arms around her waist.

She shifted backward, sinking her buttocks between his thighs.

He grasped her hair and kissed her neck, her nape, her shoulders.

"My husband," Bella whispered, a pleasant sensation spreading through her limbs, feeling how she was giving herself to him.

"My wife," murmured Gershon, his voice shaking. "I can't believe what my lips are uttering."

He fluttered his clenched lips over hers, and then brought them down again to her neck, to her cheeks.

"Not like that, Gershon," she whispered softly and lifted his head with both hands. "Like this," she said, opening her lips and sucking his into her, immersing them in her mouth.

"It would be better if we got into bed."

They got in, he on one side and she on the other of the wide bed redolent with the deep scent of passion from the petals strewn over it. Gershon lay on his back, his arms at his sides, and stared upward, scanning the gloom of the ceiling. Bella lay on her side, turning her breasts to him, longing for his touch. He did not move. If you don't do something this night will end and we will leave this room just as we came to it, Bella thought, and slowly slid her left hand over the sheet until it touched Gershon's warm body.

He started in alarm.

"It's only me," Bella laughed, putting her warm hand on him.

Gershon did not say a word, but she could hear the sound of his breathing as she began caressing him, learning the lines of his body, if only he would reach out and touch her.

In the end she took his hand and laid it on her breasts.

"Touch, Gershon, touch," she told him, "from now on this is all yours."

Gershon turned his body towards her, his face, which for some reason seemed tortured. Hesitantly, he reached out to touch her face. She closed her eyes in tense expectation. With his outstretched finger he began moving along her hairline and forehead, the outline of her eyebrows, the curve of her nose. With his finger he sculpted her image, learning her secretly, embarrassedly, gently. Then he laid his broad hand on her neck and caressed it, and lowered it to her breasts and belly, and upwards again, afraid of coming to that place.

She moved her body closer to him and as if by accident touched his member with her hand.

His Honor lay there, flaccid and still, like an inoffensive appendage.

Gershon shifted his body away from her.

"Perhaps we should go to sleep," he said, pulling the blanket over his body.

"No, Gershon," she whispered hesitantly, "not tonight of all nights."

"I don't know what to tell you," he said suddenly in a cold, clear voice, from which all traces of sleepiness had vanished, "but I've never done this before."

"Neither have I," she laughed.

"You laugh like a little girl," Gershon said.

"It's you who's behaving like a child," Bella replied, and began tickling him all over his body. "Child! Child!" she shouted.

Gershon twisted and turned under her tickling until he began returning tickle for tickle. In no time at all they started laughing joyfully, tickling and slapping one another like two children at play, Gershon telling her not to laugh so loudly lest they be heard outside. As they frolicked Gershon finally felt his member coming erect and hardening. All at once he reached down to her pudenda, and his probing touch turned her laughter into moaning and led his member into her.

An amazing warmth and softness like a thousand velvets enveloped and surrounded him, and he began galloping inside her, striking inside her in a frenzy, showering kisses on her lips as she writhed beneath him, clasping his hand over her mouth so her animal-like cries, her moans, would not be heard, their scream as they climaxed simultaneously, mingling one with the other, discovering their lust.

Then he withdrew all at once and rolled onto his side.

He lay panting, listening to his still-pounding body as it slowly calmed. Only then did he notice that what he had taken for moans of passion had become sobs of weeping.

Gershon lifted himself into a half-sitting position.

"What's the matter, Bella?" he asked concerned, fearing he had hurt her or harmed her in some unknown way.

Bella did not reply, trying to stifle her tears with deep breathing. But the tears burst from her unceasingly, soaking the pillow, the bedclothes, the mattress.

"What's the matter?' Gershon persisted.

"Nothing's the matter, Gershon," she finally said. "They're tears of joy."

Nobody had prepared him for this. Only a few moments ago they had been one flesh and now they were like two strangers, and he knew nothing of her world.

He looked at her in surprise, keeping silent, then closing his eyes.

She embraced him, drawing his body close to hers.

He lay beside her completely frozen. Within a few moments he started snoring softly, his chest rising and falling under the blanket.

She held him for another moment and then moved over to the other side of the bed, abandoned in the bed, in a strange room, with the man who had claimed her virginity but who had not penetrated her soul.

Twelve

On the day that Reine-Chaya restored her soul to her Maker, Leah was brought to bed of a daughter.

Seven days later, Leizer awakened in the last hour before dawn, got out of bed while his wife was still sleeping the sleep of the just, and took the straw basket with the infant in it out of the room. He threw on his coat and hat, arranged the tiny blanket round the baby, and clutching the small crib to him, he slipped out of the house.

Had she given birth to a son, Leizer would not have waited even seven days to remove the child from his life. But since it was a girl he allowed Leah to nurse her for a week before putting his thoughts into action. He started walking rapidly toward Danzig's big orphanage, hoping that the child would not wake up and start crying, which might arouse the suspicions of passersby.

During that week Leizer had taken care not to call the child by name, just "It", and Leah, knowing her husband well, realized that she did not have much time. He was intent on separating her from her daughter. If she wanted to protect her infant daughter she must forestall Leizer. And so, when he brought home a straw basket, ostensibly as a crib for the baby, but in fact as a carrier of orphanhood, beneath the blanket she had sewn she hastened to hide a letter, saying that the child's name is Esther, the daughter of Leah Kochmann of Mattenbuden. Due to her husband's demand and her fear for the infant's life, she had been forced to give the child up to the orphanage. She was filled with gratitude to the women of the orphanage who would care for her daughter, and as a mark of her thanks she enclosed eighteen coins. When she was able she would visit her daughter, nurse her, and pay more for her upkeep if only they would keep her safe and well.

As Leizer made his way to the orphanage, he was unaware that beneath the blankets covering the newborn child, Leah had hidden what she had hidden.

Leizer did not dare to return home that day, and paced back and forth in his workshop, imagining that he could hear Leah's cry as she awakened with a smile on her face and her breasts longing to give of their milk to the infant, and now the crib has gone, the child has gone, her husband has gone, and her heart is already telling her what has happened. He only returned home that night, opened the door like a thief, and saw his wife sitting in a torn mourning garment, not looking at him to greet him.

For many days not a word passed between them. Leizer would wake up and escape to his workshop, seeking to avoid the accusing, tortured look in her eyes, and each morning she would turn onto her side, pretending to be asleep, letting him drown in his guilt. She, of course, was fooling him, and stole to the orphanage whenever she was able to nurse the baby. But she did not forgive him for taking her daughter from her and compelling her to raise the child as a kind of wet nurse who came to her daughter surreptitiously, gave her the breast, and afterwards left her in the hands of other women.

A short time later, while chatting in the timber market by the port, Leizer heard by chance that Reine-Chaya, the wife of Shmuel Bergman from Altschottland, the woman from whom he had stolen the ring to cure his wife Leah, had died on the very day the infant was born. On hearing this he was beside himself with terror.

Not long after he left her daughter on the orphanage doorstep, the old malady returned to assail Leah. One night, as she lay in bed beside Leizer, she felt her leg quivering strangely and then stopping. A few days later, the strong smell of carpenters' glue began to fill her nostrils, even though Leizer's workshop had long since not been close to their house. In the way of people seeking to forget their troubles, at first she thought it was foolishness or signs of fatigue from her pregnancy and the birth. But slowly she began to notice that these episodes had become a regular occurrence, and she realized that the falling sickness had returned, albeit in relatively mild attacks, but in a different form. Odd tremors would suddenly pass through her arms and legs, causing them to be thrown here and there without her being able to control them.

One evening, as she served a bowl of soup to Leizer, she was suddenly gripped by such a spasm that her arms began to fly uncontrollably in all directions. The bowl of scalding soup danced in her hands, landed on Leizer, and bounced from him to shatter on the floor.

Leizer screamed as the boiling soup burned his body, and jumped up in fright, tearing off his shirt as he did.

"You could have killed me!"

"I'm sorry," Leah said, "I don't know what happened to me. My hand suddenly jumped."

"You don't know what happened to you?" Leizer screamed in a mixture of rage and pain, "you're not wearing the ring. That's what happened to you. Where's the ring?"

Leah stood frozen in the middle of the room, looking at him in silence.

"In the basket of the child you took from me," she replied in restrained and measured tones, knowing how deeply the blow would strike.

"What?" he yelled as he grabbed her with both hands and started shaking her back and forth.

"You wanted me clean the way I used to be, without being pregnant, without a child," she said, shaking off his hands, "so that's how you got me. With everything I had when we first met."

Leizer looked at her incredulously, and then began running around the house maniacally, grabbing objects and throwing them against the walls, venting his anger on them instead of her.

"Is this why I saved you from death? So that now you can die slowly, in agony, right before my eyes? Is this what I deserve? Is this your gratitude, Leah?"

"You have killed me, Leizer," she answered quietly. "You saved me to kill me a second time, when you got up like a thief in the night and took my daughter away."

With a sudden movement Leizer raised his hand to slap her. But the hand stopped in midair and fell laxly to his side. He fell into a chair.

Wordlessly, Leah moved to him and laid her hand on his head, on which graying hair surrounded the bald patch in the middle. Leizer felt the warmth of her body which he yearned for close to him, so close, and reached out and clasped her to him, his face to her belly.

"You can't love a woman and hate the fruit of her womb, Leizer," said Leah quietly.

"What am I to do, Leah, what am I to do?" he mumbled into her belly.

"Let me visit the child, nurse her and nurture her every day at the orphanage."

"And you won't bring her home?" he asked timidly.

"Not as long as you live, and may you live long," she replied.

"As you wish," he said, "the main thing is that we stop living like two strangers filled with hatred."

Thirteen

When Bella and Gershon returned from their honeymoon, they decided to live in the Bergman family home. Shmuel, Gershon's father, was still observing the year of mourning, and was in need of help in maintaining the household and raising his younger sons. So Bella went to see her mother, from whom she knew she would obtain the best advice on how to run the household without being seen as out of place or setting anyone against her.

When Berta saw her daughter getting out of the carriage that had brought her, her heart lurched in her breast. Bella's face revealed that she had returned from her honeymoon in great distress. It was enough for her to see the way her daughter dropped into a chair in the kitchen.

"What's the matter?' asked Berta, standing beside her daughter and clasping her head to her belly.

Bella sighed, but right away regained her composure and shook off her mother's embrace.

"Nothing. It's just the journey here."

"My heart tells me what your lips won't," Berta said, and sat down facing her daughter. "Did he behave badly toward you?"

"God forbid, Mama," replied Bella quickly, "he's a well-mannered man. The hotel was fine too. The owner welcomed us in person."

"There'd be the devil to pay if he hadn't," said Berta, "your father paid him extra just for that."

Bella raised her eyes to her.

"What did you think? Your father doesn't leave things like that in other people's hands," Berta said.

Bella lowered her head.

"*Das gefelt mir nicht, mein kind*," said Berta, taking her daughter's hand. "I can see that you're not right. What's the matter?"

"Mama," Bella sighed, "either he didn't know what to do, or he did know and didn't want to."

"*Oy zu meine jahren*," said Berta through clenched lips. "But in the end he did what he was supposed to do?"

"Yes," Bella replied embarrassedly, "like a child."

"What do you mean?" asked Bella, raising her voice. "I won't allow that kind of behavior toward my daughter!"

"No, no, Mama," she said, hurriedly correcting herself, "it was all right in the end. We even laughed about it. But I had to offer myself to him, otherwise he would have gone to sleep like a dead man."

"He should come here and watch the horses. Maybe he'll learn something from them!"

"The day he comes to watch the horses, I'll get warts on my hands," Bella laughed, "he busies himself only with his books."

"You don't get grandchildren from books!" said Berta, cutting her short. "You must put something in the water or his food so that the man in his heart wakes up."

"Put what in his water?"

"*Paksheiveh*," Berta replied. "It's a weed you have to pull out with the root, wash it, and boil it in rainwater. Then you filter the liquid and put it into a glass of wine. He'll drink it and be a man."

"How do you know about all this?" Bella inquired.

"What do you think," Berta laughed, "that you're the first woman to have a man without vigor? We used to brew this potion, or give the man figs to eat, or grind up a piece of an ox's or ram's horn, and put it into wine: one glass in the morning and another in the evening."

"But he doesn't touch wine, Mama," Bella said.

"He doesn't touch wine? *Nu, schon*, then I'll buy you some *spingard* oil to rub on his you-know-where. Then he'll rut like a goat, I promise you."

"How can I do that?" asked Bella in alarm. "Rub it on his you-know-what?"

"Well, what do you want, for him to do it himself?" thundered Berta. "*Parve is a parve*. If you don't do something, then he'll do nothing. He'll just study, eat, and get as fat as a pig."

"I can't."

"Believe me, you can," Berta replied, "what do you think, that your father was such a *kaliker*? If he'd known how much *paksheiveh* he drank he would have slapped me senseless!" she added, laughing.

Her expression turned grave. She got up, preoccupied with her thoughts, and began pacing the room. "But of course," she murmured, "why didn't I think of it before?"

"What didn't you think about, Mama?"

"The ring. His mother's ring. You have to get hold of the ring."

"I don't understand."

"Do you remember how the ring glowed on the day we first met her, and we talked to her in the synagogue courtyard?"

"Yes," Bella replied.

"Do you remember the stories about the ring, how it saved her from her illness?" asked Berta, continuing to weave the thread of her thoughts.

Bella nodded.

"And how she died after the ring was stolen?"

"But what's that got to do with anything?"

"The ring. You've got to get the ring back, Bella. If you want to be his wife and the mother of his children, if you want to be the head of the Bergman family, not only in this generation but in the next too, you need that ring. It possesses a secret, a certain power, and you need that power. Without the ring you'll just be the daughter of a Danzig horse trader."

"And where am I to find it? Bella asked. "It was stolen. How am I to find it?"

"Whoever stole that ring knew very well what he was stealing," Berta asserted, "he didn't take anything else."

Bella looked at her mother, not understanding what she was saying.

"So it was a thief from here, from Danzig. And Danzig isn't all that big a city," her mother added. "We must find out who else in the city suffers from that illness, and that way you'll find your ring. It's yours by right. Promise me you'll find the ring."

"All right, Mama, all right," Bella said, trying to pacify her mother. "Now, can one get anything to eat here?"

Mother and daughter sat eating and talking for a long while. Bella sought advice from her mother about running the Bergman household, and her mother told her she'd come and see how she was managing with the house, and the three little boys, and her *shvigger*, Mr. Bergman, and the cook that Reine-Chaya had left behind and who, if you asked her, she'd have dismissed as swiftly as possible, because there's one thing you don't inherit and that's servants and cooks. But before that she must learn all the dishes that the *shvigger* likes, because what he eats, his sons will eat too.

While his son Gershon sat reading and writing on philosophical topics, Shmuel Bergman was drawn into his grief. He became thinner, ate but little, and most of the time was immersed in his misery. Yet he was scrupulous about one thing: each morning he would rise early, go to the synagogue, and recite the mourner's *Kaddish* for his wife.

Except for the wedding of his eldest son, which was celebrated modestly as was seemly for a wedding following the *shiva* mourning period, he did not attend a single joyous occasion. He spent long hours in the synagogue, remaining there after morning prayers, feeling that only within the walls of that building he had a raison d'être. After the last of the congregants had left the synagogue, each hurrying off to his day's work, he would slowly go up to the women's section, dragging his weary feet, passing row after row of seats until he came to that of his dead wife, Reine-Chaya Bergman of blessed memory, whose name he had had embossed on a copper plate, and he would stand there, stroking it. Then he would raise his head to the air of the world, gaze at the light reflected in the synagogue's stained glass windows, his lips murmuring words from him to his wife in the next world.

And exactly one year to the day after his wife's death, he too was gathered unto his people.

Fourteen

Afterwards, Gershon would sleep alone on the couch in his father's study, waken amid the thousands of books surrounding him in the semi-darkened room, and barely taste the food that either Bella or Hinda brought him. Wild, hard stubble, with early gray glinting in it, covered his cheeks, and his eyes were sunken in their sockets as if the Angel of Death had passed his hand over him and severed him from himself. Sitting not as a man, a husband, an elder brother, and the owner of the family estate, but as a sort of vegetable that did not know what had befallen it. He would lie on the couch all day, or sit at the desk for a while, gazing at the pages before him, and immediately submit to his cowardice and lie down on the couch.

Had he believed in the next world he might have found some solace in his soul. But Gershon, a disciple of the Jewish Enlightenment movement, did not believe in it by any means. They, his father and mother – thus his upbringing told him – are lying beneath the sod. They are no longer here. They are not with him and are not hovering over him. They lived, and they are dead. The belief in the finality of death only heightened the dread that enveloped him, the dread of the constancy of life that goes on, in any creature, from beginning to end.

For thirty days Bella let him wallow in his grief like a legless horse. For thirty days she held herself in check not to shake him out of his mourning, but let him stew in it, to exhaust it. She did not even trouble him with the unveiling of the gravestone, but sent Meir, his younger brother, to the Danzig burial society to choose a suitable stone for his father now resting beside his wife, decide on the inscription, the lettering, and when the unveiling would take place of the gravestone of her beloved and respected father-in-law, respected by the entire Danzig community, and just as his funeral had been attended by many people, so he was entitled to a gravestone unveiling worthy of his name.

But after the unveiling, on their return from the cemetery, deep in their grief, they got out of the carriage with Gershon lagging behind them and thinking of again closeting himself in his father's study, she grasped his arm and stopped him.

"Gershon, no."

Gershon looked at her with his lost, dull eyes without a word.

"The thirty days are over, Gershon," she said, "you are not going back into that room. Do you want to continue sinking until you die yourself? Please, here, in the living room. Not behind a closed door. You're not alone in this world, and I will not become a twenty-nine year-old widow. You've got a household and three brothers to provide for. If there is still life in you, take control of yourself. Now, give me your hat and coat and sit down in the living room. Look outside a bit, at the city. Perhaps you'll remember that you've still got a life to live."

Gershon listened to her biting, incisive speech, and remained silent. He only took off his hat and coat and handed them to her, and went and sat down in an armchair by the big window, sat and gazed at the darkening Danzig sky, the darkening street, the lamps coming on one after the other in the city streets, and for the first time since his father's death he suddenly felt how he was reconnecting with himself, and he opened his mouth and quietly asked if there was anything to eat.

Bella smiled to herself contentedly, knowing that this evening she had won one battle of all the battles her life had brought her, and she went to make something light to eat. A bowl of borscht. She came out of the kitchen carefully bearing the steaming bowl, and placed it on a small side table in front of him. Then she brought him a linen napkin and a soupspoon, and placed them on the table too. Gershon felt the old and familiar feeling of hunger rising from his stomach, and began sipping the red, sweet and sour soup, with its flavors of sugar and chopped garlic and black pepper that she had liberally sprinkled into it, and each sip gradually opened up his constricted heart.

After he finished eating, he straightened his back and looked at Bella who was sitting facing him, watching him in silence.

"Thank God you're here, Bella," he said, and immediately closed up again.

Bella looked at him with surprisingly soft eyes which showed a little compassion, love, and gratefulness, and asked him if he would like something more. He nodded slowly, and she went into the kitchen and came back with a plate piled with liver, a small dish of horseradish, and four slices of bread to dip into the sauce, to eat – and heal.

During the days that followed Bella brought craftsmen to the house. She took them upstairs to her late father-in-law's study, and on her orders they dragged out the pieces of old furniture that had served him. Then she instructed them to repaint the room in gayer colors, not the turgid green that had covered the walls before.

While she was renovating and redecorating the study, Gershon was forced into sleeping with her in their bedroom again, and that only hastened his return to the living. He started reading again, talking with his brothers, taking an interest in what was happening in the world, and even looking at the journals sent to him as always, keeping abreast of the situation of Zionism and the Jews, and matters of the people and nationalism, the Enlightenment and its opponents.

At the same time, Bella had a beautiful escritoire brought specially from Hamburg, gleaming with the lacquer on its heavy oak wood, and a new reading armchair, and long bookshelves made of superior wood that were fixed to the walls of the study, which now seemed spacious, and then she arranged the many boxes of her husband's books by subject and in alphabetical order. Only when she had finished, when new curtains had been fitted on both sides of the wide window, and the clear light of a winter morning shone into the room, flooding the decorated vase she had placed on the sill with a huge bunch of fresh flowers, their colors echoing those of the embroidered carpet she had spread on the floor, only then, as she scanned the beauty of the room and her heart swelled within her, she called Gershon and asked him to come into the study she had remade for him, the study of a philosopher and educator, a man rich in thought whose life and wife had led him to a life of study and writing of philosophical matters. And Gershon, who had turned the corner and even put on some weight, stood on the threshold, assessing the fullness of the life she had managed to breathe into the room, which previously had been a small room of mourning and gloom, and he told her that he thanks God for bringing her into his life, and he will always be grateful that she was at his side during those difficult times, and had actually pulled him back from the brink, and he embraced her strongly.

That night he came to her bed passionately, as a man whose potency had been restored. While she was happy to have him, her heart told her that his gratitude is one thing, but these rapid fluctuations between joy and sadness, virility and impotency, a sense of life and the depths of desolation, would be part of her life for many years to come, since they were like the swinging pendulum of an old grandfather clock.

One day Bella returned home from the tailor's – Danzig Modes, where she purchased her husband's suits – her arms loaded with parcels. Hinda opened the door, her eyes blinking and half hinting.

"Your mother's with Gershon again," she whispered.

Bella quickly put down the suits and hastened inside. "Mama, I'm home," she called as she swung open the heavy door of the study, just as Gershon was handing her mother a brown paper-wrapped package. Her mother quickly stuffed it into the pocket of her dress.

"What's all this, Mama?" she inquired curtly.

"How are you, Bella?" asked her mother, all innocence.

"What have you got there?" Bella asked, moving to her mother. "Take it out, show it to me."

"Nothing," her mother replied, as Gershon's eyes roamed the air as if following the flight of an insect.

Bella pulled her mother's hand out her dress pocket. A bundle of banknotes fell from it and fluttered to the floor. Her mother bent down to gather them up, but Bella stopped her with a hand.

"I thought that the donation business in this house was over, Gershon" she said angrily to her shamefaced husband, who tried to bury himself in the upholstery of his chair.

While Berta Litvinovsky's husband was totally immersed in his horse trading business, doing what he had done best all his life – buying young animals, training them, and selling them to the Danzig police and the army – his wife did her best to frequently visit the home of her daughter and son-in-law to help her daughter manage her household, and also to pass the time. Since her son-in-law's father had been one of the managers of Mattenbuden community's fund prior to the union with Altschottland, she was approached from time to time by Jews who had come from Russia, penniless refugees, to indirectly intercede with Gershon and perhaps squeeze a few coins out of him to provide for widows and orphans. Berta, who still remembered her and her husband's time as refugees, would visit the house when her daughter was engaged in matters outside the home, and ask Gershon for a little charity from his late parents' estate, as his father had done before him.

Had it not been for his mother-in-law, who from time to time would ask him for charity in his parents' name for one refugee family or another, he would have forgotten the world outside. But Berta, who was attentive to the suffering of our brethren from the Diaspora, would sometimes come on behalf of a woman looking for her husband, or for poverty-stricken parents collecting a dowry for their daughter, or to provide for a young Torah scholar, or a Jew traveling to the Holy Land, and thus she succeeded, much to her daughter Bella's chagrin, to get Gershon outside his four walls, and even concretize the situation of Diaspora Jewry. Gershon knew that his wife fervently objected to *schnorrers* and requests for charity, so he would give the money to her mother surreptitiously.

Berta crouched to gather up the banknotes from the floor.

"Don't touch them, Mama," Bella stopped her, "if there is money on the floor in this house, let it stay there!"

"How can you speak to her like that? She's your mother," Gershon said quietly.

"Don't interfere between me and Mama," she cut him off, "you just take care of your inheritance. It won't be there forever. You're still not earning anything from all your lofty thoughts to permit yourself to give and give like some graf!"

Gershon looked at her without replying. He knew that at moments like this it was better to leave her alone in her rage, and let her vent it.

He picked up a book and pretended to leaf through it, stealing a glance at his wife and mother-in-law who had remained frozen where they stood.

"Come, let's go downstairs to the kitchen, Mama," said Bella, breaking the silence. "We have things to discuss."

They left the room, Bella slamming the door behind her, finally leaving Gershon alone in his study. He didn't dare argue with her because he knew she was right. His inheritance was indeed large, but it is the nature of wealth to disappear if it is not taken care of. And in the meantime his brothers were growing and he had to consider them too. Meir, the elder, was already studying medicine at the University of Hamburg, but Nathan and David were still at the gymnasium and must be cared for.

On his wife's advice, he divided the inheritance into four – one part for him and her, and one for each of his brothers – and set up three funds in which he kept the inheritance money for his brothers when they grew up. The only thing Gershon and Bella kept for themselves, at her behest, was the collection of religious artifacts that had accumulated in the house since the time of his great-grandfather, and was now their property. Bella was right. Every donation he gave to his mother-in-law for Jewish refugees took food from their mouths. For however hard he strove, he had still not found work suited to his education and talents, and he spent most of his time writing articles for journals. Even if they elicited numerous responses, the money he was paid for them was nothing compared with the time he invested in their writing. Bella was right, but it was difficult for him to withstand the importuning of his mother-in-law, his mother's friend, who had she been alive would surely have acceded to all her requests, and even added money.

As he sat thinking about all this, Bella and Berta were verbally knifing each other in the kitchen.

"Don't you ever shame me in front of your husband like that!" Berta told her daughter across the heavy, safe, wooden table separating them. "I'm your mother, and don't you forget it!"

"What kind of a mother are you if you take from my mouth to give to others, and in secret yet?" Bella screamed. "What do you think, that he's a milch cow? In the end there'll be nothing left!"

"Heaven help us!" Berta said, sotto voce. "You don't look all that hungry!"

"I've got to worry about us, not the *Ostjuden* living in the streets!"

"*Ostjuden*?" her horrified mother shouted. Your father and I were once *Ostjuden*! Your blood is *Ostjuden*! Never forget that!"

"If you're so eager to give," Bella said, "then take from Papa."

"You've got a cheek!" her mother replied in a hard voice. "Your father hasn't been working with animals for forty years to provide for all the Jewish People! But your husband doesn't work, he's got a large inheritance, thank God, and he sits there all day with those *bichelach* of his. I've yet to see any *glick* come out of it for you!"

"My husband's an intellectual," said Bella, cutting her off, "it's his vocation!"

"Yes, yes, an intellectual," Bella snorted contemptuously, "*a schvacher kinder macher* who can't have children!"

Bella was incandescent with rage. "What's that got to do with it?"

"He's not a man!" her mother said venomously, "if he doesn't work, then at least he should give me a grandchild!"

"You will not insult my husband in this house!" said Bella, pounding the table, so enraged she was but a second away from attacking her mother.

"You can boil like a pot with an egg," Bella said smugly, "but it's the truth, Bella. You deserve a child and I deserve a grandchild."

Bella was beside herself with rage.

"Do you think I don't want a child? That this belly doesn't want a pregnancy?" she yelled, slapping her stomach.

"And what are you doing about it?" her mother shouted back. "Have you brought him back to your bed, or is he still spending his time alone on the couch in the study? And what about the ring? Have you looked for the ring?"

"The ring again? You'd think that your grandchild will come out of the hole in a ring!"

"You don't understand anything!" her mother replied. "You need it to be the lady of this house like his mother!"

"I'm not his mother, I'm his wife," said Bella quietly. "And apart from that, I've been looking for it in pawnshops. There's no trace of it."

"Pawnshops? Go to doctors, find out who else suffers from this sickness. That's where you'll find answers!"

"All right, Mama, all right," Bella murmured, feeling as though all the wind had been taken out of her sails.

"Look for the ring. Without it you'll never be whole," said Berta, gripping her daughter's hand tightly. "His father was a Kabbalist. That ring had powers. You've got to have that ring!"

Bella nodded. Berta's words were etched deeply in her heart.

Fifteen

Like many other things that begin randomly, with an imperceptible quivering of the soul until they become a dybbuk, Bella, too, was suddenly assailed by an obsession that accompanied her from then on and embittered her life – to obtain the ring, come what may. Things like that do not happen in one fell swoop, but once they gain momentum they become a passion that knows no bounds. Some might say it was Bella's inflexible nature that led her into such a sense of urgency, or the circumstances of her upbringing and education. She was, after all, the daughter of a family of horse traders.

Bella was blessed with a highly-developed sense of the value of things. From the moment the running of the household passed into her hands, she made sure that the maids polished the art works fashioned by her late father-in-law, and which were always on display in cabinets in the parlor. Only on festival eves did she allow some of the artifacts to be taken out – wine goblets and silverware – and used at table, but the jewelry and ornaments made in this house, which she found in a carved wood box that her mother-in-law had kept by her bed, Bella zealously kept secret.

Of all the things that had come into her possession, only one ring was missing.

She felt its absence all the time: when she and Gershon were invited to a ball at the Danzig Opera House, and she took out the jewelry box from its hiding place for the event, or when she was buffing and counting, for the thousandth time, the gold and silver pieces in their showcases, the antique clocks, and the exquisite objects. She felt its absence in the evenings when Gershon would leave the house troubled, as if before an important meeting, and return late at night, emptied and calm, but holding a secret within him. She felt its absence when he avoided her touch when they were alone, and she felt its absence every time she told her mother a little about what was happening between her and Gershon, and her mother would repeat that the ring symbolized her union with Gershon, the hold of family on family and status on status. She would be Mrs. Bergman only if she wore that ring on her finger.

Not only did she feel the absence of the ring, which she had seen but once, but was troubled with dreams about it. One night she dreamed about a hand coming down from heaven, holding a long, twisted thread coming down from heaven to earth, and tied to its end, swinging, a gold ring. When she awoke with a start she saw the face of her mother-in-law looking at her from the land of the dead, and on her lips the same request.

At the time, Gershon's mind was occupied with completely different matters. He read Theodore Herzl's *Der Judenstaadt*, kept abreast of the preparations for the First Zionist Congress, and debated with intellectuals and sensation-mongers in the Danzig, Berlin, and Hamburg press. At night he would wander, wrapped up in his overcoat, along the quays of Danzig Port, looking for sailors. Therefore he only detected the change in his wife when that nervous and uncontrollable tremor passed over her face, a kind of sudden, involuntary tic that would appear in her beautiful face, and immediately vanish.

At first he ascribed her irritableness to something in the house not precisely arranged to her liking. He saw how she tyrannized the servants, making sure that they put everything in its place. But once he heard that she had begun frequenting pawnbrokers' shops and inquiring about a ring fashioned from ten pieces of gold, he realized that what was troubling his wife was no trifling matter.

He tried to behave gently with her, giving himself up to her completely, but in the end he was unable to ignore her annoyance, and sought to talk to her.

The opportunity to do so presented itself one evening after dinner. His brothers had gone about their business, and the servants had left the dining room and gone to their quarters. Gershon poured two glasses of wine for them.

"Bella," he said, "you know that I love you with all my heart."

"Yes," she replied, "but what are you trying to say?"

"I'm not trying to say anything other than I love you."

"You've never needed to declare it," she said, "so if there's something else it would be better if you said it."

"I'm worried about you," he said quietly, setting his wineglass down on the table, "this matter of the ring is worrying me, Bella."

"What's so worrying to you about the ring," she replied belligerently, "it's me who dreams about it at night, not you."

"You're letting it dominate you."

"The ring is not dominating me, but I'll dominate it," she replied assertively. "That ring is ours; I promised your mother it would come back to us, and I fully intend to keep that promise."

"You promised her, and I'm grateful for it," he said, "only that way was she able to leave this world peacefully. But I've heard that you're frequenting pawnshops looking for it, and I'm asking where this is leading you, Bella. Just see how you're looking."

Bella fired him a sharp glance.

"How I'm looking? I'm looking fine. Or perhaps you think otherwise?"

"No, no," he said, backtracking, "but it's troubling you so."

"Of course it's troubling me. I'm troubled by it, and by running this household, and looking after your grandfather's and father's ornaments, and also by keeping my promise to your mother. I'm troubled by it, but I won't give up until I find the ring. No one had any right to take it from us. Understand this: whoever stole the ring killed your mother and father, Gershon. He's got to return the ring and pay for what he did. It's not a matter of vengeance or consolation, it's about justice. And justice must be served."

"It's about superstition," Gershon said, "whoever stole the ring is a thief, not a murderer."

Again he avoided his wife's flashing eyes, picked up yesterday's newspaper, and pretended to read it. From behind the paper he heard Bella get up and leave. Then he heard her walking to and fro between the rooms of the house, muttering to herself angrily, lighting a cigarillo, going out onto the long balcony, and then coming inside again. He knew he would be unable to stop her searching for the ring. It would be better to leave her alone until she despaired of finding one ring in a big city.

He did not know that Bella, who had exhausted her search of the known pawnshops in the city and also of the smaller ones in the suburbs, had made up her mind to renew her search, this time not in any rational manner, thinking that the thief had surely sold the ring, but by means of the stories around it – to visit doctors and inquire who in this city suffers from the falling sickness, to tighten the circle around anyone who might have stolen the ring out of belief in its healing powers.

While Bella was trying to tighten her search for the ring, Leah Kochmann's life began closing in on her. The strange attacks of falling sickness that had beset her did not pass, and the power of the ring, which she had deposited at the orphanage as surety for her daughter, was not with her. But her heart would not allow her to endanger her daughter's life by taking back the surety, so she tried to cure herself with medicines she concocted at home. When she saw that they were of no help, she went to see a specialist.

Dr. Heckhart's diagnosis was that she was suffering from rare complications of epilepsy, and after trying in vain to help her with various salts he summoned her back to his surgery and informed her that he was unable to help her. The sickness would be with her for the rest of her life. And Leah, who was in the prime of life, left the doctor deep in thought. She did not want to end her days in this sickness, but at the same time she refused to even consider saving herself at the cost of neglecting her daughter. After all, she told herself, it was due to the ring she had hidden in her crib that her daughter was fed and well treated at the orphanage. How could she take that away from her in return for her own life?

At a loss, she went back home and found a stranger on her doorstep, his face downcast. He was a messenger who had come to deliver terrible news. Leizer, her Leizer, was dead.

The timber lift that had crushed Leizer Kochmann bringing about his sudden death was driven by a Pole who had earlier had some beer in one of the taverns by the port. He was a god-fearing man, and when he heard Leizer's screams he stopped the machine, got down, and stood there thunderstruck at the sight of the pile of timber, from beneath which peeped the shirttail of the best of the city's carpenters.

The drunken Pole shouted for help, calling the artisans working nearby to help him shift the timber from Leizer. But when they moved all the planks and trunks and beams, they saw Leizer, his body bent like that of an animal.

The Jews stood there, and started arguing about who should go to the burial society and who should go to Leah and give her the terrible news.

When Leah heard that Leizer was dead, a terrible cry burst from her lips. Then she went to her husband's things in complete silence, took out his prayer shawl, and asked the bringers of the tidings to place it beneath his head.

And that was how she buried him.

Sixteen

Bella abhorred illness and the world of the sick. Sick people always terrified her and she would try and keep away from them, as though their very closeness might infect her. And there was no shortage of sick people. The *Ostjuden* flooded the streets of the city. They were not satisfied with the quarters designated for them and swarmed like locusts into the more affluent neighborhoods, with their threadbare clothing and black *kapotas* redolent with the sweat of small synagogues. Some had even fallen so low that they slept on benches on the boulevards, a patched coat beneath their head and a box for collecting coins at their side.

Since she detested anything from which the smell of sickness rose, Bella Bergman also kept her distance from doctors' surgeries. Even though some were renowned in their field, she avoided visiting their surgeries so that she would not have to encounter the sicknesses of others, even though they might be wealthy and of some social standing.

But after visiting all the pawnshops in the city, she now had to overcome her revulsion of sickness and death, go from one specialist to another in Danzig, and elucidate her request. Could the doctor tell her whether he has or has had a patient suffering from the falling sickness, whose attacks are irregular and even occur after an interval of many years, and who wears a ring on her finger.

Most of the doctors turned her away, either because of respect for others, or because they had not seen such a patient, or because their attention was quite naturally on their patients, not what they were wearing.

One evening, almost on the brink of despair, Bella visited the surgery of the renowned Dr. Heckhart, where a surprise awaited her.

"Why would madam be seeking information of this kind?" asked the doctor.

"To right a wrong from the distant past."

"Madam is aware that full confidentiality over his or her body is an individual's right?"

"I am, Doctor, but I am also aware that the person wearing that ring is a murderer."

"A murderer?" replied Dr. Heckhart loudly. "How so?"

Bella related the story from start to finish while the doctor listened gravely.

"There is nothing more remote from the practice of medicine than that story, which possesses more than a hint of magic," he said. "A ring made pieces of gold from virginal yeshiva students saves people from sickness? Because of such nonsense you accuse another of murder?"

Bella stared at the doctor, piercing him with her gaze.

"I, too, do not believe in such claptrap, Doctor. But this is not about my beliefs but those of whoever stole the ring in order to save herself from the illness."

The doctor's expression softened.

"I see, madam. So, only to assist in solving what appears to be a kind of crime, and that, of course, if to some extent we accept the validity of magic, I do have a patient whose manner fits your description. Truth to tell, she visited me not long ago because of particularly severe attacks of the sickness, after not having suffered one for many years. I remember her telling me about a ring, which according to her belief can save her from her attacks, but that it is not in her possession. I was unamazed when I heard her story, just as I *am* amazed at hearing it from you."

"Why?" Bella asked with hope in her heart.

"Because superstitions are suited to a woman like her."

"A woman like her?" Bella wondered aloud.

"Well, she's a whore," said the doctor, embarrassed.

Bella shuddered at the thought of a whore wearing her ring, but restrained herself and listened to the doctor's story about Leah Kochmann, her origins, and the history of her sickness. He also mentioned that as far as he knew the woman lived in the Mattenbuden quarter and that she had recently lost her husband.

Leah went directly to the orphanage from Leizer's funeral to recover her daughter and the ring. She came there in her widow's weeds, with a fine black lace veil falling down to cover her face.

When the orphanage matron saw her, she realized that something had happened. She welcomed Leah Kochmann with all due respect, because she had left such a valuable surety, had proved her devotion to her daughter from the moment she was born to that very day, and because she was the only one who had a name and face and address, unlike the other women whose children had been gathered up from the street to this home, Jewish and Gypsy children, German and Russian, poor nameless and homeless orphans. Of all of them, there was only one child there that had a name, Leah's little daughter, Esther, whose behavior was also different from that of the other children because she had some idea of who her mother is, and was not growing up as a foundling.

"Good afternoon, Frau Kochmann," the matron welcomed Leah, who sat down at her large desk, the desk at which each day the children who had transgressed stood to receive their punishment.

"Good afternoon, Frau Halblicht," Leah responded, adjusting her small hat. She was unused to such headgear.

"I understand that I should offer you my condolences," the matron said.

"My husband," Leah replied, "died suddenly. I have just come from the cemetery."

"I'm sorry to hear it," Frau Halblicht tut-tutted, pale light falling onto her face from the window facing the inner wall in the yard, and giving her features the look of a bird of prey instead of that of a compassionate matron.

"I've come to take my daughter back, to raise her as I always wanted to," Leah said, "Esther and the surety both."

"It's not that simple," said the matron, "there's the matter of payment for several months' upkeep."

Leah opened her black purse, took out the banknotes she had readied and silently handed them to the matron. The matron counted them meticulously, nodded, and placed the bundle of notes in her desk drawer.

"That apart," the matron continued, "the girl is almost ten. Although she knows you as her mother, raising a girl at that age after not being with her during the most important years of her development is not all that easy."

"It's never easy," Leah smiled, "but thank God, there are a lot of mothers in this world and they all raise children,"

"You yourself were an orphan from a young age," the matron continued, "do you know what you're letting yourself into?"

"Thank you for your concern, Frau Halblicht," Leah replied quietly, "but she is the only daughter I have. There aren't any schools for motherhood in the world. Together we shall learn how to be mother and daughter."

"I have no doubt you will," Frau Halblicht smiled, her face illumined by light and shadow, as if half of it were an angel of light and the other an angel of darkness. "But should you be in need of advice from me, my door is always open to you."

"Thank you, Frau Halblicht," the mother replied.

"I'll send someone to call her," the matron said, "but remember – you must ready yourself for a strange reaction from her. For you, this is a wish fulfilled. For her it's being uprooted from everything she's known as a home. My friendly advice, Frau Kochmann, is not to give the child too much freedom. She needs to be in a framework."

Leah told Frau Halblicht about her plans to open an eating place, enroll her daughter at the state elementary school in Danzig, and put together a strict daily timetable for both of them so that the girl would grow up close to her and not wander the streets on her own.

The matron went on to advise her on how to behave with her daughter.

"Order, cleanliness, discipline," she stressed, "she must know there is a limit for everything, even the smallest things, so that her soul is properly shaped.'

As they spoke, the matron ordered a member of the orphanage staff to bring the girl, and to wait with her while she packed all her belongings.

The child was brought into the room wearing a tight-fitting dress and short white socks, her hair drawn back and tied with a ribbon. The woman who brought her took the little hand from her own and gave her a small push into the room, into which, the girl knew, one only came to be punished. So as she came inside and saw her mother, she hesitated on the threshold.

"Come, Esther," the matron said in as kindly a tone as she could manage, "come and say hello to your mother."

With tentative steps the child walked toward Leah. The mother held out her hand. The child put her small hand into her mother's as she looked at the matron, wondering what was going to happen next.

"Esther," the matron began, "you know that you're a special girl because you have a mother who always comes to visit you and brings you presents and clothes, isn't that so?"

The child nodded, but removed her hand from her mother's and placed it in her own lap.

"All these years we have looked after you and raised you so that your mother could save enough money to raise you herself," the matron went on, beckoning the child to come closer.

The child went to her, cautiously and hesitantly. Frau Halblicht stroked her head, then lifted her onto her knee, which she had never done before.

"Today is a great and happy day for you, my child," she said gently. "Your mother has come to take you to a small house just for the two of you. From now on you will be living with your mother."

The child turned to her with an alarmed expression.

"But what about all my friends?" she finally asked tremulously.

"You can visit them whenever you wish," the matron smiled.

The child clung to the matron, who put her down from her lap. "Go to your mother," she said, "go on."

The child stood beside her mother, her head lowered and her heart filled with fear.

"Hug the child," Frau Halblicht ordered Leah, who was sitting frozen on her chair. She had buried her husband only that morning and now she had to deal with her little daughter's fear of her, her mother.

Leah held out her hand to her daughter, but Esther stayed rooted to the spot.

"Lower yourself to her height," the matron whispered through clenched lips. Leah got up from her chair and knelt in front of her daughter, looking her straight in the eye.

"Esther, my Esther," she said painfully, "you'll love our house. There's a little room there just for you."

""Can I bring my Grimeh?" the child asked, which was the worn rag doll that had been with her since her childhood and with which she slept in her little bed.

"Of course you can," Leah smiled. "And if you like, we can make her some new clothes."

The first hint of a smile lit up the child's face. Leah took her into her arms, and the child could feel how the embrace was almost suffocating her and tried to free herself from the strong grip.

"Go to the girls' room," Frau Halblicht told Esther, "and collect all your things. We'll be waiting for you here."

The child left the room with the woman who had brought her and was waiting outside. The matron looked at Leah. She seemed exhausted from pain.

"Now that we're alone," she told Leah, "I shall return your surety."

She opened her desk drawer, took out the wooden box containing the ring, and proffered it to Leah. Nodding her thanks, Leah took the box and opened it with trembling fingers. The ring lay there, turbulent and gleaming, as if it knew its time had come.

She put the ring on her finger, and it closed around the flesh as if it were reaching its objective, and she felt new powers coursing through her. Now fortified, she raised her face to Frau Halblicht who could see the immediate change that had taken place in her, but did not say a word.

Seventeen

It was school holiday time, the best opportunity for Leah to get her daughter used to her and her way of life. As soon as she brought the child home she took her into her little room and encouraged her to arrange it as she wished, and even to set up a play corner to her taste. As she entered the room Esther saw that there was no house for Grimeh, her gray doll, and so she went outside with Leah, found a wooden box, washed it, and asked her mother to buy some paint for her so she could paint it properly. The mother was pleased with her daughter's practical attitude and initiative, gave her a tin of paint, and watched attentively as she painted the box and with her brush painted a window, a door, and a red-tiled roof. Perhaps something of Leizer's golden hands had been strangely passed down to this child, she thought, for if not, where had the ability to hold a brush come from, the ability to imagine things in her mind and turn them into a reality of cloth and wood?

A few days after she brought her daughter home and the ring had stopped the attacks of her sickness, Leah, more energetic and filled with greater vitality than she had been for a long time, embarked on bringing her plan to fruition: opening a small inn close to the Port of Danzig.

She did this in the building that was formerly her husband's carpentry shop. It was spacious, with two rooms, a kitchen, and even a toilet. She brought in workers who had worked with her husband, emptied the building of the tools and timber, and brought a builder who broke down the wall between the rooms and made them into a long, wide sitting room, with four long windows at the front opening onto the street of the port. Then he painted its walls, repaired the floor, and built three wide steps at the entrance and a fine door. She then called in carpenters who had known her late husband, and in return for the tools and timber they made her a high serving counter of dark wood with shelves behind it, twenty small square tables with four fine chairs at each, and kitchen cupboards. As they worked, Leah sat and sewed twenty fine checkered cotton tablecloths and she bought cooking utensils and tableware, small candlesticks and candles, and made herself a splendid inn that would provide for her and her daughter. Before she began to welcome Leizer's friends and acquaintances, who brought with them more and more port workers, at the front she put up a sign made of a tree trunk section sawn lengthwise and lacquered, which bore the name "Leizer's" in eye-catching lettering, which would be a memento of her late husband.

While the school holiday lasted, Leah would take her daughter with her to her new inn and let her help with light work in the kitchen. She sat her on a low stool beside her, and while she was cooking her dishes in the big pots, her little daughter would sit with infinite patience peeling dozens of potatoes with her tiny hands, and then put them into a pot of boiling water to turn them into a purée with fried onions and fat, so it would be soft and tasty. As she did so the child would sit and tell her stories from the orphanage, or stories that just came to mind, and Leah would sing fragments of songs she remembered from her childhood. Together they sat, singing pieces of children's songs in Yiddish, laughing and enjoying themselves, and Leah, who had waited for this moment all her life, was filled with happiness over everything she had accomplished.

But at night everything was different. From the moment she put the child to bed the little one was assailed by terror. The shadow of the tree in the window seemed to be an evil man bent on tormenting her, and every rustle of the autumn leaves in the evening breeze sounded like his approaching footfalls. The ships' sirens in the port terrified her, lest they were coming to take her away from her mother, and the screeching of the night birds frightened her. And so, almost every night Leah would succumb to the little one's pleas and take her into her bed, where the child clung to her and fell asleep with a thumb in her mouth and her head between her mother's breasts.

These displays of affection by her daughter filled Leah with both joy and fear. On the one hand, she was very happy that her daughter displayed such closeness to her, finding in her protection and refuge from the evils of the world and her own fears, which had apparently intensified in the long nights at the orphanage. But on the other hand she feared that her daughter's behavior presented a kind of sickness or dependency, and she wondered what would happen to this child when she grew up. Would she be able to withstand the rigors of life without her, as she herself had previously, fatherless and motherless, and forced to make her own way.

But when school reopened and she returned to the company of friends her own age, these signs slowly diminished until they disappeared completely. The child would go to school eagerly, and come home no less excited. With eyes alight she would tell her mother about everything she had learned that day, the teachers and her schoolmates, new words they had learned and a story they had been told, and she would devour with gusto everything her mother put on the table before her.

Several years passed, and before Leah's very eyes the child became a young girl. She came home despondent from school one day, went into the kitchen, and threw her satchel into a corner.

"What's the matter, Esther?" the mother called, wiping her hands on her apron.

The girl shrugged, her eyes downcast and her hands on her behind, as if trying to conceal something.

Leah took the girl's hand from behind her back and saw a dark stain spreading over the bottom of her dress.

"What's this, you've soiled your underwear?" she shouted, pulling her daughter behind her into a corner away from the window overlooking the port.

The girl shook her head.

Leah drew her closer.

"Come, let's get this dress off you and see what's happened."

"I didn't do anything," the girl said, terribly embarrassed, "but all of a sudden there was blood and dirt there."

The mother could not believe her ears, but removed the girl's dress. What she had suspected had indeed happened. Filled with joy she removed her daughter's underwear, raised her hands and without thinking what she was doing, slapped her face twice, once on each cheek.

"Why, Mama?" the child wailed, "I haven't done anything!"

"Silly girl," her mother laughed, "it's from happiness. It's so you'll always remember the day you became a woman!"

Puzzled, the girl wiped away her tears with the back of her hand, not understanding what all the commotion was about. Leah said that if she sat beside her while she was cooking she would explain. Openmouthed, the girl listened to her mother. When Leah had finished revealing some of the secrets of the world, she told her daughter that when she finished what she was doing they would go to a seamstress who would make her some new dresses, and that from now on she should stop playing with Grimeh because she was no longer a little girl, but a little woman, and little women play other games.

The girl did not want to hear of it because she was bound to her faded doll, but she slowly came to like her new-found status in her mother's eyes, who began dressing her like a woman, not a little girl, and even sat and showed her her makeup box, and explained which color is used where, and what is suitable for which occasion, and even allowed her to make up her own face, but only on Saturdays when she was not at school and strangers could not see her.

Time passed, the girl continued to grow and started to develop breasts. The frequent changes that took place in her body worked wonders on her: from a stooped, orphanage child she turned into a beautiful young woman. But as happy as Leah was with her daughter's beauty, her fears for her fate heightened. She knew how drunken sailors would open the hatches on their ships at night and call out to passing girls to "come and taste our borscht", and how men roamed the boulevards after all the cafés had closed, looking for women to spend the night with. She therefore forbade her daughter to leave the house after dark.

One day a Jew from Lodz happened along to her inn and told her about how an elegantly-attired man and wife, wealthy Jews from Buenos Aires, Juana and Moshe Geist, had come and charitably consented to take five good Jewish girls whose parents had sent them, to find a match and work in wealthy Jewish homes in Argentina. Leah listened to his story and began making inquiries about what was going on among the Jews of Argentina. She discovered that this country had opened its gates to emigrants from all over the world, including Jews, and she heard about the settlement program of the Jewish Colonization Association and about Baron Hirsch.

A few days later, while on her way from her house to the inn, Leah saw an unusual poster stuck onto the trees lining the wide boulevard, onto house walls, and even in the display windows of some of the shops. The poster showed the face of a young girl, the daughter of respected Jewish family from Altschottland, Perla Hildesheim, thirteen years of age, just like her own daughter, who had been declared missing. "The police and her parents seek the assistance of the enlightened public in finding the lost child," Leah read, "and any person conveying information on her whereabouts to the Danzig Police will be rewarded by her parents."

Leah read the poster and was seized by fear. What had happened to that poor girl, she wondered, and how could her parents bear the uncertainty of the fate of their little daughter who had vanished – so she heard later – when she had gone out to play with her friend in the street outside her home.

During the next few days the whole city was in uproar. People everywhere were talking about the lost girl, and Leah, who was deeply touched by the unfortunate girl's fate, talked with her daughter and made her life difficult so that she would beware. Instead of her coming back from school to the inn alone, she made sure that someone would escort her, or went to bring the girl home herself. Her daughter, who was already grown up, complained about her mother's excessive concern but did not dare flout her authority.

A week later, Leah saw a commotion in the street through the window of her inn. She hurried out and saw the mounted police of Danzig in full gallop, in their stiff uniforms and steel helmets, moving aside the people gathered to see what was going on.

Leah went up to one of her watching neighbors and asked him what had happened. The amber and textile retailer, whose shop was close to her premises, told her that the police had found the body of the missing girl close to the port, lying naked as the day she was born, defiled, in a puddle of sewage between the old quays. On her skin, he said, the murderer had deeply incised a Star of David.

Leah clasped her hands in shock. What she had feared had indeed come to pass. She had hoped that this was not what would happen to the girl, but now the heart heard and refused to believe, such a young girl, only God knows how her last hours had passed, what crudeness and bestiality and torture she had endured.

That night she took her daughter, sat her down at a table in the inn after the customers had left earlier than usual, put her heavy arms on the table and rested her face, sweaty from cooking, on them.

"Esther, life in the city is becoming difficult and dangerous," she said, wiping the sweat from her brow, "and I'm very worried about you."

"What have you got to worry about?" the girl asked, "I'm here with you all the time."

"Yes, but every so often you go out shopping or walking around the city with your girlfriends."

"There's nothing to worry about."

"That girl they found by the port an hour ago didn't worry either."

"I don't go near the port at night."

"You're the same age, you're beautiful, you've even got breasts. Don't tell me that some man hasn't looked at you or said something."

Esther bowed her head and said nothing.

Leah didn't need any more than that.

"Have you ever heard of Argentina?" she asked her daughter with some urgency in her voice.

Esther shook her head.

"Argentina is a new country, big and free. It's a country where Jews aren't persecuted."

"Why are you telling me this?"

"Because there are other places to live apart from this damned place!" she replied, almost shouting.

"Do you want us to go there?"

"A lot of people from my town are living in Argentina," she replied, ignoring the question, "and now they're accepting Jews into the colonies to start a new life."

"So?"

"I want to send you there."

The girl looked at her in total shock, as if not comprehending.

"I want you to start your life afresh, without persecution, without fear. I don't want you to end your life like that girl!" she said, covering her daughter's hand with her own.

"Don't touch me!" Esther said, removing her hand.

Even if she hadn't known of her mother's shock when the policemen came into the inn and told the people sitting there about what they had found in the port that night, her mother's suggestion to send her away again aroused fear mingled with rage in her.

"I'm your mother!" Leah told her, forcefully and angrily.

"If you were my mother you wouldn't be thinking about sending me away on my own to another country! What kind of mother are you? One who leaves me time after time?"

"But I'll follow you," said Leah, trying to mollify her.

"You're not a mother, you're a whore! I was told that a long time ago!" the girl screamed.

Leah raised her heavy hand and gave her daughter a resounding slap. The girl fell to the floor weeping. Leah bent over her daughter to comfort her, but in vain. Her daughter wailed in tears like a crazed pup.

The events of that night engendered in Leah such great fear for her daughter that she resolved to send her away from the city, even though she would hate her mother for doing so for many years. In the end, she told herself, she will understand that everything she did was for her sake.

The very next day Leah sat down and wrote a letter to the Jewish Colonization Association in Paris, in which she told them about herself and her daughter, and requested that they examine the possibility of joining one of the first groups of emigrants for Argentina organized by the Association. She did not know then that the JCA, which was looking for only those emigrants who could learn manual labor, had a selection process and screened out educated people, intellectuals, or non-productive professionals. What would they want with a carpenter's widow who owned an inn in the port?

Eighteen

Like a spider scurrying toward its prey, from a distance yet with presence of mind, Bella Bergman sought to ensnare the whore living in the Mattenbuden quarter and running an inn in the port. It did not enter her mind to take a carriage directly to her house like one of the woman's vile customers. She wanted to get to that contemptible woman only when she would be unable to escape her.

For the time being she investigated this woman's history and origins from afar. The first thing she did after recovering from the shocking discovery was to visit the Danzig Jewish burial society.

The burial society premises were located in a low building adjoining the Great Synagogue of Danzig. She had never been inside. Even when her mother-in-law and father-in-law had died, Reine-Chaya and then Shmuel Bergman, her brother-in-law Meir had dealt with all the burial arrangements. She so abhorred death that she had never imagined herself crossing the threshold of this place, a pit of loss and extinction.

But where fear fails, revenge takes over, and Bella's desire for revenge was so fierce that it helped her overcome her fear of death.

She stood on the threshold and knocked on the door, which was opened by a young gravedigger who resembled a raven in human form from whose lips came a short cry, since he was unaccustomed to looking directly into a woman's face. Behind him stood a few yeshiva students, as sweaty and flushed as he, who looked at her – and immediately covered their eyes with their hands, which emitted a smell of fresh earth.

The flock of gravediggers hurried away, leaving Bella facing a stocky, thickly-bearded man wearing a simple hat. The elderly gravedigger looked straight at her, just as she was looking at him. It was clearly evident that he had no fear of the living.

"Frau Bergman," the old man greeted her.

"How do you know my name?" Bella shot back.

"There are two people who know the names of all the Jews of Danzig," the gravedigger smiled, "the midwife and the gravedigger."

Bella grimaced.

"I know your name," the old man went on, "and I also remember your face. It was me who buried your brother who was cut down in the prime of his life."

Bella felt that her legs were giving way. The old man offered her a chair by the table, a big wooden table at which he and his fellow gravediggers had been eating, tearing chunks off a big loaf that stood on it.

Bella sat down, taking care not to soil her dress with breadcrumbs and bits of soil.

"I apologize for the mess," the old man said quietly. "We gravediggers are unaccustomed to company, and certainly not the company of a woman. How may I help you, Frau Bergman?"

"I adjure you in the name of my dead brother, Heinrich, to let me read your records."

"My records are open to you, as they are to all," the old man replied. "There is no secret in a person's name once he leaves this world, so there is no need to swear an oath. But what are you looking for?"

"The names of the people who died in recent months. To find out who died and where they are buried."

"And why would you wish to know that?" the old man asked.

"To rectify a wrong," she replied, intentionally using language that would pluck at his heartstrings.

"Are not the donations made by you and your husband to the living sufficient, that now you wish to provide for the dead as well?" he smiled.

"We would like to make a donation toward setting gravestones on the graves of the unknown," she said.

"A commendable deed," said the old man, "there are many unknown here from among the Russian refugees, without a relative to put up a stone on their graves."

The old man took out his ledger from a cupboard, involuntarily wetting a finger on his tongue, and began leafing back. "Here," he said, "this is where the list of the deceased in recent months begins."

He swiveled the book so she could read it. Bella moved down the list with a finger in the air, taking care not to touch the pages stained with a gravedigger's saliva, moving from the name of one dead person to the next.

"This won't tell me anything," she said. "Can you tell me something about each one, those who were poor and those who weren't?"

"Of course," the old man replied, and began going through the names of the deceased one by one.

In the end he came to the name she was looking for.

"This is the name of Leizer Kochmann," he said. "He was a master carpenter, clean-handed and pure of heart. He did a lot of work in Altschottland."

"Where did he live before he died?"

"In Mattenbuden," the old man replied. "Incidentally, I think your father-in-law knew him."

"What do you mean?" Bella asked tensely.

"Before he was crushed by a *goy*'s machine, this master craftsman made beautiful furniture for the homes of Jews in the quarter, and every so often he visited their homes to repair one thing or another. And I think he did so for your father-in-law."

"Did he live alone," Bella asked, "or did he have a wife and children?"

"He had a wife, but it would be better if I did not mention her to you," the old man replied, closing the book in embarrassment.

"Why not?"

"The Almighty forgives us everything," the old man said, "but before she was his wife and the owner of an inn in the port, she sold her body to strangers."

Bella clenched her fists.

"I thank you for your help," she said, her voice choked. "Now I shall speak to my husband about a suitable donation for the graves of the unknown, and I shall inform you about it tomorrow."

"I am most grateful," the gravedigger nodded, "most grateful."

Only when she was by the door she asked, almost casually, on what Hebrew date the carpenter had died.

The gravedigger told her, and fell silent.

After she left, the old gravedigger lapsed into thought. He did not trust that woman. Her look was not the look of a philanthropist, but of an evildoer. "May all curses, oaths and prohibitions, and all manner of evil eye cast upon you or upon any member of your household be removed," his lips began murmuring, "the evil eye and evil inclination and unfounded hatred remove man from the world."

Nineteen

There are all sorts of people in the world of the Almighty, blessed be He. There are the nobles, the landowners and their sons, and there are the poor. There are rabbis and yeshiva students whose life is devoted to the Torah, and there are tanners and leather merchants who smell of carcasses all week long and only on the Sabbath eve do they wash their bodies and drip perfume onto themselves, and then the smell of their occupation does not waft from them like a contagion. There is the matchmaker who wherever he goes the people immediately start whispering that the time has come to match Mr. So-and-So with Miss What's-Her-Name, and there is the gravedigger, who when people see him walking heavily, wrapped in his thoughts like a shroud, with the terrible splendor of death all around him, they immediately make way for him, fearing that he is approaching their house. For the gravedigger is a man that people prefer seeing only in the cemetery, and if they see him walking down a city street they are instantly affrighted and think he has come to bring bad tidings to one of the households, and then from their neighbor's house or theirs, Heaven forbid, will come such a cry that even the night birds will flee their nests in terror. Therefore, a gravedigger who knows his work and the nature of his vocation in the world, knows that if he has to go to a Jewish house he should go under cover of darkness so that no one sees him and will not see where he is going, and for what purpose.

This is what the old gravedigger of Danzig did. From the moment he realized that he must go to the home of Leah Kochmann, the widow of Reb Leizerel Kochmann, he timed his arrival there for late at night, after all the congregants had returned from the synagogue and shut themselves up in their houses. When he knocked on the door of her little house with his aged hand and she opened it, wondering who could be disturbing her daughter's sleep at such a late hour, she was surprised to find on her doorstep Reb Asher Feinstein, of whom it was said that in his youth he dug so deep that the soil of Danzig opened its mouth and sang songs of praise and thanksgiving as it received his dead.

Leah asked her uninvited guest in, and Reb Asher kissed the mezuzah and entered, leaning on his stick. He sat down in the small sitting room corner, facing the likeness of

Leizer Kochmann on the wall above the sideboard, a flat-headed man wearing a hat, smiling with flashing eyes, in an oval frame like a huge egg.

As he looked at the lifelike portrait of Leizer, Leah quickly drew the curtains over the windows. Then she stood fearfully over her visitor and offered him, in a somewhat quivering voice, a glass of tea after his long walk. She had not seen him since Leizer's funeral, and in the way of all people she had also hoped not to meet him again so soon. And now he was actually in her house facing her, this compassionate man, whose eyes reflected the sorrow of the world.

"Your late husband was a dear man," murmured Reb Asher as he stroked his beard.

"You remember him," Leah said softly, sitting down opposite him.

"I remember them all," the old man said smilingly.

"And what has brought you here?" she asked, avoiding his eyes, thankful that her daughter was sleeping the sleep of the just in the other room, so he had not come, Heaven forbid, to bring her some terrible news about the girl.

"I have come in the Almighty's name," Reb Asher told her, "on a mission of religious duty."

Leah heaved a sigh of relief.

"Tell me, Madam Leah," Reb Asher said, straightening up slightly, "did your husband ever give you a ring to keep secret from anyone else?"

"How do you know that?" she said, rising from her chair.

"Before I tell you, would you be so kind as to show it to me for a moment?"

Leah went to the cupboard where she kept the ring hidden when it was not on her finger, took out a small, delicately carved wooden box, and opened it before Reb Asher.

Reb Asher sighed deeply as he reached out a trembling hand to examine the ring closely, and decide on what his eyes saw and his heart told him. Very carefully he took the ring and looked at it. The ring looked back at him, sending its deep, venomous light into his eyes. He moved it away slightly, looked at the inner face, and saw the unmistakable mark: the verses engraved by Reb Zerachia, of blessed memory.

"What is it?" Leah asked, frightened by the expression on his face,

His lips began murmuring verses from the Psalms as if he were standing on the edge of a grave, not sitting in the house of a Jewish woman.

"What's the matter, Reb Asher, what's happened?" she asked him.

"Did your late husband tell you from where he obtained this ring?" he asked.

Leah nodded fearfully, and told him how on the day that Leizer brought her the ring she had asked him how he had obtained it, for it was made of pure gold and inlaid with precious stones, and it was surely very valuable. And he had evaded the issue and told her that he had found it in the street in the Mattenbuden quarter, where some matron had probably lost it. But after a time she had asked him again how he had come by the ring, and he told her he had bought it in a Danzig pawnshop. It was then that she knew he was keeping something from her.

The more Reb Asher heard, the deeper his heart sank within him like lead. It is one thing to visit a person's house to inform him of a death, but it is quite another to come to the home of a widow and tell her that her late husband, whom she so revered and loved, was a thief, and as a result and to his discredit, had also become a murderer.

"Madam Leah," he said, "this ring has certain properties. Did you know that?"

"Yes," she replied, "he brought it to cure me, and the moment I put it on my finger I was indeed cured of my severe illness."

"There used to be a very righteous Jew here who was a goldsmith, Madam Leah," he told her. "He knew the secret of joining the letters of the Torah, and in his artifacts and jewelry he would embed all kinds of properties and talismans. His name was Reb Zerachia, and this ring was fashioned by him on the intructions of the Rabbi of Kotsk, words of the living God."

"But what's all that got to do with me?" Leah asked, looking into the abysses of the eyes sunken into the depths of Reb Asher's face, from which something suddenly flashed, not the darkness of death but the cogent wisdom of the living.

"This ring, Madam Leah, was sent by the goldsmith with his son to a Jewish township in Poland, Sedlec, where the goldsmith's son, Shmuel Bergman, married a Jewish girl from a good home who suffered from the same illness as you, and like you was cured of it the moment she received the ring," Reb Asher added. "This ring is that girl's wedding ring. Her name was Reine-Chaya Bergman, and I had the privilege and sorrow of burying her."

"But why are you telling me all this?"

"The owner of the ring is dead," Reb Asher said, "and in its absence the ring that saved you, killed her."

Leah clutched her head as if wanting to let out a great cry. But not a sound came from her mouth that alternately opened and closed. The old man held out his kind hands to console her, but she got up and started pacing the room as if terror-stricken.

She walked around mumbling until she stood facing the portrait of Leizer on the wall, and stared at it with brimming eyes. She looked at for a long time, her body shaking with choked sobbing, and then tore the picture from the wall, clasped it to her bosom for a moment, and then threw it onto the floor, shattering the glass.

"Leizer!" she shouted, stunned with pain, "What have you done to me, Leizer?"

"What's the matter, Mama?" They suddenly heard Esther's voice, who had jumped out of bed frightened in the other room, and now stood in the doorway in her nightgown, embarrassed by the sight of the old man sitting facing her mother, his hands outstretched in trembling entreaty, and her mother standing facing him, aquiver with shame.

"Nothing, nothing, Esther, go back to bed," the mother said, trying to control herself.

The daughter looked at her mother for a long time and then went back to her room, where through the half-closed door she listened to fragments of the conversation between her mother and the old man.

"I am very sorry for you, Madam Leah," the old man said quietly, "but if he did such a thing for you, your late husband obviously loved you very much."

Leah was too upset to utter even one syllable. The old man proffered her the glass of water she had given him and was still half full. "Drink a little. It's not good to be without water on hearing such news."

Leah barely sipped the water, she felt that her whole world had suddenly collapsed in ruins. For years she had kept the object that had brought her relief and taken her out of her past. Now, all that time another woman had suffered torment in its absence until she died, and she had had no idea. Her good, beloved husband who had brought her the ring, had deceitfully concealed this from her in order to save her.

She suddenly emerged from her musing, picked up the box with the ring and handed it to Reb Asher.

"Take it," she said, "take it and return it to its rightful owner."

"Slowly, Madam Leah," Reb Asher murmured, "I know you are a decent woman. But this ring heals you, and the woman who needed it is no longer with us. What has been done cannot be undone, as they say. Do not give up your succor so quickly, Madam Leah."

"Then why did you come and tell me this?" she shouted painfully. "Why torment me?"

"To warn you."

"Warn me of what? About who?" Leah screamed, a wave of wrath and helplessness engulfing her.

"About that woman's daughter-in-law, who is looking for you," replied Reb Asherkeh Feinstein. "She came to see me and showed interest in your husband's grave. I could see she is an ill-tempered woman. I came to warn you, Madam Leah, not to take the ring from you, because you have need of it and it will better serve the living than the dead. But that woman is hard on your heels and she will not rest until she has the ring. And if, Heaven forbid, she lays hold of it, this ring will again bring death instead of healing, and this time to you, Madam Leah, may you have a long life."

The old man ended his speech and completed the mission that had brought him to this house. He was sorry for this woman who had known great anguish in her life, and now he had come and added to it. But he knew he had done the right thing by telling her all this, for by so doing he had perhaps saved her life. And the main thing – he had helped guard the hidden intention of the Rabbi of Kotsk, that the ring be one of healing, not of grieving and death, that it bring to its wearer a cure, not sorrow and terror.

Twenty

After the gravedigger's visit to her home Leah felt that life was closing in on her from all sides. She was unable to bear the thought that her salvation had been bought at the cost of another woman's life, a good and righteous woman who had never wronged a soul, and she was unable to come to terms with the knowledge that her late husband, Leizer, had left her – apart from a house and a workshop and a livelihood and a good life – such a legacy of blood. She suddenly saw her dead husband in a different light, not as a man whose love guided him, but as a devious man living under cover of his artifices, and even though they were acts of love intended to save her from prostitution and sickness, she could not countenance them. Her dead husband, the man who had lifted her out of her previous life, the man with whom she shared her bed and for whom she had relinquished raising her daughter like any other mother, that man had intentionally stolen a healing ring from another woman for her, and in so doing had sentenced that poor woman to death and had made her, Leah, his accomplice.

But more than anything she was consumed with concern for the fate of her only daughter. If thus far she had feared that she would come to harm at the hands of drunken sailors or lustful, anti-Semitic *goyim*, now her anxiety took on the form and features of that daughter-in-law, the one described to her by Reb Asher, searching for the ring and who, in the end, would reach her to exact vengeance for her dead mother-in-law. Who would believe that she had nothing to do with the crime, and who would stop the city police from throwing her into jail, leaving her daughter without a father and mother, without a soul to protect her and her innocence. From her own experience she knew what awaited orphans abandoned to their fate, alone in the big city, and how far evil could reach if they had no one to turn to for help.

She felt anxiety closing in on her. She had always suspected that the ring Leizer had given her was not his property, but now that she knew beyond doubt that it had been stolen and caused the death of another woman, she was incapable of putting that ring of death on her finger. Now she would have to act swiftly and cunningly; if she could not save herself from this misery, then at least she must save her daughter.

The more she thought about it, she came to the conclusion that the perfect solution would be to send her daughter to Argentina. There was a big, rejuvenated Jewish community there where Jews could maintain their way of life without fear. In any case, Jewish intellectuals were already urging European Jews to emigrate to Argentina, and her daughter would easily find her place among them. Not only that, Argentina was very far away from Danzig and should anything happen to her, the news would not reach there and cause Esther any distress. As she pondered, she checked how much money she had managed to salt away and realized that it was not enough for her to go with Esther, and because of the urgency she would also be unable to wait for a reply from the JCA. She would just have to await the arrival of the first ship from Argentina in Danzig, and get her daughter aboard to save her.

Fortunately for Leah, a few days later a ship from Argentina docked in the port. It was a freighter that had brought frozen beef packed in ice lockers and skins for tanning and sale, and was to return to Argentina carrying modish clothing, European stud stallions, and piles and piles of amber. A day later one of the ship's passengers happened along to Leah's inn, a man whose Spanish rolled off his tongue just as fluently as his Yiddish.

Leah scrutinized the foreigner who sat at the square wooden table closest to the bar. His small mouth was almost hidden between his groomed mustache and the small beard beneath his bottom lip. While his thin mouth was busy chewing and swallowing, apart from a glint of cunning in his brown eyes, there was also a hint of quiet sadness that invited trust.

He ate with great attentiveness to detail and it seemed that he wanted to demonstrate his foreignness, that this inn beside the port, which was illuminated by candles whose light was absorbed by the wooden walls, was not the kind of place in which he was used to dining. His every movement displayed a certain stylish elegance.

The other diners also felt the foreigner's presence. Every now and again they turned their heads and gave him a quick glance. But he pretended not to notice anyone; he only heightened the grunts of pleasure that escaped his lips.

Leah sent her renowned dish, leg of lamb in apples, with her daughter. Esther approached the table and placed the hot food, sizzling in an iron skillet, on the table, turning the handle away from him. He shot her an inquiring glance and immediately diverted his look – right into Leah's eyes. He realized that those eyes wanted something from him, but he did not know what.

Leah let him finish the dish thanks to which her reputation had spread throughout the city. She only came over to him with a glass of tea, also surprising him with an ashtray and a small bowl in which she had placed a fine cigar from her stock hidden under the counter.

He stole a glance at the men sitting behind him and looking at him disgruntled, thanked her for the cigar and with a broad gesture invited her to join him. As he did so he took a small penknife from his jacket pocket, opened one of its blades, and deftly cut off the end of the cigar.

Leah took out her box of matches from her apron and lit it for him. He began puffing on the cigar, exhaling the first cloud of fragrant smoke. The men behind him coughed, and shortly afterward started to get up and leave.

"The osso bucco was splendid," he said, exhaling a fragrant puff of smoke. His voice was soft and fluent with a hint of a foreign accent.

Leah looked at him. "We call it leg of lamb."

"And your secret is the orange zest you use in it," he asked-stated, smacking his lips.

"The gentleman understands secrets," she replied with a reserved smile, "but to cook in a city like Danzig you need a lot of secrets. You have to know where to gather them – all these secrets – and how to mix them all in one pot."

It was clearly evident that her words had given him confidence.

"Is that young girl your daughter?"

"Yes."

"What's her name?"

"Esther."

"A name like that in times like these, here, is like a mark on the forehead," he said.

"I gave it to her when she was born. My husband made me put her into the only orphanage there was, a Christian one, where she grew up. The name helped the nuns to distinguish her from the other infants, but now it has become dangerous," she said, and sighed. "I hear you're from Buenos Aires. A Jew?"

"A Jew," he confirmed, "Manuel Zind," he said, and shook her hand.

"Is it true that over there they're looking for young girls for housework with Jewish families?"

"Yes, it's true," he smiled.

"And what's life like for the Jews there? Good?"

"Jews are engaged in all branches of commerce in the city," Manuel told her, "and many of them have become very wealthy."

"Do they observe Jewish tradition there?"

"Wherever there's a Jew, there's a synagogue," Manuel laughed. "The Sabbath is the Sabbath and a festival is a festival."

"How can I arrange for my daughter to get work there?" Leah asked, a spark of hope igniting in her heart.

"You are in luck, Madam," said Manuel, smiling, "I have come here precisely to find young girls and bring them back to Buenos Aires."

"To work for Jews?" asked Leah, wanting to be sure.

Manuel nodded and fell silent.

"So take her away from here," she said quietly.

"What?"

"Take her away from here," she repeated, as if wanting to hear herself actually uttering the words. "I've looked after her myself for years, but this city is getting worse by the day. I don't know what's going to happen here. I only know, like any mother, deep in my heart, that I must send her away from here as quickly as possible!"

Manuel puffed on his cigar, silently gazing into her eyes.

"She's a good girl. God gave her intelligence and beauty and also a good pair of hands. She's young. Fourteen, that's all. I don't want to find her one evening thrown into some ditch at the edge of the port, the way they found another Jewish girl. Dead. Defiled. Take her away from here."

Manuel had never imagined that he would encounter such an entreaty under such circumstances.

Although Leah could see his doubts, she did not understand the reason for them.

"Wait here," she said, and went to the bar and opened the door behind it.

A few minutes later she emerged from the inside room, making sure that all the other customers had departed into the night darkness, and sat down beside him, fumbled in her apron pocket, and brought out a wad of banknotes.

"Take it. For travel expenses."

He tried to protest, but she would not allow him to say a word.

"For my part, the matter is closed," she said decisively. "You're sailing in the morning, aren't you? So tomorrow morning you'll come back here to take her aboard the ship."

Manuel nodded, stunned by the force of the despair with which she had thrown her daughter upon his mercy.

If she had only known what she was doing.

He got up, picked up his hat from the chair beside him, and put it on. He strode toward the door, and only on reaching it turned round, and over her shoulder he saw the girl looking at him inquiringly from the far end of the room.

"The leg of lamb really was excellent."

"Tomorrow," Leah said, closing the door behind him.

Where wisdom fails, necessity takes over. Leah did not deliberate for long. From the moment she decided to get her daughter Esther out of this city before the troubles that Leizer had left her to confront caught up with her, she knew that she would hide the ring in her daughter's belongings. Apart from the money she had given to the foreigner, this ring was the only thing she was able to give her, and she wanted to send her daughter away in the knowledge that she was protected from evil. If, sometime in the future, she needed money, she told herself, she could always pawn the ring and use whatever she got for it. She also preferred that this ring not be with her when trouble came knocking on her door, because of one thing she was certain: that wealthy family, the Bergmans, would come and demand the ring from her.

She could not close her eyes that night. For half the night she stood preparing the satchel for her daughter, and then she went to bed, thinking feverishly about the other things her daughter might need for her long journey. She got up, tired and troubled, adding another bundle of stockings to those she had already prepared, went back to bed, seeing in her mind scene after scene since her pregnancy to the present, a kind of broken film of the chapters of a partial, incomplete motherhood. The days when she would leave the house when Leizer was already in his workshop, hurrying to breastfeed her little daughter at the orphanage; the pain that would pierce her each time she had to detach the infant from her breast and hand her back, sated and with closed eyes, to the matron; and the day she came to take her daughter, how she walked through the streets of Danzig, an older, inexperienced mother, holding her little daughter's hand, who was wearing a floral dress and a thick gray coat, one hand in her mother's and the other clutching a faded rag doll; how she sat beside her in the inn, helping her and dwelling on her stories; and how she developed at school, sharing everything she had learned that day; and how she had grown into a young girl, and then her thoughts wandered to the ring, to Leizer, and the woman she doesn't know who is stubbornly looking for her, who had even gone to the cemetery, and again she was filled with dread, and so she lay dozing in her bed until dawn started to break and it was time to wake her daughter and give her the harsh news that she must again be separated from her, and in the company of strangers sail to an unknown country in which there were so many Jews from Russia, Poland, and Lodz, and they all had traveled there with dreams great and small, individual dreams and dreams of a nation, and Leah began talking to herself and praying to God to protect her daughter from any evil that might befall her on the journey, that she should reach Buenos Aires safely and learn the new language, and write to her how all is well with her, and how happy she is with what her mother had done.

But Leah did not delude herself. She knew that her daughter's initial reaction would be one of shock, and that much time would pass before she was capable of forgiving her in her heart for again sending her away.

Sighing, she went into her daughter's room and opened the curtain over the window, letting the blue, early-morning light flood the room.

Esther lay in her bed sleeping deeply. As the light touched her face, wandering over her beautiful, fine, black eyelashes, she started blinking. Leah stood by the bed for a moment, looking at her with pain-filled eyes, and then touched her arm, shaking her gently.

"Esther, it's time to get up," the mother whispered.

110

"It's still early," Esther replied, "let me sleep a little longer, Mama."

"You've got to get up," her mother said in a more assertive tone, and pulled the blanket from Esther. "Today is a big day. Today you're going on a long journey."

Esther got up puzzled, confused by her interrupted sleep, her hair disheveled, and in her nightgown went to the toilet and to wash her face.

As she came into the kitchen and sat down at the table, to which her mother brought a glass of tea and a slice of bread, she noticed the big bundle standing ready in the corner.

"What's that?" she asked, taking a first sip of tea from the glass in her hand.

"A bundle for the journey."

"Who's going?" Esther asked, yawning.

"You," Leah replied, looking into her daughter's eyes. "Soon a man called Manuel will be coming to take you to Argentina on a ship."

Esther put the glass of tea onto the table and looked at her mother. Leah did not move. Esther widened her eyes, her mouth, tried to say something, but remained silent.

"What?" she finally said in a strange voice. "What are you saying?"

"I'm sorry," her mother said, "but I've got no choice. I'm in great danger and so are you. You've got to go away. You've got to go now."

"I'm not going anywhere!" Esther said, raising her despairing voice.

"You can shout until tomorrow," her mother replied decisively, holding back her pain, "But you're going. You aren't going to stay here and suffer like I did when I was your age."

The daughter did not manage to say a word, and burst into bitter, broken weeping.

While she was still weeping there was a knock on the door, and Leah left the kitchen to return with a stranger.

Esther peeped at him for a moment through her tears, and then threw herself, in her nightgown, onto the floor and started banging her head on the ground. Her mother rushed to her, gripped her forearm resolutely, and pulled her up. She shook her to calm her down from the hysteria that had gripped her, and with her other hand took her daughter's coat and threw it over her, nodding to Manuel to help her with the baggage. The three left the inn, Leah dragging her daughter behind her, slamming the door with her free hand.

As they proceeded through the main gate of the port, along the quays, past the fish stalls to the deep bay where only big ships could anchor, the porters and stevedores looked at them in amazement. An elderly woman, heavy in appearance, dragging a frightened girl after her, accompanied by an elegant foreigner carrying a suitcase and another large satchel, a shiny gold ring on his finger and his black hair combed back sleek with brilliantine.

They finally reached the ship and stopped at the foot of the gangway. The mother shook her daughter, grasped her head and turned her round to face her. She looked long into her eyes, and then tried to kiss her cheek.

The daughter turned her face away.

"I hate you," she whispered.

"You'll get over it," the mother said, "it's all for your own good."

Manuel signaled to one of the sailors to come down from the deck and help with the luggage of this pest, and after the sailor had loaded her luggage onto his back, he grabbed the girl's arm and dragged her up the gangway. When they reached the deck, the girl turned toward the mother. On seeing her daughter's anguished face, Leah covered her face with her hands in an expression of pain and sorrow.

The daughter turned her back on her, and Manuel forced her inside the ship. This one isn't a dog, she's a wild horse, he thought, as he dragged her along behind him until he locked her inside a big meat locker in the hold.

Leah remained on the quayside, looking at the big ship being loaded with the last of the crates and boxes, and now the stevedores were hurrying down the gangway from high above, and smoke was coming from the funnel, and the siren blared. She stood, tears imprisoned in her throat, mumbling a silent prayer that seemingly came from her of its own accord, the prayer before embarking on a journey, praying to God to protect and save her daughter, and she went on standing there until Manuel came out on deck and waved that everything was fine. Only then, when she saw his hand raised to her, and she raised her own hand for a moment to tell him she understood, did the fat tears begin pouring from her eyes, and she bowed her head and sobbed silently, not knowing if she would ever see her daughter again, but hoping that she had done the right thing for her. She stood there, choked, until the ship disappeared from sight. Then she filled her lungs with air and mustered the strength to return to her little house on her own, she and her hopes, she and her memories, she and her troubles.

Twenty-one

Like a caged animal Esther sat on her luggage in the big meat locker into which a little light and air came from an aperture in the ceiling, and inside which was only a bucket of water and another for calls of nature. At first she tried banging on the door, hitting it again and again with her fists, hoping that someone on deck would come to her aid. But none of the sailors answered her calls. In the ship's hold were many more such lockers designed for carrying frozen beef to Europe, but which were now filled with meat of a different kind, young women like Esther being shipped to their ruin. The sound of her banging was muffled by the dull rumbling of the ship that came from deep within it as it propelled itself forward out of Danzig Port, loaded with people and goods, into the open sea.

The ship rocked from side to side, plowing through the high waves, throwing Esther from one side of her cell to the other and putting her stomach into turmoil. A wave of nausea rose in her, and unable to stop it she vomited her breakfast onto the floor. Her mouth filled with a disgusting sourness. She stumbled to the water bucket, holding onto to wall with both hands, and scooped up some water in her cupped hand to wash her mouth out.

The water had a brackish taste of rust, warm and musty like water that had stood for many days in the ship's belly. She spat it out and went back to lie on her luggage, not knowing what she could do next except stare at the aperture in the ceiling, her mind empty of thoughts, and she, still stunned by what had happened to her all at once that morning – being torn from her world.

A few hours later, when the ship was already on the open sea, evening began to fall. She could discern this by the amount of light coming in through the ventilation aperture, until the cell was completely shrouded in thick darkness. Suddenly she heard footfalls approaching the door, and before she could get up it opened and three muscular sailors came inside carrying a lamp and smelling of oil mingled with the strong stench of alcohol and sweat.

Esther crouched in a corner of the locker, her back to the wall. They grimaced at the stink of the vomit she had cleaned up with a piece of her clothing. One stood with his back to the door, blocking it with his big body. The second stood facing her, and the third sat on the floor next to her as she clutched her knees to her chest, not understanding what they were doing there and what they wanted of her.

"We've come to have some fun with you," said the sailor sitting beside her in Spanish.

Esther looked at him wonderingly and then shrugged to show that she didn't understand.

"To give you a good time," laughed the one facing her, his hand slowly sliding to his groin.

"Can't you see she doesn't understand?" said the big sailor blocking the door. "The little Jewess doesn't speak Spanish!"

"Then she'll definitely understand this!" laughed Pedro, the sailor facing her, quickly unbuttoning his trousers and taking out his large member and wagging it to the laughter of his friends.

Esther covered her eyes with her hands.

She had never seen such a thing.

Late that night Pedro, Paolo, and Jorge, their faces flushed, came up the companionway from the lower to the upper deck where Manuel was waiting. Hearing their voices he turned to them with a calm, frozen expression on his face.

"Did you do what I told you?" he asked the sailors.

"Yes," Pedro said, "we tore the little slut apart."

"We opened up the virgin for you," Jorge chuckled, "from all directions."

Manuel shot him a stern look. "I don't need to hear the details."

"Whatever you say," Pedro said, "now what about the..." he added, rubbing two fingers and a thumb together.

Manuel handed him a wad of notes, which he began counting. There were thirty pesos.

"There's some missing," he said.

"There's nothing missing," Manuel replied, stubbing out his cigar under his heel.

"You said twenty each, that's sixty pesos," Pedro said, handing the notes to Jorge. "Count it."

"That's all you're getting," Manuel said, "you've had enough fun."

Jorge raised his eyes to him. "*Judeo mierda*, you shitty Jew!" he said, taking a step toward Manuel. His two friends held him back.

"What did you say?" Manuel asked, slipping his hand to his belt where his snub-nosed Belgian pistol was stuck.

"He didn't say anything, Señor," Pedro said quickly.

"Very good," Manuel said, "if you say one word I'll hand you over to the police the moment we dock. I've got them all in my pocket, you know that."

The three nodded. They knew that this man was a Jewish pimp and that the ring of Jewish pimps was well-connected to the Buenos Aires police, and that they let them take their girls off the ship with no problems. The three knew this and didn't want any trouble.

Jorge stuffed the notes into his pocket, mumbling a few more words, and the three turned and left him for their quarters.

Manuel slowly straightened his shirt to hide his pistol, and rubbed his hands.

He was eighteen in Poland when he was sold the dream of Buenos Aires. The son of an observant Jewish shopkeeper who hoped his son would become a Torah scholar, and of a religious housewife who spent most of her time cooking and looking after the ten children she had borne because they knew nothing about the use of *preservativos*. It didn't even enter their mind. Most of his brothers and sisters were older than him, some of them married, and he saw full well how they were mired in the poverty and degeneration of the town, doing what they could to barely provide for their families. It sickened him. His eyes looked toward the big world across the sea, and although his parents tried to persuade him to study Torah, he was friends with the *goyishe* children, playing with them and hitting them, and so in his childhood he was dubbed with a nickname that stuck to him ever since: Emmanuel Shaygetz. While his peers and younger siblings attended *cheder*, he would run off to play with the children of market traders or run around the streets of the town with the *goyishe* children. This was how he heard stories about the big world from the adults, and discovered that the world did not begin and end in Czernowitz, his town.

When the migration of Jews from Poland and Russia began, he heard stories about Jews emigrating to South America. There was always something exotic in these stories and they always mentioned great wealth. Back then who did not dream of having a rich uncle in South America who could send him money and rescue him from life in the town? But Emmanuel decided to take his destiny into his own hands and fled his parents' home, leaving behind a note in broken Yiddish to the effect that he had gone to seek his fortune across the sea, on a ship bound for South America, and that they shouldn't come looking for him because they would never find him.

On the ship he met some other boys like him, impatient young Jews who were prepared to sail on a freighter and do any work they were given, just so they could get to the New World. On the ship, where he worked as a deckhand, he met men who were to become his close friends, and who also became members of the pimps' Varsovia organization, later to become the Zwi Migdal Society.

On the voyage, which lasted for weeks, they had time to sit together at night, drink eau-de-vie, cognac, and whisky, and listen to the sailors' tales of the sea, especially the one about the seabird it was forbidden to kill because it was the soul of a woman and whoever killed it would have his eyes pecked out at night by it, or stories about the anger of the sea god at sailors, which whipped up great storms.

On reaching Buenos Aires, Emmanuel joined other young men who frequented the taverns where he discovered the flourishing *Blancas* industry. The possibility of making easy money and living like a king attracted him. He took a loan from his friends to sail to Poland and bring back a few women. The agreement was that he repay the loan from his profits, which was an excellent arrangement.

Deep in thought, Manuel sat on the upper deck, twisting the heavy gold ring on his finger, which bore his engraved initials, M.Z. Then he stretched, took out a coarse Cuban cigar and smoked pleasurably.

He had a few hours to wait before going below deck to the young girl's cell, to discover, seemingly by chance, the catastrophe that had befallen her. If he went down right away it would appear implausible and he would lose the opportunity of discovering it in amazement and regret, to display compassion toward her, thus making her his forever.

Tomorrow he would give the same treatment to the other young girl he had picked up in one of villages near Lublin, he thought to himself. It was designed to prepare them for what awaited them when they disembarked and went into the city. Unlike other women his friends from the organization had purchased at auction, naked, he had chosen these two for himself, and they would be taken to the house right away and put to work. They would not suffer the shock of public auction, forced to parade naked on the platform before the pimps, judges, police officers, city dignitaries, and the madams, the *porteras*, who would examine each of them closely, pinching their breasts and buttocks, and estimating their price. For if they weren't raped on the ship they would be like mad dogs, clawing and cursing and trying to escape from the room where they were held, not understanding that any policeman who caught would take them right back because their papers were in the hands of the people who had brought them, and in any case, most of the policemen were paid handsomely by all the members of the organization.

Still sitting on deck, gazing at the star-studded sky over the great sea, Manuel thought with great satisfaction about how his life had turned out. He was only thirty and already owned his own small brothel with a *portera* who knew her job, and his own collection of pistols. He had no aspirations of owning a brothel with seventy or eighty whores, like some of his friends. He was quite happy with a small house and a few good girls who knew how to provide service to the customers, and him with an income. But to do that you had to know how to train them right from the start.

Esther heard footsteps approaching and then the bolt sliding back. The door opened, flooding the cell with blinding light, and Manuel came in carrying a tray of food, and closed the door behind him. He looked around, his eyes screwed up against the pale light coming in through the aperture in the ceiling, and saw her lying frozen on the floor, her face scratched and her eyes wide.

He put the tray down next to her and bent over her, examining her face closely. Her eyes showed no sign of recognition. She had evidently taken it very badly, he thought, but she'll get over it. Like all of them. Like most of them.

He brought the cup of water to her lips. Esther blinked, but did not raise her head.

With his left hand supporting her head he slowly lifted her until she was sitting. Then he slowly fed her some water from the cup in his hand without asking anything. She, too, did not say a word.

After she had drunk, he stood up, took his linen handkerchief from his pocket, wet it in the turbid water in the bucket, and painstakingly began washing her face, just like a sister of mercy.

Esther's whole body shrank from his touch. Now and then a tremor ran through her body but she did not speak, only her eyes said it all, as did her hands clutching the blanket to her as if trying to hide her young, wounded body.

He finished cleaning her face, stuffed the handkerchief back into his pocket, and held the plate with a sandwich on it to her mouth. Esther shook her head slightly in refusal. She was still incapable of eating. But her nostrils flared, a sure sign that she was tempted by the food, Manuel told himself. He would leave her the plate. She would eat in the end. Like all of them.

He put the plate back onto the floor, and lightly held her back with his left arm as his right hand gently stroked her head. Only then did she burst into tears, mumbling fragments of words, clasping him, her tears wetting his chest, the tears of a young girl who did not know how this had happened to her, and who else in the world she could trust.

"Don't say anything," he said, taking out the handkerchief again and drying her eyes. "I know what those monsters did to you, but don't worry; from now on I'll take care of you, just as I promised your mother. Everything will be fine. Cry, child, cry until you feel better. Everything will be fine, I promise."

With boundless patience he let her cry and tell him, in confused sentences, what had happened to her. Then he got up and fetched her another cup of brackish water, the main thing was that she drink and replenish the fluids in her body. Still stroking and holding her, he already knew – from now on she was his, body and soul.

She slowly calmed down, and again he offered her the food. At first she just sniffed the plate, and then took the sandwich in both hands and wolfed it down. When she had finished he offered her an apple. She would feel stronger after eating. He needed her to have her strength, for tomorrow they would be docking.

Everything was meticulously planned and calculated, just as he had been told by the Geists before he left on this journey, the first in his life: only one day must elapse from the deed itself to when the girl starts work. That way the fear is still fresh in her mind and she will not rebel. Just remember to make sure she doesn't harm herself or throw herself overboard.

The girl slowly calmed down, and he laid her gently on her luggage and covered her with the blanket like a caring father. Then he kissed her forehead and stood there for a few moments until her eyes were quiet once more, her eyelids closed from fatigue, and she fell asleep.

Now he had to give the treatment to the other one, he thought, and he left the big locker quietly, bolting the door behind him.

Twenty-two

Bella waited for the right time to speak to her husband about the various tradesmen and artisans who had previously provided services in his father's house. One evening they were sitting in the living room, and Bella was ostensibly examining a piece of embroidery and looking at Gershon who was reading the newspaper, scrutinizing yet another article about Zionism.

She cleared her throat once, and then again, until she managed to attract his attention.

"What is it, Bella?" Gershon asked, folding his paper into half, then quarters, and placing it meticulously on his knee. "You will agree, I hope, that things between us have improved of late."

"Yes," she replied with her freezing smile, "life seems completely different since we've been sleeping together again."

Gershon gave her a half smile and rubbed his thigh, suddenly enjoying the feeling of his flesh under his hand. "So what is it you want to say?"

"You know how this big house and everything in it gives me sleepless nights," she said.

"Yes, you really do devote your all to it."

"I'd like to ask you who the artisans were that worked here in the past. I'm finding it hard to find good craftsmen of the old school. I'm afraid of leaving the house and its contents in the hands of overly reckless workpeople."

The unexpected question surprised Gershon, but he was quietly pleased. His wife's mind was filled with household matters instead of the bitterness that had filled it.

"What do you want to know?" he asked cautiously, wondering whether her concern for the house signaled that the ring madness had passed. "What kind of artisan are you looking for?"

"All those who came and went here in the past," she replied quietly.

Gershon's heart swelled. Only infrequently had she asked him to share the memories of his childhood and youth. He began by telling her about his old governess, almost a family member, who would come to his parents' house every day to look after him and his brothers until his mother had finished her daily activities, and about the knife-grinder from Mattenbuden who would tramp the quarter's streets shouting his wares; the women who cleaned the house, and one in particular, whose expertise was polishing brass and glass, and how each ornamental plate or chandelier she cleaned would gleam in the sunlight; and he also mentioned the cook and the porter, and the decorator whose hands were expert in creating designs in paint that looked like wallpaper, and the carpenter with wonderful hands who could repair antique armchairs, and wardrobe doors that were off their hinges, and by the way, the poor man died not long ago, killed by a lifting machine that crushed him.

"That *poor man* stole your mother's ring," she interrupted sharply and dryly.

Gershon opened his mouth but said nothing.

"Yes, yes, Gershon, that poor man stole the ring. It was he who murdered your father and mother."

Gershon was astounded. "But he was a good Jew, an artisan, a man with clean hands!"

"Your good Jew lived with a whore. A whore with falling sickness," she went on, looking right at him.

"So what?" he protested.

"Tell me, where's your head? He heard the stories being told in the city about the ring, and that's what led him to burgle the house and steal it!"

"But there were no signs of forced entry," Gershon said, quailing before his wife's rage.

"He visited this house often and knew every loophole in it. I wouldn't be surprised if he had a key or another way of getting in."

Gershon fell silent. Of all the occasions when she had tortured herself over the ring, now her words seemed logical. If she is right we can demand the return of the ring from the carpenter's widow.

"So what are you thinking of doing?" he inquired carefully.

"I shall see," she replied evenly, "I shall see."

"Just don't put yourself in any danger, you don't know what this woman is capable of," he said, not knowing exactly to which woman he was referring.

Bella gave him her cold smile. "How I detest your concern, Gershon. I've told you more than once – you're not my father. You're only my husband."

She went out onto the veranda to think and smoke another cigarillo. Gershon looked at her back and smelled the sickening stench of tobacco smoke that wafted into the house, clinging to the heavy curtains, the carpets, the chairs, her body. He could even detect the smell through the heavy perfume she used. But as was his wont, he did not dare say a word to her. And anyway, his mind was on other matters.

Twenty-three

Everywhere Gershon went, be it the cafés where he met like-minded friends, or the Great Synagogue where he paid his respects to his parents' memory, or to attend to matters in the city, he came across increasing numbers of refugees, snuffed-out people, wandering the streets of the big city, standing out in their strange attire and their laughable appearance, people with no ground beneath their feet, without a past, without a future, without a place to go back to, rejected, degraded. But even he lived his life at night as one of the rejected, walking the streets, the parks, leaving his house on the pretense of having to think, but in fact extricating himself from the feeling of siege he felt because of his wife's silent demand for congress, forcing him to her for the act of love. Fleeing, getting himself away from her and the house where he grew up and was married, the home in which his whole life was housed but not his longings and desires, for those passions have no place there and they, which grip his heart forcefully, turn him, too, into a refugee like them. Whereas they had been forced from their country, he fled himself, his world, where he was bound to adapt himself to life as a married man, a husband, a philosopher imprisoning his feelings within his opinions, ever restraining himself to never again go to the darkness of those parks, to the fleeting figures in the gloom, strangers who come and give what they give, take what they take, and vanish into the darkness.

He shared his inner world with no one, especially his wife, but simply diverted all that lust to his writing, his ideas, his thoughts, which were increasingly disseminated among the Jewish public, endowing him with the status of a philosopher who was certainly worth reading and hearing.

The article he wrote that gained the greatest attention in the press of the time was the one in which he set out his ideas on emancipation. "The ingathering of the exiles about which the pragmatic Zionists dreamed is but a pipe dream", he wrote. "Now is the time to change the material woes of the majority of the Jews in the Diaspora countries by acquiring land and establishing Jewish nationalism, even in transitory countries".

A short time after this article was published Gershon received a letter from one of Baron Hirsch's people, which bore the seal of the baron himself. Gershon looked at it, turned it over slowly, carefully slit it open with his letter knife and with pounding heart read its few lines. It contained a proposal from Baron Hirsch that Gershon assist him in organizing the settlement of Jews in the broad expanses of Argentina.

For Bella, the very idea of leaving Danzig was like a sort of death. This idea, which Gershon eagerly explained to her as someone who had had sufficient time to let it mature within him, of leaving the city where she was born and had grown into adulthood, cast a dark terror over her.

His frequent homilies about the journey, about his desire to emigrate to Argentina, from the journals he placed on her desk with their articles about Baron Hirsch's plans, all clearly demonstrated to Bella that he would not renounce his original intention, and not only that, he was preparing the ground for realizing that intention.

Bella put on a long, form-fitting white dress with a plunging neckline, and gathered her braids under a wide-brimmed white hat. She carried a small matching handbag. She summoned a carriage and drove to her parents' home to consult with her mother. Berta, who since her daughter's marriage was unaccustomed to such unannounced visits, watched her worriedly from the window, but when she saw her alighting from the carriage so elegantly attired, her demeanor resolute, the concern vanished from her face.

"You look wonderful," Berta said, kissing her daughter, "it's a shame that Papa isn't here to see you looking like this."

"Excellent," Bella replied, "I must speak to you alone."

"What's the matter?" Her mother tensed, following her into the big farmhouse. "Is he giving you trouble again?"

"Let's sit down first," Bella replied, walking into the spacious parlor at the front of the house. Pleasant summer sunlight came into it through the windows bordered with curtains her mother had made, and sunbeams played over the wood floor, the furniture, the saddles ornamenting the walls, and her brother's old collection of riding crops standing in a tall container with his portrait hanging over it. Her yearning glance lingered over her brother's picture, and then she sat down on the wide sofa, the sun casting golden rays over her face. Her nostrils suddenly picked up an aroma wafting through the kitchen door.

Her mother noticed her daughter sniffing, and smiled. "You've come on the right day. I'm just making the heavy rye bread that Papa loves."

She went to fetch her daughter two slices of the warm bread with a glass of tea and a dish of forest fruit jam.

Bella was filled with the smell of this house, its warmth, recalling the great simplicity in which they had lived within its walls, whose surrounds were constantly drenched in the smells of forage and horse droppings, but inside was the fragrance of paradise from her mother's kitchen. She drew it in and exhaled it with a silent sigh.

"Tell me what's happened," her mother urged her, pushing the refreshments toward her, "and eat slowly, it's still warm."

"Gershon received a letter from Baron Hirsch," Bella said, spreading jam onto a slice of bread. "The baron has asked him to go to Argentina to set up a network of Jewish schools."

"Mazal Tov! Mazal Tov!" her mother cried, rubbing her hands. "Oh, what a pity Papa's not here! What news!" At the same time she noticed a cloud over Bella's face. "You look like you're in mourning, I don't understand."

"It's a different country, Mama, another continent," Bella replied, a trace of despair in her voice. "How can I go?"

"What do you mean?" Berta said. "By boat, like everybody else."

"Stop it, Mama. You know exactly what I mean. I'm not leaving Danzig for some barbaric country!"

"Barbaric?" Berta asked. "They raise the healthiest horses and the best cattle in the world there, there are huge expanses of land. It's a new, developing country and people there become extremely wealthy."

"But where in Buenos Aires will I have a slice of bread like this from my mother's oven?" Bella smiled, her mouth full.

"Oh, really," her mother scoffed, "you've been used to the Bergman family's rolls for a long time."

"I'm not leaving you and Papa for another continent," Bella said, dabbing her lips with a napkin.

126

"I married you to that boy so you'd have a good life, Bella, not so you'd stay tied to your mother's apron strings!"

"What's so bad for me here?" Bella asked. "If he wants to go, let him go. I'll wait here until he comes back."

"Like a widow, God forbid," her mother nodded. "Bella, you've got to go with him. Don't forget he's your husband."

"Sometimes I really do forget," Bella replied caustically.

"So that's why you should go with him," her mother persisted, "a change of air sometimes helps a man. Anyway, he'll be completely in your hands over there. Be sensible, be practical, Bella. You really will be the lady of the manor there."

"And you'll stay here and grow old on your own?"

"Oh, Bella, Bella," her mother smiled, stroking her hand with her warm one, "*Zey nisht a narish*, don't be foolish. Every mother wants a husband with such status for her daughter. Baron Hirsch has invited him, and you're thinking twice? Do you have any idea who the baron *is*? He's married to the daughter of the richest banker in London and his heart's as big as this house."

"What's that got to do with me?" Bella asked. "He's spending his money on land for Jews, not on his employees."

"I can see that you really should talk to your father so he can explain something about business to you," her mother tut-tutted. "What are you thinking? That you'll be living in a wood hut? That you'll earn pennies? Is that what your intelligence is telling you? Don't be childish. Take what God gives you. And don't worry about us. I'll have a daughter in Argentina I'll be able to visit every year. It'll be a pleasure for me. Do you understand?"

They talked a while longer until Bella got up to leave. "And don't say a word to Papa," she warned her mother at the door, "I don't want him having all kinds of aristocratic imaginings. I'm not going anywhere just yet," she said, kissing her mother's cheek.

"We married you to an aristocrat's son so you'd become an aristocrat. So stop talking rubbish. The main thing is that it should be good for you."

"It will," Bella laughed, and started walking toward the waiting carriage. "In Danzig." Her mother replied with a wave.

"Rubbish," she murmured as the carriage moved off. "In Danzig. Rubbish," she repeated, and then resolved to visit her son-in-law the very next day on the pretext of obtaining a donation for a Jew, and toast the good news with him.

A few days later Gershon made up his mind to take the advice of his mother-in-law, who had called on him on the sly, and write to Baron Hirsch. He wrote that the baron's proposal appealed to him and that he believed in the notion of organized evacuation. He also felt that the baron had granted him a great privilege – being part of this endeavor, not only in words and ideas, to bring about change in the situation of the Jewish people in the Diaspora. Yet in his personal life he was encountering difficulties in bringing this idea to fruition with his wife, for whom the Spanish culture and language were alien. She was born, had grown up and lived all her life in Danzig. But, he wrote, should his wife be able to meet the baron and his wife and become aware of the sincerity of their intentions and their integrity, and also leave Danzig for a while, which she had never done, and at the same time taste the flavor of travel from one country to another, it would certainly help in getting her to accommodate the idea of traveling to Argentina, whose name at present she only had to hear for her to shudder in disgust.

Baron Hirsch was sensitive to peoples' feelings. He sought to bring about a momentous historic event, but he knew that the basis of any change lies in the heart of the individual. If this Gershon Bergman could maneuver his wife, he thought, then he was surely suited to the role intended for him – to negotiate with the Argentinean authorities and representatives of the colonies' settlers in order to establish a network of Jewish schools.

So it happened that two weeks after sending the letter, Gershon received an official invitation bearing the baronial seal from Baron Hirsch and his wife, inviting Gershon and Bella Bergman to visit them at their modest home in Paris.

The letter was received by Bella, who was at home when the special messenger bearing it arrived. The envelope was addressed in bold print to her and her husband, so she excitedly tore it open, and was amazed to see that the baron himself had taken the trouble to write the letter, its cursive, meticulous script revealing both wisdom and eloquence, and right away, perhaps involuntarily, she started thinking about what the villa of one of the world's magnates looked like, and what life was like in that palace, and how they would be entertained there. When Gershon came home she opened her arms to him, happier than usual, suddenly pleased that he was her husband. Perhaps there was some benefit in all the long hours he spent closeted in his study, reading and writing in such profound seriousness, as if he were planning the future not only for him and his household, but for all the Jewish people.

Twenty-four

The moment Bella set foot in the spacious home of Baron Moritz Hirsch she comprehended the great importance of their relations with their new benefactor. Baron Hirsch captivated her with his conduct. He and his beautiful wife, Clara née Bischoffsheim, treated them with great respect and even held a festive dinner in their honor, to which dignitaries from the Jewish community were also invited.

At table, the baron and his wife seated Gershon on the great benefactor's right and Bella on his left, with the baroness beside her. The four were seated at the center of the table with all eyes upon them, and many of the other guests at the long and splendid table wondered who this lucky couple were, whose company the baron sought, until the baron tapped on his crystal wineglass with a silver spoon.

"My friends, my wife and I are happy to have you at this table with the eminent Jewish philosopher, Gershon Bergman, and his lovely wife Bella."

Blushing, Bella lowered her eyes in embarrassment.

"If what I have in mind comes to pass," the baron went on solemnly, "they will travel to Argentina with our colleagues and take upon themselves the task of establishing an independent Jewish education system." He then raised his glass and asked the company to drink a toast to the couple's success.

After they were again seated, the liveried servants, with bow ties at their throats and dark pressed vests tight on their proud chests, began serving salvers of delicious food.

The baron looked at Bella warmly.

"Thank you, Baron," she said quietly, "there really was no need."

He smiled at his wife and for a brief moment laid his hand on Bella's.

"A beautiful woman should be told so to her face," he said, clinking his glass with hers, inviting her to taste the fine wine sparkling in the gleaming glasses.

Moritz Hirsch passed the rest of the dinner in perfectly natural conversation with the other guests without weaving a single thread of it with her. But later, when a short pianist began playing gay dance music in the salon, he took her arm and asked Gershon's permission to talk to her outside for a while, while he, Gershon, should mingle with the other guests. Gershon nodded obediently and followed the baroness, who took him under her wing, as the baron and Bella walked out of the large dining room and sat at a round wooden table on the verandah, while servants quickly brought a bottle of wine, two glasses, and the baron's pipe.

"You're a striking woman, Mademoiselle Bergman," the baron said as he filled his pipe, again making Bella blush embarrassedly.

"Thank you, Baron."

"Moritz," he said.

This familiarity puzzled her. After all, he didn't know her at all.

"You're a clever woman, Bella," he said, "and I'm sure you already understand that I am unaccustomed to being refused. I have set my mind on sending you and your husband to Argentina."

"In that case you should be speaking to my husband," Bella replied, a hint of assertiveness creeping into her voice.

The baron smiled. "I know where the power lies."

"As you wish," she said, "but then you must accept me as I am, warts and all, with none of the trappings of royalty."

"You really are a woman after my own heart!" he laughed in reply, moving to refill her glass.

She gently moved her glass aside. "You are evidently used to drinking, but I must keep my head clear."

"I ascribe great importance not only to your husband, but also to you in this great venture," the baron said.

"I'm no philosopher."

"Great plans have no need of philosophers, they need deeds. You're a practical woman, precisely the one your husband needs when he faces a diplomatic mission. A woman who knows how to forge relationships, bring people together, and how to grease palms."

"I don't understand where this trust you have in me comes from," Bella replied.

"It's not a matter of trust, it's a matter of eyes," the baron laughed, puffing on his pipe. "Incidentally, what were you expecting, that I'd send you to a life of poverty on a remote farm?"

131

"My thinking hasn't reached that far," she replied, and after hesitating briefly she asked if she might be permitted to smoke a cigarillo.

"Of course, of course," he replied expansively, "I didn't know you were a smoker. What can I say? A woman after my own heart!"

He lit her cigarillo and went on talking, telling her about Recoleta, the most affluent quarter in Buenos Aires, to which he intended to send her and her husband, only if she consented, to live amid all the comfort and splendor that the city had to offer, a new port city, almost as big and as international as Danzig, but younger.

"I'm not a woman who's accustomed to grandeur," Bella said, "I was brought up to be happy with what I have."

"Modesty *and* pragmatism," the baron said, "that's how a woman should conduct herself."

Next morning Bella found a silver tray outside their door and on it a German translation of the manifesto disseminated by the baron among Russian Jewry. Atop it lay a card inscribed with the baron's cursive hand and signed by him: "For Bella Bergman, a woman after my own heart." Lying on the card was a long-stemmed red rose, the stem green and thorn-less, and the flower open like a woman's lips.

She opened the manifesto and began reading.

"To my brethren in Russia," the baron wrote, "I stand ready to do everything in my power to relieve your distress, but you must help me to do so. Emigration need not be like disorganized flight whereby people fleeing danger descend straight into ruin."

Bella hummed in agreement and went on reading: "I address you with a caution. You are the descendants of a people that has suffered greatly for hundreds of years. Bear your heritage in submission a while longer. Be patient and give those who seek to help you the possibility of so doing."

Bella's heart was filled with fear. What would happen if she gave her consent to her husband and his benefactor and agreed to leave Danzig and live in exile, far from everything she had known? Did it not mean that she would be voluntarily accepting the fate of an uprooted woman?

The word 'uprooted' horrified her. Uprooted from her country, her family, her memories, her language, trapped in the vast abyss gaping before anyone relinquishing his world for dreams of distant and better worlds.

These fears gave her no peace. She wandered the palace, up and down the sweeping staircases along which old paintings hung, and her heart was heavy. The longer she was there in that beautiful marble palace, lined with huge, colorful carpets trodden by bankers, philanthropists, and businessmen, the more her heart wilted within her.

Each day she passed the numerous works of art collected by the baron and his wife, observing the odd mixture of Jewish and Christian paintings. She was particularly taken by a large oil painting depicting Mordechai the Jew and Queen Esther writing the Book of Esther, and beside it one by Bernardino, which showed the Magi announcing the birth of Christ, and a huge, brilliant tapestry with a scene from the life of the goddess Artemis.

She stood shocked in front of a huge painting in one of the salons that depicted Roman soldiers conquering a city and taking its women captive. She wondered what exactly in this violence fascinated the baron and baroness, and then she told herself that people whose business dealings are so extensive and world-encompassing must also aspire to greatness and power.

In another great room she looked at sculptures of the god Pan, a nymph, Ariadne and Hercules.

"Those are variations of classical sculptures discovered in excavations of the fifteenth century," she suddenly heard her host saying. She was surprised to see the baron, who had accompanied her without her knowledge as she wandered among the many art treasures. "They are copies fashioned by artists in Florence, and it was they who heralded the Renaissance. That little one was made in France by Giambologna in 1529."

Bella was captivated by the beautiful sculpture, with its embracing figures of Nexus and Arianna, and inquired how the Florentine sculptor had managed to create such a striking copy.

"He first made a clay model, covered it with wax, and then put it into a vat of molten bronze," the baron explained. "The bronze filled the hollow sculpture, and when it had hardened he broke the outer clay mold and took out the sculpture."

No less than she was impressed by his vast store of knowledge in which there was a hint of pride of possession of these exquisite objects, Bella enjoyed the attention he heaped upon her.

But there is a time for softening the heart and a time for hardening it, a time for softening a woman's heart and a time for business. A few days after their arrival at his home, Moritz Hirsch invited Gershon into his office for a téte-à- téte. The baroness made sure that she kept Bella away by inviting her to take a stroll to see the cultural sights of Paris. They left the house in all their finery, with wide-brimmed hats, looking for all the world like sisters.

After exchanging the customary pleasantries, the baron told Gershon that his wife's anxiety was perfectly natural, and that he should pay attention to it for it is characteristic of people when circumstances place them before the need to leave their homeland.

"Would you also expect such difficulties from those who have already sailed to Argentina?" Gershon asked him.

"A person uproots himself from his life, from everything he has known, so it is only natural that the first thing he feels is great anxiety and a need to be secluded."

"A secluded Jewish settlement is the last thing we need," Gershon said, "that has always been the nature of Diaspora Jewry. Seclusion due to the instinct of survival brings with it the exact opposite."

"Precisely," the baron said, thumping the desktop, "and that is the idea behind sending you to establish a school network in Argentina. Give them religious instruction but bring them closer to the language, the culture, and the history of this new place, for the sake of…"

"Assimilation," Gershon interrupted him, "emancipation and assimilation."

"Indeed," the baron replied, repressing his feelings. This young man was too hasty to impress him, yet he did not seem lacking in manners.

"Look," he said, picking up a document from his desk, "Wilhelm Lowenthal has just returned from South America. The authorities there have decided to encourage Jewish emigration to Argentina, and have even appointed a representative in Europe. We will be able to establish a superb Jewish settlement only if we know how to properly screen those chosen to settle there."

"Did you say 'screen'?"

"We do not need intellectuals among them," the baron replied, "but young workers capable of labor – and having children."

"What about the aged and infirm?" Gershon asked apprehensively. "Will they remain in the towns and villages in Europe, subject to persecution and pillaging?"

"The great plans of nations require the sacrifice of individuals. As we bring succor to an entire people, some individuals will suffer."

Gershon could hardly believe his ears. The cold pragmatism concealed behind his host's cordial veneer chilled him. The notion of selection seemed horrifying to him, and he could feel himself rebelling against it. The sharp-eyed baron noticed his darkening expression.

"Speak your mind, Gershon Bergman," he said after a brief silence, "you are not entirely fainthearted, just as I am not just a man with a heart of iron."

"What do you mean?" Gershon stammered, feeling as if he had been caught red-handed.

"Don't allow your anger to besmirch my reputation, leaving you simon-pure in your own eyes," the baron smiled. "We're both human beings, and we both have both sides in us. I too would not dare to leave the aged and infirm, helpless widows and orphans in a place rife with anti-Semitism. I shall take them to Argentina a short time after their children. A drop of cognac?" he asked, suddenly changing the subject and its tone, and taking from his escritoire a bottle of fine cognac and two balloons.

"I don't usually drink."

The baron laughed. "Then you'd do well to get used to it; they say that the Argentineans are a people that knows how to drink."

He poured himself a drink, his hand cradling the balloon half-full of the brown liquor, warming it, swirling it, and sniffing it delicately, and then throwing it back in a single swallow followed by a long sigh of pleasure.

"Perhaps you'll change your mind?"

"If you insist," Gershon replied, not wishing to offend his munificent host, "but just a drop."

"Just a small one," the baron laughed, pouring him a generous measure.

Gershon raised his glass, almost spilling its contents, and downed it in one. He paused for a moment, not knowing how to deal with the liquor searing his throat, and was then subjected to a bout of embarrassed coughing while the baron pounded him on the back as a father would a son, lest he choke, heaven forbid.

Gershon blushed, either from the liquor or the discovery of how unused he was to this ritual, but even so he felt a pleasant warmth coursing through him.

"Tell me, if you would, my friend," Moritz asked with a warm, fatherly look, "why haven't you got any children?"

Gershon was surprised. "I was far too occupied with raising my young brothers and with thoughts of the national future, and my wife, as you can see, is a difficult woman."

"Since our Lucien passed away," the baron said softly, "I have known no peace."

Moritz Hirsch's only son had died suddenly years earlier.

The baron laid a hand on Gershon's. "Have children, Gershon. There is nothing more important than having a son." For a moment it seemed that he wasn't there, but someplace else. "Believe me, Gershon, wake up, bring a new living soul into the world. It will change your situation completely."

Gershon laid a consoling hand on the baron's, feeling for the first time that perhaps he had found in him not only a patron and benefactor but also a friend. He was enveloped in good feelings of closeness toward this man. A man in whom a combination of authority and compassion endowed him with genuine fatherly attributes, yet how potent were his vision and power of leadership.

"First I must persuade my wife to agree to the idea of emigrating to Argentina," he said, feeling that he could trust this noble man and reveal his innermost thoughts to him, "but I've no idea of how to go about it."

"With cunning, Gershon, with cunning," the baron smiled. "Your wife is afraid of the new, the uncertain, but she does have a taste for worldly pleasures. She is an inquisitive woman who in the end will be glad to discover the world. Perhaps I'll send her, as a gift from my wife and myself, a Spanish tutor to give her a taste of the local language and culture and thus heighten her partiality for the entire venture."

"Thank you," Gershon replied, suddenly feeling uncomfortable with his benefactor's overweening closeness as they sat in Hirsch's semi-darkened office, two men in a seemingly warm, soft-looking room.

"Then let's shake on it," the baron crowed, "a Spanish tutor. That will surely be interesting."

"Most definitely," Gershon said, seeking to escape before the baron recognized his great, real weakness, his weakness for the company of another man, older and more authoritative than he, who would embrace him. He felt the desire building in him to be swallowed up within this man, to be clasped in his kind arms, to rest his head upon him as if he were his son, while he, the baron, was his kind, loving father.

As he mused, the baron got up and gave him a cordial fatherly hug as if reading his innermost thoughts. Momentarily, Gershon submitted to his embrace and then detached himself from him in great embarrassment, and took his leave, leaving the office with pounding heart.

Twenty-five

In the days that had passed since their return to Danzig, Gershon continued, secretly, lest he arouse his wife's ire, with all the practical preparations for their emigration to Buenos Aires. These included an initial work plan for the establishment of a Jewish school and deciding on the subjects to be taught, the number of hours to be devoted to Jewish studies and manual labor, the local language and culture, and all manner of plans that would change the moment his feet stood on Argentinean soil.

Not much time had passed since their return home when a special messenger from Baron Hirsch knocked on their door accompanied by a small, foreign-looking woman. To her chagrin, Bella discovered that she was a guest sent to them from Argentina by Baron Hirsch without her knowing anything about it. Her name was Mademoiselle Violette, Señorita Violette in Spanish. Her first name was Eva. She was a short, broad-faced woman with big, laughing eyes and thick black hair. Her features had a slightly Latin cast, and indeed, her mother was from Italy and her father from Spain.

Bella was surprised by her unexpected appearance, but she was unable to turn away a guest sent personally by the baron, and she also found it hard to resist her captivating smile and the softness in her quiet voice. She was angry with Gershon for not preparing her for their guest's arrival. She realized deep down that her coming was a sign that Gershon's intentions of emigrating had reached the practical stage. But in deference to Baron Hirsch, and also due to a certain interest in this woman who had brought with her a whiff of a distant continent, she welcomed her as an honored guest and made her at home.

At the time, Meir was studying at the University of Hamburg, and his lovely, bright room, which faced the boulevard, was carefully furnished and vacant. Bella ordered the servants to take the guest's baggage to Meir's room.

"It's a disgrace," she told Gershon when they were alone in their bedroom, "nothing was ready for welcoming this guest. It's a disgrace!"

"I'm sorry," Gershon replied in a mollifying tone, "but the baron specifically requested that she be a surprise for you."

"You should know by now that this is not the way to please me," she said, G145 turning her back to him and lying on her side with her face to the wall, trying vainly to fall asleep.

Gershon carefully got into bed on the other side, keeping his distance from her so as not to provoke her anger again. He lay there with his eyes open, tired, but smiling inside.

The baron was right. This woman would melt her heart.

In the days that followed Bella Bergman and Mademoiselle Violette started talking. Bella wanted to make her stay in their home pleasant, to thank Baron Hirsch for entertaining them in his home, and she was curious to discover what her guest had brought with her. Mademoiselle Violette, Eva, had never before left her own country, and Bella promised to show her all the sights of the city and its environs, an international port city, with its influences of every regime, and also the influences of foreigners that had come to it from over the sea for commercial purposes, and had fallen in love with the city's special, vibrant atmosphere.

"That would be a great privilege," Eva said in broken German, "I will be like your pupil."

Bella smiled and offered her a cup of tea. The woman raised her hand. "We only drink tea after the siesta."

"Siesta?" Bella asked, pouring herself another cup from the ornate china teapot she used for serving tea, together with her mother's homemade biscuits.

"What you call *schlafstunde* is our siesta," the woman smiled. For you it comes from culture, for us it comes from the heat."

"Is it so hot in your country?" Bella asked.

"As hot as hell itself. But life stops for a few hours and comes back to life in the evening. And evening begins with drinking *mate*, which is a kind of very strong tea served in a wooden cup with a straw."

Bella listened to her guest's descriptions of her culture. It seemed unlike any other she had known, and it fascinated her.

Eva noticed this.

"And you, Señora Bergman, have you ever been out of Danzig?" she asked with feigned innocence.

"Only once, not long ago, to Paris. We were the baron's guests."

"The world is full of surprises, Señora Bergman. On the side of the world I come from everything seems the same but different. We, too, have respected ladies like yourself who know how to dress and entertain people from high society. But ours are very happy."

"What do you mean?"

"True, I've only been here two days," Eva replied merrily, "but it seems to me that our country is far happier. People laugh a lot more there. Perhaps it's because of the heat, perhaps it's the blood flowing in their veins."

In the days that followed they would sit in the lounge every morning and talk until noon. Toward evening, Bella would link her arm with Eva's and together they would go to a café, the theater, or just stroll down the streets.

Then quite easily, as if involuntarily, they started to teach one another their own language. Eva, a clever woman by her own lights, started pointing out various objects in the room and asking Bella what they were called in German. At the same time, Eva began teaching her the names of the same objects and terms in Spanish. This was not teaching per se, but rather becoming mutually acquainted and even a game.

Bella boasted about her private tutor who had been sent specially by Baron Hirsch, whereas Eva was happy to get to know the pleasures of a European city as the companion and protégée of one of the most respected ladies in the city.

One thing was unapparent, since Bella took pains to conceal it. Deep in her heart she was preoccupied with something else entirely. The date of the murderer's memorial service was approaching, and she knew that she would not agree to leave the city until she had recovered the ring.

Twenty-six

On the tenth of the Hebrew month of Tammuz, the first anniversary of the murderer's death, she knew that the time had come. The widow would surely be at his graveside with his friends, acquaintances, and relatives. It would be easy for her to blend into the crowd attending the first memorial service, which was usually larger than those at the following ones.

Bella carefully inspected her wardrobe and chose a simple dress, the only one of its kind she had, dark and plain. Then she took a kerchief from the bottom drawer, the same one she had worn when going to the Great Synagogue with her mother. On her feet she wore joyless flat black shoes. She completed her mourning attire with a small black handbag, faded with use, which she borrowed from her cook.

Her husband was surprised to see her dressed like this. She explained that she had spoken with the old gravedigger and decided to obey the commandment of visiting the graves of the poor. Gershon was astounded by this decision, but said nothing. As always, his wife's hidden motive would only be revealed to him in the fullness of time.

The old cemetery of Mattenbuden was small and crowded. The graves were packed so closely that there was barely a piece of ground to stand on. Unlike the new Altschottland cemetery, here there were no grave plots that looked like cathedrals or vaulted chapels, and no tall black granite tombstones inscribed with gold lettering. All the graves were simple, and their stones looked as though they had been gnawed by the teeth of time.

Bella walked between the rows of graves until she came upon a small group of people standing in an isolated area of the cemetery. From a distance she could see the old gravedigger's back, and knew she had come to the right place.

She moved forward slowly, trying to hide in the congregation as if she were only an acquaintance wanting to pay her respects to the deceased together with his family.

But her appearance made her stand out, with her distinctive features and simple clothing. Not only that, the deceased had not been a gregarious man and among his friends there were none who were strangers to his widow.

Leah was very tired. Her soul was weary. She would have liked a little rest instead of having to deal with the woman lurking behind the row of mourners encircling her like a temporary, brittle wall. But she knew she had to face the woman for her daughter's sake.

The rabbi continued with the service, moving from one psalm to another, intoning them in the same droning monotone he used for the dead every day of the year. The dead are all different but are given equal respect. A few psalms, then chants according to the name and the letters of the Hebrew word for 'soul', the memorial prayer, and the 'God, full of compassion' prayer. That's it. Now she had to turn and face that woman.

"Excuse me, Frau Kochmann?"

Leah pretended not to hear, as if her mourning attire covered not only her body but also her ears. Her arms folded, clutching a black kerchief, the skin of her hands cracked from hard work.

These are not the hands of a whore, but of a cook, Bella thought.

Leah noticed that she was inspecting her fingers. She raised her hands and turned them over and back, as if examining them in the light.

Bella followed the movement of her hands. And then it came to her. These fingers were bare.

"You know why I'm here."

"The gravedigger warned me," Leah replied, vainly trying to speak calmly.

Bella flashed a look of anger at the retreating gravedigger's back.

"You've no reason to hate him," Leah went on, "if it weren't for him I wouldn't have known that the ring was stolen."

"What do you mean?" Bella asked.

"The man lying here in the ground brought me the ring to save me from a sickness. He didn't say from where. He just put it on my finger and cured me."

"And you didn't know anything?" Bella asked, placing a hand on her chest, gripped by a strange feeling of compassion.

"I didn't know and I didn't want to know. I was naive. I didn't understand why I couldn't wear it in public. The only times I did I covered it with a bandage so it wouldn't be seen."

"Your man was clever," Bella said quietly, "but he was a thief. A thief and a murderer."

"Don't you say things like that about my husband! Not here, not at his graveside!"

"It's what he was."

"No!" Leah cried. "He loved me and wanted to save me from the sickness and take me away from the clients that came to me day and night. He wasn't thinking of anything else when he took the ring. Nothing else!"

"That's a great shame," Bella said, "a great shame. But now give me the ring…"

"It's gone." Leah whispered.

"What do you mean, it's gone?" Bella was stunned.

Leah gestured her to sit on one of the gravestones.

The dead beneath the stones don't know anything anyway, Bella told herself, finding a light-colored stone, less dirty than its fellows, and sat down on its edge. "What do you mean, it's gone?" she asked again.

Leah sat down on the ground.

"I sent it with my daughter," she said.

"Where to?"

"Another country. Far away. To Argentina."

Leah told her the story of how the ring had cured her, her time with her daughter, and the sickness that was attacking her again of late since her daughter's departure. She did not tell her the identity of the man with whom she had sent her daughter abroad.

"I gave my daughter the ring to protect her," she told Bella. "I am not protected. You can do with me what you wish. But I'm no longer alive. Without my daughter I'm dead. And that's why you can't do anything to me."

Bella slowly got up from the gravestone and smoothed her dress. "You have started a war between us," she said. "I shall recover that ring whatever the cost."

"Leave me alone and go back to your life, Madam," Leah replied, "there's nothing for you here."

Bella turned and left the cemetery, leaving Leah slumped on the ground by her dead husband's grave.

Twenty-seven

Like all his men and women friends, Manuel traveled from Buenos Aires to Poland to bring back young women for sale. Some of them went back to the towns in Russia, Poland and Hungary where they were born and from whence they had come to Buenos Aires, while others went to other towns and villages. Manuel did not even consider going to Czernowitz because he did not want to return to his past. He also preferred young city-bred girls with some education and knowledge of the world, rather than village girls who didn't know a thing. He purchased his first women at the auctions held twice or thrice weekly in the city. He decided to bring the new ones himself to cut out the middleman, and also to see the world.

The two young girls he brought with him from Danzig didn't know each other. One was Esther and the other Miriam, a poor girl he had picked up in a small town near Lublin. Both were intended for his business, not for auction among his friends, and so they didn't see each other during the voyage. They were smuggled into the meat lockers where they were locked up until the ship docked.

They boarded the ship unmarried virgins. They were not to know that they would disembark no longer virgins and married by virtue of forged documents. They also were not to know that the man they were married to was already married to several other women who were already resident in the same house, groaning beneath the bodies of strange men. They certainly did not imagine that the man they perceived as their savior, who had to each of them separately, as if he were a redeeming angel in their time of travail, given the feeling that he was the only one able to protect her, and in the end also penetrating her and making her his forever – he who had brought down this catastrophe upon her in the first place.

The day before they reached Argentina and disembarked, Manuel appeared with a bottle in one hand and a gold ring and marriage papers in the other, and married each of them without the other's knowledge.

The two women discovered one another only when their cells were opened and they were taken down the gangway, walking on both sides of Manuel, clutching their bundles, their heads bent and their eyes becoming accustomed to the clear, autumnal morning light of Buenos Aires.

They descended to the quayside and walked on to the plain wooden desks of the two uniformed immigration officers. Manuel handed over their passports and marriage papers; one the wife of Manuel Alfonso Zind, and the other of Manuel Juan Zind. The officers scanned the documents and exchanged glances. These bigamists were well known to them, bigamy planned to put women up for sale in the brothels. But inside each document they found a twenty-peso banknote. They nodded to him, lifted their wooden stamps from their holders, and stamped the passports.

"Good luck, Señor," one of the officers said.

"Just a moment," said the other, "what about inoculations?"

Manuel gave him a look that left no room for doubt.

"Fine, fine," the first officer hastily silenced his colleague.

Manuel nodded his thanks and exited the port with the two young women.

Outside stood carriage drivers waiting for fares, and Manuel signaled to one of them. The young driver hurried over and with his strong arms gathered up the girls' baggage and helped them load it onto the carriage.

"Where to, Señor?" the driver asked, lifting the reins and cracking them, making the horses straighten their backs ready to trot off.

"322 Calle Junin, Las Clavas," Manuel replied brusquely, already tired from the journey, longing to get home and rest.

"A nice place," the driver said, "the señor has good taste."

Manuel smiled to himself with satisfaction. Within a short time his house had gained a fine reputation in the city, so much so that it had come to the ears of carriage drivers.

The two girls sat in the simple wooden carriage, with tiny bells tinkling from its sides in time with the horse's trot, and remained silent. They looked at the tumult on the quays of Puerto Madero, and after a few moments they left the road running alongside the port, and then the scenery of the city was spread before them.

They drove down unfamiliar streets with decorated, marble-clad buildings, until they came to a big square. From the square extended wide boulevards crisscrossed with smaller streets. They trotted up one of the boulevards, and on almost every corner stood small shops and simple wooden stalls where chunks of beef, large sausages, omelets, and sugared peanuts sizzled in hot skillets. The smells filled Esther's nostrils, and the saliva flowed in her mouth. She had not eaten since the previous night and was very hungry.

They trotted on, passing an avenue of stalls in a fruit and vegetable market, until the driver brought the carriage to a sudden stop.

"I'm sorry," he said, pointing at a large carriage crossing the road right in front of them, drawn by three pairs of horses and with dozens of people crammed into it.

"*Concha de su madre*," Manuel exclaimed, and spat through the window at the *colectivo* that had crossed in front of them without its driver even noticing the commotion he had caused. "May his balls fry."

"They don't give a damn about anything," their driver said, and whipped up his horses.

After a long drive they reached a quarter that seemed familiar because of the Jews they saw there. They were unmistakable. Jews wearing *kapotas* and *streimels*, and the women with their heads covered, just as it was in their own country.

The carriage drove up Calle Junin until they came to a four-story building at the end of the street.

The driver quickly dismounted, opened the door for Manuel and the girls, unloaded their baggage and placed it by the locked iron gate. Manuel took a wad of banknotes from his pocket, handed it to the grateful driver, and sent him on his way. He turned to the gate and tugged the bell-pull hanging from the right-hand side, beneath the illuminated sign, Las Clavas. When nobody answered, he pulled the bell again until its sound filled the courtyard.

"*Dios mio*," an older woman's voice called, "who's so hot that he can't wait?"

Irritably she opened the gate, her expression changing when she saw who was standing there.

"Manuel!" she cried joyfully.

"*Hola*," he said, kissing her on both cheeks.

"*Hola*," Roja-Rosa replied, returning his kiss. "*Estas son las nuevas*, are these the new ones?"

"*Si, claro*, yes, of course," Manuel replied, "help me get them inside."

They walked through the tiled courtyard to the patio from which emerged more women who encircled Manuel with shouts of joy. He greeted them and immediately silenced them with a gesture so they would not frighten the new arrivals. With blind obedience they detached themselves from him and went back into the big room to await their clients.

There were buildings similar to theirs in the street, those belonging to Walter, Angel, Ziskind, David, and Israel. In each of them were women who had been brought there in the same way from all over the world. In each house there were men who knew when to caress, and when to hit, who traded their women like animals and treated each one as if she were his one and only. It all depended on the time, the circumstances, and the behavior of each of them. The main thing was that they generate income, not shame their owners, and not become pregnant.

And for this to happen they had to start work the day after their arrival at the house, without further delay. Without time to adjust, rebel, or think.

Twenty-eight

On the death of his aged father, Frank Abramson came back to Danzig, which he had left in his youth. Due to the length of the funeral and the *shiva* mourning period he was in the city for a whole week, and Gershon made a point of calling at the Abramson home every day to console his friend. During these visits he would lecture fervently on emancipation and Zionism, the Liberals' struggle against the Zionists, his most recent thoughts on the evacuation of Russian Jewry and other such matters of paramount importance, while Frank gazed at him half painfully, half inquiringly.

Gershon feigned not to notice the guarded, hidden question in Frank's gray-blue eyes, which were as beautiful as they had been in his youth. But deep in his heart he could feel how his friend, who had grown into a sturdy, noble man, was pulling him as if with ropes.

Bella Bergman accompanied her husband to the funeral and also on one of his visits to the friend of his youth. When she was introduced to Frank he offered her a chilly hand and greeted her with a grieving but restrained nod. She wondered why there was no wedding ring on his finger, and why the editor of the liberal Jewish newspaper's son had remained a bachelor.

On the conclusion of the seven-day mourning period, the night before his return to Hamburg, Frank surprised Gershon by coming to his home to say goodbye. He said that he felt a need to do so because Gershon had taken the trouble to visit him at his home throughout the week. Furthermore, he had not seen his friend's house, the Bergman house, since their childhood, and who knows when he might see it again.

Gershon showed Frank into his study and with bated breath closed the heavy door behind them. Frank noticed the excitement gripping his friend, but was in no hurry to pick its fruit. First he took in the study which he remembered from their youth when they were looking for a hidden corner where they would not be seen.

"Did she do all this?" he asked, gesturing at the shelves housing the dusty books, as ramrod-straight as soldiers on parade, the tasteful antique cabinets, Mr. Bergman's escritoire, and the couch, a nice-looking couch that seemed particularly soft.

Gershon hemmed and nodded.

"A talented woman," Frank said, bitterness and Schadenfreude mingled in his voice.

"Thank you, Frank," Gershon replied, wondering which subject he could broach to bring him back to everyday matters. But Frank placed a finger on his lips. "Shhh…," he whispered, and moved over to Gershon on the other side of the desk, who started as if bitten by a snake. Gershon tried to say something, but Frank forestalled him, gathering him to his chest in a strong embrace.

"That's good, that's good," he whispered in Gershon's ear, who was quivering at his touch. "I've been waiting for this all week."

Gershon raised his face to that of his beloved friend and gazed into his eyes, at his brilliantined hair, his nose, his ears. Frank clasped his head and kissed him ardently, not giving him time to breathe or say anything.

They stood clasped in each other's arms, two suit-clad men in their thirties, the smell of male perfume emanating from them, kissing with abandon, Gershon sucking at his friend's smooth neck, and Frank groaning and moaning, stroking his hair, embracing him and slowly pulling him backward to the couch in the corner, falling onto it and dragging Gershon on top of him.

"No, no," Gershon said, trying to lift himself from Frank's body, "we can't."

But Frank had already loosened his waistband, roughly pulling down Gershon's trousers and underwear, freeing his painfully erect member and taking it into his mouth as Gershon groaned with pleasure, moving his body back and forth with his penis in the hot mouth of the friend of his youth, sinking completely into the pleasure of the act.

But Frank had other plans. He got up from the couch, stood behind his friend, pulled down his own trousers, lubricated his own member with saliva, quickly parted Gershon's buttocks and jammed himself inside him.

Gershon groaned, confused with passion and pain, no longer knowing what he wanted or what he was saying, while Frank put a hand over his mouth lest he say anything at all. The love of his youth had inserted his wonderful big penis into him and Gershon moaned and groaned until he emitted a great cry, and then, just as they both spent themselves, the door opened and Bella came in.

She had heard the cries coming from the study where the two were closeted and feared that something was amiss, which is why she had unhesitatingly opened the door without knocking. She stood frozen by the scene. For one rare moment the power of speech had deserted her.

"Pederast!" she said in a snake-like hiss, "Pervert!"

Gershon tried to lift himself up from the couch, extending a hand toward her in a gesture of desperation.

"Don't touch me," she said, backing away, "now it's all clear. Your impotence on our wedding night, your sleeping alone, those nightly walks, and now this!"

"No, Bella," Gershon tried to say, but she silenced him.

"Don't you dare say a word to me, Gershon. I'm leaving this house tonight and going back to my parents' home."

His words were left unuttered. He looked helplessly at his friend, Frank Abramson, who moved to stand facing his wife, dressed and unembarrassed as if nothing had happened.

"Don't threaten him," he told her in a strange, icy voice, "go back to your parents, but when you get there tell them about their righteous dead son, Shlomo-Heinrich, who used to fuck children in the stables."

Bella swayed as if she had been poleaxed. Gershon quickly dragged an armchair behind her so she could drop into it, not to the floor.

So shocked was she that her lips moved soundlessly. Only after a long moment did she find the strength to shout.

"Snake! Get out!" she screamed at her husband's childhood friend, "How dare you desecrate my brother's memory and ruin my marriage! Get out!"

"I'm going," Frank replied with tense restraint, "but you take care of your husband, Frau Bergman. If he has kept the truth about your brother from you for all these years, then he really must love you."

"You'd better leave, Frank," Gershon whispered.

"I'm leaving, my friend," Frank replied, "but remember one thing. Don't let anyone, even your wife, have complete control over you. It's a recipe for pleasing others, but not always yourself."

He left the study, knowing that he would never see his friend's face again.

Gershon closed the door behind him and went back into the study, falling onto the couch he had occupied earlier with his friend. He sat facing his stunned wife, holding his head in both hands, not daring to say a word.

"Is what he said true?" she finally asked.

"Why desecrate the memory of the dead," he replied, trying to fend off her question.

"That dead man was my brother and I have a right to know. Is what he said true?"

"When he was ten. He did it to him when he was ten," Gershon whispered, "and afterwards Frank came and did it to me."

Her heart breaking with the pain, Bella bowed her head and started sobbing. She remembered full well how her dead brother occasionally brought a youth or boy to stroke the horses in the stables.

Gershon reached out and tried to stroke her head. She did not say a word. Only he could feel the searing touch of her hair, and he drew back his hand.

"Bella...," he whispered, "I kept it from you all these years because I respected you. Because I loved you."

She burst into tears. She felt torn apart and twice betrayed by the two most significant men in her life, who had seemingly conspired – one from the grave – to bring her world down in ruins.

Gershon did not know how he could help her overcome her pain, how he could explain his love for her, his admiration of her assertive behavior, and the way she managed their life together. But he did know that now he should disappear, and so he tiptoed out of the room, leaving her sitting there, shamed, in his damned study, in the hell she had designed with her own hands and was now a prisoner in it.

The days that had passed since her visit to the Mattenbuden cemetery, and since she had regrettably been compelled to face up to her husband's true nature, were very difficult for her. She felt as if the hand of fate had gripped her and torn her from everything she had known and considered as her home, her life, rocking her and shaking her in the air without her having a secure handhold. From life in a world of certainty, her life had suddenly been swept up into chaos with which she did not know how to cope, and this caused her deep distress.

Her change of mood was clearly evident to all who visited her home. Eva, too, noticed it. They would routinely meet each day for a Spanish lesson and then go for a walk through the town together. But now several days had passed and Bella continued to postpone their daily meeting, her face downcast, withdrawn into itself, and she would send one servant and then another with various excuses, asking her to go for a walk by herself today because she was still not feeling well. And in much the same way her husband walked around her surreptitiously, endeavoring to absent himself from the house for hours, sequestering himself in his study for entire evenings, from which he emerged just before morning, his hair unkempt and his head heavy, as if his sleep had been assailed by terror. Eva also noticed that the couple habitually slept in separate beds, but she thought that perhaps this was just another of the local gentry's customs.

After a few days of being immersed in herself and shutting herself away, Bella felt her strength returning. Not only that, a new thought about what she was to do in the very near future began to germinate, but she was still unable to utter it and she needed further information before she made a final decision. She sent a servant to Eva's room to tell her that she wished to go to a café with her to talk.

Along the way Bella did not utter a word. When Eva tried to start a conversation, she stopped her with a gesture.

She only started to talk once they were seated at a secluded table on the café's large terrace, and after the bow-tied waiter had taken their order.

"You're probably wondering why I asked you here," Bella began, gesturing at the spacious, crowded café.

"I'm always happy to come into town with you," Eva smiled.

"I'd like to speak to you about something personal."

Eva's eyes widened.

"Eva, my husband doesn't yet know for sure, but I've decided to go to Argentina with him."

"What's happened?" Eva asked in surprise, since so far she had only heard why Bella would not even consider leaving Danzig. "What's made you change you mind all of a sudden?"

"Fate sometimes taps on your window once, then twice, until you hear the tapping and realize that this is the last time you can go along with it," Bella replied, folding her linen napkin neatly on the table. "My husband needs a change of surroundings. All his life he's been shut up in the world of thinking. Do you think he'll feel more alive in Argentina?"

"Of course he will," Eva laughed. "In Argentina everyone lives three times as much as people do here. Everything's bigger. Joy and pain, sadness and beauty. Do you follow?"

"I think so," Bella replied.

Eva's eyes were flashing. "The weather in Argentina is more extreme, the temperature rises and falls all at once. That's why people live more at night than they do in the daytime. More in winter than in summer, and most of all, they laugh and enjoy themselves. Over there, all of life is a drama. Over there we don't live small, only *grande, muy, muy grande.*"

Eva suddenly seemed different, more radiant and joyful.

"And are all the women in Argentina like you? Full of life?"

Eva laughed. "They love love, and love loves them, if you get my meaning."

"And do the men there know how to treat a woman?"

Eva leant over and whispered something in her ear. Bella blushed to the roots of her hair.

"Like stallions," Eva said in a loud voice, and laughed. "The weather makes everyone love like animals."

"Just as it should be," Bella blurted, and laughed.

Eva laid a hand on Bella's. "I've never seen you like this."

"There's a reason for everything," Bella said, "and don't say a word to Gershon, I want to tell him myself, but when I feel the time is right."

"I won't say anything."

They sat there for a long time, sipping wine and talking about men and women, women's customs in Argentina, their favorite dishes, the quality of the cloth from which their clothes were made, cloth from the West compared with that of the Indians, the mixture of cultures, the Sunday markets at San Telmo and La Boca, the atmosphere of the city and its uniqueness. Eva's words sounded so full of vivacity that Bella began to feel new forces filling her broken heart. Perhaps Buenos Aires really did hold a miracle for both Gershon and for her.

Twenty-nine

In the days that passed since the incident with Frank, in his distress Gershon did his utmost to stay out of his wife's line of sight, avoiding her penetrating look that elicited guilt feelings in him. Meanwhile, Baron Hirsch's messengers continued to knock on his door with letters in which the baron reported on the purchase of the first land, the establishment of Mauricio and Moises Ville, and the arrival of the first Jews at the colonies. 150 had come on one ship, and 234 on another, and after them another large shipment of 817 souls on a third vessel. Time was already of the essence to begin setting up the independent education system for their children. Agitation was rife among the settlers as might be expected of people uprooted from their home and taking their first steps in a country that was different, vast, and strange for them and their culture, and so it was of the utmost importance that he and his wife arrive in Buenos Aires no later than September this year. Gershon read the missives and was filled with a sense of expectation and personal commitment to the baron, and he could also feel how his soul was longing to get away from everything he had known and endured here in Danzig, how he longed to go out into the expanse of the world and get away from the world of words and writings, so much so that he actually felt physical pain, but he did not know how he could speak about it to his wife, especially after what she had discovered about him.

He shut himself up for hours in his study, torturing himself with thoughts of how to mollify her and how she might be persuaded to go with him without causing her to create a hullabaloo or, heaven forbid, tell any of her relatives about her discovery. That would generate a wave of rumors that would be the end of him, he told himself, and was filled with dread. But as usual at times like this he did not go and speak to his wife, but picked up a book of poetry, sinking his pain and longing into the words of another. Then he sat down at his desk, took up a pen and began drafting random jottings he called "On Ideals and the Heart's Desire", in which he described the great flood that swelled his heart every so often, a flood that had no explanation or origin in the soul, a longing for something unknown, as yet nameless, without shape or form, that is not in realness but in the inner reality of the soul, and which could not be translated from pure heart's desire into something tangible, for then it would be negated and indecent, impairing the nature of the yearning to which it had given birth and from which it was born. And so on and so forth, fragments of transparent, circumspect musings, wandering along the fragile borderline between what could be uttered and what could not, between an idea and its impermanent, fleeting realization in condemnation of the flesh and the material, but this time he picked up his writings and took them downstairs to the parlor, where he seemingly forgot them on the small tea table in a sufficiently prominent place to which Bella's eye would be drawn, and then, troubled with thoughts as was his wont, he went out to wander outside, swearing that his feet would not lead him to a place of lust and wantonness, but just to walk randomly while his wife sat and read what he had written.

On his return that evening, his wife was indeed waiting for him in the parlor, and the dim light that fell on her face endowed her with the appearance of a dozing hawk. He came in and threw himself into an armchair with a deep sigh.

"I read what you left here," Bella blurted after a silence. "It's the first time I've read anything of yours that I was able to understand, connect with, unlike all your essays on ideas. Just a man's musings. It's beautiful."

He looked at her bleary-eyed from lack of sleep. "I'm tired, Bella. I'm tired, and my soul is tired too."

"That's clear from what you've written, and from your seclusion."

"I'm tired," he repeated, as if he had no other words in his vocabulary. "I'm only thirty-three and I'm as tired as my father was in his dotage. I've no strength. Not to run away from here, not to quarrel with you, not to live with you in an atmosphere of suspicion, alienation, and hostility."

"No one has ever hurt me as you have," Bella said quietly.

"I know," he said, feeling his stomach churn, "but I didn't want to hurt you. You've been precious to me since the first time I saw you. All I ever wanted was to fulfill your wishes. To be your husband. To be a whole man in my own eyes…"

"And in the eyes of your mother and father," she cut him off, "in the eyes of the whole world, Gershon, without thinking about the side of you that embitters your life as it now embitters mine, without making me part of it. Living a double life, a daytime life and a nighttime life, a life outside and a life inside, stealthily, secretly…"

"I beg of you, Bella," he whispered, "I didn't want this for myself. I don't know where it comes from, but I still want to be your husband."

"And what are you going to do about yourself?" she asked.

"I don't know. I only know that I want you, I want children, a family, and I want a little peace. Yes, peace. Peace within me and peace around me. That way I shall be able to endure my life," he said, barely managing to finish, as involuntary weeping, thin and silent, bubbled up from deep inside him, mingling with his words. Weeping for his willingness to sit facing his wife and beg for his life while denying and relinquishing his deepest passions. But he had no other way. For what could he do? Extricate himself from his own life and remain with his desire, but denuded of everything he had known and been surrounded with for generations?

"This has been a difficult time for me too," Bella said slowly, her inner turmoil clearly evident beneath her words. "I could have gotten up and left. But I stayed with you, because you're a kind of unfulfilled, almost sham promise for me, of happiness and wellbeing."

He raised his head and looked into her eyes as she went on speaking, trying to maintain the clear preciseness of her words without raising her voice.

"Our parents brought us together at a young age," she went on, "into this turmoil of marriage, without us knowing its deeper meaning. But I'm willing to persevere, Gershon, on condition that we have a family and don't remain as two strangers, living in separate beds and separate rooms. Let's try and build something together, otherwise there's no point in it. For that, Gershon, I'm prepared to go with you to Argentina."

Her words flooded him with happiness and a deep wave of gratitude. He embraced and kissed her, tears of joy flowing from his eyes. Now she allowed herself to cling to him, and for a long, rare moment even laid her head on his chest, hearing the pounding of his heart racing within.

"I'll never go out at night again, I promise," he said without being asked, "I'll strangle that desire inside me."

"I don't want to hear that. Don't make any such promises. It's impossible. Just promise me one thing: that I shall never, but never, have to witness that again, Gershon. You want to feel a man's touch? Go ahead. But not in my home, not in my city, not anywhere near me. Go wherever you want, do whatever you want, but always come back home to be my husband and a father to your children. Do you understand?"

Gershon nodded. He could not have hoped for more. He did not understand from where she drew the spiritual fortitude to say these things. But now he knew that he indeed had an exceptional wife.

"Let's celebrate," he said, surprising them both. "Tonight we have a real cause for celebration."

"At this hour?"

"Right now!" Gershon replied, laughing like a little boy as he grasped her arms.

Shortly afterward, elegantly dressed, they left their home and went to a restaurant on Danzig's main street, which was well known for the large number of diners that flocked to its door until late at night. The great joy that Gershon felt at hearing her decision, and her knowing that her agreement fell into line with her search for the ring, also gave Bella a sort of relief. She allowed herself to drink two glasses of champagne, and even accepted his invitation to dance a waltz with him. On their return home they made love, which had not happened for a long time.

Thirty

Throughout the evening there was a steady flow of men to the room.

Esther lay on her bed, detached from her body, allowing the men to come into the room one at a time, say something in a language she didn't understand, undress, and mount her as she lay silent, frozen, not even uttering a single groan. Thus she shielded herself, distancing her consciousness from her young body that was being defiled and gradually corrupted. But after a few long minutes during which no one came in, she allowed herself to slowly reenter her body, suddenly feeling how swollen and painful it was.

The place between her thighs burned as if a white-hot rod had been inserted into it. She barely managed to remove her knickers, lift the hem of her dress, and inspect that place that was now distended, red, and exuding a mixture of blood and bodily fluids. She limped over the bucket of water standing there in the room, her leg muscles completely cramped, dampened a towel and cleaned the painful place. Reflected in the small mirror was an unkempt, fatigued young girl, her eyes filled with horror at everything she had gone through that night. And then, as if a latent force were grasping and pulling her from inside, she picked up her clothes, which were still in the bundle her mother had prepared before her departure, and on unsteady legs went to the door and flung it open.

Facing her she saw the Buenos Aires sky, a clear, star-studded sky. A pleasant breeze touched her face, but she wasted no time on the enchantment of this sight. She looked left and right, and seeing no one in the long corridor, started running along it and down the stairs, passing barefoot through the patio and past the half-open doors of the big entrance hall, the sound of drinking and merrymaking coming through them, women's voices mingling with the low voices of men, and unfamiliar music. As fast as she could she ran to the big iron gate through which she had passed only the previous day, grasped the big iron handle in her small hand, and tried to open it.

But the gate did not move under her shaking, not even with the blows of her hands on its hard heart.

"Help!" she shouted in German and Yiddish, the only two languages she spoke, "Help!" With her last remaining strength she banged on the iron gate, which replied with a dull, gong-like sound.

"Who are shouting for, child?" she suddenly heard a man's voice behind her.

She turned to see Manuel facing her.

"Let me go!" she screamed, attacking him with her fists, "Let me go!"

Manuel pushed her off with such force that she fell to the ground. Roja-Rosa arrived on the scene to see where all the shouting was coming from.

"What's going on?" she asked.

"The usual," Manuel replied, "the little bitch tried to escape."

Roja-Rosa stood over Esther. "Get up."

Esther didn't budge.

"Come, I'll help you," Roja-Rosa said, holding out her hand, "we'll go upstairs together, you'll wash and get dressed like a human being."

Esther got up slowly, firing a malevolent look at Manuel.

"This one's a wild dog," he said to Roja-Rosa in Spanish, "make sure you treat her accordingly so I won't have to," and went back to the clients sitting with the girls in the salon, quaffing wine, unaware of what had taken place outside.

"Come," Roja-Rosa put her arm round Esther's waist, "let's go upstairs."

Esther followed the older woman up the stairs, went into the room and fell onto the bed, exhausted.

Her room was the last of those that lined the corridor. It had one window barred with a decorated grille. On it flapped a flowered curtain, and over that a heavy black drape to either darken the room completely of leave it half lit, as necessary. The door locked from the outside. There was a wide iron bedstead flanked by bedside tables, and on them candles in candlesticks. Beside a low wooden cupboard stood a pail of water for washing, a stack of towels and a tray with a carafe of drinking water and glasses.

Roja-Rosa locked her in and returned some time later carrying a tray with roast chicken, rice, and boiled vegetables, a few slices of bread, a cold drink, and some strange-looking fresh fruit.

"My name's Rosa," the elderly woman said, "but everybody here calls me Roja-Rosa because of my red hair."

Esther was silent.

"Eat," she said in Spanish-accented Yiddish, "and then sleep. I'll be waking you early in the morning."

But Esther was unable to touch a thing. "I want to die," she replied in Yiddish, "that's what I want."

"Then get a rope and hang yourself. Let the maggots have you."

"I want to go back to my mother," Esther replied.

"Your poor mother's got no idea where she sent you," the old woman said. "If she knew, she'd die."

"I'll write her a letter."

"You'll break her heart," the older woman replied.

"But he took me away from my mother to work for wealthy Jews!"

"He's the only wealthy one here," Roja-Rosa chuckled, "we're only his servants."

"But he saved me on the ship!"

"He saved all of them on the ship."

"I don't understand."

"There's nothing to understand," Roja-Rosa replied, "it's a sort of business. And now you're here."

"That can't be!"

"I know it's hard for you," Roja-Rosa said, "it was hard for all of us at the beginning. But you'll get used to it."

"Never!" Esther screamed.

"You'd do better to listen to me," Roja-Rosa said brusquely, "I'm the only one who'll explain it to you nicely. He's got other ways of teaching you how to behave."

Esther recalled the three sailors who had come into her cell on the ship, and fell silent.

"They leave the money downstairs. With Manuel or me. Love they get from you."

"Stop it!" the girl shouted, "I don't want to hear it!" she screamed, covering her ears with her hands, rocking her head back and forth, voicing animal grunts from her throat as if with them she could block out the forthright words the woman facing her was saying.

Roja-Rosa slapped her.

"I'm sorry, but sometimes there's no other way."

"What kind of a place is this?" the girl asked, perhaps to herself, perhaps to Roja-Rosa. "What kind of a world is this?"

"It's a world with its own rules," Roja-Rosa said. "You don't make trouble with a man and you don't leave here without permission. If you want to live, you keep those rules. Believe me, I know what I'm talking about," she said, turning to her and moving her hair from her face. On her neck was a thick, ugly scar. "I tried to run away and got this. Since then I've learned what's permitted and what's forbidden. You're a pretty girl. It'd be a pity if your face was ruined."

Esther did not reply, she just looked at the scar on the woman's face, a long, deep, thick cicatrix on the skin of her neck.

"Now eat, the food's getting cold," Roja-Rosa said, moving the tray closer.

Esther looked at the tray and kicked it away in revulsion. The food scattered over the floor.

"If that's the way you want it, you can lie in your own filth," Roja-Rosa said, her heart lurching in her chest. "Just remember that you asked for it."

She went out, locking the door from the outside. With a heavy heart she went downstairs to the courtyard. Manuel was right. This girl had to be taught in the way she had chosen herself, she told herself.

As she entered the room, Manuel gave her an inquiring look.

"*Sin agua, sin pan*, no water, no bread," she told him.

Manuel nodded.

Roja-Rosa made sure that the other girls knew about it, so that none of them would interfere until Esther's rebelliousness had been quelled.

Nothing in her youth had prepared her for what she had been through so far. She was very tired. Tired from the journey, the voyage, the rape, from the total shock she had experienced. She lay down on the bed, staring at the whitewashed wall, the wall she had gazed at every time someone had come to her throughout that day. Even when one of those dirty, nameless men had remarked on this, she had been unable to tear her gaze away from the white texture.

But the wall did not crack under her gaze. Its skin was thick and through its pallor she could see its stone pores, breathing like living tissue.

The food she had kicked away was still scattered on the floor. She got down from the bed heavily, crouched on the floor, picked up a piece of chicken and bit into it ravenously. She devoured all the food from the floor, feeling her strength returning.

Feeling stronger, she unpacked her belongings and arranged them in the small wooden cupboard. A small box suddenly fell out from among them. She picked it up and opened it. In it lay an object whose gold was dark and whose light shone brightly.

A ring.

Esther took the ring and examined it closely. Then she went back to rummage through the bundle it had fallen from, where she found a few zlotys wrapped in an old newspaper – and a letter. The letter told her the history of the ring, how it had come into her mother's possession, how it had helped her, and what its cost had been.

She looked at the letter and the ring for a long time, not knowing what to think. Her naive mother. Telling her stories about a ring without even imagining the disaster she had visited upon her. How she hadn't suspected a thing, how she had trusted that man and entrusted her to him. Esther was too tired to cry or to try and run away again, but inside she felt rage against her mother, her dead, unknown father, the whole world, mixed with gratitude to her mother for sending her away with money and a ring, giving her at least one item of value to remind her of her and protect her with her very memory. Something that was hers alone, which she would not let anyone take away, for it reminded her of her youth and her mother, the house to which her life had almost been bound before she was taken from it to face her dreadful fate.

Thirty-one

All the next day she was locked in her room. Nobody came, not even Roja-Rosa or the other girls. She awoke, washed her face and opened the curtain over the window. A fresh morning could be seen outside. Facing her window were houses, most of them three-storied, with lots of windows which, like hers, were barred. Down below, as far as she could see from where she stood, was a street, a city street that was quite busy at this hour of the morning. People in gray clothes walked from place to place. A woman carrying her baskets, a man wearing a gray jacket, a laborer in work clothes. She tried banging on the window and shouting, but no one down below heard her. Then she had second thoughts, went to the door, and started banging on it wildly. She hit it with all her might, kicked it and shouted, and then put her ear to it. She heard no footsteps hurrying down the corridor toward her.

She looked around, wondering how to attract somebody's attention. The room was so carefully organized that she was unable to find anything she might use to smash the window.

All that day she lay in torment on her bed, her hunger intensifying, and read and reread her mother's letter. She had not washed herself since all the men had come to her, and her flesh, especially that place, was red and swollen. But once more she was unable to wash herself in the dirty water standing in the pail.

It was only in the early evening that she finally heard footfalls outside the door and the rattle of a heavy bunch of keys.

Roja-Rosa came in carrying a tray of food. She didn't say a word, but just lit the candles in the room, driving away the evening gloom, and placed the tray in front of her. Like a starving animal, Esther devoured every morsel.

When she had finished eating Roja-Rosa asked if she would like to wash herself. Esther nodded, feeling renewed energy flowing through her, replacing the weakness of hunger. Roja-Rosa smiled, went to the cupboard, and took out a towel from the bottom.

"Come downstairs with me and we'll get a pail of hot water. We've just boiled some for everybody. But Esther – no tricks," she warned, and opened the door.

Esther followed her without any intention of resisting. She just longed to feel the touch of hot water on her body.

They went down to the courtyard where a wood fire was blazing merrily beneath a large cauldron of water. Roja-Rosa took the pail and filled it, the hot water sending off clouds of steam. Then she passed it to Esther who took it obediently and followed her back to her room.

She put the pail down in the corner. Roja-Rosa tested the water with a fingertip and like a caring mother told Esther to wait until it had cooled down. Then she signaled the girl to strip, but she was incapable of doing so. She was unable to expose her defiled body even to this woman, and Roja-Rosa had to peel off her clothing as if she were her little daughter. She gently removed all her clothes, letting her cover her swollen pudenda with her hands, stroked her head gently, took a glass and began pouring water over her back. Then she wetted the soap and brought it to Esther's body. Esther shrank at her touch as if refusing the touch of a stranger, even the hand of this woman.

Roja-Rosa began soaping the girl's back, and the girl still covered her private parts. "It's all right, *niña*. I'm like a mother to you."

After washing her, she wrapped Esther's body in a towel, stood her up, damp and feeling better, and told her to get dressed properly. She took out a pair of clean knickers and a brassiere for her, and a nice-looking floral dress from the cupboard.

"Here, put that on," she said.

Esther put on the dress and stood facing Roja-Rosa, who inspected her closely.

"Very nice," she said. "You're very pretty. Now dry your hair and we'll go down and meet the others."

Esther did what she was told without a word. She enjoyed Roja-Rosa's personal care, but at the same time found it confusing. It was this woman who had sent men up to her throughout that day without any consideration at all, without looking in to see what had become of her. And now this same woman appeared to be a caring, supportive mother. Esther did not understand it, but recalled the scar that Roja-Rosa had showed her the night before. She had evidently been through all this herself, she mused.

As if reading her mind, Roja-Rosa began answering her unasked question. "We all went through this, and some of us went through it in worse houses with men not as nice as Manuel. I know exactly what you're feeling."

"How can you do this?" Esther asked.

"We've no choice," she replied. "We're held here like slaves. Like their dogs. They've got our documents, and they're in with the police so it's impossible to run away. That's why I'm telling you to be like me, like all of us. Let them do what they want so that every morning you'll be able to live and be happy with us like a big family."

"But how can I?" Esther whispered. "Until yesterday I hadn't been touched by a man…" Then she fell silent, remembering the rape on the boat.

"We were all interfered with on the boat first. For them, it's like a school. For us, it's like the grave. But enough, let's not talk about sad things. Now it's time to eat and be happy a little. Come, let's go downstairs."

She held out her hand. Esther put her little hand into her warm one, and let her lead her to the salon on the ground floor, where the voices of the men and the sounds of drinking had receded, and the music was fading.

They entered a big hall comprised of three adjoined rooms. There were couches there, and numerous seating corners with tables next to them. It was illuminated with red light cast from standard lamps in every corner and large chandeliers with glass drops hanging from the ceiling. All over the room there were vases with colorful flowers, and on the couches sat eight or nine women, most of them only slightly older than Esther, exhausted after a long day's work.

On seeing Roja-Rosa and Esther come in they jumped up to greet them.

"*Hola*," called a young woman whose sharp, white face was circled by short blonde hair. She was wearing a close-fitting evening gown, and a pair of earrings made of two ivory rings.

"Somebody bring the girl something to eat, please," she called to the girls. "Don't forget that this is her first day here."

"Sure," called Clara from the other side of the room. She was a woman with a fuller figure, not tall, with a big, smiling face. Her hair was black and her thick, black eyebrows arched over a large nose that fitted her thick lips and wide mouth. "Come, Estella, let's go to the kitchen and find her something!" she called to a slim girl, who was busy reading a newspaper. She was wearing a pleated dress tied at the back with a matching ribbon, and her face was sad and weary.

Clara and Estella went off to the kitchen, and while they were preparing some food for Esther, Roja-Rosa sat her down next to another woman wearing a Bordeaux velvet dress. Her wavy black hair fell to her shoulders. Her eyes were made up in blue and black, which deepened even further the already deep expression in them.

"This is Sophia, who except for me has been here the longest," Roja-Rosa said.

"What's your name?" Sophia asked in a gravelly smoker's voice.

"Esther," she replied quietly, embarrassed by all the women around her.

"That's like a mark of Cain," Sophia said, "we must find you another name for work."

"It's my name," Esther replied, looking at them, uncomprehendingly.

"It's not a good name for the clients. Not for the *porteños*, and certainly not for Jews."

"*Porteños*?" Esther asked.

"The natives," Sophia replied. "Most of them are *goyim*, but there are a lot of Jews here too and they come to our house. They don't need to know you've got a Jewish name. It'll make them feel like they're coming to their mother."

"My name is Esther."

"I know! I know!" Another jolly-looking woman wearing a light-colored dress that set off her round face, her smile, and her tinkling laugh, jumped up from the couch facing them.

"This is Felicia," Roja-Rosa said, "she's always laughing."

"Call her Olivia!"

"Olivia?" Sophia said, frowning. "Why Olivia?"

"Just look at the color of her skin. It's olive-colored," Felicia laughed. "She's got a special skin color. And so pretty!"

Without thinking Esther touched her face. Until now she had never even given a thought to the color of her skin. But two things were clear: her skin color was only olive in this light, and she would not give up the name given to her by her mother.

"Maybe Nina's better," Sophia said, inspecting the girl's face. "Nina sounds sexier, and it's shorter."

"My name is Esther."

"A stubborn girl," Sophia smiled at Roja-Rosa, who nodded. "She's even tried to run away already," she said, yawning.

Clara and Estella came in carrying plates of food unfamiliar to Esther. They put them down and tried to explain what each dish was, but Esther paid no heed. She was still hungry and simply attacked the food with her fingers, and began eating with gusto, grimacing each time she tasted something strange and unfamiliar, ravenously devouring everything that tasted good. Sophia observed her with some queasiness.

"What's this, eating with her fingers?" she said severely. "She must be taught table manners!"

"All right, all right," Roja-Rosa laughed," let her eat in peace. Not all in one evening."

Esther was still bent over her plates, biting into a piece of chicken and then a potato, filling her belly with tasty, nutritious food, until she was completely sated. Only then she straightened up. Roja-Rosa smiled and passed her a linen napkin, gesturing that she wipe her mouth and hands, and Esther did so.

"Would you like a cigarette?" Sophia asked, fitting one into her holder.

Esther shook her head.

The girls put a tango record on the gramophone, and bright, pleasing music filled the room. They got up and began dancing in couples to the sound of the captivating, soothing music.

Sophia told her that the vocalist was telling the story of an Argentinean man's love for his dancer beloved.

"In a lot of songs there's a man and woman who are lovers," Sophia explained, "and they always suffer, poor things. They love and suffer."

The girls dancing in the big, empty room, empty of male presence, evoked in Esther a scene from her distant childhood, a scene of a little girl with her rag doll, abandoned in a corner of the orphanage's big yard. They're like orphans, she thought, exactly the same, just a bit older.

An unbidden tear fell onto her cheek.

Sophia noticed. "What's wrong?" she asked.

"I remembered something," Esther replied quietly. She was about to say more when Roja-Rosa suddenly started screaming.

"Good God!" she shouted, clasping her head in her hands. "How could I have forgotten? Where's the other new one?"

"There's another one?" Sophia asked wonderingly, stopping her drumming on the table beside her to the rhythm of the music with her long-nailed fingers.

"Yes, yes, Miriam," Roja-Rosa shouted, "I'm going upstairs to see what's happening with her. "This one," pointing at Esther, "kept me so busy with her trying to run away that I completely forgot the second one"

She quickly ascended to the upper floor, hurrying to the locked room that housed Miriam, the other girl Manuel had brought on the boat.

She tried to open the door, but it did not give. Roja-Rosa ran to the banister and called down, "Sophia! Clara! Felicia! Come up and help me. I can't open her door."

The women hastened upstairs, each of them trying to push the door open, but in vain.

"She's dragged something heavy against it," Sophia said, "we'll have to push something heavy against it from this side, all together, to move it."

Roja-Rosa looked at her in fright and gestured to the girls to follow her. They went downstairs and together carried up a wooden bench and placed it against the door at Sophia's instructions.

"Stand on both sides, and shove it forward," she said.

The girls formed ranks on both sides of the bench, grasped it as if it were a battering ram and began swinging it against the door. This time the door creaked and opened slightly, revealed a narrow crack between it and the lintel.

"A bit more," Sophia said, "one, two, three, push!"

Straining, they did as she said, pushing the bench further inside until the door opened wide enough to afford entry to a woman. Roja-Rosa, her hands clasped as if in silent prayer, walked hesitantly to the door, glancing at Sophia, who returned an understanding and approving look.

She went into the room she had forgotten to visit that whole day. It was illuminated by the pale light from the doorway, but even so she could see the girl lying on the bed, a silhouette folded into itself. With great trepidation Roja-Rosa touched the girl's face, the bed, the soft, damp sheet.

"A candle!" she shouted. "Bring a candle!"

Estella ran to get a candle from her room, lit it, and gave it to Roja-Rosa. "There's blood on your hands, Roja-Rosa!" she shouted in fright.

The new girl, Miriam, was lying in a large pool of blood that had soaked into the bedclothes. She was not moving.

The girls all screamed in fright. Roja-Rosa yelled at them.

"Quiet! I can't think what to do with all that noise! Shut up!"

Sophia went to the girl's bed, took her slashed wrist and searched for a pulse, her own hand covered in the blood still oozing from the severed veins.

"She's still alive," she said quickly, "tear the sheet into strips. Maybe we can still save her!"

Roja-Rosa went quickly to the wardrobe, took out a clean sheet, gave one end to Clara, and they started tearing it into strips and giving them to Sophia, who bound the girl's forearms with them. Her right one, her left one, and then her legs.

"She's cut herself in four places," Sophia said quietly, "she really wanted to die, poor thing. Get some water. A bucketful."

The girls quickly did as she said, and Sophia poured the cold water over the girl.

The semiconscious girl opened her big black eyes, too weak to say anything.

"Thank God," Roja-Rosa murmured, "Blessed be the reviver of the dead. Clara, get a glass of water. Sophia, see if there's any liver left over from last night's supper. If there isn't any, get some from Angel's house. Flory, make her some tea, and you," to the other girls, "what are you standing there for? Let me be alone with her for a moment."

The girls withdrew to the corridor, murmuring quietly amongst themselves. After a few minutes Sophia returned bearing a plateful of chopped liver. Roja-Rosa's right, she told herself, liver's good for loss of blood. She went into the room to see Roja-Rosa supporting the girl, carefully feeding her water, drop by drop, from a glass. The new girl's head lay on her shoulder, her eyes frozen, and her thin, pale lips barely opening to taste the reviving water.

"Here," Sophia said, offering her the plate. Roja-Rosa signaled with her eyes and Sophia smeared some of the liver onto her finger and brought it to the girl's mouth.

The girl clenched her lips. Sophia didn't give in and held the plate under her nose; let her smell it, she told herself, let her sniff the aroma of food from her mother's kitchen. It will only make her feel better.

The aroma from the plate slowly wafted into the weakened girl's nostrils and from there into her consciousness and memory. She opened her eyes in total surprise, and with two fingers Sophia pushed a bit of the liver into her mouth, which opened like the beak of a feeble chick.

They sat there for a long time, feeding the girl and making her drink until she recovered. The blood on her arms and legs had congealed, and they were able to remove the tourniquets that had saved her life.

"It's a shame about the sheet," Roja-Rosa sighed, "it was new."

"You're lucky she's alive," Sophia said, "you know what Manuel would have done to you if she'd died."

Roja-Rosa sighed again and unconsciously touched the scar on her neck.

"Child, child," she said, taking Miriam's head in both hands. "Don't ever do anything like that to me again. He'll kill me instead of you!"

The new girl remained silent. She was too weak to speak, but her eyes scanned the room, the two older women who had helped each other to save her life, and she wondered why they had bothered if they too, like her, were trapped in this place. What was the point in saving her life if it meant returning to this place, a place of pain and shame.

She opened her mouth, but no words escaped her lips.

"Shhh…" Roja-Rosa restrained her. "It's better you don't talk. Rest. We'll take you to another room so we can clean this one up."

She inclined her head to Sophia, and they helped the girl onto her feet, and between them led her down the corridor to a vacant room, and laid her down on the bed.

That is how Esther was reunited with Miriam, who had descended the gangway with her two days earlier. Next day, when she was able to encourage her to talk a little, she learned that Miriam was a rabbi's daughter, and that Manuel had collected her from a small town near Lublin. If the rape on board ship had been a shock for Esther, and also the first day of forced labor in the brothel, for Miriam it was hell on earth. It was as if Satan in person had shown his face in the guise of Manuel, who had persuaded her poverty-stricken parents to give her to him to work in the homes of God-fearing Jews in Buenos Aires.

Unlike all her companions, her gentle soul had been unable to withstand this terrible experience, so she had smashed the china plate on which a meal had been brought to her the previous day, taken one of the long, sharp shards, and slashed her wrists and ankles again and again, sawing at her flesh as if it were the flesh of an animal.

Thirty-two

Next day they were awakened by Roja-Rosa a little later, but she still chivvied them to dress quickly and go downstairs. "We've got a lot to do today," she told Esther as she opened the curtain in her room, letting in the bright sunlight, "so get up quickly."

When Esther went downstairs she saw that all the other girls were already there, each busy with a different job. Clara and Estella greeted her gaily from by the big concrete tub in the courtyard as they washed underwear on a scrubbing board half sunken in soapy water. Bianca, the pale-faced girl, was sitting on a stool peeling vegetables into a big bowl at her feet, every now and then wiping the sweat from her brow with the back of her hand. Felicia was arranging firewood in a stone fire pit in the middle of the yard under the big cauldron in which they boiled water for washing, and Roja-Rosa came to the door and called Esther to her for breakfast.

"Be careful," she managed to whisper, "he's here. Don't tell him what happened last night."

Esther nodded slowly and followed her into the big room where, at a long rectangular wooden table on which there were plates, some already used, stood a basket filled with toast, a clay bowl of boiled eggs, a bowl of salad, a jug of sour cream, a carafe of fresh orange juice – and Manuel, elegantly attired in a business suit, fresh and alert, looking at her as he spread butter on his toast.

"*Buenos Dias, niña.*"

"*Buenos Dias* is good morning," Roja-Rosa told her, "say it after him."

"*Buenos Dias,*" Esther murmured, and sat down at the far end of the table.

"Come, eat," Roja-Rosa told her, giving her a plate and cup and heaping the plate with two pieces of toast, an egg, and salad. "Eat so you'll be strong. Be a good girl and everything will be fine, *niña.*"

Manuel did not say a word, he just sat there following her with his eyes as she lowered hers and with her fingers ate everything she could lay hands on. He watched her with a mixture of astonishment and disgust at the way she stuffed the food into her mouth without using a knife and fork, and he almost said something but then remembered that her mother had told him she had been raised in an orphanage, so he closed his mouth and didn't say anything. Only afterwards he whispered to Roja-Rosa that this girl must be taught some table manners so she wouldn't shame them in front of the clients, and then went off to the third meeting of the group of friends convened by Noé Traumann to finally sign the founding documents of the organization.

When she had finished eating, Roja-Rosa called her outside. She was carrying a heavy tin can and a box of matches. They walked to the fire pit where earlier Felicia had arranged the firewood, and Roja-Rosa put the can into the flames that flickered and heated it until the wax it contained started bubbling over. Then Roja-Rosa quickly took it from the fire using two long thin sticks as tongs, put it down beside her, and signaled Felicia to bring the strips of cloth she had readied earlier.

Felicia called the rest of the girls, and they all stood in a smiling circle around Esther, lifted their dresses, took some wax on a small twig, and spread it onto their legs, arms, and armpits, and after each smear of amber-colored wax they bound it with strips of cloth, and then pulled it off in a swift movement to the accompaniment of squeals and laughter as they plucked out their body hair.

Esther stood gaping at them. She had never seen anything like it.

"Come on, try it," Roja-Rosa told her, "look, everyone does it here. Now it's your turn."

Esther shrugged in refusal. It seemed both unnecessary and painful to her.

"Lift your arms up," Roja-Rosa ordered her. Esther did so, revealing her armpits with the black tangle of hair that had already grown there.

"See? A real forest," Roja-Rosa laughed. "Do you want people saying you're a savage? Any self-respecting woman in our profession does it. Come on, it'll be your first time."

Esther persisted in her refusal, embarrassed by doing such a thing in front of them all, and in any case she was answering a drive to refuse that rose from within her, as if her consent to this act would make her one of them completely.

Roja-Rosa looked at her with a darkening expression. "Don't make me force you to do it. It'll only hurt all the more."

But Esther did not budge, so Roja-Rosa signaled the girls who swiftly grabbed her arms and legs, one lifted her dress, another smeared on the hot wax, and a third, with expert hands, bound the strip of cloth and quickly tore it off, making Esther scream as if she had been slaughtered on the spot.

"Poor thing," Felicia laughed, "it's your first time, poor thing," stroking Esther's head, who shook off her hand. "What are you scared of, I'm not going to touch the hair on your head," she laughed.

"Now the legs," Roja-Rosa ordered, and the girls did their work on Esther's legs, which she tried to free without much success, kicking them here and there until in the end Roja-Rosa slapped her, but less forcefully than before.

"Calm down already, *niña*," she said. "You're making me do things I don't like doing."

Esther didn't know what hurt more, Roja-Rosa's slap or the scalding wax on her skin.

"I'm not your property!" she screamed. "Do you understand?"

Instead of a reply came another slap, this time on her left cheek. Roja-Rosa stood facing her, her cheeks aflame.

"No, *you* don't understand!" she shouted. "Do you think I enjoy this? We're all like you! So shut up and take it like a woman!"

"Never!" Esther screamed. Clara stopped her with a gesture. "Shhh... Don't let anyone outside hear you. It'll go badly for you," she said, and her friend Estella nodded in agreement.

But Esther was not to be silenced. "Why don't you run away from here?" she screamed at them. "Why do you stay here at all?"

As she screamed, not knowing if it was due to the feeling of imprisonment or because of the scalding wax on her body and the girls plucking her hair out with it, the windows of the tall building adjacent to theirs opened, and the heads of their women neighbors, all of them Jewish, looked out.

"*Kurvehs! Kurvehs!*" the neighbors screamed, spitting at them from above. One of them lifted a pail of dirty laundry water and emptied it over them.

Roja-Rosa went outside brandishing a stick. "Get out of here and shut your filthy mouths before I set my husband on you!" she yelled.

Her threat worked like magic. One after another the neighbors closed their windows, mumbling lurid curses in Spanish and Yiddish.

Roja-Rosa looked at Esther. "See what you've done? That's all I needed, for those bitches to put their heads out and curse us. Now get back inside!" she said harshly, pushing Esther before her. "You'll stay locked in your room today. You won't see anybody until tomorrow. That way you'll learn your lesson!"

A deep male voice belonging to Manuel was heard from behind her as he came into the courtyard. "What's going on here?"

"The new girl doesn't yet understand where she is," Roja-Rosa sighed. "I haven't got the strength for this, Manuel. The cleaning, the washing, teaching the new ones, and running this house."

"Everything will be fine," Manuel said, gripping Esther's arms so tightly that he stopped the flow of blood in her veins.

He dragged her up the stairs after him. Roja-Rosa clasped her head in her hands and shouted after him that he shouldn't do it, but he paid her no heed. His blood was boiling after yet another confrontation with Angel, the owner of the brothel opposite, which had miraculously ended without bloodshed.

At the door of his house Angel used to stand his *portera*, to whom he was married. She was a fat, meaty woman called Rachel who wore tight-fitting clothes far too small for her, revealing the dimensions of her big body. Every evening she would stand at the door of his house, her face heavily made up and wearing bright lipstick, calling out seductively to every passerby who came to the street still undecided about which of the houses he would visit. And this enraged Manuel. Angel was stealing clients from him and the other men from under their nose, and the illuminated signs that they all put up over the doorway of their brothels were of no help, and neither were the strings of colored lights and the sound of music coming from inside – nor the musicians they paid generously just to play every evening to attract clients with their lively music. Angel's wife with her big mouth and huge breasts dimmed all their lights.

That morning some of the men had met at Noé Traumann's house to discuss the final details of the establishment of the organization he had worked on, the first of its kind in the world that would bring all the city's Jewish pimps under its aegis for mutual aid for them and their wives. When Angel mentioned his wife in passing, Manuel attacked him furiously, feeling he had been harmed more then anyone because his house was opposite Angel's.

"You keep your wife inside the house so she doesn't steal the neighbors' clients!" he shouted at Angel, who was sitting sipping vodka.

Noé Traumann had poured them all vodka at the start of the meeting to put them at their ease so they wouldn't argue over every detail.

"You're jealous because I've got prettier women," Angel laughed, looking at the others for confirmation.

Nobody joined in his laughter. They too had had enough of him and his stratagems.

"I'll show you what jealousy is!" Manuel shouted as he got up infuriated and stood facing Angel, who quickly put his hand on the butt of the revolver tucked into his waistband.

"Gentlemen," Noé Traumann swiftly intervened, "we're having a meeting, not settling personal scores!"

"Then tell him to beg our pardon," Manuel shouted, grabbing Angel by the throat as the latter pulled his gun and waved it threateningly in front of him.

"Enough! Stop it!" Noé banged on the table.

Two of the men jumped on Manuel, dragging him back as Angel brandished his gun, possibly menacingly, perhaps just in fun.

Manuel sat down, his face suffused with anger. Angel calmly replaced his pistol in his waistband. The annoying smile had not left his face throughout the incident, and this drove Manuel absolutely crazy.

"Bastard!" he hissed, and spat at Angel. "I'll show you what stealing clients is!"

Angel quickly wiped off the spittle and shifted his chair away from the table. "If you're a man, come outside!"

Manuel tried to get up, but two pairs of hands forced him back into his seat.

"Gentlemen," Noé Traumann stood up. He was a tall man whose gray hair was thinning and whose face showed the first signs of the cancer gnawing at him. "This is an example of why we need the organization. To resolve problems like this. So that no one raises a hand or pistol against his brother or disrespects him."

"He's my brother?" Manuel shouted. "He's a thief and the son of a thief!"

"Enough, Manuel, enough," Noé stopped him. "We'll fix this matter and all the other matters and disagreements between us. The city is big, thank God, and there's work for all of us. But first we need a proper organization with a mutual aid fund, a committee to adjudge cases like this, and the main thing – proper management for bringing in fresh meat and its auction."

The others nodded in agreement. Peretz Stauber asked if the papers were ready for signing.

Noé took out a bundle of documents. "There's just one thing left to do," he said, as he handed out the articles of association to those present, seven in number. "We have to decide on a name for the organization."

"*Gemilut Hasadim*, The Benevolent Society," Peretz suggested, "so it sounds Jewish."

"The Society for Jewish Aid," said another, continuing this train of thought. "The way they have in their society, we'll have in ours."

"We'll have everything they have," Noé Traumann said, "but first we need a name."

"Most of us are Poles," someone said, "so let's call it Varsovia, Warsaw, and honor our city, eh?"

Noé Traumann looked at them. No one had voiced opposition. He raised his pen and said, "Then Varsovia it is."

He quickly inserted the name of the organization into the document before him and asked them to sign at the bottom of the founding documents, which they all did since they were all familiar with the articles from previous meetings.

Noé collected the documents and invited them all to drink a toast.

"Today," he said, "we have made history. Today we have founded the world's first organization of Jewish *rufianes*. You will see that many will join us and follow in our footsteps. Mazal Tov, brothers! May our endeavor be blessed!"

They all raised their glasses, clinked them and gulped the liquor. Their spirits were particularly high. They felt they were at a historic moment that would change their lives forever and the lives of those to come after them. The world's first organization of Jewish pimps had been founded.

When Manuel returned from the meeting, the anger that had welled in him from his confrontation with Angel still remained, but it was mingled with happiness at the establishment of the organization. But when he saw Esther going wild in his courtyard again, only one day after she had tried to flee, he could feel the anger rising in him again, a wild anger with no direction, no proportion. He dragged Esther up the stairs and shoved her into her room. Roja-Rosa, who had anxiously followed them down the corridor, stopped in her tracks at the sight of his menacing expression.

Manuel closed the door behind him.

"Get your clothes off and lie on the bed," he ordered Esther who was quaking with fear.

She did not move.

In one movement, Manuel pulled off his trouser belt.

"Get your clothes off and lie down!" he yelled, and whipped her body so hard with the belt that she fell onto the bed, her dress in disarray. He whipped her twice again on her clothing, taking care not to mark her face and chest, and then ripped off her dress. Enraged, he tore off her knickers and brassiere, revealing her in all her nakedness, sprawled on the bed, frightened, staring at him with her big eyes, her thin body shining in its whiteness, her big, full breasts and her *concha* open to him.

Manuel quickly took off his trousers and spread her legs with his strong hands. He lay atop her with his full weight giving her no chance of escape, and with one strong thrust of his erect cock, and her enveloping him like a shell, he began fucking her wildly, pinning her arms to her sides as she moaned and groaned beneath him, her eyes shut, and he screaming at her to open them and see who is fucking her because he's the boss, and this is what he'll do every time she opens her mouth and tells him 'no'.

He went on pushing himself inside her, wallowing in the honey of her young body until he came with three or four brief shudders, spilling his thick semen inside her and spending his anger. Then he released her arms and got up, pulled on his trousers and buttoned them in front of her.

"Now you know who's the man of this house," he hissed, panting, "and don't you ever make trouble again, do you hear? Because if you open your dirty mouth again I'll cut you. Understand?"

Esther carefully closed her legs and whispered a weak "Yes."

"Very good," he said. "Now clean yourself up. I'll be bringing your clients today, not Roja-Rosa, not anyone else. And you'd better keep your eyes open when they're fucking you, because if I hear you've closed them, you'll have me to deal with."

The girl did not reply, she just staggered to the pail of water in the corner, took the towel from its hook on the right, wet it, and began toweling her groin slowly.

When he saw she was doing what she was told he calmed down somewhat, turned on his heel and left the room, locking the door behind him with two turns of the key.

That day he brought thirty men to her. During the first hours they were a few high school pupils and two students. Then he brought several poor Jewish emigrants who each paid only two pesos. Then the better clients began arriving, and they too were glad to try out a new girl, trusting Manuel and his taste in women. He brought them upstairs one after the other, without mercy, without a break, knowing that this was the only way to get her used to her work and quell any resistance until she realized that she was his, completely his, the way all the other girls had realized it, each in her turn.

Thirty-three

The helplessness, the desire to die, the voices that whispered, enough, enough already, put an end to it all, what are you suffering for, better to slash your wrists or pour kerosene over yourself and light it, for what are you suffering so much?

All these voices calling on her to kill herself, telling her give up, give up, you can't vanquish your fate so why are you fighting, who are you holding on for, lying here for three days and receiving man after man, and all they want is to enter your young body.

The horror that can only be dulled by food and wine, for when the belly is full and the head reeling it all becomes easier, and the music that makes you happy and generous, the difficulty of enduring this life for one more moment, God, don't let me live in this shame, don't torment me, Almighty God, don't let me end my life this way, God, God, God.

The overcoming that comes from the body uncontrolled. To get up, to wash, even if the filth is inside you, to look into the mirror and tell yourself that everything will be all right, that it won't go on forever.

Esther finished cleaning herself and dried herself with the big soft towel, and over her wrung-out body put on the red dress that Roja-Rosa told her was suitable for evening wear, combed her hair, and inspected herself in the mirror. She then took a deep breath and opened the door, promising herself not to breathe a word of what she felt but to behave quite naturally and relaxed, and as she did to check where she was incarcerated and perhaps find a way out of it. She walked carefully on the high heels that Roja-Rosa had given her which added to her height and forced her to walk mincingly, and went out into a pleasant evening whose light touched the hedge surrounding the house and its walls, softening the place until it seemed that it was a large and pleasant family home.

Her room was one in a row on the second floor of a splendid-looking house, in a passageway with a long roofed verandah. At the end of the passageway a staircase descended to the ground floor and a tiled forecourt filled with plant pots in which climbers, flowers, and herbs grew.

The house was built around a large courtyard in the Italian style. The ground floor was built of a patio that gave onto the rooms, but unlike on the upper floor its rooms were spacious. There was a kitchen, a dining room and lounges, large high-ceilinged rooms connected by doors. When there were parties, the heavy wooden doors were opened, turning the row of rooms into one big hall.

The courtyard was encircled by a high plastered brick wall that separated the house from the neighboring ones. There was an iron gate at the entrance that was topped with a bell.

Nobody gained entry without first being checked by Manuel, Roja-Rosa, or one of the older women.

Seemingly relaxed, tall and beautiful, she went down to the big room where most of the girls were sitting together with Roja-Rosa and Sophia, but not Perla who was already working. They looked at her in astonishment. One of them even whistled, and another yelled, "What a beauty's coming down the stairs!"

Esther smiled at them, believing that except for her and Roja-Rosa, nobody was aware of what had happened earlier with Manuel.

She looked into Roja-Rosa's eyes, who lowered them. "Are you hungry?" she asked in her warm motherly voice.

Esther nodded, filled with gratitude toward this woman who was gradually revealing all her facets to her, not just a hard, tough concierge, but also a housemother, the girls' mother, the most senior of all of them.

"Come with me," Roja-Rosa said.

Esther followed her through the dining room and into the kitchen, which looked like the kitchen of a large family. There were two big stoves beneath a window overlooking the backyard, with wood countertops on both sides. Above and below them were cupboards in a U shape, on hooks on the wall there were cooking utensils on one side, and pots on the other. As she took covered plates from the refrigerator, Roja-Rosa told her where everything is, and Esther, chewing on her food, nodded.

"I know what that's for," she said, "it's for eggs, and that's for cake."

"How do you know?" Roja-Rosa asked smilingly.

"My mother's got an inn in Danzig, and I used to help her in the kitchen."

"*Muy bien*!" Roja-Rosa chortled. "So you know how to cook?"

"A bit," Esther smiled, "but not like here. Different food."

"Cooking's cooking and food's food," said Roja-Rosa, pleased that this girl had come to them. There was evidently something in her, not only problems.

"Would you like to help me cook for the whole house?"

"Yes, why not," Esther replied, "but on condition that you teach me what I need to know about cooking here. I'm used to something different."

Roja-Rosa raised her up from her chair and embraced her warmly. "Just look how lovely you are now. Come, and I'll show you a few more things."

She signaled her to follow her into the yard and explained where they did laundry, how to hang it out, and when to ask her for foodstuffs and clothing, cleaning materials and makeup.

On seeing that Esther was calm and collected, Roja-Rosa felt that this was the right time to teach her a few more things important for their profession, and she asked her to come back upstairs with her to her room. Once they were behind the closed door, Roja-Rosa opened the drawer in the small wooden table under the mirror, and took out a small wooden box that Esther had not seen earlier.

"We haven't got much time. Men will start arriving soon. I'll show you what you must do when a man comes to you," she said, and opened the box.

Inside it was a kind of odd-lookin bladder. Roja-Rosa took it out and stretched it between her fingers. "Do you know what this is?"

"Esther shook her head.

"It's called a *preservativo*. It's so you won't get pregnant."

Esther did not understand a thing.

Roja-Rosa searched her apron pocket and took out a carrot. She handed it to the girl. "Hold it in your hand, straight."

Esther did so.

Roja-Rosa took the contraceptive and showed Esther how it fitted over the carrot. "Now do you understand?"

Esther looked at her wordlessly.

"Every time a man comes to you, you've got to put this over his organ. Only then do you allow him in. If you don't, you'll have a child. Understand?"

Esther was silent.

"They know it's what they've got to do," Roja-Rosa went on, "all the men we brought you got one of these before they went up to your room. The men don't like it but you've got to put it on every one of them."

Roja-Rosa looked inquiringly at the girl, hoping she had understood.

"If a man doesn't want it and goes inside you without it, you go right to the pail and wash yourself inside. Then you do exercises to force out what he left inside you. Understand?"

Esther shook her head.

Roja-Rosa sighed. She gestured her to go to the pail of water in the corner, pulled a low wooden stool from under the bed and told her to sit on it.

"Spread your legs."

The girl didn't move.

"Spread your legs, I said," Roja-Rosa repeated, raising her voice. The girl opened her legs before Roja-Rosa in terrible embarrassment.

"If a man doesn't want it, you sit down on this stool and wash your body with lots of water, inside too, like this, with a glass," she demonstrated. "Afterwards you've got to move your body a lot to get it all out. You should do it if you don't want to drink bad water against pregnancy. Believe me, you don't."

Esther nodded.

Roja-Rosa sighed again. "Men will soon be arriving. Be beautiful and behave well."

Roja-Rosa left Esther in her room and went downstairs. Before the first clients arrived she took down an iron pot and began concocting the abortifacient liquor. She took equal parts of vinegar, lemon, and oil, added honey and one ricinus seed, a little iodine and a glass of alcohol, and stirred it all together. Then she sprinkled in a little gunpowder from a pistol cartridge and some green herbs from her garden, and then let the concoction simmer and bubble for a long time. The new girls, she knew, were accident-prone. In the shock of an encounter with a man they might forget everything and become pregnant. She had to make sure this did not happen, that they stayed fit for work.

That evening she was allowed to sit with the other girls in the big room so that a man could pick her out according to his taste. But once he did she had to smile and do as she was told without a word, take him upstairs to her room, and let him do with her as he wished. She thought it was terrible, but bearable compared with the alternative she had experienced during the previous nights – that Manuel and Roja-Rosa would bring one man after another to her room. This way at least she could sit with the girls for a while, talk with them and look at Miriam, the other young girl who had been with her on the boat, her face as sad as that of a fragile doll.

Very late at night, after the last of the clients had left and the music ended, the girls all gathered around her. They told her to strip. Sophia, the only one who understood her without her saying a word, closed the door to the courtyard and dimmed the light that flooded the house throughout the night, leaving just a few lamps that cast their warm light over the floor and walls.

"Don't worry," Sophia said, "we do this with every new girl. Don't be shy. We're all sisters."

Esther began unbuttoning her dress and the girls helped her take it off without tearing it. Then they helped her with her brassiere. She was shy standing in front of them, her hands over her breasts, wearing only her knickers, until Sophia nodded at them too. Esther hesitated momentarily, lowered her eyes, and then removed them.

The girls examined her naked body from top to toe. Her big beautiful breasts, developed before their time, were magnificent, two huge pale breasts with a deep, wide cleft between them that continued to her rounded belly that looked as soft and pleasant as a down pillow, her splendidly wide hips that seemed sculpted by a gifted artist, her thick hairless calves, her lower leg muscles, her foot, and then her head again, her flowing loose hair, her rounded face, long sharp nose, inclined toward her lips, her pink sensual lips, her eyelids lowered in shame over her eyes, her long lovely lashes that blinked in confusion, so feminine, feminine and soft, at the peak of her youth yet so stubborn. Her full, curvaceous body that seemed like flesh inviting a touch, but with a gentle hand, the hand of a lover, not the rough hand of a migrant or laborer.

Perla brought a candle close to Esther's face.

"You're beautiful," she said, a catch in her voice. "I don't know who made you like this. You're simply wonderful," she said, and reached out to stroke Esther's hair. "But this hair needs something doing with it," she added, glancing at Sophia who was also captivated by the sight of Esther's body, as if she were seeing her own reflection from the days when she was still young.

"Yes," Sophia said, emerging from her musings. "It needs to be put up. Come and see," she told Esther, taking her to the mirror on the other side of the room, and stood behind her and gathered her hair into a pile above her face.

Esther laughed. "It's strange, I look like a lady."

"That's exactly what you should look like," Sophia told her. "You're not a little girl anymore."

"I can't have a tower like that on my head," Esther said, turning her back to her.

"Would you rather wait until Manuel cuts your hair?" Sophia asked, sharply and assertively. "Don't think he hasn't done that."

Perla went to Esther and gathered her hair into a knot again, holding it in a kind of ball and pulling strands out of it. "Well, what do you think?"

Esther looked at her reflection. "It's better."

"Now we can see your face," Perla said, taking a hair grip from her pocket and inserting it so it held Esther's hair in its new style. "The clients want to see your face. Always remember that."

"And with your eyes open," Sophia laughed, remembering what Roja-Rosa had told her: the clients had come away, one after the other, from having sex with such a beautiful, well-developed girl, but they had all complained that she had lain beneath them with her eyes closed, her lips clenched, and her body rigid.

"Let them do as they want," she replied, "as long as they don't expect me to look at them while they do."

Sophia's laugh was redolent with nicotine. "It's a man's nature, child. He wants you to see him doing it to you. He needs to feel strong. *El porsador.* Do you understand?"

"I don't want to know," Esther replied, loosening her hair, "and I don't want any changes either."

"You're obviously going to learn it all the hard way," Sophia said, and left the room.

"What do you need this for?" Perla asked her. "Why do everything the wrong way round? In the end he'll go crazy with you, girl."

"Let him. Let him kill me if he wants. He can't do any worse than he already has," Esther hissed.

Roja-Rosa heard what she said. She took pity on this girl who had no father and had spent most of her life in an orphanage.

"Our world has rules just like outside," she told her. "In our world a man is a man. You don't say no to him, do you understand? Look at your sisters, at how well they behave, and how every evening, every evening, he takes a different one to walk with him to the theatre, in the street, to a café, dressed like a queen. Don't you want to go out a bit and see the city?"

"I do. But not with him and not like that. As if I'm for sale. Only with you, Roja-Rosa."

"We've got a rule here. For the first three months nobody leaves the house," Roja-Rosa told her, "but I'll talk to him and see what can be done. That's on condition that you dress properly and keep your eyes open, understood?"

Esther nodded slowly, thinking that this was a small price to pay for getting out of this house and seeing the city.

"Go to sleep now. All of you, get some sleep," Roja-Rosa ordered.

The girls got up, dragging themselves in one tired bunch up the stairs, and one by one got into their beds.

Thirty-four

Buenos Aires was a big city, but she would only discover it through the men that came to her. For as time went by and Manuel and Roja-Rosa observed her obdurate, rebellious character, they tightened their yoke on her. They had no alternative other than putting her up for auction, but then, Manuel knew, he would lose much of her value and his investment in her. First they would do better to exhaust all their educational methods – imprisoning her in her room for a few days, with or without food, beatings and rape, immersing her head in a pail of water after a whole day's work, or increasing the number of inferior clients she received.

"One way or another she'll learn," Manuel told Roja-Rosa, "otherwise she'll have me to deal with again, and that will certainly not be worth her while."

And Roja-Rosa, who knew full well what this man was capable of when he was really angry, continued to talk to Esther, slowly drawing her closer through her first kitchen tasks and the new clothes she bought her.

Once the clients discovered her, she became a firm favorite because of her beauty and proud bearing, and they began asking for her again and again, only her, to go with only her. Thus Esther came to know a regular group of men instead of the many casual clients that came to the house.

Juan Bautista, a short balding man, came to her every week, sometimes day after day, and always looked sweaty and troubled. His hands were stubby and thick, their skin like used sacking, cracked and furrowed with thin lines.

Antoine, a gentle-looking and warmhearted man of about thirty would come to her with great shyness. But once he got into her bed he would assail her with bites and trace the lines of her body with his long, thin middle finger, at whose tip was a small, ugly wart he was born with that he used for his pleasure. With that finger he would dig inside her before inserting his manhood.

Another man always stopped outside to clip his nails. One day Roja-Rosa yelled at him to desist from doing this at the entrance to the house because nail clippings are the food of the earth demons, and wherever they fall becomes a site for their feasting. He laughed and said that his nails grow overnight, and he did not want to be seen as discourteous. Had he given some thought to the number of crooked-nailed *marineros* this house had already served, he would not have made such an effort to demonstrate his nobleness.

And there was the theatre designer, Miguel de San Amejo, a tall man whose groomed mustache and small beard hid his face and ugliness. His fat fingers, five sweaty sausages, rested on her flesh, exuding an unpleasant dampness. Each finger bore a ring that pressed into the layer of fat beneath it.

"Where are those rings from?" Esther asked him.

He laughed. Even his smile oozed fatness. "I'm a great expert in buying in the markets. Whenever I have time I walk around the market. One day in the secondhand clothing market I saw a tray full of rings. They were all made from tiny silver teaspoons that had been worked into all kinds of shapes. I bought the whole tray. As time went by I gave some of them away. I only kept these five," he said, showing her his fleshy hand with its five worked silver teaspoons on it.

Esther swore that this man would never lay a hand on her again. For her part he might be the wealthy scion of an aristocratic family or a master silversmith, but he would never touch her again. Neither his sweaty hands nor his rings.

What she didn't know was that one of the two sailors she had been with that morning had left her some lice with which she infected Miguel. Since then, whenever he heard her name he would spit and say, "*hija de puta!*"

The months went by until 'The Angel', as all the girls called him, came to her. He was a young man with long, smooth, blond hair that fell over his handsome face and eyes, which were as brown as two wells of compassion. He had an upturned nose and thick lips, and his lovely head was set on the stem of his neck that rose from a pair of fine shoulders. To his credit it should be said that from the moment he came to Esther he was smitten by such harsh guilt feelings that she had to calm him down and persuade him to do what he had come to do, for if he didn't her owner would beat her. So he relented, but immediately afterward he begged her to flee this dreadful fate with him and accept his help to return to her own country. Every time, after the act, he would display his anguish to her.

One day an idea flashed through her mind, which she had thought about during her first days there, and now was the time to put it into action.

"I really do need help," she whispered as she sat beside him on the bed, stroking his thigh.

"You only have to ask," he replied, excited by the thought of being able to do something for her that would ease his tortured soul.

"I need a pen and paper to write to my mother about what is happening to me here," she whispered, "and I need you to take the letter out without anybody knowing, otherwise they'll kill me."

"You're a brave girl," The Angel whispered as he stroked her cheek. She gave him a long kiss and he embraced her ardently. "I'll bring what you asked for next time, but don't say a word to anyone. I don't want any trouble with him," he said, nodding in the direction of the door.

A few days later he came to the house, asked for the new Jewish girl, and went up to her room with her. From his coat pocket a took a sheaf of folded writing paper and two new pens, and adjured her to sit down and write to her mother quickly so that he would not have to leave neither pen nor paper with her, lest she be caught, Heaven forbid. And Esther sat down and wrote a brief letter in Yiddish to her mother, telling her everything that was happening to her, while The Angel sat glancing at his watch, fearful that somebody might come upstairs to see why he was staying so long in her room, while at the same time feeling his groin, for he had come filled with lust, but in the end he turned his back on the writing girl as he spilled his seed onto the floor accompanied by several short, choked grunts. The he got dressed, took the letter in its envelope on which she had written the name and address, said goodbye, and left.

Esther was left standing for several long minutes alone in her room, clasping her hands in silent prayer that the letter should reach its destination, and perhaps bring her salvation.

Thirty-five

Gershon liked being on the road, not only as the antithesis of his life in Danzig, but simply traveling, devouring the vast expanses of Argentina on his way from one colony to another when he could observe the beauty of this country, its scenery and people, and still he was not sated. Two huge haystacks standing erect and rounded in the dusk light, on a vast harvested tract of land, the last sunlight endowing them with their deep golden hue; evening falling on distant fields, darkening their green to a tone bubbling with vitality and menace; a farmer on his way home, a hat on his head and the red gaucho kerchief around his neck, sitting atop his high cart loaded with grain, urging on the pair of oxen harnessed to the wide yoke, pulling the cart along the dirt road; a family sitting in their yard by the fire, and the father, an elderly, thick-bearded man, wrapped in his poncho against the evening chill, reaching out with his sharp knife to the big slab of meat hanging beside him, slicing off chunks for *asado*, as his young son watches fascinated, his face shining in the firelight; or a greenish natural pool in the shade of a stand of trees, illuminated by the blue dawn light.

The train chugged its way over the pampas from village to village, and the men, the very special men of this country, some of whom seemed to be made of *dulce de leche*, their skin milk and honey, their eyes green or blue and their hair chestnut or light, or the other men of mixed race in whose veins flowed Indian or Spanish blood, dark skinned, their features like those of gods aroused from their slumber. Even though he did not allow himself more than a stolen glance at them lest he feel his weakness, still he could feel himself falling in love with this country, its sheer size, its scenery, the landscape still untouched by human hand.

It was hardly surprising, then, that his trips became more frequent as his efforts on behalf of the Jewish settlement increased. He invested all his energy in them, and his repressed lust. But his wife Bella had no idea of this because she was preoccupied with something else entirely. When the second consecutive month without a period went by, she realized she was pregnant.

When Gershon came home and heard the news he was overjoyed. As the pregnancy progressed he began to somewhat reduce his trips away from the city to be with her.

Bella was thirty and this was her first pregnancy. As she got used to the morning sickness, the strange bouts of hunger that assailed her at odd hours causing her to devour all kinds of foods, she found it hard to adapt to the sudden weakness, the ebbing of her strength that deserted her in the middle of the work she so loved – arranging her father-in-law's ornaments in the parlor. She would suddenly feel that she was about to collapse and have to put down whatever she was holding, and the duster saturated with detergent, and sit down with a sigh. She realized that this was part of being pregnant, but at times like these she could not recognize herself. She was able to get up after a good night's sleep, and then a short time later feel all her freshness and energy dissipating as a great tiredness overcame her, as if the child inside her was sucking out all her strength and emptying her.

It was a completely new feeling. Once again she was not in control of her body. Somebody else was now dictating the pace of her life and her speed of thought, her mood, and her daily routine.

The servants and maids took note of these side effects and strove to be at her side insofar as she allowed them to. Eva, too, the childless spinster who had linked her own destiny to that of this woman, had become her most trusted friend. She endeavored to be with her for most of the day, to be at her side and answer her like an echo. And what other option did Eva have? Nobody was waiting for her in her small, silent, empty house, to which she would return late at night as if it were just a place to sleep. When Bella asked her to she would sometimes stay over to sleep in her house. Then they would get up together and have a good breakfast, either in the big, well-lit dining room at the window overlooking the yard, or beneath the climbers covering the patio, sitting and talking with a few sunbeams breaking through the thick foliage and dancing over their faces, highlighting the dishes, the milk jug, the bowl of fruit on the table.

It was in one of those conversations that they sat thinking about names for the baby. Whether she had a son or a daughter Bella knew she would have to name it after either her dead brother or her mother or father, may they live long. But those names are unsuitable for this country, she told Eva, sharing her thoughts.

"Then you should give it two names," Eva advised, "one Argentinean and the other Jewish."

"That sounds sensible," Bella said, sipping from her glass, "but I don't know any Argentinean names."

"That's what I'm here for," Eva chuckled.

"If I have a girl I want to name her for a flower. Something that brings a beautiful flower to mind."

"Flora is a flower in Spanish," Eva told her, "but every flower has its own name. Rosa, for instance, or Margarita, Lila, Dahlia, and so on."

"I like Margarita. It sounds very musical, very Spanish."

"And what if you have a boy?" Eva laughed. "Will you call him Tulip?"

"If it's a boy I'd like something with character. A religious name, or one with an attribute."

"Angel," Eva replied almost instantly, "that's a lovely name."

"Yes, but what if he isn't such an angel?"

"You're right. It's a name with a commitment. Maybe Santo. No. No. Alejandro!"

"What does Alejandro mean?"

"Defender of Man, Alexander the Great."

"That's a fine name!" Bella said, slapping her hand on the table. "That's my son's name!"

"And there's Alonso, a noble man."

"That's a bit weak."

She had lately become even more tired. Her belly, too, was far more distended than expected in a first pregnancy. The housemaids, particularly the eldest, Isabel, looked at it as she passed and exchanged surreptitious remarks.

One day Bella noticed this and summoned Isabel.

"What are they saying every time I pass them?" she asked her.

"That you've got a double pregnancy."

"What do you mean?"

"You've got a belly that's too big for just one baby, Señora."

"Nonsense," Bella replied, patting her stomach.

"Believe me, I can see these things. You're having two babies, not one."

Thirty-six

Her womb yielded twins, two boys, one after the other, squalling and wrinkled, both weighing slightly less than expected, for they had shared the space and nutrition inside her, but they were perfect and healthy.

As soon as the news spread the house was filled with flowers. Strangers flowed to the house as did bouquets and flower arrangements from everyone who had contact with her husband. Notes and greetings cards were pinned to the flowers, and each time another bouquet came the maids would loudly announce its arrival.

"*Este dulce sueño de niño*! This bouquet is the child's sweet dream!" one of them rejoiced, holding a big bouquet with gold, white, and blue flowers bound with a dainty ribbon.

A few minutes later another messenger arrived with a big basket of flowers. Their blossom looked like big purple stars.

"*Esta canasta para la nueva mama*! A basket of flowers for the new mother!"

All this commotion tired her. Giving birth to the boys, whom she named Alejandro, Defender of Man, and Amado, The Beloved, had changed her entire routine. She nursed them both, and in the meantime the happy Gershon had made arrangements for the double circumcision ceremony.

Were it not for the festive event in which she was restored to her old self, dressed in her finery and wearing her jewelry, even the ring would have been forgotten for a while.

But it was then, as she stood beside her husband, averting her eyes from the awful work of the *mohel*, at the moment when her two baby boys burst into tears as they were initiated into the Covenant of Abraham, that the old gold ring resurfaced before her as if it were not a ring but the mouth of a womb, an old, ancient, primeval womb, alternately contracting and expanding, drawing in and expelling words, stories and people. The numerous people came to congratulate her and shake her hand and kiss her, smiling at her with faces filled with flattery, but she was in a completely different place, her wide eyes staring straight ahead in what appeared to the people around her as a sudden physical weakness, or a kind of detachment caused by anxiety or depression. She stood there, not saying a word, until one of the guests went over to Gershon and in a whisper drew his attention to her delicate condition. Gershon quickly sent Eva to her, who took her by the arm and gently led her out of the room and upstairs to her bedroom, shutting the door behind them.

Bella went to the window, gazing vacantly at the wintry view, a wide and quiet city street whose houses now stood washed by the rain, with their dark brown stone walls and gray roof tiles.

But she saw only one thing. That opening, with its concentric rings of flesh and muscle, pulsing and opening like a tunnel or a dark crevasse, calling her to it, to enter it and be swallowed up inside it without leaving anything of herself, to answer the call of this monster of darkness from the depths of time and the darkness of generations, to compensate it for the two children it had given her, to give it herself as a sacrifice, and her lips began murmuring, "The ring... the ring..."

Eva touched her forehead.

"You're burning up," she said, and hurried to get her a glass of cold water.

But Bella paid her no heed. She was in thrall to the dark magic of the ring whose other side had suddenly been revealed to her. Not as an exquisite object but as the demanding maw of a monster.

When the last of the visitors had departed, Gershon, tired out, hurried to his wife's room and tapped quietly on the door. Eva came out, despondent and worried.

"What's the matter with her?' he asked.

"I've given her something to relax her. She's sleeping now, she needs to rest."

"It's obviously all been a bit too much for her. Emigrating, the pregnancy, and now the birth and the circumcision," Gershon whispered.

"What's 'the ring'? She didn't stop mumbling 'the ring, the ring...'"

"That's what she was saying?" he asked, refusing to believe that this damned madness had beset her again.

"What's it all about, Señor Bergman?"

"She tortures herself because of the theft of the wedding ring I was to put on her finger," he replied shortly.

"I don't understand, she's wearing it. The ring with the small stones."

Gershon shook his head. "This is another ring, a very special and ancient one. The one she wears is only a substitute. I'll tell you about it tomorrow, Eva. Meanwhile perhaps we should arrange for a wet nurse for the boys."

"You're right. In her condition she won't be able to feed them. I'll try and find somebody today."

Gershon thanked her with a nod, left her, and wearily went to his room, wondering why Bella had suddenly remembered the ring right in the middle of the circumcision ceremony. Why now of all times, when they were so happy together, in a new city, with two newborn children, had the madness of the ring assailed her again? Would it never leave her?

Seven days and seven nights Bella Bergman lay in the grip of fever, hanging between life and death. On the orders of the doctor who had been rushed to her, the maids, supervised by Eva, gave her cold baths to bring down her body temperature, but in vain. The doctor drew blood for testing and stood helpless at her bedside. "This is a specific type of fever," he said, "one I've never come across. It's not malaria or any other known fever." He turned Bella on her side, searching vainly for the bite mark of a mosquito or another insect. Then he took her pulse and temperature again, mumbling to himself all manner of possibilities. He greatly desired to save this woman whose twin sons needed her. But he was unable to discover what she had and was unable to conceal his helplessness. He packed up his instruments, said something about consulting his colleagues, and hurried out of the room.

Eva accompanied him to the door. Isabel, the senior servant, closed it behind the doctor who was fleeing for his very life.

Isabel was a poor Indian woman in the prime of life who worked hard and long in the Bergman household, generally leaving only late at night, slowly making her way to her little house in La Boca where her elderly husband and six children awaited her like starving chicks.

"It's better he's gone," she told the worried Eva, "this isn't a matter for a doctor. I'll go now and get her something myself."

Eva looked at her, puzzled. She should not argue with the wisdom of these native women, she thought. They were born from the soil of Argentina and knew its secrets more than anyone. She herself was descended from a mother like this and an emigrant father, and in her home, too, there was a mixture of ancient demons and imported magic, spells from which the smell of sun and rain emanated, and fears originating in another, turbulent continent in which wars had been waged between countries and peoples.

She went back up to Bella's room, soaked a flannel in a bowl of water and wiped her brow and parched lips. Bella was so weak that she was unable to even raise her head to drink.

It was only late that night that Isabel returned.

The room was in semi-darkness, illuminated only by the pale light of a single lamp. Eva was dozing, but when the door opened and Isabel strode in quietly, she shook herself awake and raised her eyes to her.

"Help me lift her up," Isabel whispered, as from her bag she took a strange object oddly-woven from colored straw.

Eva carefully lifted Bella onto her side. Isabel swiftly tucked the woven object under her body, and gestured to Eva to lay her down again. Bella shifted back and forth, feeling that she was lying on something prickly, and turned back onto her side, mumbling the names of Danzig streets in her sleep.

Then Isabel took out another woven object and hung it over Bella's bed. "Now she'll be fine."

"What was it you put there?" Eva inquired.

"Have you moved so far away from us that you don't know?" Isabel asked, frowning. "We call it The Dream Keeper. But it imprisons dreams."

"What do you mean?" Eva asked, imagining dark-faced jailers chasing broken dreams through the air with butterfly nets,

"It catches the bad dreams and doesn't allow them to stay. Now I must go. My husband and children are waiting for me. What can I do, I've got a home too."

"*Claro*," Eva replied, shrugging, "the main thing is that it helps her."

"Of course it will help her."

Eva spread an embroidered wool rug and some cushions at the side of Bella's bed. As she sank into sleep at her friend's side she imagined she could see dark bubbles emerging from the top of Bella's head and being trapped in the woven colored straw hanging in the air above her head. She fell asleep letting this chain of scenes fade within her, sinking ever deeper into the sleep of dreams.

In the morning Bella awoke, put one foot out of bed and almost stepped on her devoted friend sleeping at her bedside. At the touch of Bella's foot, Eva opened her eyes in alarm. Bella was sitting up in bed, her face tranquil.

"Good morning, Eva. I slept a lot. How long *have* I been asleep?"

"A week."

"Good God!" Bella exclaimed, starting. "What about the children?"

She found standing difficult. Eva got up and helped her onto her feet. "Slowly, Bella, slowly, you've been in bed with a high fever for a week. Walk slowly. First get used to walking again."

"But the children, what's happened with them all this week?"

"I brought them a wet nurse," Eva replied, "it was the only way of keeping them alive."

"Another woman's nursing my children?" Bella screamed. "How dare you!" More than anything else Bella's angry voice convinced Eva that she had pulled through.

"You were lying here dying, Señora," she said harshly. "Now let's go downstairs and I'll fetch you something to eat and drink. Afterwards you'll see the boys."

Bella followed her silently, looking around her with eyes filled with wonderment as if she had awakened to a reality that was familiar yet only dimly remembered. Everything seemed familiar. The walls of the rooms, the old portraits in their elliptical frames hanging on the wall leading down from the second to the ground floor, the splendid old furniture, the glass-fronted cabinets in which various ornaments gleamed in the sunbeams that cast luminescent shards of morning light upon them, the potbellied decorated china vases filled with bouquets.

She was back home again. But she was unable to answer the question of where she had been all this time. She recalled only fragments of dreams and scenes that were intermingled. A dark tunnel, the mouth of a road, a dark hoop spinning before her at

198

tremendous speed, growing and approaching infinitely, threatening to swallow her up. She blinked, ridding her mind of the image, looking at Eva again.

"What's the matter?" Eva asked as they walked toward the kitchen.

"Nothing. I just remembered something," Bella smiled weakly, holding out her hand to her friend, asking for support. Eva linked arms with her and led her into the kitchen where they were greeted by the cooks with shouts of joy. Isabel did not say a word, but looked right into Eva's eyes with her warm ones, a smile of deep satisfaction on her face,

In the days that followed Bella immersed herself in raising her children. Preoccupied with nursing first one then the other, her breasts filled with milk and the two infants falling upon them several times a day, sucking out all her vigor with hungry mouths, crying with hunger and burping when sated. But after feeding them and putting each one back into his crib, she noticed that her breasts were as empty and flaccid as empty sacks.

But not only her breasts, her body was changing from day to day. Her belly, which had been hugely distended, now looked cleft and wrinkled. The skin, which previously had been taut over her belly looked like an old, gray, crumbling piece of cloth, and was covered with flakes of dry skin. She was so ashamed of how she looked that she refused to expose her body to Gershon, neither in daylight nor at night, and she kept herself from him almost completely.

At the same time Gershon traveled away from home far less frequently. That being so he felt, as men do, the need for release. One night, after she had consented to let him share her bed, he tried to caress her body and seemingly by mistake his hand encountered her belly covered with flaky skin. He started, withdrew his hand, and asked what it was he had touched. Bella answered quietly that with the dual birth the skin of her belly had been spoiled, but the Indian maid had concocted a herbal ointment for her which she was rubbing onto her stomach, and it was already much better. This she told him, and turned her back to him, letting him reach his climax by rubbing himself against her body from behind.

Bella saw that she was unable to cope with nursing and the changes that had taken place in her body, and asked that the Jewish wet nurse – whom she had gotten rid of – be brought back. Begrudgingly, but with acceptance, she saw how the wet nurse approached her babies' cribs, lifted out one and then the other, and nursed them with her milk. Only after becoming accustomed to her unassuming and devoted presence she began sitting on the bed beside her, one feeding one infant and the other the second, and then changing over so that the babies would not become used to the taste of one and not the other.

At the same time they started talking. Berta Himmel told her that her husband had left Russia for Argentina first, leaving her behind to wait for his call. After almost a year of expectation she managed to raise the passage money to follow him to Argentina, thinking in her innocence that she would find him right away and be reunited with him. But on reaching Argentina she discovered that he had not stopped there, but continued to another South American country leaving no trace. Left alone in the crowded Jewish emigrants' hostel on Calle Pueyrredón, she scraped a living from selling matches and the like in the street. One evening she was seduced by the touch of a strange man, a Jewish emigrant from Poland, and became pregnant. On hearing of her pregnancy he packed his bags and left, leaving her with a swelling belly. After the birth she was unable to go back to selling matches in the street, so when she heard that a Jewish woman had given birth and then fallen ill and her boys needed mother's milk, she had seized the opportunity to wet nurse them for the few coins with which she could feed her own son.

Bella told her a bit about Danzig, imparting information about herself and her husband only sparingly, but trying to pay this woman double her fee to help her settle in better surroundings and get out of the dank hostel. She had heard about the hostel from Gershon who had visited it on several occasions with the leaders of the Jewish community, and each time he had been shocked by the harsh conditions in which Jews were living, in dark and crowded yards with clotheslines strung between the buildings, and hordes of children in their rags sitting on the stairs, infested with lice and sickness, sores and wounds, gazing helplessly at any approaching stranger who might perhaps bring them salvation.

It was from this Berta Himmel that Bella first heard about Rabbi Hirsch who had come to Buenos Aires and served in no official position in the Jewish community. Berta spoke his name in awe. Bella wondered what a rabbi had to do with a cheap and crowded emigrants' hostel, but Berta told her about his wonderful deeds, his compassion and kindness, and how he uncomplainingly lived with them in the filth of their lives and without acting superior because of his learning, teaching the children some Torah even in the crowded conditions they lived in, and many other stories about him that Bella filed away in her memory.

As they sat nursing the babies and talking, in the kitchen Isabel the maid and Eva talked about the Señora.

"We must take care she doesn't fall ill again," Eva said one evening, as they got ready to leave the house.

"I've been thinking about that too," Isabel replied, carefully folding her apron, hem to hem and fold to fold, and putting it into the small cupboard. "But I'm off home. Would you like to walk with me a while?"

Eva was happy to accompany her instead of crossing the quarter by herself on the way to her house at the far side of the city. She put on a coat against the night chill and left the house with the maid.

"Her husband thinks she's forgotten the ring she lost," Eva said as they walked down the street, "but she hasn't."

"What has been lost gives no peace," Isabel replied, "the heart doesn't forget, only the head. The heart doesn't."

"It may attack her again."

Isabel halted. "She must be given a lot of rings."

"What do you mean?" Eva asked, feeling her nose freezing in the terrible cold, grateful that the rain had stopped at least.

"You should tell her husband to buy her a new ring every time. She should start collecting rings until they calm her."

"But she wants one particular ring," Eva said. "How can that help?"

Isabel smiled, revealing white teeth in the darkness. "When she has enough rings they will call the other ring to come back."

The magical logic in Isabel's words seemed strange, just like the time she had brought her the Dream Keeper. And that had aroused Bella the very next day as if she had never been sick at all, and so, Eva thought, there are evidently some things in sacredness that are beyond human ken and which should be accepted at face value.

Thirty-seven

Not thirty days had passed since the birth of the twins and Bella Bergman was presented with a second opportunity to encounter the ring, but this time not in sickness and distress, rather out of abundance. Gershon asked her to hold a redemption of the firstborn dinner for the dignitaries of the Jewish community, and while she considered whether to accede to her husband, it was Isabel, the pagan housemaid, who insisted that the Jewish custom be observed.

What did an old Indian woman have to do with the custom of redemption of the firstborn, Bella wondered. But Isabel explained that her people observed a similar custom, and that one had to give the Great Spirit a gift so that it would release its grip on the child's soul. And if firstborn twin boys are born at exactly the same time, the gift should be appropriately big to propitiate the Spirit of the World, so it should not claim its due from the souls of her two sons.

"It will also be an opportunity to entertain everyone who hasn't yet been here," Eva added. "It will help with your and your husband's contacts."

Happy to have reached agreement with his wife, Gershon invited everyone who was anyone to his splendid home to honor him on the redemption of his firstborn sons.

Whereas the circumcision ceremony had been held with in the presence of only a few guests, this time they invited numerous Zionist dignitaries and government officials to their home, and accordingly they had to arrange a sumptuous dinner despite all the Jewish dietary restrictions. The three women sat down and planned the dinner down to the last detail. Which of the servants and cooks would be in charge of each part of the meal, and what dishes would be served for each of its courses. Isabel would be responsible for the round brown confection made of risen dough that browned slowly in the coal-fired stove until it turned into rolls whose crispy crust crackled to the touch, and its inside as soft as butter, and the *empenadas*, those pastry pockets of secrets that every woman stuffed with her own special filling for herself and her family. She performed magic with her *empenadas*. Some she filled with potato and fried onions, and others with ground chicken and olives; some had ground beef with raisins and pine nuts, while others were filled with vegetables piquant with Far Eastern spices she bought specially at the spice market. Eva took on preparation of the root vegetables indigenous to Argentina, which were cooked unpeeled – sweet potatoes and carrots, onions and garlic and white potatoes lying big and brown in clay casseroles and cooked in the oven, emitting the deep, intoxicating aroma of roots cooking and softening together.

Bella went to the market to order meat for *asado* that would be kosher but varied, with chunks of prime beef marbled with fat, and *chorizo*-like sausages made from carefully koshered meat, kidneys and slices of chicken breast, lamb and veal of a quantity sufficient for the Buenos Aires gourmands who judged their hosts by the quantity of meat piled onto their plate. At the same time she summoned a builder of grills to construct a sufficiently large and long *parilla* on which a large quantity of meat could be grilled, and he built it in the big yard along the wall surrounding the house.

While the three women were busy with their respective tasks, another cook was preparing large quantities of *chimichurri*, the sauce without which no *asado* was worthy of the name, which she made of garlic, parsley, vinegar, salt water, pepper and cumin seeds, thyme and paprika, while a maid took the knives to a sharpener in readiness for the great feast. And while they were engaged in the great, complex operation of preparing the redemption of the firstborn dinner for more than two hundred guests, the youngest maid prepared desserts for the approaching party, which included *alfajores* filed with *dulce de leche* and dusted with coconut flakes, and bowls of sugared almonds, and *grafiniades* cooking slowly in caramel and filling the house with the sweet burnt smell of melting sugar, thickening and coating the small nuts.

They toiled for a whole week until the great day arrived. Round tables were set up in the garden and covered with white tablecloths and tableware and beautiful flower arrangements, with servants in white uniforms helping the guests alight from their carriages, while the hosts, Gershon and Bella Bergman, as befitting their status, stood at the door with the twins in their cradles, and Eva beside them to ensure that their crying would not disturb the evening's proceedings, welcoming their guests with a kiss on both cheeks in the local manner and receiving their gifts, each according to his munificence, a ring from this one and a pendant from that one, a piece of precious jewelry from another, all intended for the redemption of the firstborn, in which the infant is completely covered in piles of jewelry, with all present loudly intoning the traditional blessing, and afterwards giving the rabbi his fee in coins, then leaving their hosts with all the exquisite objects soaked in the blood of their sons.

Yes, yes, their sons' blood, this is how it was seen by Isabel, who followed the ceremony anxiously, and when she saw that the blessings were over and all the piles of gold and precious stones were removed from the boys and put into two wooden boxes for safekeeping, and a wad of banknotes was slipped to the rabbi, she clutched her head in her hands, seeing disaster overtaking the infant boys and this house, because the custom had been altered.

After the dinner, Bella and Eva sat down in the big salon, and with trembling hands Bella opened box after box, one inscribed 'Amado' and the other 'Alejandro', and looked happily at the many pieces of jewelry on which sunbeams danced joyfully, as if they too were amazed at what they saw. While they were thus engaged, Isabel hurried in.

"It's not good to keep these things in the house, Señora," she said with some urgency.

"What do you mean?" Bella asked, astonished. "Where do you want them to be kept?"

"In the place of your god," Isabel explained, "these belong to the Great Spirit, not to you."

"There's no Great Spirit in our synagogue," Bella laughed, "only collectors of dues, beadles and a cantor."

"I don't understand your god," Isabel said, "but keeping the Spirit's possessions is a great sin. It's dangerous!"

"Calm down, Isabel," said Bella, trying to placate her, "we're Jews. Our God is very different to yours. Your superstitions don't apply to us."

Eva heard this, and again her soul was torn in two. She was sufficiently educated to reject all the nonsensical beliefs in ancient curses and customs that must not be broken, but the same beliefs flowed in her blood without her even knowing whence they came. Furthermore, with her own eyes she had seen how the Indian maid had saved her friend from certain death from the fever.

"May God protect you and the children," Isabel said in a sharp voice that lacked even a hint of inner conviction or optimism. She was convinced that if they kept these things in the house, the fate of the two unfortunate boys would be sealed before they even managed to say 'Mama' or 'Papa', but she knew there was no point in pursuing the matter. The Señora was perhaps familiar with the demons of her own country, but not with those of Buenos Aires.

Thirty-eight

Bella Bergman was so delighted by the sight of the jewelry collected for her two boys that she decided to establish a collection she could enjoy and later bequeath to them. She made sure to inform Gershon, Eva, and all her visitors that in future, on holidays and festivals or any other joyous occasion, she would prefer jewelry above all else. For jewelry is made of precious stones that do not fade like flowers, beautiful though they might be, and do not break like a glass or china jug, or do not wear out like clothing. A piece of jewelry is valuable not only because of its material worth, but because of the artistry of its polishing and decorations, and it is always pleasing to look at as it gleams in the sunlight, revealing the depth of its hue, or by candlelight, for then it doubles the flame in its blue or purple eye, bringing out tones of a hidden hue from the precious stone that lay hidden in the ground for a long time.

The family's visitors learned of her love for jewelry, especially for rings and brooches. Anyone who met Gershon knew that if he wanted to reach an agreement with this man he should bring his wife a gift.

Bella was a forceful woman. She walked through the world as if she were slicing it with her body like a knife. Her noble air, the knowledge of her status that radiated from her, and her manners, all made settling in this city easier for her, a city that knows how to respect any person from whom power and authority or the smell of money emanate.

Nobody knew what had happened to her in her childhood that had made her so acid-tongued, so hard. The women of the community said she was hewn from a rock, not a womb. They did not know that she had become so embittered only on her wedding night when she discovered that her wedding ring had been lost forever.

But when Bella welcomed a visitor to her home, and he opened his purse or took from his coat pocket a jewelry box and surprised her with a ring, a scarf or an expensive brooch, a hint of a smile would cross her face.

Her reactions were always restrained.

More than anything she loved objects with a story. An object that is just a thing of beauty can dazzle the eyes, but one with a story is different thing entirely. The greenstone brooch, for instance, a beautifully fashioned silver brooch with a huge greenstone in the middle, was brought to her from America by Max Nordau. He spent an entire evening at their home, telling them about a small mining town situated on both sides of a road from the mountains to the ocean, in a region where the greenstone mines were located. He told them how he stopped his car and had gone to look at the souvenirs on sale at the roadside stalls. His glance had lit on this silver brooch, which immediately intimated to him with its green eye that it wanted to come with him to a very special lady in Buenos Aires, Argentina, "to rest on your dress, Madame."

She also possessed a small gold brooch in the form of a crocodile, which Gershon had brought her from one of his trips to the provinces, and a lily brooch she had been given by the Jewish Agency emissary from Florence, the city of Lorenzo de Medici, the noted patron of the arts.

She kept the brooches in lined wooden boxes in her room. She would never leave a brooch or ring on the dressing table. The moment she took them off she would return them to their box, always taking care to remember the number of pieces she had lest the housemaids covet, heaven forbid, one item or another.

One day Isabel presented herself and asked to tell her something.

"What do you have to tell me?" she asked dryly. In her view Isabel was filled with superstitions.

"I had a dream. About you, Señora," the maid replied. "I dreamed that a small basket came to you, and in the basket that floated on the water was an old ring."

"Floated on the water?"

"Yes, like the basket of Moses in the Old Testament," Isabel said. "But instead of a baby there was a ring inside it."

Bella strove to conceal her excitement.

"Your ring is calling you," Isabel. "It's close."

"Yes," Bella replied, "it's just a pity that you didn't dream about where it is. That would have made everything so much easier."

"It is coming on the water. On a ship. Look for someone who came here on a ship."

"Everybody comes here by ship or train. How can I find anyone like that?"

"Look for a Jewish woman," Isabel said, "she's coming like a Jewish woman."

Bella gave her a probing glance, remembering her conversation with Leah Kochmann in the Danzig cemetery. She thanked the maid for her dream and its interpretation, and sent her away with a request to check if the servants had picked flowers from the garden for the numerous vases dispersed throughout the house. Afterwards she stood rooted to the spot for a while and then decided to devote some time to this strange dream. Without a word to anyone, of course.

That night, as Gershon slept in his room – here too they had separate rooms, and only on the rare occasions when they had intercourse would he come to her room – that night, as the sound of his snoring came from his room, she sat down at her dressing table in front of the big mirror. She took a big crystal candlestick whose slim base was decorated with leaves fashioned in silver, and lit a tall yellow candle in it.

Bella sat in the dark looking at the candle as she screwed up her eyes to see how its light split into Stars of David, cat's whiskers, and tiger's eyelashes, as she immersed herself in her musing. Slowly it dawned on her that the water the maid had seen in her dream was the Atlantic Ocean, and that the wooden box in which the ring lay was the boat that had brought the daughter of the whore and the murderer to Argentina.

It meant that the ring was close to her. Closer than ever.

She didn't know how to begin searching for the girl. She didn't even know her full name. If the girl is Jewish, she would have to search among the Jewish émigrés, she thought, and she began thinking about the synagogues of Buenos Aires, the Once district, the *conventillos* where the émigrés lived, those crowded buildings where families of Jews lived in poverty because of their stubborn insistence on living in the big city and not going to work on a farm in the colonies. She had never visited those places, but then she recalled the wet nurse's story about that strange rabbi, Rabbi Hirsch, who had come to Buenos Aires without a congregation or rabbinic office, and who taught Gemara in one of the émigré *conventillos*. He's the man I need, she told herself. He knows the émigré community, and certainly those who had stayed to live and work in the city. So she summoned the wet nurse and asked her to arrange a meeting with Rabbi Hirsch on a matter of some urgency.

On the appointed day she dressed as befitting her standing, got into the house carriage with the wet nurse, and together they drove down the boulevards and streets of Buenos

Aires. They passed Plaza de Mayo, around which drove *tranvias a caballo*, wide wooden coaches harnessed to a pair of horses, and private carriages, and they drove up the boulevards to the edge of the city where the houses were more crowded, leaning against one another, as if should they be separated slightly there would be a real danger of them collapsing, tiny houses whose flat roofs and walls were neglected and yellowing. There was much activity in the alleyways between them. The numerous Jews who had settled in these cheap dwellings conducted their social and commercial life, learning and foolishness in their alleyways and yards.

The wet nurse signaled the driver to stop and gestured Bella to follow her. They made their way through a crowd of men, women and children, some standing, some sitting in the narrow passage they called a yard, who looked with interest and suspicion at the elegant woman entering Rabbi Hirsch's yard.

Bella walked between them slowly, looking at their faces and attire. A poor girl wearing a simple cloth dress and a cloth kerchief covering her head like a rain hood, and beside her a kneeling man holding his little son's hand wearing a checkered cap and a threadbare jacket, and at their side a tall woman with sharp, handsome features, wearing a dress with a plunging neckline and her hair rolled back and gathered on her head, and behind her a doleful, dark-complexioned man wearing a hat, a simple scarf around his neck and his hands stuck deep in his pockets to protect them from the cold. The miasma of smells that filled the small yard made her nauseous, the dense, cloying smell of cooking and the stench of sewage that flowed unhindered at the edge of the yard, the smell of frying fish from one of the rooms mixed with the cheap perfume of a passing woman who also looked back at her to see who she is and what she wants. Another moment, she felt, she would be sick. But the wet nurse took her arm and pulled her after her into another alley between the houses, at the end of the patio. Even darker and narrower, where people no longer gathered. There, in the middle of the alley that had a sort of tin roof whose gaps were stuffed with old clothes, stood the rabbi's room.

The wet nurse knocked on the cracked wooden door.

Rabbi Hirsch opened the door. "Please come inside," he said. He was short and slightly stooped, with a wild black beard, wearing old trousers and a shirt from beneath which peeped the tassels of his ritual *tallit katan*. On his head he wore a black yarmulke and a strange look blazed in his eyes.

The rabbi closed the door leaving them inside a small, narrow, dank space in which disorder reigned. Clothes and cloth were piled one on top of the other and from beneath them peeped sacred books. There were two wooden tables and a low stool standing around a simple iron bedstead on which there was a mattress covered with coarse ticking. The atmosphere was gloomy and suffocating.

Bella sat down facing the odd rabbi and had difficulty breathing. "Perhaps we could open the door or a window?"

"Of course," he replied, and quickly opened the door a crack enabling some air and a little light to penetrate the room. "How can I help you, Madam?"

"I'm looking for a Jewish orphan from Poland, from Danzig."

"I am honored you have come here," he said and sighed, tugging at his beard. "I have been told that your husband is a great worker for the Zionist cause."

"My husband doesn't know I'm here," she said quickly, realizing her mistake but unable to retract her words. "This girl is the daughter of a whore from Danzig. Her mother stole a ring from me. My wedding ring. I want it back."

The wet nurse glanced at her, puzzled. Until that moment she had not known why Bella had asked her to arrange a meeting with Rabbi Hirsch from the *conventillos*. She waited a moment then said that she had to go to the toilet, and added that she would wait for Bella outside the yard. Bella nodded her thanks.

"Ay, ay, ay," the rabbi groaned, "life here is so hard, Madam."

"I am always happy to help," Bella said, looking him in the eye.

"And what you are asking calls for a great deal of time for searching, questioning, and enquiries, and there are many mouths and hands along the way," the rabbi added.

Bella had prepared herself for this eventuality. "Here, Rabbi, a little something for you." The rabbi looked in amazement at the wad of banknotes she offered him, and immediately tucked it into the pocket of his shabby trousers, his eyes gleaming even more brightly than before.

"It is written in the Torah," he said, "that the daughters of Zion must not walk with stretched forth necks and wanton eyes."

"I don't understand."

"A Jewish woman who wears jewelry and paints her face is perceived as a harlot. Like Dinah in Genesis."

"But what's that got to do with the girl I'm looking for?" Bella began losing patience with his casuistry and allusions. It was evident that he was not a real rabbi and if he were, he was a rabbi of the lowest order, living in a wretched room, holding out his hand for money and then bursting into a strange medley of Torah quotations.

"You said that the mother was a whore in Danzig," the rabbi said. "Like mother, like daughter, Madam. I will have to search in the right places."

The rumors of the trade in Jewish women had reached her ears too, horror stories that did the rounds in the community, about the brothels of Calle Junin in the Once district. She could not make the connection between the figure of a rabbi, even this one, and brothels, either simple or splendid, and yet it was certainly logical that in a big, strange city like Buenos Aires where unemployment was rife, that the whore's daughter might find herself following in her mother's footsteps.

"Don't worry," the rabbi smiled, patting his trouser pocket, "with God's help all will be well. Go on your way and I will start making enquiries in the right places for you, and I shall send you my answer through Berta who brought you here."

She thanked him and left the room into the dank air of the narrow yard, again making her way through the many refugee Jews thronging the alley, and got into her carriage. Only when she sat down was she finally able to breathe deeply of the protected air of the house carriage, urging the driver to hurry and get her away from the suffocating street to the center of the city.

Thirty-nine

After Mrs. Bergman left, Rabbi Hirsch remained alone in the room. He closed his eyes and began swaying back and forth, praying ardently to the Almighty, blessed be He, to grant him the fortitude to go the houses of the *mecklers* in search of the daughter of thieves and help that righteous woman.

Bella did not know that not only was Rabbi Hirsch a Hasidic rabbi, but also a fallen Hasid, that is a Hasid into whom a dybbuk had entered in his youth, and because prayers and exorcisms had been to no avail, his despairing parents and rabbis had unanimously decided to send him to Argentina, where perhaps life would be better for him.

Rabbi Mendel Hirsch had been a young, golden-haired blue-eyed boy, his features gentle and soft, when he was sent to study at the great yeshiva of Lithuania. Even at the commencement of his studies there he stood out among his colleagues with his diligence and erudition, until the heads of the yeshiva set him above his colleagues and treated him as a great Torah prodigy. Unfortunately, one night when sleep deserted him, he entered the synagogue at a late hour to take a book and say a midnight prayer by his bed, but as he went into the study room, the door closed behind him and he was engulfed in total darkness that swallowed him and the room.

Mendel Hirsch sat in the dark, his heart affrighted and his soul not knowing who or what it was, and he began thinking all kinds of thoughts to raise his spirits. But because of his fear an opening in his soul was unlocked, and a dybbuk entered it and seized it so strongly that it never left it again. And why is this story written in Hasidic language? Because Rabbi Hirsch himself, even though his everyday language was the vernacular, his inner language and that of the dybbuk was that of a fallen Hasid, and the same dybbuk that had taken possession of his soul began uttering obscenities and cursing.

The next day the yeshiva rabbis found him sitting on the ground, his head covered with sackcloth and ashes and his eyes rolling in their sockets, his lips mumbling unthinkable nonsense. They immediately threw a bucket of cold water over him. Mendel Hirsch shook his head and began talking to them, thick-tongued, in all sorts of broken verses containing words of Hasidism and words of heresy and apostasy, and then he stood over them and cursed them, until he unexpectedly fell to the ground, unable to move or speak, like someone suddenly frozen. Then his yeshiva colleagues carried him to his room and laid him on his bed without the mattress, on a wooden board like a dead man, until he recovered.

Mendel Hirsch awoke from his troubled sleep and did not remember anything of what had befallen him. But from that day on he began complaining of melancholy, he would hardly eat, sometimes for days on end, barely eating a morsel and drinking a little water.

The rabbis saw what was happening to him and feared he might starve to death. And because they recognized the signs of a dybbuk possessing him, they discussed his case and even though they did not believe in dybbuks, all the signs were there, and so they were forced to hand him over to Hasidim who knew how to save his soul.

They sent a messenger to the Hasidic sect in Koznitz, and with him a question for the Maggid: What should they do with an educated student who had been assailed by a Hasidic spirit that threatened his very life? The Maggid of Koznitz heard that the leaders of the *Mitnagdim*, the opponents of Hasidism, were seeking his counsel, and said right away that they should bring the student to him and he would see what he could do for him.

For seven days and seven nights the yeshiva emissaries drove in a horse-drawn cart, and in it rocked and swayed Mendel Hirsch, his flesh scrawny and his eyes shining with an alien light, his lips mumbling strange sounds and barks like the dogs of the field, until they reached Koznitz completely exhausted, and handed him over to the Maggid.

The Maggid saw what was before him and immediately ordered that the boy be locked in a room. Next day the Maggid gathered all his followers in the synagogue to recite psalms, and they brought the boy to the synagogue and stood him in the center so that his soul would be enveloped in the music of the psalms and perhaps thus he would be revived.

All the Maggid's followers stood and recited the psalms of the third day of the week in a loud and righteous voice, and they recited them twice, for according to Genesis the third day is twice-blessed. The boy was silenced of all his mumblings and pricked up his ears until it seemed that his sanity had been restored.

But the moment they stopped singing his mouth opened with a great bleat and he began responding in kind with all sorts of poetry and melodies in the holy tongue, things he could not have known, until it seemed to the Hasidim that the spirit of a cantor had entered him, and there were some who reached the point of grief from the words of wisdom he uttered. But those words were mingled with crude sounds and nonsense.

The Maggid saw that he had encountered a powerful and cunning dybbuk, and he ordered that the boy be taken back to the room and tied to his bed.

They laid Mendel Hirsch on his bed and tied him down with thick ropes, and all the time he was singing sacred melodies in a clear, pleasing voice as if he were a cantor in the middle of the Yom Kippur service. After prayers the Maggid came into the room and without further ado slapped the boy hard on both cheeks, and asked him who he is and what he wants.

"I am the dybbuk of the Cantor of Radzin," chortled the dybbuk inside the boy, "and I seek Mendel's soul."

"It shall not be given to you," said the Maggid, and he began swaying back and forth, enumerating all the awe-inspiring names of the living God and thundering at the dybbuk to leave the boy as it had entered him, through the tips of his toes.

The dybbuk fell silent, and began opening cracks in the boy's toes, spraying thin jets of blood from them.

"So, Maggid," it said, "does it befit you to spill the blood of an innocent man in this way?"

The Maggid was affrighted and said, "Go back, go back."

The boy's toes immediately returned to their former state.

The Maggid left the room and secluded himself and prayed and thought about what he should do.

He began thinking of the stories he had heard of the powers of the Seraph of Mohelnice who in one day had exorcised two dybbuks from the body of a yeshiva student, or the saintly Rabbi Shalom of Belz who had sent a boy with a dybbuk to look for a priest in Lemberg, and when he found him he attacked him and beat him, and the dybbuk passed into the priest.

In the end he decided to send this possessed young man away from Poland to Argentina. Let him go far away and there attack some Jewish *meckler*, and thus bring redemption to his soul.

The Hasidim washed and dressed him, took him in a cart to the port, gave him a prayer book and phylacteries to bind the good parts of his soul, and prayed for his success and a good life, and sent him across the ocean.

On the boat the young man's spirits improved. The dybbuk had vanished as if it had never existed. But his face had aged before its time due to the travails of the journey, his beard grew wild and his eyes burned with a strange fire.

When he disembarked at the port of Buenos Aires with all his companions on the voyage, they took pity on him and took him, like a brother in times of trouble, and put him up with them at the émigré hostel. For although he was mad, he still possessed great erudition in the Torah, and now and again would also quote Hasidic epigrams.

Truth to tell, he confused them completely, for they did not know whether he was an educated *Mitnaged* or had rediscovered his Jewish self.

But he lived with them in the émigré hostel for a whole year and taught their children Torah and Gemara. And if he felt unwell or suddenly emitted strange sounds as if he had swallowed a dog and the dog had awakened inside him and barked, they would take the children away from him until his spirit was calm again.

To the Jews in Argentina the attacks by the dybbuk he had in Poland seemed like holy visions, and they began consulting him, or the dybbuk within him, on numerous matters. And the dybbuk would give them proper answers, beautiful good answers, because it needed Mendel Hirsch's body in order to exist and it still had to maintain what the Maggid of Koznitz had imposed on it.

Now, after Bella Bergman's visit, Rabbi Hirsch sat down and began thinking disgraceful thoughts.

This city possessed a special quality of duality. There is the divine Buenos Aires and there is the everyday Buenos Aires. In the everyday Buenos Aires there are the same streets as in the divine Buenos Aires. But their names are given in broken lettering and are read backwards. In them live the same people that live in the divine Buenos Aires. Like the Jews in the divine Buenos Aires, they too observe the commandments and bear children, bring them into the Covenant of Abraham and live and grow and die. And when they pass on they are buried in a cemetery. But their cemetery is not our cemetery, for they are unclean. They belong to everyday Buenos Aires, the *unterwelt*, the netherworld of the land of demons where they speak Spanish and Yiddish, but deal in harlotry. They, The Unclean, possess a strong power of attraction with which they attract not only the wealthy and Torah students, but also good young Jewish girls, who see the face of some *meckler* and do not notice that it is gray and his heart black, and they are seduced into following him from Poland and Danzig and with him board a ship bound for the land of the sun. But instead of reaching Buenos Aires and finding a Jewish husband to build a Jewish home, they wallow in the filth and dung of the *unterwelt* and only get to touch the flesh of a Jew when they take on the image of Lilith.

He pondered these thoughts in a new language because he was taking one thing for another and was confused by all the languages that dwelt within him and in the houses of the émigrés of Buenos Aires. And now he also had the money to start frequenting the forbidden houses of the city.

He got up and began wandering among the Jews' *shandheizer*, dressed as was dressed and growling as he growled, striking terror into the hearts of men and women alike, but each time waving his wad of banknotes at them and pacifying them. The men in charge of these houses would shrug and say something to themselves, the main thing is that he paid, and so long as he paid good money then let him go with one of the girls and do whatever he wants. And so every evening he would go with a good Jewish woman to observe the commandment in her room, on occasion in small forbidden houses and on others in big forbidden houses where there was a great deal of hubbub, so much so that they did the act in the big room, separated from the others only by a curtain, or even on the roofs, the men separated from each other only by a kind of rush screen, and the whole rooftop would be filled with the sighing and groaning of Jews spending themselves. Then the dybbuk inside him would awaken, dance and groan, lick its lips and start singing all kinds of Hasidic melodies in a loud voice, until it struck terror into the people there who would want to throw him off the roof.

Forty

For more than a year Leah Kochmann waited for a letter or a sign of life from her daughter Esther until one day the postman knocked on the door of her inn. He came early in the morning when she was cooking before the arrival of the first hungry customers. Leah opened the door and saw the postman in his pressed uniform proffering a light blue envelope from another country, and her heart leapt with joy.

Leah sat down at the table nearest the door where the light from outside spilled in relatively liberally at that hour of the morning, carefully slit open the envelope with a knife and started to read. Going by the date at the top of the page, the letter had been written several months ago.

She read slowly, the excitement of actually receiving a letter delaying her complete understanding of what she was reading. But the more she read and reread with eyes wide with astonishment and shock, she suddenly understood what she was reading and a terrible cry of pain escaped her lips, a cry that people utter when a relative dies and the cries tear them apart from inside, escaping from the depths of the chest and breaking out until they reached the ears of her port worker neighbors, who rushed inside to see what had happened.

Leah sat there, her face pale. One of the neighbors gave her a glass of water and forced her to drink it, and another poured her a glass of schnapps, because eau-de-vie helps in such situations, and he made her drink half of it. Weakly, she put the glass on the table, feeling the schnapps coursing through her veins, somewhat quelling the terrible rage roiling inside her but not dulling the intensity of her pain at all. It was not for this that she had torn her daughter from her bosom and sent her to Argentina. No, only not that. What kind of cruel trick of fate had brought down this calamity on her head? Who had allowed her only daughter to fall into the hands of such cannibals? Whoever heard of such a thing, that after all the tribulations she had herself experienced until she abandoned prostitution, her own daughter would fall into it. How had she trusted that man who seemed so kind and well-educated, and it transpired that he was a wolf in sheep's clothing, a damned scoundrel who dared to defile her daughter, the sun's rays should burn both his eyes. Almost collapsing with rage and pain, Leah wondered what she would do now: sell her house and inn, board a ship and sail to save her daughter from the hellhole? And if she did, could she restore her lost innocence and stolen virginity? She knew that there is no healing for a woman whose body has been sold and defiled over and over. Even if she were fortunate enough to find her a husband, the licentious shadows of the despicable men who had come to her would haunt her and defile her soul. And what could she do now to save her daughter from that fate after he had seized her in his talons?

Even her friends and acquaintances wrung their hands on hearing the news, albeit they asked one another how she, of all people, had not thought about all this beforehand, and had sent her daughter away with a strange man as if she herself was not sufficiently experienced in life to expect such things, poor woman. They suggested she go and see the communities committee and tell the community leaders what had befallen her and request their urgent assistance in finding a solution and salvation for her daughter.

And she did so the very same day. She changed her clothes, took the letter, and drove in a carriage to the communities committee office, where the heads of the committee greeted her as they had already greeted numerous women and mothers from other towns and cities who related the same horror story. A daughter who had legally married a Jew from Buenos Aires, with a feast and guests, and a rabbi and marriage license, and a short time later they had heard that the man was already married and had only wed their daughter to obtain an entry visa to Argentina for her and put her up for sale like meat; or two friends from the same street in Lodz who had been handed over to an elegantly-attired couple who spoke *mamaloshen*, and who said they were leather traders and had come to find Jewish girls for a match with young Jewish men in Buenos Aires, and selected only the most intelligent and good-looking girls; or another man who introduced himself as a young widower who was sick of his loneliness and had come to find a good Jewish wife and found her in a town not far from Warsaw and married her, and now she was with him in conditions of captivity and wanted to die due to her grief and pain; and more and more stories like them that had started to accumulate on the committee's desk, indicating what appeared to be an organized movement for trading in young Jewish women by Jews, may their names be erased, who exploited the good nature of their brethren and stole their daughters and thoroughly debased them.

The committee listened to Leah's story and showed her more letters and inquiries from other women and mothers, and told her she should not travel to Argentina for it was a real *unterwelt*. She would do better to stay at home and save her money to help her daughter through the committee, since they were overwhelmed with horror stories like her daughter's, and they sent all the material to Mr. Gershon Bergman who was presently in Buenos Aires on behalf of Baron Hirsch, and they assured her that they would do everything, through him and with the help of the benevolent baron, to save her daughter and all the other girls.

And so the committee forwarded her daughter's letter to Gershon, together with the letters and inquiries of other women, and requested him to make discreet inquiries so as not to cause anti-Semitism, about how much truth there was in this story and what could be done for these girls who were openly traded as slaves in the Jewish quarter of Buenos Aires.

From the moment she received the letter, Leah's life was not worth living. She was mad with worry and helplessness and despair. She did not open her inn, she just sat there as if in mourning, her door half open, but the pleasing aromas no longer emanated from it. People would pass her door, nod, cluck-cluck, and tell the whole story from beginning to end, how she was once a whore and had married a man and bore him a bastard daughter, and she too had become a whore, *die ganze meiseh in a fer worter, aber mit a sach risheh*, the whole story in a few words but with great wickedness, and everything they said about her only added to her bitterness.

Leah was like a bereaved mother, dejected and weeping bitterly, and the little money she had was dwindling as if she had not worked at all, and all her thoughts were centered on her little only daughter; she was filled with guilt feelings that she had not kept her with her, and had even had the temerity to think that if she sent her to a distant land some good would come of it. She would surely have continued to wallow in her pain had not the old gravedigger of Danzig heard what had befallen her, and come to see her again.

In the year that had elapsed since his last visit his back was bent even more, and he leant on his stick and his young nephew, who brought him to the door of Leah's inn and waited for him outside while they talked.

The old gravedigger stood in the doorway, extended his hand to the mezuzah and kissed it reverently, and then came into the room leaning on his thick stick, where Leah was sitting at the table, her head supported by a hand and her eyes staring into the distance like two sacks of tears, her long hair unkempt, the skin of her face drooping like that of an old woman, and the old gravedigger stood looking at her until she raised her head and saw who was standing there.

"Reb Asher," she murmured weakly, "why are you here?"

"There is anguish that pierces the very hub of the universe," Reb Asher said quietly as he slowly sat down, releasing a deep sigh and laying down his good friend, his stick, to rest at his feet.

"I have nothing to offer you to eat, Reb Asher," Leah said, embarrassed, "perhaps a glass of tea?"

Reb Asher laid his old hand on the table, its skin furrowed like a layer of soil, its fingernails cracked from digging the soil of the graveyard and its sinews tired from carrying so many stretchers of the dead, and Leah stood looking at it as if it were the hand of God.

"Come sit with me, Mrs. Kochmann, sit down and tell me how you are."

But instead of words, such weeping erupted from her that one would not wish upon anyone in the world, because weeping like this was like a groan that had lain inside Leah for many days and now made its way out to burst from her lips.

Reb Asher had heard much weeping in his life and his heart had been assailed by great pain, so much so that with the passing of the years he had become inured as slate to it, but he had never heard weeping like this before.

"Cry, Leah, cry," he told her, his aged heart twisting inside him. Why, O why, Almighty God, did you have to further burden the yoke on this woman's shoulders, he asked himself. Where is your mercy, O Almighty God, that you have worsened the fate of one woman?

When her weeping lessened somewhat, he raised his old, sad eyes to her, eyes whose rims were wrinkled with age like mountains surrounding a lake, and he said, "Leah, oy Leah, may God preserve your soul and the soul of your daughter, for I warned you about the ring and its power."

"But I sent it with my daughter to Argentina," Leah replied through her clasped hands, "so it would be with her in time of trouble! Who knows if that rogue has not taken it from her and left her with nothing," and she began weeping anew.

"What were you thinking of when you sent it with her to Buenos Aires," the old gravedigger murmured, "for it is a stolen ring, a ring of blessing that became a cursed ring."

"What was I to do?" I had no money because the *meckler* took it all for her passage."

"And now what can we do to annul the decision?" the gravedigger asked.

"Is that why you came here, Reb Asher," Leah asked in a different tone, "to deepen my despair?"

"Heaven forbid. I came to see how I can help you."

"I'm sorry, Reb Asher," she said, softening her voice, "I can't make head or tail of anything. All I can think of is my daughter. The communities committee promised to help but I haven't heard anything from them. I'm dying from worry."

"If only her father were alive," Reb Asher said, "he could have helped you."

"What? What did you say?" Leah jumped up, her eyes suddenly blazing wildly, "What did you say?"

"If Leizer were alive…" the old man repeated, astounded by the panic that had seized her.

"Oy, Reb Asher," Leah said as she grasped his hands, "you are the wisest of men. You have brought me salvation!"

"How?" Reb Asher asked in astonishment, "I haven't said anything."

"Because her father is still alive! He's still alive!"

The old man feared that her grief had relieved her of her senses. "How can he be alive, since I buried him with my own hands?"

"Leizer wasn't her father," Leah shouted, "he was Mendel Grunem's youngest son who was brought to me one night to learn what a woman is!"

The old man brought his hand to his mouth. Of all things, this was the last he expected. He knew that Leah had been a whore but had not imagined that her daughter was not the daughter of the master carpenter, of blessed memory, but of a boy in the past and a wealthy man today.

"I'll go and see her father tomorrow and tell him everything," Leah announced, "and I'll beg him to help me save her!"

The old man heard, but did not say what he was thinking, fearful of her frustration when she went to the home of the wealthy man who had married years ago and had a wife and children of his own. He would surely throw her out or deny paternity of the unfortunate girl. But Reb Asher took a deep breath and told her that until such time as help came from the girl's real father, she must reopen her inn and not spend all day in her grief, and not only that, she would be earning a little money that she would probably need to rescue her daughter.

But Leah was no longer listening. A great wave of joy engulfed her obliterating any possibility other than that she had found what she was seeking, someone who would rescue her daughter, and she was so overjoyed that she implored Reb Asher to stay until she made something to eat for him, and Reb Asher, who was wise in the ways of people and saw how she had shaken off her pain and sadness, accepted, on condition that he might invite his nephew, who was waiting for him outside, to join them.

Leah brought the boy in and hurried into her kitchen. A short time later, from the small kitchen wafted a smell of paradise, and the old man and his nephew, and anyone passing Leah Kochmann's inn, knew that her good spirits had been restored and her hands were busy cooking.

When Reb Asher and his nephew left the inn, and were standing sated at the door, the old man heaved a great sigh. "That is a dear woman, my son," he told the boy, "remember that when I am no longer here, and you assume leadership of the Jewish cemetery of Danzig. It is good that I filled her heart with joy, but it is a false joy, and great troubles will yet be laid on her doorstep, and she, the innocent, knows nothing of them because sometimes pain and sometimes joy can blind her."

The boy listened in silence, and took his arm and led him, step by step, until they were on a city street.

People standing there saw the old gravedigger being led from the port by his successor, as they say, who had learned all the sacred work from him, and they started talking among themselves, saying that if the old gravedigger had come so far, then he must have brought bad tidings, and they wondered to whom he had gone this time, and from which house a great cry of pain and fright would come, and since they heard nothing, but only smelled the wonderful aroma of cooking wafting in the air, they remembered the flavors of Leah Kochmann's inn. And they began feeling their mouths filling with saliva and their bellies grumbling, and they flocked to the door of the greatest of cooks and filled the cashbox that day, a day of pain mingled with joy.

Forty-one

The home of David and Tirzah Schindler stood on the edge of the Altschottland quarter. It was a villa surrounded by lawns and thickets, and was hidden in the shade of a wall. They had previously lived in another house, but following the death of Mr. Schindler, who had owned a Danzig bank, his only daughter Tirzah and son-in-law David had inherited the spacious home, where from time to time they would lavishly entertain the luminaries of Danzig's wealthy elite.

But David was not a Schindler but a Grunem, the son of a corn merchant named Mendel who had one squinty and one laughing eye, and his features were all a grimace and a wink. But even his father Mendel allowed his son to change his name from Grunem to Schindler, which was not customary for Jews, because he wanted with all his heart that his son not only become part of Mr. Schindler's dynasty, but also his heir. And if Mendel Grunem allowed his son to annex himself to his father-in-law, may his saintly memory be blessed, what would people say? As a matter of fact all their remarks stopped when Mendel, too, adopted the mannerisms of a wealthy man, wearing a velvet-lined coat and taking superior snuff from a solid silver snuffbox. This habit became so rooted in him that his mustache and fingers were stained with the brown juice whose smell is deep and intoxicating, and it delights the mind and strengthens the heart not only on Yom Kippur but every day of the year. He also began contributing generously to the synagogue, but on condition that he and his son be allotted seats among the wealthy, very close to the Ark, right in front of the Almighty and facing the large congregation so they would know who Mendel Grunem and his son are, the wealthy man who owned the third-largest bank in Danzig, whose brain is sharp and mind clear, who does business with the great and noble of the world.

Mr. Schindler was in full possession of his faculties when he died, and he inserted a clause in his will stipulating that after his death his bank would pass to his only daughter Tirzah, and to her alone, and only if his future son-in-law would prove talented in the money business and would climb the ladder rung by rung by dint of industriousness and diligence, only then would he have a part in the bank. But this part would never exceed one fifth of its value, and the remainder would be in the hands of his daughter in perpetuity for his future grandchildren, should he have any. And in any event, the bank would actually be managed by his good friend Advocate Citrin, but he too was placed under the supervision of a board of directors whose members would always include three of the leaders of the city committee.

When the spindly-legged young David Grunem was brought before Mr. Schindler, and his father stood there hat in hand, and in honeyed tones sought a position for him as a junior clerk in the bank, Mr. Schindler looked at him. Before him he saw a young man who had been raised in the home of a Jew and a merchant, for whom finance was no stranger and who would be like putty in his hands. He deigned to take him on, and over him placed one of his senior employees who would introduce him to the management of money, and would be strict with him.

David Grunem, whose legs were as spindly as two canes and whose chest hair was sparse, took his work seriously, and the more his hands came into contact with money his skinny body fleshed out and he became a human being. And he was so diligent and devoted to his work that he hardly raised his eyes from the bundles of banknotes, the promissory notes and interest calculations before him – except on one occasion. A young girl with beautiful eyes was standing in front of him, looking at him with her clear eyes. She was short in stature, but her features were beautiful and her curves peeked out from her neckline, and David Grunem, who since that one night with Leah Kochmann had never enjoyed the taste of a woman, felt his cheeks burning and his member swelling.

Then the loud voice of her father, Mr. Schindler, was heard calling her from his office, "Tirzah! Tirzah!"

The girl moved away from David Grunem, who sat there, his heart pounding wildly and his head whirling. But the father, who had come out of his office and was standing in the doorway, managed to see his daughter standing by the desk of David, the son of the corn merchant who was in financial difficulties.

The father stroked his daughter's head with his heavy hand on which he wore a big gold ring, and said, It's nice of you to visit your father in the middle of his day's work. And Tirzah's eyes were still locked onto that young man. And the father smiles to himself and thinks, Well, my daughter has found a worthy match by herself, and he made up his mind that from now on he would supervise this young man and make him truly worthy of her, not only in accordance with her heart, but also in his eyes, and more particularly, his wife's.

From that day forward fortune smiled on David. The owner of the bank in person took him to become his personal aide who accompanied him to all his meetings and on all his journeys, and learned from him everything he could. And to this end he summoned the merchant Mendel Grunem, gave him a large sum of money and told him, I have my eye on your son and am about to make him my personal aide. But, for God's sake, make sure he dresses like everyone else.

Mendel Grunem bowed, almost falling over with the pride that filled his heart and with the joy that his plan had succeeded even more than he had imagined it would, and hurried off with his son and bought him landowner's clothing, and even took him to a watchmaker's and bought him a gold watch and chain to put in his waistcoat pocket so that all the people of Danzig might see that he had no ordinary son, but the aide of a wealthy man. He also bought him a monocle, a false monocle with plain glass, so he could stick it into his eye very punctiliously as he counted stacks of money and wanted to strike terror into the hearts of the people standing trembling before him for a loan or to forfeit a pledge.

Mr. Schindler passed happily from this world, leaving to his son-in-law and trusted aide not only his daughter but also his home and bank, and he also managed to see the birth of his two grandsons, but not that of his granddaughter. And before he restored his soul to his Maker, he even managed to teach the eldest his Torah portion and attend his bar-mitzvah at the Great Synagogue of Danzig.

And why must all this be related if not to say that when Leah Kochmann reached the gate of David's house, an old woman who seemed like a walking vessel of pain, she knew nothing of all these momentous matters, only that he was the son of a corn merchant and had become a wealthy man in his own right, and here he is living in Altschottland, probably as gaunt and pallid as he was in his youth.

She stood at the front door and tugged the bell pull. A uniformed butler came out to her and inquired who she was and what she wanted. The gentleman of the house, she said, and he replied, He is not at home. He is at the bank on so-and-so street, and meanwhile she looked past him and saw that because of the sheer size of the house she couldn't see to the end.

Leah was fearful lest she had committed a solecism, but in her despair she told herself, What should I do if not this, and on tired legs she walked from street to street until she came to the Bank of Danzig, which then was located in a tall building, and she saw her reflection in the window, and she was exhausted by the walk and all the anguish that had recently beset her, so she primped her hair as best she could and walked into the bank, determined to meet the owner in person.

The clerks' eyes swiveled toward her as they wondered what she was doing there. Going by her simple attire and her face, which was the face of a poor woman, not a wealthy one, it was clear that she was unaccustomed to such places.

Leah plucked up her courage and went up to one of the clerks who was older than the rest and whose eyes were like those of a beaten dog, and asked him where she might find the owner of the bank, please.

The clerk looked at her and asked, And why might Madam need the owner of the bank?

"I have a gift for him," she replied.

The clerk told her to wait there and the servants would take it to him.

"No," she said, "the gift is big and heavy and I do not actually have it with me. I have to tell him about it and he will have to collect it himself."

The clerk stood up and offered her a seat. "Please sit here while I go to my master and see what he has to say."

Leah thanked him weakly and sat down, looking around at all the splendor of the world, at the room's wood-paneled walls, the large, heavy, hand-carved desks that smelt of a good woodworker, and suddenly she was flooded with yearning for her Leizer who had died and left her like this, alone, as a beggar.

The clerk went to his master and told him about the woman and her gift.

David Schindler followed the clerk to the door of his office, which had previously been his father-in-law's, to take a look at the woman, and after straining his eyes and his memory and realizing who she was, his face paled as the blood suddenly fled it.

He was assailed by such a weakness that the clerk had to help him back into his office. When he recovered he told the clerk, "Go and tell her I'm not here, that you mistakenly thought I was and I've gone to Brussels on business. Go, tell her whatever you wish, but get her out of here."

The clerk took fright and did his master's bidding, wondering who this woman was and what was her hold over his master.

Leah saw the deception in his expression, but thanked him and left the bank on trembling legs. She made up her mind to return day after day until she saw the young boy who had spilled his seed inside her, become a wealthy man, and now was chary of seeing her.

Day after day for two weeks she took herself to the Bank of Danzig, either before she opened her inn or after she closed it, went inside to the same clerk with the same request. The clerk, on his master's orders, would come back and turn her away. But after two weeks David Schindler's luck ran out when his faithful clerk was taken ill and did not report for work, and so Leah went inside and strode down the corridor right to Mr. Schindler's office, and surprised him where he sat filling his pipe after a hard day's work. David smoked a pipe before departing for home because his wife Tirzah detested the smell and he had promised her never to smoke in her company.

David Schindler saw who was standing before him, jumped up as if bitten by a snake, and quickly shut the door after her, hoping that no one had seen her come in.

"I've been knocking on your door for two weeks," Leah began, "aren't you ashamed in the slightest?"

"I'm a married man, with a bank and a wife and three children on my head. Why have you come to bother me?"

"A little courtesy wouldn't come amiss," Leah replied, and sat down. "Now sit down and listen to what I've come to tell you, and don't be frightened. I haven't come to threaten or disrespect you, but to ask for your help."

Leah told him what she told him.

He sat opposite her as pale as a corpse, his hands gripping his pipe so hard that he unintentionally broke it and cut his hand. Leah jumped up clutching a kerchief to help

228

him, but he shoved her back, took out a pocket handkerchief, and bound it around his finger until it stopped bleeding.

"She's not mine," he said, rejecting her story out of hand, "I was only a boy!"

"A boy a boy, but the father of a daughter!" Leah replied, raising her voice.

"She's not my daughter," he said, trying to sound restrained and calm, "I shall never acknowledge her as my daughter."

"But your daughter is a captive in the hands of criminals!" Leah cried.

David glanced at the heavy wooden door to make sure that no one could hear her cry. "Pardon me," he said purposefully, "but I must go home. My wife and children are waiting."

"You bastard," Leah hissed. "When you sprayed your seed into me you weren't as strong as you are now. But yours is a sham strength, Mr. Banker!"

"Are you threatening me? Go, go back to where you came from. Were it not for my father, may he rest in peace, I would never have seen you and I wouldn't have gotten myself into such trouble!" He suddenly realized what he had said, thought for a moment, and then said, "Now get out and never come back!"

Her rage boiled within her. In another moment she would have slapped this insolent gentleman, her daughter's father, who dared deny his paternity and was even ejecting her from his place of business. She got up, so angry and despairing she was unable to speak. "May fire rain down on you and consume you and your wife and your children," she cursed him, "may the torments of hell come down on you just like they did on me and my daughter if you don't know how to stand up like a man and face the fruit of your loins!"

She spat on the floor and left his office, with her look searing all the magnificence that surrounded him.

"Detestable witch," his lips murmured as she left the bank. But as he did he suddenly felt a giant's hand gripping his heart, and panting he clutched at his chest, his forehead sweating and his body shivering from cold and heat, and he fell convulsed to the ground. Not many minutes went by and the Angel of Death passed through Danzig and saw that all his bodily orifices were open from fright and fear, and he rubbed his hands, rejoicing that he had come to the premises of a wealthy man, and such a young one, and quickly snatched his soul.

David Schindler died in his prime from a heart attack that was both inexplicable and unexpected for any of his doctors or friends. He left a shocked widow and three weeping children in mourning in a great house in the Altschottland quarter, and a bank. But he also left another girl, she and her mother, who heard of his death and thought at that moment that her world, too, lay in ruins, for the wellspring of hope had dried up.

From that moment Leah's health deteriorated as well, and the old sickness that had lurked in her aging body for years, again attacked her with a vengeance.

Forty-two

Their isolation was intentional. Each of them found herself talking only with her sisters and Roja-Rosa, exchanging only a few words in Spanish or Yiddish with the men that came to them. Which is why it was so easy to control them.

They would meet in the big kitchen every morning, drink something and start cooking. At first each of them made what she had learned from her mother. Chicken soup and roast beef and *cholent*, *gribenes mit schmalz*, *mamaliga* and other delicacies. Later they learned from Roja-Rosa how to make *empenadas* and prepare meat for *asado*; how to make piquant *chimichurri* and kosher *chorizos*. When the siesta was over at four in the afternoon, they would report for the duty forced upon them, silencing their cries. It was their way of surviving the hurt, the exploitation, the destruction.

Esther was happy in the mornings which reminded her of her mother. She asked Roja-Rosa to show her how to make *empenadas*, and this request proved to Roja-Rosa that she was starting to get used to the house. But she made one stipulation: they would cook together in Spanish.

This girl hasn't been out of the house since she got here many months ago, thought Roja-Rosa. Buying ingredients for the *empanadas* would be a good excuse to take her out for a while, to walk among the passersby. She agreed what she agreed with Manuel, and next day woke Esther up earlier than usual and told her to put on something nice, because today we're going out.

Esther, of course, excitedly did what she was told.

When they left the house into Calle Junin the sky was painted in a clear, cold blue, and although there were some thick white rain clouds, the sunlight burst through them and played on their faces.

Esther looked around at the long street teeming with people. At this hour of the morning they were all on their way to work, and for the first time she was able to gain an impression of the tumult and hubbub of this city.

There were a number of houses similar to theirs in the street, which Rosa-Roja pointed out. From the window of one of them she saw a mournful-looking woman, who waved to her. She was like her. She could see it in her face.

231

Roja-Rosa grabbed her arm and scolded her. "What are you looking up for, look down, at the shops, the people."

"I am," Esther said, "I am."

"We're in Once now, the Jewish quarter," Roja-Rosa told her and pointed at the shops across the street. "All the shops here are Jewish-owned. Most of them deal in cloth. But there's also a butcher, a greengrocer, and a moneylender. We're going to the butcher's and the greengrocer's. We don't need the moneylender," she laughed.

They passed shops with bolts of cloth standing or lying in their windows, leaning against the frame. Brawny young men wearing yarmulkes were busy unloading new bolts from a tricycle standing outside one of the shops.

Jewish women, some wearing a head covering, went from shop to shop carrying their baskets. But not one looked at them. And when she looked at one of them, the woman immediately averted her eyes as if she were not there.

"That's the way they are," Rosa-Roja told her, "you'll get used to it."

"What's the matter with them?"

"For them we're unclean."

"Unclean?"

"It's what they call us. The Unclean."

Esther bowed her head. She had never thought of herself in those terms. She viewed herself as a young girl who had been abducted from her mother's house, a victim, not a collaborator. But she kept silent, knowing there was no point in saying anything.

Roja-Rosa led her toward the butcher's shop, but when she saw through the window a few women inside, she took Esther's arm and stopped her from going in. "It's better not to meet with Jews in these shops, it embarrasses the butcher."

They waited until the shop emptied and only then went inside.

"*Vus hertzach*, how's it going?" the butcher greeted them in Yiddish.

"*Muy bien*," Roja-Rosa replied intentionally in Spanish.

The butcher sharpened his knife on another one. "What would you like?"

"A kilo of ground beef for *empenadas*," Roja-Rosa replied, pointing at a cut of succulent beef in the window.

"*Esto es carne*, that's meat," she said to Esther, pointing at it. Then she pointed at the other kinds of meat hanging there: "*Pollo*, chicken, *carne de lomo*, fillet of beef."

"*Pollo, lomo*," Esther repeated.

After buying the meat they went and bought flour, raisins, pine nuts, and fruit. By the time they got back to Calle Junin Esther felt tired. Reality had assailed her with unfamiliar scenes and language, with unaccustomed names.

But when they reached the house and went into the big kitchen, her friends surrounded her with questions about where they had been and what they had done and how did it look.

She smiled tiredly and began telling them. About how they had been ignored in the street she was loath to talk. Why burden them with that as well, she thought.

Sometimes, when Manuel and Roja-Rosa were out in the city on various errands, either to arrange papers for one of the girls or to buy supplies, the girls would seize the opportunity of being on their own, put one of their favorite tango records on the gramophone in the corner of the room, open wide the windows to the yard, take each other's hand and dance.

These were rare moments of happiness for them. Not tangoing with men, when they had to please them with their nimbleness of foot and then with sex, but when they held each other in their arms, singing aloud in Yiddish, and together dancing the steps of the dance they loved so much.

The women neighbors would open their windows, spit and scream at them, and then slam the windows shut.

Most of them were religious and the habits of these girls seemed outlandish to them. A woman who plucks hair from her legs and removes her mustache? Whoever heard of such a thing? When they saw them wearing new clothes with wide-brimmed hats and small parasols, evening bags of fine leather, jewelry they would be given only to see and be seen in every evening – especially the one who accompanied Manuel to the theater or a café on those rare evenings he chose one to accompany him to where he met government officials and bohemians, military men and financiers – the neighbors would simply go out of their minds.

But what really drove them mad was hearing the tango.

Because the tango would always come together with songs in Yiddish, and the girls would dance together, singing their favorite songs, songs of longing and yearning, of compassion and sadness, in that tone that tore at the heartstrings of anyone hearing them. That drove them crazy.

So long as they were different women who dressed differently and behaved differently, they were able to stand them. But when the girls started singing in Yiddish, the neighbors realized that the difference between them was not all that great. Both, the girls and the neighbors, were traded against their will. But the girls had been raped on the boat and since then had been forced to have sex with strange men, while they, the women neighbors, were forced to have sex only with their husbands by virtue of their arranged marriage, and had to respect them as well.

It was during one of those hours that they were surprised by Miriam, who until then had been considered a quiet one, when she started singing her own words to one of the familiar tunes. The girls stopped in mid-dance and listened. She stood among them, her eyes closed, singing the heartbreaking words in her lovely voice, and as if in thrall to sadness they began swaying to the rhythm. Even Sophia, whose heart was already roughened by the scenes in the brothel, sang the words woven by Miriam from the depths of her grief. It was magical, arousing all the hurt in the heart and putting it into words and music.

A deep silence reigned in the yard when Manuel and Roja-Rosa came back. Each of the girls was busy with what she was doing, one doing laundry and another ironing, one cooking and another cleaning, one dusting the furniture in the lounge and another picking flowers in the garden, and none of them speaking to the other. Manuel and Roja-Rosa did not know that they were not silent at all, for they were quietly repeating the words of the melody composed for them by Miriam from within her broken heart, the heart of a rabbi's daughter who had fallen into the clutches of a pimp.

It happened a few days later that one of the girls started singing the words quite unintentionally in the evening, when the lounge was full of clients. The tune was drowned out by the voices of the chatting men, but when the rest of the girls heard what she was singing they joined in. They sang the words of this song in the arms of the men they were dancing with, but instead of casting the girls from their arms and going back to their places, the men grasped them even tighter as if the song reminded them of their home and past. Afterwards they stood and applauded and asked Manuel to tell his girls to repeat their song again and again. And Manuel, who was also deeply affected by the words of the song whose tune he knew but whose words were unfamiliar, told them to stand together and sing their song, and he saw how it filled the hearts of the men with such imagined compassion that he immediately realized he had a business opportunity on his hands.

When the clients had gone, Manuel sat the girls down and asked them, gently and candidly, where the song was from. They looked at one another, not knowing what to say, until they saw Miriam nodding slightly.

"You've got a poet here," Sophia, the most authoritative of them all told him, pointing at Miriam.

"Her? Her of all people?" Manuel asked wonderingly, looking at the girl he had picked up on the road near Lublin, the quiet, black-haired one with the beautiful but sad face. She's as silent as a pickled herring, one of the clients had complained to him, and now she had suddenly revealed such a talent.

Manuel asked Miriam to write words to other tunes for the clients. Later, he told all the girls that from now on they would sing for the clients every evening, to touch their hearts, as he put it. Only then he felt his stomach grumbling and remembered that he hadn't eaten since he got back from his engagements.

"Roja-Rosa," he called, "what have you made today?"

A few minutes later she was at his table holding platters, signaling to the girls with her eyes that they should let the boss eat in peace. He tore the bread with his thick fingers, ate, and stared at his plate, still hearing the words of the song as they aroused in him memories of his childhood in the small town. A good deal, he mused as he swallowed spoonful after spoonful of the scalding soup. This will be the only house in town where the women dance *and* sing. Now we'll see Angel and all the other brothel keepers talking, he sighed with pleasure, either from the soup or his thoughts, and then decided to go a step further and replace the gramophone music with a live trio. That would be the best. The girls singing, the musicians playing and attracting ever-increasing numbers of clients.

Warm-eyed, Roja-Rosa listened to him and nodded smilingly.

A few days later the atmosphere of the house was changed. Now the girls sang as they danced with the clients, while three Jewish musicians, refugees happy to earn a little money every evening, played the tunes they had recently learned, happy tunes that were different from the old Yiddish songs they knew, in the unique tango rhythm that bewitched and captivated all its listeners, enabling them to draw out the notes so as to pluck at the heartstrings with longing and yearning for things that once were and are now no more. But the eye follows the ear and arouses the heart, and the soul goes out to it, to the chorus: I had a girl, so beautiful with eyes all lashes, I had a girl, her body all flowers, and her smile my heart dashes.

Miriam's face was lined with the hunger she had experienced in her youth, but it was still long and lovely. She was dazzled by strong sunlight, and sometimes at night was assailed by a fever. But her brain was sharp and her mind was like an open law book.

This quality frequently led the girls to share their problems with her, whether they be about an item of clothing that two of them claimed was theirs, or because of a gift that a wealthy, satisfied client had left for one of them, while another claimed ownership of it. There was something in her character, in her ability to see things rationally, to weigh desire against desire, wish against wish, and decide one way or the other, and usually wisely and intelligently, that led the girls to seek her counsel in every quarrel and dispute. Sophia did not like this. She was particularly irked that this weakling, who on her first day had committed the most considered act and slashed her wrists so she almost died, was now assuming a highly respected role in the house, while she was even unable to do the sex act properly, just lying beneath the clients like a log, without a sound, so that they quickly reached their climax and hid from her withering gaze. The rabbi's daughter, as the clients called her, simply terrified them.

Sophia was also enraged by Miriam's tendency to fall pregnant, since again and again she was smitten with unwanted pregnancies, avoiding work with her nausea and physical pain, causing Manuel and Roja-Rosa to rush the Indian woman to her, a healer in times of trouble who worked in the street at the time, to scrape yet another unwanted baby from her womb. It was inconceivable that the many clients her singing brought in should fall on her sisters, while she pretended she easily became pregnant but simply forgot or avoided putting a *preservativo* on her men. This is what Sophia thought as she looked at the skinny rabbi's daughter who composed her songs and fetuses to avoid the fate shared by everyone here.

Sophia's loathing of Miriam was most apparent when they were alone in the house, when Manuel was at Association meetings and Roja-Rosa was out shopping. Sophia would find all manner of pretexts to plague this rabbi's daughter who had two left hands, but whose mouth was full of words.

And so it was one morning as they were hanging out their washing, and Miriam's, who was on the top floor above Sophia, started dripping onto her washing which was already nearly dry.

"Look at where your drawers are dripping, you swine!" Sophia yelled from her window.

"You're so bitter that your mouth is as black as a sack of tar," Miriam replied.

"If I'm a sack of tar, you're a sack of babies, you filthy cow," Sophia screamed, causing the neighbors' heads to pop out of their windows, accompanying this dialogue with their spitting.

"Even germs are scared of lying between your legs, bitch," Miriam called down.

Esther came into the room and swiftly pulled Miriam away from the window. "Are you crazy? Why are you even answering her?"

Sophia stood in the window smoking, as if victorious. Let the neighbors see who has more power and seniority in this house. Bitches. At the same time Esther was trying to comprehend what had happened to Miriam, whose self-restraint was well known.

"That jealous cow is doing everything she can against me," Miriam told her.

"Let her do whatever she wants," Esther said. "Why do you need this quarreling? It can only harm you!"

"What can they do to me? Put me up for auction at the Hotel Palestina and sell me to another brothel keeper?"

"It's not worth it. You don't want to go to a house that's even worse than this one."

"Nothing's worse," Miriam retorted, "they're all the same."

"You get special attention here," Esther said in a softer tone, "anywhere else you'll be just a piece of meat."

Miriam pinched her breasts and cheeks whose skin was lax and tired. "Look at this body."

"With a little effort you too can look different," Esther smiled, and took her friend to her room where she applied to her face the green avocado cream she had mixed on Roja-Rosa's advice, to protect and preserve her skin.

Miriam sat in front of the mirror, horrified by her green face.

"Do you want some on your arms and body too?" Esther asked her.

"Heaven forbid. I look like a monster as it is. All I need is for Sophia to come in now."

"She uses it too," Esther told her, "but in her case it doesn't help."

They laughed coquettishly and carried on talking. There was a special closeness between them since they had been on the same boat and married the same man, they had both been raped by the same bestial sailors, and both had been chosen by the same man to work in his brothel, and not be sold.

Only one thing separated them, she thought, and Miriam knows nothing about it. Until now she had completely concealed it. But now she felt that a special closeness had been formed with Miriam, and she wanted to share her secret with her.

"I've got something to show you," she said, going to the wardrobe and from the bottom taking out a small square wooden box that she placed in front of Miriam.

"What is it?" Miriam asked, not daring to open the closed box.

"Open it and look."

Miriam opened the old jewelry box. On its deep blue velvet lining lay a ring that sparkled with an odd light, effervescent in a kind of vitality.

"What is it?"

"My mother's wedding ring," Esther replied, carefully taking out the ring that sparkled with a light she had never seen before. "Look at how it's flashing. Something bad is happening."

"What are you doing with your mother's wedding ring?" Miriam asked.

"She hid in the things she got ready for the journey," Esther replied, looking fearfully at the ring that seemed like a spring of blood. "Something's wrong."

Miriam gestured to her to replace the ring in its box and she closed the lid. "It's only a ring."

"No, it's not," Esther replied, shaking her head, and then sat down and related the tale of the ring to Miriam, seeing how her eyes widened in terror and wonderment.

Since she had been brought up to keep away from anything smacking of the arcane, because of the Four Who Entered the Pardes and so on, and because she didn't want to believe in the existence of lofty forces over which humans have no control, Miriam preferred living in the visible world, even when it embittered the soul like their present world. But without doubt this object possessed a special quality.

"Maybe you should tell Roja-Rosa or Manuel about it?" she asked, feeling a strange tiredness descending on her and her eyelids becoming heavy as if seeking to lead her into the worlds of dreams, the worlds of the past.

"All I need is for them to know," Esther replied, horrified. "They'll take it right away."

"It's dangerous," Miriam murmured, amazed by the power of the ring's influence.

"It's all I have left from my mother," Esther whispered, stroking the box with her fingers, feeling the ring's warmth passing through the wood and into them.

Miriam closed her eyes and began murmuring unclear words that slowly took on the form of a song. It was beautiful and sorrowful, the song of the ring. Except for her and Esther, no one knew for whom it was sung, who the girl with the ring was. But the song was etched upon the heart of anyone hearing it afterward, and so it passed from house to house and person to person until it became one of Buenos Aires's most loved songs, and from there it sailed to distant lands.

If you wish to weep, then listen
To the story of Nina, daughter of a rabbi old,
One day a stranger came and gave her
A stone mounted on a ring of gold.

Body and soul she followed him,
Innocent was she, and not old.

He dragged her down into the filth
And gave her up to be sold.

Nina, Nina, where are you, still a child at most,
You who knew not the taste of a man,
You became a kind of ghost.

Day after day she labored hard and long
And became a famous lady,
Everyone in the city knew her
And called her 'Red Nina'.

Until one day that selfsame ring
Her heart it filled with rage aroil,
With a knife she cut his head off
And buried it deep in the soil.

Nina, Nina, what have you done, still a child at most,
You who knew not the taste of a man,
You became a kind of ghost.

To the jail she was taken away,
Manacled both hand and foot,
But then she tore out both her eyes
Leaving only two black holes.

And since that day the ring it glows
Before the eyes of the rabbi's daughter, the blinded whore,
And from the darkness again emerges
The face of the man who loved her.

Nina, Nina, what have you done, you woman-ghost,
Inside your two eyes there you lie,
As in the grave, alone.

Rabbi Hirsch heard this song on his first visit to Manuel Zind's brothel, and it immediately captured his attention. At first he didn't understand why. The girls there sang various songs about their bitter fate, dancing with the men as if they were not weeping for themselves, carried away by the rhythm of the music, tapping their feet here and there on the tiles. Of all their songs, why did this one catch his attention? But after hearing it again and again, he felt his heart bound up with the character of the rabbi's daughter who had become a whore and a murderer. He was so attracted by the beauty of the women here that he did not realize that the song was about a ring with the power to cause terror and rage.

Forty-three

When Esther's letter reached Gershon Bergman he didn't know what to do about it. He read and reread it, wondering how he might deal with the story it contained. First, he thought, it is not certain that this is a collective story. Perhaps it's just the little story of one or two girls. Second, should what the letter contains prove to be true he would be unable to rectify it on his own. But he made some discreet inquiries among his diplomat friends, especially the Swiss consul with whom he was on particularly good terms, and discovered the full picture. Buenos Aires and neighboring Montevideo had become centers of white slavery through which numerous Jewish women passed. The traders, all of them Jews, went to Vienna, Budapest, and Danzig, from where they brought women and sent them by sea to every part of the globe.

Vienna was an international center of white slavery. There were hundreds of agencies in the city whose purpose was to take women under various pretexts and enslave and trade in them with brothels throughout the world. The Jewish traders did not stop at women from Bohemia and Hungary but sent out their tentacles to Jewish women from Russia, the Caucasus, Kiev and Petrov, and the Polish cities of Warsaw and Kalisch. And these unfortunate women were sent not only to Buenos Aires, but also to Alexandria in Egypt, to which traders came to purchase them for brothels in Cape Town and even in India and China.

This picture made him shudder so violently that he immediately wrote to Baron Hirsch and related the scope of this phenomenon.

On receiving the letter Moritz Hirsch was shocked. A short time later he began financing the *Ezrat Nashim* (Women's Aid) society in London, whose aim was to fight white slavery. At the same time the Jewish Colonization Association people, including Gershon Bergman, established a branch in Buenos Aires so that these women would have somewhere close to turn to.

Meanwhile, the press began publishing reports on the phenomenon, and the Jewish community, which until then had done nothing more than call the pimps and their women "unclean", was now unable to ignore the scope of what was going on.

So long as they were shut up in their houses, the women could only hear about what was going on through the rumors and stories circulating about the power of 'The Association'. The brothel keepers made sure that their women heard stories about girls who had tried to escape from one house or another, were caught by the police, and because of the Association's close ties with them in various districts, were returned to the men from whom they had escaped. They were then punished by being put up for auction. They were forcibly stripped and paraded on a platform, naked as the day they were born, before an audience of white slave traders and *porteras*, policemen and government officials, who were there to enjoy the show. Roja-Rosa told the girls this story, either because she had been so shocked to see it with her own eyes, or because she knew that this way she would banish any thought of escape they might harbor.

When did the girls of this house hear about the fate of the girls from another house, and the proliferation of the city's brothels? Mainly in the evening, when Manuel, like any brothel keeper worthy of the name, chose a woman who had proved her diligence and loyalty to the business, and who looked good, to accompany him to a café or the theater. The Excelsior, Ombu, Soleil, and Nuevo Mitra, the city's numerous Jewish theaters were all very active and hosted theater companies that traveled between the provinces and the capital. The most glittering evenings were those on which the theaters hosted the stars of Jewish theater from Europe. All the girls wanted to attend them. If they didn't sing songs from their countries of origin there, in their mother tongue, then at least they would be able to see and be seen among the who's who of the city's high society.

Each time, Manuel and Roja-Rosa chose one of the girls to go to the theater, either to attract new clients or to give them all some small sense of life. Manuel never took the new girls lest they try and escape into the crowd. The more senior girls won this honor and they would come back and relate what they had seen, what had happened, how the audience was dressed, and how they were treated.

Among the old hands was Flory, Manuel's preferred companion because of her laughter and abundant physical attributes that were clearly evident under her dress. She went to the theater most frequently, and on her return her face was always suffused with enthusiasm.

"The women were dressed as if for a wedding," she would say, "in skirts and a wrap and a modern hat, or in dark, lace-trimmed evening dresses. They were all wearing expensive jewelry. And the men in suits and black bow ties. And there were even some older women in tight-fitting dresses over their fat bodies and a little mustache, and there were a lot of children too, in black suits and berets, and Bertha Gerstein looked like the daughter of God onstage. And she was followed by Marie Karsin with her angelic voice who answered her, and then came Ben-Zion Vitler who sang in such a strong voice that it broke your heart, and even the men in the audience wept." And so on and so forth, going into the minutiae of what went on and who was there, and how, every time a latecomer entered the hall, all the heads swiveled from the stage to the door to see who it was, what he was wearing and where he sat, for the real stars were always the people in the hall, not the ones onstage.

From the stories of the girls chosen to accompany Manuel, the others discovered that there were not only plays but also music recitals at which funds were raised for building the community's educational and charitable institutions, which is why it was important for the brothel keepers to be there and be among the donors.

One evening, a short time after leaving the house, Manuel and Flory came back, their expression bleak. Roja-Rosa opened the door and on seeing them return so early, immediately asked what had happened. Manuel mumbled something and went to the bar. Roja-Rosa made to follow him, but Flory stopped her and told her to be careful. He's very angry about what happened to us. Leave him to have a drink until he cools off.

"What happened?" Roja-Rosa asked. "What can possibly happen at the theater?"

All the girls gathered round to hear what Flory had to say. She sat down, untied the ribbon under her chin, flung her hat away, and burst into tears.

"They were standing outside with placards and drove us away."

"Who's 'they'?" Roja-Rosa shouted. "Who dared do such a thing?"

"The socialists," Flory mumbled, "the workers from Zalman Sorkin's organization were standing there with placards saying 'Rufianes Out!' and they wouldn't let us into the theater!"

"Only you? Only you and Manuel?"

"All of us," Flory sobbed, "all the owners of the houses with their women. Angel, Noé Traumann, they threw us all out!"

"It's hardly surprising," Sophia interjected, "they call us unclean. It had to happen sometime."

"All their women must have seen it," Roja-Rosa murmured, "all those envious women neighbors, and their husbands who come here looking for a woman at night."

"And not one person took our side. They all stood there shouting 'Rufianes Out! 'Rufianes Out!' I was so ashamed!"

"Enough!" Manuel's loud voice was suddenly heard as he came in, his face flushed with drink and rage. "Haven't you got anything to do but sit here gossiping?"

"I'm sorry," Roja-Rosa said, signaling the girls to disperse.

"They'll regret this," Manuel said. "Everything they don't give us, we'll do better. Don't worry," he said to the girls, "we'll have a better theater, with better actors and singers than theirs, you'll see."

He took another big swallow of his vodka and told Roja-Rosa that he was going to meet the other men to discuss the situation. He put on his coat, took his revolver, and left, leaving them all astounded.

Forty-four

The scene at the theater was a turning point in the Jews' attitude toward them. But the *rufianes* knew nothing of this until Yom Kippur, when it became abundantly clear.

It was on that day that all the brothel keepers agreed to go – each with his wife and children – to the Sephardi synagogue to hear the blowing of the *shofar* and pray to God like any other Jew. This was self-evident to them: a Jew is a Jew in any circumstances, even a Jew who does work like theirs has a Jewish heart and soul. And like every Jew, Manuel and Angel and Noé and all the rest, and their wives of course, wanted to have a small taste of the Day of Awe. All dressed in white for purity, wearing a prayer shawl and carrying a prayer book they walk to the synagogue, attend the Yom Kippur Eve service, hear the voice of the cantor raised in supplication, and feel that heaven opens before them and God welcomes them all willingly and mercifully, each person with what he has done and will do, for they are all Jews and they are all His children.

For the girls this was a special occasion. Yom Kippur was the only day of the year when they did not have to work. All the feverish preparations were completed by Yom Kippur Eve – the white dresses, kerchiefs, scarves, hats and prayer books, which Manuel bought at a religious bookshop in Once and brought to the house. Each woman wrote her name in her prayer book. Of all of them, Miriam was the most excited, for since she left her parents' home she had not had the opportunity of holding a prayer book and attending a synagogue.

With the advent of Yom Kippur peace descended on the whole house. The girls sat down with Manuel to eat the pre-fast meal, and they went to their rooms to dress. As evening fell, a line of horse-drawn carriages was already waiting outside, which Manuel had booked to take them all in a fitting manner, like real ladies, to the new Sephardi synagogue on Calle Camargo.

As Manuel's carriages drew up outside the synagogue there were other carriages already standing there. The major brothel keepers had gone a step further and hired two or three *colectivos* so there would be enough room for all their women. It was only then, with each of the women sitting in her carriage and seeing more and more carriages gathering in the square fronting the synagogue, each one carrying men and women and

246

children in their festive attire, that they suddenly understood the true, vast scope of the Association, and the size of the other brothels spread throughout the city. It was amazing. Several hundred men, women, and children, all dressed in white, standing in front of the two-storied synagogue with its magnificent dome, its long windows decorated with beautiful stone arches, and above the ground floor windows, two stars that looked like Stars of David.

"This is nothing," Manuel whispered excitedly to Roja-Rosa, "wait till you see the magnificence inside. How beautiful the Ark is, with a *menorah* on each side and gold inscriptions around it."

The synagogue door suddenly opened, and from it peeped the sparsely-haired head of a rat-faced man. He looked here and there, scanning the large crowd with his tiny, darting eyes, and then opened his mouth and started shouting, "*Los impuros! Los impuros!*", and then withdrew his head, slamming the wooden door behind him.

A few moments later a great commotion was heard from inside the synagogue. The door was opened wide, and a crowd of men, women, and children, all in their finest attire and ready to begin the Yom Kippur evening service, came out roaring wrathfully, "Rufianes Out!"

They stood there, defending the synagogue door with their bodies, their faces alight with holy wrath as if the men and women from the brothels had come to defile or loot the source of their sanctity.

Noé Trauman came out to stand in front of the crowd. Of short stature and sickly-looking, but dressed like a landowner, wearing a striking, gold-embroidered prayer shawl and holding a beautiful blue velvet phylacteries bag and a thick prayer book, he looked like a rabbi or cantor.

"We are all Jews! We all worship the same God!" he shouted at the roaring crowd. His voice was drowned by the wrathful chanting of "Rufianes Out! Rufianes Out!" that came not only from the men, but also the women who waved their fans and hats, and from the children, even the children.

A gunshot was suddenly heard.

The crowd was silenced as if God in person had descended from heaven in a chariot of fire.

Eyes darted here and there to locate the shooter, and then they lit on Angel standing by his carriages and women, blowing into the barrel of his revolver and then sticking it back into his waistband.

"Now talk," he told Noé Trauman, who nodded irritably, cursing this idiot who had come to the synagogue carrying a gun on Yom Kippur Eve.

But this was not the time to talk to Angel and rebuke him for his action. The atmosphere was so tense it could have been cut with a knife.

"Your God is our God. Your place of worship is ours. Your Yom Kippur is our Yom Kippur. We want to worship, to be Jews like any other Jew, that's all," he said, trying to persuade them.

The crowd suddenly parted, and from it stepped a tall bearded man in a black top hat, and dressed in a dark, beautifully tailored suit. He looked like a wealthy company owner or an esteemed philosopher. His eyes were sunken from anguish and study, and his ears protruded from his red side whiskers.

"You have no place here," Rabbi Halperin thundered, "you have no place amid this pure host!"

"Rabbi..." Noé Trauman began, trying to reason with him, but his voice was immediately drowned out by the shouts of the angry crowd, reveling in the blood, the insult, "Rufianes Out! Rufianes Out!" they shouted as if at a mass exorcism.

Noé turned on his heel, his face filled with disappointment and pain. He looked at the other men, each with his women by their carriages, and flicked his eyes. They all exchanged glances, and then, as if by common consent, they gathered their women and got back into their carriages.

"Where to?" Manuel asked Noé.

"I've no idea," he replied, "let's just get away from here."

"Come to my place," Manuel said in a spur of the moment decision, "everybody."

"To Calle Junin!" Noé Trauman called from carriage to carriage, "to Manuel's!"

Some of the men looked at him, disgruntled. In comparison with them, each of whom had seventy or eighty women, Manuel owned only a small house with only ten. But at that moment there was no point in having a prolonged discussion about where to go for Yom Kippur, so they drove off in a long column, a column of outcasts, to Manuel's house, accompanied by shouts of joy and exultation from the synagogue congregation that was still standing and shouting "Rufianes Out! Rufianes Out!" until the last of carriages disappeared from sight.

Manuel sat in his carriage feeling his heart torn apart with shame, pain and anger. That a Jew should do something like this to a Jew, stand there and drive him away in front of all the men and women gathered there, before God whom they all feared, God who hears the prayers of all and the suffering of all and the sins of all, and always forgives, that a Jew should do something like that to another Jew outside the House of God? Even God knows that even the filthiest man in Buenos Aires possesses a Jewish heart and a Jewish soul, and what's so terrible if a Jew does a favor for another Jew, travels abroad and brings him the most beautiful women, and at his expense brings them here and teaches them to be good to men hungry for a woman, and makes sure they're clean and healthy, for that they should be grateful, not drive him away from the House of God on the holiest day of the year, and shame him in front of everybody as if he were a gentile or unclean.

We'll show them yet, he thought, proud of his swift decision to invite them all to his house. We'll arrange chairs in the big room and worship on our own. He suddenly remembered that he had neither a Torah scroll nor a *shofar*, and Yom Kippur without them is not Yom Kippur.

An idea flashed through his mind. He stopped his carriage abruptly next to the carriage of his neighbor and rival up to that day. Angel heard the squeal of brakes and immediately halted his own carriage, looking tensely at his rival.

"What?" he asked through the window.

"We haven't got a Torah scroll or a *shofar*!" Manuel called.

His neighbor looked at him for a moment through half-closed eyes, and then a smile spread over his thin lips. "Don't worry," he said. "Go back to your house. You'll have everything you need right away!"

He sped off in his carriage, causing all the men and women in the column to look after him in wonderment. Why is he driving through the city streets like Jehu a moment before Yom Kippur Eve?

The carriages arrived one after the other at Manuel's house. The passengers alighted slowly, gathering and pushing through the narrow gate to the yard, filling the spacious patio and the big rooms with a flood of white finery, the women scanning the house for this was the first time they had seen one other than their own, and Manuel's girls greeted them with welcoming shouts and gesturing at their house with great pride.

No more than forty minutes later Angel burst in, his face flushed and his eyes flashing. He made his way between the guests wrapped in a splendid prayer shawl, his gun in one hand and the tail of a *shofar* in the other, and both arms embracing a large, splendid Torah scroll, complete with a crown.

"Where did you get that?" the men asked, swiftly helping him to put the scroll down lest it fall.

"What you can't get with brains you get with brawn," he winked. "From a ritual objects shop in Once."

The men went into the big rooms that opened up into one another, and helped arrange the chairs and couches in rows facing east. In front they placed a fine table over which Roja-Rosa quickly spread a Sabbath tablecloth. On the table they carefully placed the Holy Torah, and then stood back and regarded their improvised synagogue with satisfaction.

"Everybody, please come inside," Noé Traumann called from the table, and banged on it in the manner of a synagogue cantor, as if this were his longtime occupation. "The service is starting!"

The men, women, and children crowded into the big room, some standing and others sitting facing Noé Traumann. He opened the prayer book and began praying aloud. Noé left the blowing of the *shofar* to Angel, to honor him with the inauguration of the ram's horn he had brought, and when the time came Angel stood beside him and blew it, filling the whole house with the sounds of *teruah* and *shevarim*, as if the voice of God were bursting through the walls, the ceiling, and echoing back to the congregation.

That was the first time that all the members of the Association had gathered under one roof. The righteous of Buenos Aires had cast them out of their synagogue, but instead of harming them, they had brought them together through the potent force of insult.

It was only after Yom Kippur that it emerged that in those precious moments before the inauguration of the festival, Angel had hurried to the ritual objects shop in Once, smashed the display window to smithereens with the butt of his revolver, taken the Torah scroll, the *shofar*, and the prayer shawl, and left the owner a wad of banknotes on his table, with a note saying, "This is for the Torah scroll, the *shofar*, the prayer shawl, and the broken window. Happy New Year, The Unclean". Thus he signed it, celebrating his brilliant triumph.

The service on Yom Kippur Eve marked the beginning of the synagogue of The Unclean, their cemeteries, and the other institutions they established to provide themselves with a Jewish life to replace the one so shamefully stolen from them. After that Yom Kippur they also decided to accelerate the establishment of the Association's club.

A short time afterward they purchased a two-story building on Calle Cordoba, and in a few stormy meetings decided on its interior design. The first floor would accommodate a synagogue, a ritual bath, an assembly room, and a conference room. On the second floor would be another large meeting room, a dining room, and the Association's office. They left the big garden around the house as it was, but extended the patio abutting it and planted tall, striking palm trees around it, which climbed far above the roof and the wall surrounding the yard.

All the Association's members took part in this enterprise. Each of them sought to outdo his partners in the building of the holy site. Each member wanted his contribution, be it money or various objects, to surpass that of his colleague, as if its size attested to his wealth and power. Manuel opened a donation ledger and began recording everything received for the building, especially the synagogue, which attracted most of the donations. Simon Briel donated a chandelier for the meeting room. Hermann Dreimann – a chandelier for the women's bathroom. Hermann Rathmann hauled in chairs and armchairs for the lounge, and Feivel Berliner donated six cast bronze arms for the assembly room. Hersh Kopelevich gave two columns to the synagogue, and Jose Cohen – wooden tables, an oriental stove and two oriental bronze vases. Abraham Marchik brought a mirror for the salon and a table for the synagogue, and Leon Schmaltzman – a bed and a mirror. Alberto Levi donated three bronze arms, and to his original donation Herman Dreimann added an oak chest for the Association's ballot box. Señor Rosmarin donated a fine velvet sheath embroidered with gold for the Torah scroll, and Selig Rabinesh gave some Bibles. Moshe Pariser also donated Bibles, as did Hermann

Rosenthal. Blaustein donated three comprehensive prayer books, and Señor Gaier followed suit, but with one book. David Brotstein donated a wooden dais, and Federico Gluck – the women's section balcony and balustrade. Thus they all felt that they were partners in this great enterprise, the establishment of the synagogue of The Unclean.

At the conclusion of the building, all the donors gathered in the synagogue to view the results of their labors, and their hearts were filled with pride.

"But the more they afflicted them, the more they multiplied," Moshe Pariser said, quoting the Bible, drawing a burst of laughter from the others.

"We should drink a toast," said Federico Gluck.

"A synagogue is inaugurated by circuiting it carrying the Torah, not with wine," retorted Noé Traumann, who was already very ill and could barely stand.

His words made Angel's eyes light up. "Just imagine what the leaders of the community will say when they see us in front of the synagogue, dancing with the Torah scrolls!" he exulted.

That week the houses were all busy preparing for the Sabbath. Each of the women laid out for herself and her children, if she had any, new clothes and head coverings. On Saturday morning numerous carriages gathered from all parts of the city, including those of the members of the Association, their women and children, the men in suits and hats and carrying guns, and the women in their fine dresses.

Noé Traumann came out of the synagogue and stood, solemn yet emotional, before its door, waiting for silence from the crowd. He began speaking and congratulated the Association's members on this great day. He then invited Manuel to join him, who read the names of the donors to the synagogue and their contribution. One by one the donors were called to enter the synagogue, and then came out again carrying the Torah scrolls in their velvet sheaths and topped with their crowns, each of them clutching his scroll as if it were a beloved woman.

Noé Traumann, the rabbi, the beadle, and the cantor he had hired stood before them, and behind them the congregation. The cantor began intoning the blessings, and then Sabbath songs, and the entire congregation repeated his words, circuiting the synagogue seven times, exulting and singing, their faces alight with sanctity, drawing looks from passersby who from the street observed this strange ceremony the Jews were holding for their new house.

Word of the ceremony reached the Jewish community's Sephardi synagogue during the morning service. Between the morning and evening services, while on their way home, many of them passed the new synagogue, looked on hostilely and angrily and spat and cursed. They did not dare approach because of the policemen hired by the Association who encircled the crowd gathered in front of the synagogue.

The opening of this synagogue appalled the members of the community and they began spreading rumors that Black Masses were being held there involving rituals associated with devil worship, which also included sexual acts. There was no truth in these rumors. The synagogue was on the ground floor of the building that also had a floor for social events where the Association's parties were held. Over all the years the Association was active, services were held in the synagogue on Sabbath and festival eves as were marriages and circumcision ceremonies, and even bar-mitzvah ceremonies for the Association's children. But when they had parties with music and dancing, wine and sex, the members locked the synagogue door in order not to mix sacred and profane, and it was as if they were hiding God inside.

Forty-five

Since hearing that her only hope, David Schindler who had married into the Grunem family, had died and she could see no other salvation, Leah's condition deteriorated. Instead of listening to the advice of the old gravedigger of Danzig that she devote herself to her labors and try and forget her troubles, she stopped cooking her delicacies in her inn and allowed the demon within her soul to talk to her. After all, what had she got out of all the years of hard work in the sweltering kitchen? She did not even have enough money to travel to rescue her daughter. It would be better were she to go back to what her husband had taken her from, since only in that profession would she be able to save enough money to travel from here to Argentina, knock on that contemptible villain's door and redeem her daughter from him.

One day she got up and got rid of all the tables and chairs from the inn, and placed a splendid canopied bed in the empty room. She returned to her place of business only late at night, made-up and titivated. She did this with a heavy heart. But once she had made up her mind to take action she recalled all the secrets of this profession she had learned long ago: suggestive lighting, the figure of a luscious woman in the dimness of a house, a crimson dress setting off the fleshly delights. That was enough to attract weary seafarers hungry for congress who disembarked from the cargo ships at night.

And they came to her. Only a few at first, reeling before her semi-illuminated figure in the dark street of the port, and then the rumor spread that the most experienced whore in Danzig was back in business, and what she knows about cooking with her pots and pans is nothing compared with what she does between her sheets.

Leah did her utmost so that her daytime occupation's neighbors knew nothing of her nocturnal activities. But one night a dark-skinned sailor, a real brute, visited the inn. He pounded her flesh for a long time until suddenly he felt a convulsing body beneath him, took fright and got up in the dark, and by the light of a match he struck discovered her laying there, her tongue fluttering in her mouth, froth drooling from her lips, her eyes rolled back in their sockets.

The sailor ran out, his insides turning over, and vomited his guts up at the corner of the street. Then he fled, horrified, without looking back and without saying a word to anyone about what had happened.

And that evening was the termination of the Yom Kippur fast of 1895, the same Yom Kippur of degradation and revival in the house of Manuel in Buenos Aires.

Forty-six

The moment she left her body, which was convulsing uncontrollably beneath her, she was quite alarmed; it was as if she could suddenly see her kitchen and her brothel spread below her, and she did not understand what had happened to her or even feel the weight of her body at all, but quite the opposite, she was as light as a feather, like a wavelet released from the breaker it was part of, a huge wave like a blue ringlet, and suddenly the wave was gone and she was free to discover that she was only a piece of flotsam, only a movement on the water and its waves. Thus she saw herself from above, and suddenly she felt a chilly, pleasant wind blowing through her kitchen door and calling her to rise and curl up upon it.

She gave herself up to this wind that was not from the sea, but a similitude of a wind that had come solely to take her away from there, and rode on it until she entered total darkness. Filled with wonder and awe she flew, as if in a tunnel of darkness, until at its end she saw an illuminated opening coming ever closer, and on its threshold her relatives and loved ones were waiting to accompany her. She recognized her Leizer's face, and those of her parents, her father and mother who had died when she was still in her infancy, yet it was not their faces she saw but the memory of them that still gripped her. They held out their hands into the tunnel and plucked her out, took her and with her began flying ever upward into the azure sky, into a brilliance that came from the firmament and illuminated the first hall of the next world.

She saw that she was flying weightlessly with her relatives holding her hands, and only then realized what had happened to her and was alarmed. What will I do now, she asked, how can I save my daughter Esther now I have died before my time and my body is no longer mine to come to her aid?

She immediately heard a voice from within her, like the voice of a mother, saying. Oh, Leah'leh, Leah, what you sought to achieve with your tortured body you can now achieve with a vengeance.

How, she asked herself.

The inner voice answered her, You are bodiless and can come and go wherever you please.

If so, she replied, I would like to go beyond the sea, directly to Argentina, to Buenos Aires, to the house at 322 Junin Street where my daughter is being held and from where I received her letter to me.

She had hardly finished uttering the words and she was on her way. Within a single moment she traversed continents and seas, ships and ports, cities and villages, wide boulevards, and suddenly found herself in a narrow candle-lit room. In it there is a bed, and on it lay a beautiful young woman. Her hair is combed back and her eyes are soft and clear. A beautiful dress adorns her body. She is Esther. She is her daughter.

Her excitement was so great that she flew right into the flame of the candle on her daughter's small table and extinguished it with her wings.

Esther leapt out of bed feeling a shudder run down her spine, not knowing that the presence of a dead person had caused it. She took a box of matches and went to relight the candle. She struck a match, held its burning head to the wick and lit it, looking around her, wondering, sensing the presence of someone else in the room, but after peering here and there she could see that the door and window were closed and there was no vestige of wind in the room.

So how was the candle blown out, she wondered.

As she looked around, her mother's soul moved joyously around the room at seeing her daughter, whose face was lovely and her body beautiful and her cheeks a healthy pink. But only in her eyes, oh, her eyes, there was that familiar age-old sadness, the sadness of women whose spirited white flesh is for sale, flesh that knows what is in store for it and left with no choice bows to circumstance, but which is like a cup overflowing with tears.

She wanted to open her mouth and say to her daughter Esther, Here I am, I am here before you, but her mouth would not utter the words and she began moving here and there in the room, trying to attract her daughter's attention, once by flickering quickly in the big mirror and then by knocking a small container of lip rouge from the dressing table, but instead of her daughter being happy at her being with her, Esther was so frightened by the density of movement in her room that she picked up the candlestick and fled terrified to her friends.

It was the termination of the Yom Kippur fast, some time after the breaking of the fast, the last hour of grace before Manuel would switch on the string of colored lights beneath the sign over the door of his house, Las Clavas, and before the men, fatigued by fasting and the excessive sanctity of the terrible day would again wend their way, weary and hungry for love, up Calle Junin, wandering like a bevy of angels between the brothels.

Esther went downstairs where she met Roja-Rosa who was putting the finishing touches to the lounge, arranging flowers in the big vases, flicking a duster over the sideboards lest dust of the holy day had collected on them, readying the house for the arrival of the many guests who were expected to crowd it at the end of Yom Kippur.

Esther moved to Roja-Rosa, her face as white as a corpse.

"What's happened, niña?" Roja-Rosa asked quickly.

"I was lying on my bed," Esther told her, "and suddenly the candle went out."

"So," Roja-Rosa laughed, "did you relight it?"

"Yes, yes," Esther replied hesitatingly, "but then I felt that the room was full. That somebody else was there with me. And then the rouge fell off the dressing table without me touching it at all."

"*Dios mio*," Roja-Rosa shouted. "I've told Manuel that he must check the mezuzahs in this house."

"Why the mezuzahs?" Esther asked.

"No matter, no matter," replied Roja-Rosa quickly. "Work in Flora's room tonight because she's going to a café with Manuel. Leave me to deal with your room, all right?"

Esther nodded and went upstairs to Flora's room, with Roja-Rosa following her to lock her door from the outside, saying to herself that right now she didn't have time for ghosts. This one would have to wait until later when all the girls would be busy.

Leah's soul saw all the excitement around her and was saddened. Not to cast terror into her daughter's heart had she come here, but to help her. She hid in a corner of the patio, under a green bush, curling up beneath it like a cat. She did not dare follow her daughter to her friend's room to see what she did when the first men came to the house. She also did not wish to see what her daughter went through between the sheets for she feared she would be unable to stand it, and would start going crazy in the room and frighten her daughter and her companions and, Heaven forbid, cause somebody a heart attack from fright.

So she went and lay under the bush, resting from her flight and long journey, and looked around, seeing the men coming to the house, and that there were more girls in it, some good looking and others less so, and three musicians, some kind of Buenos Aires *kleizmers*, one a violinist, the second a clarinetist, and the third with a bandoneón, placing their instruments on the floor and each one tuning up, and then starting to play a sad melody, one that was not Jewish but which touched the depths of the soul, and how the girls all around began moving their arms and swaying their hips to the music, drawing after them the men flocking inside, all dressed in their everyday clothes to distinguish between sacred and profane and between fasting and pleasure, wearing hats and berets, some with ties and others with a bandana around their neck, others with smooth trousers and others with trousers of rough material and embroidered felt shoes, all coming to the women's door in the way of men down the years, in every country, in every city.

Late at night, when all the revelers had left the house and the girls had gone to sleep, Roja-Rosa thought about following suit, but then remembered the locked room and what she had to do. She heaved a sigh, went into the big kitchen, knelt at the foot of its cupboard and took out a bunch of leaves tied with a ribbon, leaves of dried sage. She took a metal bowl, crushed the sage into it and slowly and quietly so as not to rouse the girls, went up to the second floor carrying the bowl.

Leah's soul accompanied Roja-Rosa to see what she would do.

Roja-Rosa took a bunch of keys from her pocket, opened Esther's door and went inside, leaving the door ajar.

Once inside she put the bowl onto the dressing table, struck a match, and with its flame lit the tips of the leaves.

The sage emitted a strong aroma, the fragrance of balm and myrrh that rose and filled the room with smoke. Leah's soul suddenly felt that the aroma was pushing her out of the room, from the second floor, from the house, shoving and carrying her with it, far from where it was spreading.

Roja-Rosa stood in Esther's room, she took the bowl and with it moved to each corner, wafting the sage smoke over Esther's bed and by the big mirror, lest the reflection of the dead be caught in it, and once the room was redolent with smoke she went out, locking the door behind her, confident that had there been a ghost inside it was no longer there. And if there hadn't been, then the worst thing that had happened was that the room was now filled with a pleasing fragrance that would permeate the sheets and curtains and make Esther happy.

Tired out, Roja-Rosa trudged to her room, leaving the bowl of embers outside lest it smell out her room too.

Leah's soul found itself repelled outside the house's fence, and because it did not know what to do while the aroma filled the house, it soared into the Buenos Aires sky in the last watches of the night, the hour when the first bakers begin their work, and the aroma of their bread and cakes and biscuits wafts from their shops and fills the city streets with the sweetness of freshly-baked bread.

Leah's soul inhaled this aroma deep into its lungs, the smell of fresh rolls whose name it did not know, but whose aroma she recognized, it stood in the void of the world and said to itself, What a pity I have no lips to taste this bread. Well, it's not all that bad. The girl is in good hands in an orderly city and with people.

Leah's soul was pacified, and filled with relief it flew from street to street, discovering the size of the city to which it had sent her daughter who did not yet know its size and splendor like her mother, who was now wandering its streets, enjoying its sights and smells at such an early morning hour, and it was filled with happiness.

Forty-seven

Some people know a person's soul has been taken when they see it wandering alone in the world seeking its loved ones, and there are some who cannot see souls but rather all kinds of signs of their presence around them, strange phenomena occurring all at once, because the soul seeks to catch their attention, and there are others who neither see nor hear a thing, and all they know of a person's death is by rumor. This is what happened to Bella Bergman who heard about Leah's death, not from a demon or an angel, but from a telegram.

Before leaving Danzig with her husband, Bella summoned Gershon's brother Meir and made him swear that should he hear anything about that vile ring thief he would inform her immediately. And now, hearing of Leah Kochmann's death, he hastened to send his sister-in-law a telegram informing her of what had happened and seeking her advice.

The telegram reached Bella on the day of her second visit to Rabbi Hirsch, following which she knew that nothing good would come from this charlatan. Were it not for the telegram that was waiting for her she would have been assailed by deep sorrow for placing her trust in such a man, whose eyes burned with idolatrous fire and who purchased women and drink with her money. But on receiving the missive she realized that her brother-in-law would now be able to search the dead whore's belongings and finally discover the name of the woman who had the ring.

She hurried directly to the post office and sent a telegram to Meir, instructing him to buy up Leah Kochmann's house and inn, search them, and after finding the required documents put the properties up for sale.

Not two months passed since her telegram to her brother-in-law and her receiving from him, by sea, a big package of documents he had found in an old leather satchel inside the dead woman's wardrobe, and in it some old photographs whose sepia tint had faded, and with them the identity documents of the dead woman and her thieving husband, letters in Yiddish, Leizer Kochmann's death certificate and her daughter's birth certificate, whose name was now known to her. Esther, Esther Kochmann.

Bella called her friend Eva and asked her to hide the old leather satchel in her home. Her friend, who was used to her mistress's secrets, asked no questions and simply put the satchel into a sack and hid it in her house the same day.

Now she possessed the details of the daughter who had the ring, Bella knew what she must do. On her husband's return from one of his journeys to the provinces, she began questioning him on what he knew of The Unclean about which she had read in the newspapers and journals printed in Argentina at the time.

Although Gershon was somewhat puzzled by her curiosity regarding the crime that had shaken the Buenos Aires Jewish community and which had given it a bad name, exposed it to anti-Semitism and also shocked the communities from which those wretched women had come, he told her everything he knew about it. Bella wondered how he knew so much, and he told her about the Swiss consul's report.

"Some members of the Jewish community, including myself," he told her, "approached the authorities in Buenos Aires in an attempt to limit the large number of brothels in the city and fight this phenomenon by having the emigration laws amended. Some estimates put the number of such Jewish girls in the city at three thousand!"

"Incredible!" Bella said. "Are there proper records of the girls, of these places?"

"There are partial records," he replied, "but the police take bribes and do not report on every house that's opened. Fighting them by regular means is difficult. The women are brought in not only through the port, but also through Uruguay and down the river, the men marry them and pass themselves off as their husbands."

"What's the Jewish community doing about it?" asked Bella, shocked.

"There's not much it *can* do. Last Yom Kippur they were thrown out of the Sephardi synagogue, so they founded a synagogue of their own. Then they were refused Jewish burial, so they purchased a plot of land and founded the Israelita cemetery. They are a highly organized, powerful network because of their money."

"To fight wealthy criminals you need a lot of money," Bella pronounced, "have you told Baron Hirsch about this?"

"Yes," Gershon replied, pleased with her response. "He was one of the first to hear about it. He and his wife financed an organization in London to help these women, and now they've opened a branch here in Buenos Aires.

"Which organization?" asked Bella, who knew nothing of all this.

"*Ezrat Nashim*," he replied. "They receive letters from families in Europe whose daughters have been caught up in this thing, they try to locate the girls and redeem them from the people holding them."

Bella thought for a moment.

"I would like to join this organization, Gershon."

"Haven't you got enough to do?" Gershon asked. "You've got two small children to raise. How will you find the time for public work such as this?"

"The children are already grown," she replied, "and I'm bored at home. An hour or two of voluntary work for such an important cause will only make me feel better, believe me."

Gershon knew there was no point in arguing with her. In any case he was weary from his journey and longed to tiptoe into his sons' room, kiss their foreheads and fall into his own bed. So long as she was not neglecting the boys and was not engaging in anything that might endanger her or those around her, he told himself, completely exhausted, she can do what she wants.

He consented to her plan and a short time later went to bed, sinking into a pleasant, deep sleep, dreaming of his lover, Shlomo Azaria, a young man of twenty-five he had met in Moises Ville. Shlomo, whose parents were deceased, had come to Argentina from Germany on his own and been taken into a family of Jewish gauchos who were among the first settlers there. They were happy to welcome a strong young man who would be able to help them since they had four daughters. Nobody knew of the tempestuous relationship that had been formed between Gershon and Shlomo Azaria, except for the birds of the valley that flew singing over their trysting place at the edge of some fields, inside a deep hollow lined with grass and soft straw. Apart from the field guard who once saw two men entwined with each other in a grassy hollow and was so affrighted by what he had seen, had never told a soul about it.

But what remains unspoken is clearly apparent in faces, and to his wife Gershon seemed so tired from his journey this time that she decided to leave him be and in the morning keep all the members of the household quiet so he could sleep as long as he wished and leave her to her own devices, among which was going to *Ezrat Nashim* to offer her help.

In the days that passed since then the couple were extremely preoccupied, one with reading and answering his beloved's letters, which were written with a sure hand and in fluent language, and the other with almost daily excursions to *Ezrat Nashim*.

The deeper she delved into the organization's correspondence Bella gradually comprehended the monstrous scope of the white slave trade. It had begun in the 1890s, when she was still a young woman. The first girls had been imported from Hungarian and Polish villages. Their families lived in abject poverty and the girls, dowry-less minors, were pawns in the hands of their parents in their struggle to survive. The white slavers found fertile soil in the dire economic conditions in which the Jews lived at the time, and under relentless anti-Semitic pressure. They would come to the villages, display the profligacy of the wealthy and suggest to the parents that they send their daughters with them to work in Jewish homes in Buenos Aires. They paid the parents an advance on the girl's wages. Thus many parents put their daughters and all their documents into the traders' hands. On their arrival in Argentina the traders distributed the young girls to brothels in Buenos Aires, Rosario, Mendoza, Tucuman, and even beyond the country's borders.

There were pimps who paid the traders in advance for the passage of the girls they brought them, and on their arrival in Buenos Aires they were held captive in their brothels. Girls brought for trading were held for a few days in temporary accommodations and then put up for auction to pimps and brothel keepers, brokers, and customers who attended these events for their pleasure.

The girls were forced to start work immediately and any sign of rebelliousness or mutiny brought punishment in its wake, including whipping, starvation and prolonged captivity. If they sought to buy themselves out, the brothel keepers would name sums that included their cost and not only their passage and the commission paid at the auction, which was paid to the brokers, but also their expenses for clothing and food and loss of future profits from their work. Thus any attempt by the girls' relatives or benefactors from the Jewish community to redeem the girls and restore them to a decent life, was rendered impossible.

The more Bella read the documents and testimonies, the more embittered she became. She was particularly moved by the personal cries for help that reached *Ezrat Nashim* from all over the world. In some cases the worried parents even mentioned the names of the people to whom they had given their daughters. One letter had come from a father in Lodz who had given his daughter to Moshe and Juana Geist who resided at 1637 Calle Urquiza in Buenos Aires, where the husband went under the name of Moshe Becker. Their daughter had written saying that she was indeed working in their home, not as a maid but as a prostitute, and they sought the intervention of the organization, the Jewish community and the authorities to extricate their daughter from their clutches. In her letter, written in bad Yiddish, a woman confessed that her sister, flesh of her flesh, Brendleh Kirschstein, had been given her daughter, the sixteen year-old Esther, to find her a husband and work in Buenos Aires, and it was only by word of mouth she heard that her sister owned a brothel at 138 Calle Montevideo in the city to which she had lured not only other girls from her village in Poland, but even her own niece.

Other parents had given their daughter, Breine Spiegler, to two brothers, Moshe and Lezaro Asher, without knowing that they owned a large brothel in Buenos Aires. And so on and so forth, piles of letters and requests that accumulated on the *Ezrat Nashim* desk, all stained with the tears of their senders and filled with concern and anxiety for the fate of their daughters who, in their naivety, they had handed over to people who seemed to be good, prosperous and upstanding Jews who promised them the earth but had brought their daughters down to the lowest of the low.

Bella would sometimes feel weak from the horror stories she read and would then ask herself what she was doing here in the *Ezrat Nashim* offices, and whether there was false reasoning behind what had brought her here, this pursuit of her wedding ring that was in the hands of one of those poor unfortunates. Once she even told herself that she had enough ornaments, jewelry and rings, and perhaps it would be better if she left that ring and the girl who had it alone and forgot the whole thing. But when she left the *Ezrat Nashim* building deep in thought and rode home in her carriage, she saw before her memories of the past, including her dying mother-in-law's face on her bed, her flaccid hand taking hers and Gershon's hands, binding them together with a word, and then making them swear an oath to find the ring symbolizing their marriage, the ring whose loss had killed her mother-in-law. Then another voice would rise inside her, the voice of her mother saying, "Your mission, my daughter, is to restore what has been stolen from you. Know how to distinguish between your obligations and what your heart urges you to do for those women suffering a terrible fate. You must not confuse the mind's wisdom with the heart's compassion. It is only natural that you be attentive, first and foremost, to the letters written in German and seek out in particular the rare inquiries from Danzig, for your commonsense will guide you along the right path to solve the riddle of your life, and at the same time contribute to the welfare of many other women. Would you have come to Buenos Aires had it not been for the ring? Would you have come to the aid of those hundreds of girls? The ways of fate are mysterious, and if not for your own benefit, then for theirs. You can be completely meritorious in your own eyes as you will be in the eyes of the whole world." While she was still pondering this, her head fell onto her chest and a strange sleep overcame her.

Her husband was absent from home for days on end, and once more she felt abandoned and forlorn in her married life. If before they had come together in games and amusements after quarrels or whole days of silence, now he had simply disappeared as if his business obliged him to constantly travel between the colonies and provinces to find new Jewish teachers among the emigrants coming to the city, bring them with him to the schools he had founded and adapt them to their work, education combined with the spirit of Judaism and the teaching of Spanish culture and language. Sometimes he had to actually take young men under his wing and train them to be teachers, like that same orphaned young man about whom he had told her, who had come to Moises Ville from Germany.

Since the boys were born and had grown, relations between them were correct in the extreme. Gershon would go off on his travels, working hard all over the country, and provide them with a good living and even gaining them a name and position in the Jewish community, while she was occupied with running the household, looking after the boys, and now with her work at *Ezrat Nashim*. But however busy they both were and treated each other with respect on the days they were together, physical love was missing from their relationship, and this lack surfaced each time they were together and they became like a dry morsel to one another.

Forty-eight

Some two months after Leah Kochmann's death, a letter addressed to her daughter, Esther Kochmann, 322 Calle Junin, Buenos Aires, reached the main post office that had been opened near the port. It was written by the nephew of Reb Asher, the young man who had studied with his uncle until his passing and then replaced him as Danzig's gravedigger.

"Dear Madam," wrote Bentzi Asherman in his flowing hand, "I regret to inform you that your mother, Mrs. Leah Kochmann, passed away in Danzig on the eve of Yom Kippur 1895, and was laid to rest immediately after the termination of the fast. According to her will, which she left in the hands of my late uncle, I sold her house and possessions and inn in order to transfer the funds to your good self, Madam, less burial fees and the cost of a headstone. Enclosed herewith please find the sum of 550 zlotys, together with which I offer my own sympathy and that of your late mother's friends for your loss. Ben-Zion Asherman, Yefeh Olam Cemetery, Jewish Community of Danzig."

The joy that gripped her at the sight of the letter from Danzig was replaced by a cry. Esther dropped the letter, letting the banknotes scatter in the yard, fell weeping to the patio floor and began banging her head against the wall. On hearing the commotion, Roja-Rosa peeped from the kitchen door and on seeing Esther ran to her, trying to grip her shoulders and drag her away from the wall, but in vain. It was if she were possessed by a demon, kneeling on the ground and banging her head against the wall as if trying to split it in her pain.

"Miriam!" Roja-Rosa shouted, "Sophia! Flory! Help me!"

The girls heard her cry and came out of their rooms to see what was going on. On seeing what was happening they ran downstairs, one grabbed Esther's left arm and the other the right, and they dragged her away from the wall.

"What happened?" shouted Roja-Rosa. She, who could not read or write, nodded towards the letter on the ground and the foreign banknotes fluttering next to it.

Miriam picked up the letter and read it quickly.

"Her mother," she read aloud, "her mother's died."

Roja-Rosa clasped her head in her hands. "*Dios mio*," she murmured, "God have mercy."

She signaled the girls to help her take Esther, whose body was paralyzed but whose forehead was bleeding, to her room. They sat her on the bed and wiped away the blood. Esther was like a corpse, her eyes wide with pain.

Sophia gave her an examining glance. "She's in total shock, poor thing."

"Flory, bring some vodka from the lounge," Roja-Rosa ordered.

A few moments later Flory came back with a glass of vodka. Roja-Rosa raised Esther's head and forced her to sip the fiery liquor. Her eyes were glazed which partially dulled the pain in them.

"Drink a drop more, *niña*. From now on you are like a daughter to me," said Roja-Rosa, stroking Esther's hair, who spluttered, spraying droplets of saliva and vodka all around.

Roja-Rosa dismissed the girls and continued to sit beside Esther, who was lying silent on her bed, holding her lax hand and looking into her eyes. Her pupils moved as if she were seeing the figure of her mother before her, the days of her childhood, her mother's visits to the convent, the day her mother released her from the convent and took her home, sitting with her in the kitchen while her mother cooked as she, Esther, peeled potatoes at her feet, and later, her mother waking her quickly, informing her that she was being taken away, and she struggled with her, loath to part, cursing, weeping, being dragged by both arms to the boat, turning her back on her mother who stood on the wharf and watched the vessel sail away.

Tears flowed from Esther's eyes. "I didn't even say goodbye to her," she wailed, "she died remembering me cursing her…"

"Oh, *niña, niña*," Roja-Rosa murmured, caressing Esther's cheek, "your mother loves you, believe me. Wherever she is, she loves you."

"She died because of me," the girl wept, "because of the letter I sent her."

"Letter? What letter?" shouted Roja-Rosa in horror, "who let you get a letter out of here?"

"A letter asking her to come and rescue me," Esther mumbled.

All at once Roja-Rosa let her go and looked at her with eyes in which toughness and compassion showed through simultaneously.

"How did you do it? Who helped you?"

"It's all my fault," the girl wept without replying.

"I told you when you got here. Nothing can help you," Roja-Rosa said reprovingly. "Neither you nor me."

"Now my mother's dead. I'm lost. All of us here are lost."

"Shhh… don't talk like that," Roja-Rosa interrupted her, "we're together. Like a family."

Esther clutched her hand entreatingly. "Love me, don't be angry with me, love me."

"All right, all right," said Roja-Rosa, "the main thing is that you calm down. It's not your fault. When someone has to go, he goes. That's the way it is, *niña*. The Angel of Death alone decides when to come."

When Roja-Rosa saw that Esther had calmed down somewhat, she left the room and came back with a tray of food.

"Eat," she coaxed her, "with all that crying there'll be nothing left of you."

"I can't," Esther mumbled, her nose smelling the food but her mouth refusing to open.

"You've no choice. You've got to keep your weight up. Do you want Manuel to force-feed you?"

On hearing the thinly-veiled threat Esther took the tray and began eating slowly, pinch by pinch, of the food placed before her. When she had finished Roja-Rosa removed the tray and lay her down on the bed, covering her with a blanket and kissing her forehead as if she really were her daughter. She turned off the light and locked the door to let the girl have a good night's sleep until morning. No customers, no work. The main thing was that she recover.

But in the morning, too, Esther awakened from the weeping that had assailed her in her sleep, and did not stop for days on end. She wept for her mother with whom she had been unable to become reconciled before her death and she wept for herself, left alone in the world, without a living soul to rescue her from her predicament. She wept without knowing that her letter had reached the members of the Danzig Jewish community committee, among them Gershon Bergman, and now it was in his desk drawer, while his wife, Bella, was searching for it through the piles of letters and inquiries that reached *Ezrat Nashim*.

After the first seven days of mourning during which she was left alone, Manuel's anger mounted. Every girl that didn't work, he reminded Roja-Rosa, reduced their income by one tenth.

"I haven't got a house with seventy or eighty women like some," he told Roja-Rosa as they counted the money at the night's end. "It's been seven days. Tomorrow she goes back to work."

"Give her time, Manuel. It's the only medicine for grieving."

"No time, no nothing," replied Manuel angrily. "Look," slapping the pile of banknotes, "our takings have been down for a whole week! Where can I find the money to feed all these mouths if she isn't working?'

"It's better if the customers don't see her," Roja-Rosa said.

"A touch of makeup and she's a queen again."

"You don't understand. The darkness in the heart has devoured her. She looks awful."

"Awful? Awful? Manuel yelled, "I'm going upstairs to see what she really looks like."

He stuffed the notes into his pocket and went upstairs to Esther's room with Roja-Rosa behind him. He tried unsuccessfully to open the locked door until Roja-Rosa handed him her bunch of keys.

"I've kept her locked in for a week," she said quietly, "so she doesn't make trouble."

Manuel opened the door and switched on the light. The room was redolent with the stink of stale air, and as he approached the bed he saw Esther lying there, blinking in the sudden light, her hair unkempt, a wrinkled nightgown covering her body. He saw the dark rings beneath her eyes and her numbed expression. He inspected her from top to toe and turned round.

"There's no chance of a client coming anywhere near her in this state," Roja-Rosa said, "it really would be better if she stayed here."

He hissed a curse and left, troubled by the loss of revenue and wondering about what he would do. Roja-Rosa went to the girl, kissed her forehead and covered her with the thin blanket that had been thrown onto the floor.

"Goodnight, *niña*," she whispered, "go to sleep. Everything will be alright."

It was only a few days later that Esther dared to do what she had wanted during the days of mourning. All that time she had been troubled by the thought of what would have happened had her mother not sent the ring with her, which according to her had cured her of convulsions. For more than a week she had been tortured by the thought that had she not had the ring in Argentina, perhaps it might have saved her mother. She longed to take out the wooden box from its place at the bottom of the wardrobe and throw it into the street. But she was unable to look at the object that perhaps might have saved her mother. Only now, after ten days of weeping, she felt strong enough to do so.

She opened the window, letting the fresh air and clear light flood the room. Then she went to the wardrobe and took out the small wooden box. She opened it and gazed at the ring. The stone's changing hues, a reddish-brown that flashed in the sunlight bringing out tones of green and gray and veins of crimson, captivated her. She looked at it and gradually became immersed in herself; before her rose her mother's face, the inn, the small kitchen, the window overlooking the port, the ships' masts, and the sea, big and wide and open. And suddenly she was there, in Danzig, hearing the people coming into the inn, the ships' sirens, the neighing of the horses harnessed to wagons and the sailors calling after her, Hey, girl, want to taste my borscht?

Her eyelids became heavy. Almost of its own volition her hand went out to the ring, but not to throw it away. She held it, feeling its warmth flowing into her fingers, and put it on. It fitted her finger as if it had always been there.

An hour later, in the early evening, when Roja-Rosa came to open her door before the start of work, she saw her sitting there like a lady, her long hair washed and drawn back, wearing a close-fitting evening dress, her face made up to conceal its thinness and highlight its sharp lines. She was perfumed and wore a ring on her finger, a valuable-looking, beautiful ring that cast a light on everything around it.

Roja-Rosa stared at her, stunned.

"*Dios mio*," she said, "what a beauty!"

"I'm back," the young woman smiled at her with her new look, a captivating, veiled look. "I'm ready to go downstairs."

"Where's that ring from?" inquired Roja-Rosa, "just look how it gleams!"

271

"It was my mother's. It came with the letter and the money and I shall wear it from now on."

Roja-Rosa nodded, checked the room to see if it was ready for clients, and returned her satisfied look to Esther.

"Good girl," she smiled, kissing her cheek, "let's go downstairs."

When they walked into the lounge everyone turned to look at them and then ran to surround Esther with cries of joy, happy that their friend had recovered, and how lovely she looked, as if the night itself had come to dwell in her heart.

But it was not the night that dwelt there but the knowledge that she was alone in the world, with no one on whom she could pin her hopes. This knowledge brought out in her a previously unknown strength. An unknown spirit had awakened in her – the spirit of a young woman resolved to survive at all costs, overcome the circumstances in which she found herself and turn the hardship of her life into a sort of relative advantage.

She did everything required of her. Dance the tango, entertain the customers, respect the owner. Her caution distanced her from any position of refusal or denial. She learned to do what was expected of her. The pretence of love.

She served them all faithfully. The charming men and the poseurs and the men of good name who always behaved as if they were there by mistake, the men full of themselves and those who carefully calculated each peso they spent on their entertainment, drink and sex. Quickly, with feigned passion, she unbuttoned her clothing before them as if she lived for them alone, taking her life in her hands and giving her all to obtain everything possible.

Her good attitude towards her customers spread far and wide and slowly the men began referring to her as the best whore in the city, the greatest of all. But she knew in her heart that she was a prisoner whose life had been taken from her, and if she wanted to live she must be attentive to the wishes of her guest and obey his every whim, even if he were a fleshy general whose breath stank of rotting teeth mingled with the smell of tobacco or liquor. She lived in a necessity she must fulfill each day anew.

Every morning, even when she felt despondent, she would bathe, dress and put on makeup. She finally came to the realization that she was working in the market of lust and that insolence or a foul mouth were likely to bring down calamity upon her.

272

Sometimes she would hear another voice, a voice of inner pleading from the anguished child dwelling within her. But she would immediately identify the voice of the victim and rid herself of it. She had to be hard-headed and close her heart to herself. Hearing voices such as those was too great a privilege for someone living in darkness.

Forty-nine

Bella was immersed in running her home while at the same time involving herself in community matters, but surreptitiously so she would not be suspected of instigating something futile or of superseding her husband. She knew how to maintain her standing in the city. She must meddle in the affairs of others so that no one would meddle in hers.

Wilhelm Lowenthal did not like this woman. The baron's other officials, too, did not like the Bergmans' closeness to the baron, who was already quite ill, and to his wife. In the Hirsch Foundation too rumor was rife about this woman and her husband.

Nobody knew where the gossipmongers obtained their information, but the rumors redoubled when Gershon Bergman returned from one of his trips to the provinces with a bespectacled young man who looked like an intellectual or a socialist, with a face as delicate as a woman's. Gershon introduced this young man, Shlomo Azaria, as the most outstanding teacher in the provinces and arranged a position for him in the Buenos Aires Jewish school. Quite naturally, more than he was thinking of bolstering Jewish education in the capital, he was following his heart.

A few days after returning from his journey Gershon informed Bella that he wished to invite his guest to Sabbath evening dinner at their home. They had long since agreed that whenever Gershon was home between one journey and the next, he would take the two boys to the synagogue to give them a taste of tradition, and then come home for Sabbath dinner with them. This ceremony of *Kabbalat Shabbat*, welcoming the Sabbath, was alien to Bella, but Gershon was so insistent, and in any case he was hardly ever home, so she consented. Now he wanted to invite the visitor who was alone in the city and had nowhere to go, for Sabbath dinner.

Early that Friday evening knocking was heard on their front door. Bella, who was already dressed in her Sabbath finery, glanced puzzled at the big grandfather clock they had brought from Danzig, and went to the door.

Standing there she saw a well-dressed young man holding a beautiful bouquet. She held out her hand and accepted the flowers with a restrained smile.

Shlomo Azaria stood in the doorway, stealing a wondering glance over her shoulder.

"My husband and sons haven't come back from the synagogue yet," she said. "They sometimes linger there."

"Jews," Shlomo Azaria smiled, and a mischievous spark flickered in his eyes.

She asked him in, led him into the sitting room, and motioned him to sit down.

"Thank you," the young man said politely, clearly striving to conceal his great embarrassment. He sat down on the edge of the blue velvet armchair. His eyes darted here and there in wonderment, coming to rest on the gold and silver ornaments in their tall, dark wood cabinets the Bergmans had brought from Danzig.

"May I?" he asked, gesturing at the ornaments meticulously arranged behind the glass.

"Of course," she replied brusquely, "but don't touch them. Polishing them is hard work."

He clumsily strode to the cabinets and was so excited by the possibility of having a close look at the old ritual objects that he tripped over a fold in the carpet and almost fell, but managed to stretch out his hands and check his fall on the tall narrow cabinet, of all things, which housed the Sabbath and festival wine goblets. The cabinet swayed under the blow and all the goblets rocked and fell diagonally, one after the other, on their shelves.

"Be careful!" Bella shouted, rushing to the cabinet to steady it.

The guest was so embarrassed he did not know where to put himself. "I'm sorry," he said, and reached out to rearrange the avalanche of goblets he had caused.

"No! No!" Bella shouted, grasping his arm. "Leave that to me!"

Shlomo Azaria withdrew his hand.

"Go and sit down!" she ordered him in her hard voice. "Isabel!" she called to the old housekeeper, "Isabel!"

An elderly woman of Indian extraction hurried in, wiping her hands on the apron she wore around her large body. "Yes, Señora?"

"Please bring our guest a glass of water, he's had a little accident."

"*Dios mio!*" Isabel exclaimed at the sight of the disarray in the cabinet. "Do you need any help?"

"No," Bella replied curtly. "But he needs some water to calm him." A few moments later Isabel came back, placed a large tumbler of water onto a square saucer decorated with a European landscape.

"*Gracias*," Shlomo Azaria thanked her, pronouncing the word in a foreign, wooden accent, not yet knowing how to roll the R in the manner of the *porteños*.

Isabel flashed him a smile and left the room, crossing the space between him and the lady of the house, who was standing at the cabinet arranging the fallen goblets.

A few moments later her two sons came rushing in dressed in clothes that had been snowy white when they left the house, but they now looked like two filthy urchins. They were followed by their father, mournful and downcast.

"They got into a fight with the children of The Unclean outside the synagogue," Gershon said, and then noticed his lover who had got up and was standing tensely by the armchair.

"Welcome!" Gershon exulted, going over to give him a friendly but distant embrace in the manner of a host, and added a manly slap on his shoulder.

"Go upstairs!" Bella ordered her sons who were filthy with the soil and water the children of The Unclean had thrown at them. "You do not sit at the table with dirt all over you!"

She took the boys upstairs to wash them and change their clothes, leaving her husband and his guest on their own.

Gershon looked at Shlomo. Shlomo lowered his eyes as if fearing that these walls might witness the exchange of their loving looks.

"Let's go outside," Gershon said softly. He draped his arm around Shlomo's shoulders and led him into the enchanting garden that was already mantled in the evening darkness. Stirred, Shlomo looked at the lawn bordered with flowerbeds and at the trees towering above the wall surrounding the house.

"Let's go down to the lawn," Gershon entreated his young guest, pulling him toward the dark garden.

"No, Gershon, no," Shlomo replied, pulling his arm away. "It's inappropriate."

"It'll be a while before she comes down," Gershon laughed, "you don't know my wife. She's very punctilious."

"This is her home. I'm a guest here. Let's leave it at that, Gershon, I implore you."

"Come on," Gershon whispered excitedly, a wave of passion engulfing him. All he wanted at that moment was to kiss his lover's lips amid the shadows of the garden before his wife and children sat down to dinner with them. To kiss him, to feel the rush of fear in his blood.

Shlomo was drawn into the darkness after Gershon. He let Gershon kiss his lips as his eyes darted fearfully from side to side, making sure that nobody saw them.

"There's nobody here," Gershon laughed, "you can be sure of it."

Discomfited, Shlomo detached himself from Gershon arms and strode back to the stone patio abutting the house. Gershon straightened his clothing carefully and followed him, his heart filled with joy because his lover was there with him, one way or another, in his home, in his life.

After a long, oppressive wait, Bella and the boys came down, the boys wearing fine sailor suits.

"Those damned Unclean," she said, "how did their bastard children get to the synagogue?"

"They look for trouble with us at every opportunity. Is that something new for you?" Gershon asked, and turned welcomingly to his guest. "Shall we go to the Sabbath table?"

Shlomo Azaria nodded happily. He felt far safer at the table than in the dark garden with his lover.

Gershon took his place at the table and waited in silence until everyone was seated, washed his hands, and then raised his goblet and recited the blessing over the wine. He took a sip and passed the goblet to his guest. Shlomo noticed Bella's sharp look, did not bring the goblet to his lips but passed it to her. She took a silent sip and then passed it to her two sons. After they had sipped from it she returned it to the guest, who took an apprehensive sip.

Gershon did not notice this interchange, but recited the blessing over the plaited *challah*, tore it apart and passed a piece to everyone. They ate it in silence, and Bella got up and went into the kitchen.

She came back a few moments later bearing in her shaking hands platters of roast chicken and beef, and Isabel followed her with baked potatoes and rice. They put it all onto the table and Bella stood to serve the food. She served her husband, her sons, and then herself, laid the serving spoon down and sat down.

"What about our guest?" Gershon asked. "You've forgotten him."

"Oh, I'm sorry," Bella said quickly, not knowing what had come over her. She dropped her knife and fork onto her plate and stood up again. "What would you like?"

"What everyone else has had," Shlomo mumbled, his heart pounding.

With the serving spoon Bella messily heaped his plate with a piece of chicken, a mound of rice, a slice of roast beef, and a few potatoes.

"There you are," she said, passing him the plate abruptly and sitting down again to eat in silence.

Gershon had never seen his wife behave like this with a guest, completely silent and withdrawn. But he did not say a word. They sat around the table for a long time, chewing in silence. After the meal the children went to their father, kissed him on the cheek and then went upstairs to bed with their mother. Shlomo and Gershon remained on their own for a long while, shrouded in silence, while Isabel cleared the table.

About half an hour later Bella came downstairs from the boys' bedroom and silently served them tea and a plate of homemade biscuits. Then she took her leave of the guest, saying she was tired from her day's work and would retire early.

Gershon carried the refreshments to the small table on the patio that opened up onto the garden, and invited his guest to join him in admiring the garden, while unbeknownst to him, as he sat enjoying his darkened garden, his wife was in her bedroom crying her heart out into her pillow.

She couldn't delude herself again. Their move to Argentina hadn't resolved a thing. There was no cure for this proclivity and no way out of it. But how dare he bring this sweet-faced, soft-voiced young man into her home; how dare he invite this man, who undoubtedly suffered from the same impediment, into her home – this she could not comprehend. What was he thinking, that her eyes wouldn't see? That her heart was made of iron? That she wouldn't understand, wouldn't recognize it, wouldn't know? She felt as if he had stabbed her in the heart with a long knife. And what would she do in a short while when he came into the bedroom? And what would she do if he chose to spend the night on his old couch as he had with Frank? He was probably sitting in the arms of this

278

stranger right now, the dizzying thought flashed through her mind and made her jump out of bed. She tiptoed to the door and opened it to hear either the sound of conversation or lovemaking, but all was quiet. She went back into the room and quietly opened the window overlooking the garden. She looked down and saw her husband talking with his friend, while his hand felt for the hand of this young man that was in his lap. She strained her eyes to ascertain what she was seeing, and then was filled with such rage that she picked up one of the bedroom armchairs, lifted it with all her strength to the windowsill and threw it out, screaming, "Bastard! Murderer! Pederast!"

The two men leapt from their chairs. The armchair exploded on the patio floor with a loud bang, missing them by a few centimeters and showering its fragments in every direction. Shlomo quaked in terror, while Gershon, totally stunned, looked up at the upper window from which his wife's head leaned out.

"She's gone completely mad," he said.

"Forgive me, Gershon, but I'm leaving," Shlomo said weakly. "This isn't for me anymore, all this."

Gershon did not reply. He was looking tensely to see if any of the neighbors had heard the chair hitting the ground and his wife's so distinct scream, and then rushed inside, ran upstairs to the bedroom, grabbed Bella by the arms, and dragged her away from the window.

"Are you out of your mind?" he yelled. "You could have killed us!"

"Pederast!" Bella shouted, her faced flushed with insult and rage. "Murderer!"

Without thinking, Gershon raised his hand and slapped her so hard that she fell onto the bed, crying out in pain. His hand hung frozen in the air for a second as he looked at her, not believing that he had raised a hand to his wife.

"I'm sorry," he said, falling to his knees while she wept on the bed. "Bella, I'm so sorry."

Bella did not reply. She lay on her bed, holding her choked weeping inside her with short inhalations of breath.

"Forgive me, forgive, my dearest," Gershon sobbed, his forehead on the mattress, crying like a child, not understanding where he had found the courage to raise a hand to his wife. He was to blame for everything that had happened here this evening, only he was to blame for everything. As he wept he did not hear the front door closing behind Shlomo Azaria.

Gershon discovered only next day that his lover had taken all his possessions and left the apartment he had rented for him, leaving only a brief farewell note in which he thanked him for their days together, and telling him not to search for him because he would never find him. Gershon, who knew Shlomo and his mulishness, also knew that he meant what he said. And indeed, Shlomo Azaria crossed the river to Uruguay where he found a post as a Hebrew teacher in a country town. Gershon never heard of him again.

Fifty

Bella began going out every day, dragging her feet through the streets of Buenos Aires for hours, down one boulevard to another, from quarter to quarter, as if analyzing her past and her future. She wandered for hours deep in thought, not knowing what she would do with herself and her fate. She was no longer an Iron Lady but a betrayed wife whose life lay in ruins and whose affront was etched on her face.

As if dumbly obeying an unknown command, she again began frequenting pawnshops and antique shops, rummaging through them for hours, seeking what she had lost without knowing what it was. She inspected old, beautifully carved sideboards, heavy wood cupboards with rusted hinges, old pieces of jewelry whose color had faded over many years, fine material darkened with accumulated dust. She sometimes exchanged a few words with silver-tongued salesmen who saw a wealthy woman with dead eyes and swiftly offered her something to examine from their stock.

She declined their offers and bought nothing. For many days she was also unable to tell herself what she was actually looking for, until one day she stopped outside a pawnshop in whose window were arranged rings, brooches, and pendants made of gold and silver and inlaid with precious stones.

Suddenly the memory of the ring rose before her, floating above these exquisite objects and she burst into bitter, weird laughter at herself, her life, at everything she had endured from her childhood to adulthood.

"May I help the señora?" said the shopkeeper as he came to the counter, reaching into the display window for the tray of jewelry.

"No, no," she replied, trying to quell her laughter, "I just remembered something."

She nodded her thanks, a crooked smile on her face, and left the shop, suddenly feeling how she could again look at the world with clear eyes, even though they had been humbled to dust.

People talked. People told him how she was wandering the streets, her hair unkempt, laughing and striking terror into the passersby. But he did nothing for he knew exactly what had happened to her. His wife was the manifestation of his pain, his lust, his inability to control his soul. He, to whom the baron had entrusted the running of the Jewish educational institutions network, was smitten by a young man. And what was he thinking, that it wouldn't come out? That it wouldn't destroy his world?

He could have told her to go, for at the time everyone could see that she looked like a woman who had lost her mind. He could have kept her out of sight in some institution, far from view. But then what would he say to his sons, how could he explain what had happened to their beloved mother? He just wouldn't be able to face them.

Gershon weighed up his options and then sat down and wrote a personal letter to Baron Hirsch, telling about the difficulty that had beset his wife and asking him to release him from the frequent journeys all over the provinces. To stay close to her he would have to supervise the various institutions from afar.

The baron, a man of action, surely knew that the only way of protecting the educational institutions he had founded throughout the new country was through their supervision. But he remembered the suffering endured by the couple until the birth of their children, and so he allowed Gershon to hire an Argentinean educator as the Foundation's inspector, on condition that Gershon continued to supervise Jewish studies in the network from Buenos Aires.

Grateful to his benefactor, Gershon settled into the Foundation's offices in Buenos Aires. This way he was able to absent himself from home for a few hours every day, and in the time remaining work at home and be far more involved in what was going on there, including keeping an eye on his wife Bella's condition.

Staying at home was good for him too since it reduced the time in which he could observe, against his will, the faces of handsome young men, torture himself by not allowing himself to get closer to them and love them, but he swore he would never again reach out to these boys and men, dark-skinned with dark looks, who returned an inviting glance whenever his eyes came to rest on them on his way to the office and on his way back home. Gershon traveled on the new underground railway since it was good that a public servant mix with people and not drive in his own carriage or automobile, but the journey was agony for him. One day he boarded the tram and sat down opposite a young negro with a tattoo of a naked woman on his upper arm. His short shirtsleeves were rolled up so that one could see his thick biceps and the woman tattooed on them moving as he flexed them, as if she were stretching each time he moved his elbow, and as he did he looked unflinchingly at the older man sitting opposite and staring at him through his thick glasses, licking his lips on which there was a taste of forgotten pleasure.

His presence at home began to endow the whole house with an atmosphere of calm. Bella felt that a new measure of security had been cast into her life just as she had hoped, and she slowly calmed down and got back into her daily routine.

The Hanukkah festival was approaching, and Bella polished the big silver *hanukkiah*, the eight-branched candlestick that had been her father-in-law's, and busied herself with preparing festival delicacies. The children were also excited by the approaching festival and planned what they would ask from their father as Hanukkah presents. But neither Bella nor the boys could have imagined the surprise that Gershon had in store for them. On the festival eve Gershon stood by the *hanukkiah*, intoned the blessing, lit the auxiliary candle and called upon the boys to light the first candle with him. After dining on traditional sweet and savory potato pancakes, he asked them what they would like for their festival present. The boys had kept their wishes a secret from each other, and so were completely amazed when they asked their father for the same thing, a bicycle.

Their parents looked at one another and burst out laughing.

Their father nodded, approving their request, and turned to their mother.

"And you, my dear wife, what would you like for Hanukkah?"

Bella remained silent for a moment. "I've no idea what to ask for, except a little peace."

Gershon looked at her, his eyes filled with gratitude.

"Well then," he said, "I've got something for you that will make you happy. I've rented a house at Mar del Plata so we can spend all of January together at the seashore!"

On more than one occasion she had asked him that they spend some time in the summer at Mar del Plata like their wealthy neighbors. But he preferred to spend the summer months on his frequent trips to the provinces. A wave of joy engulfed her. "But the children," she asked, "who'll help me with the children?"

"I've asked Eva to come with us and she was happy to accept," Gershon told her. "She too has never been to Mar del Plata in the summer. She'll help with the children so that you and I can have a real break."

Bella was so happy at hearing the news that she joined Gershon and the boys when they started singing Hanukkah sings. They sat and sang full-throated, enjoying themselves and laughing, until even Isabel came to see what was going on and stood smiling in the kitchen doorway, looking at her mistress into whom new life seemed to have suddenly been poured, sitting with cheeks flushed and happily singing festival songs with her husband and children.

The vacation at Mar del Plata passed pleasantly. The house that Gershon had rented was only a few steps away from the beach and was spacious and comfortable. Each morning they woke the children at the usual time so they should have a regular routine on vacation as well, dressed them and gave them breakfast, just like in the books on child raising Bella was reading at the time. After breakfast they either went to the beach together or Gershon would take the boys, leaving Bella and Eva in the house. He enjoyed being with his sons and playing with them, building sandcastles and digging tunnels in the sand. Both Amado and Alejandro were happy digging in the mound of sand Gershon piled up for them until their small hands met, tickling each other in the warm golden sand.

In the evening, after putting the children to bed they left them with Eva and went out for a walk by themselves through the streets of Mar del Plata, wandering past the holiday homes that looked like the houses in a painting of a fishing village, going down into the sand dunes, walking barefoot, hand in hand, in the night spread before them. In these moments of togetherness a new feeling filled Gershon's heart. He no longer fantasized about distant places or preoccupied himself with lofty thoughts. He was completely there, with Bella, enjoying the touch of her hand in his, her laugh, her eyes flashing in the darkness, her soft hair, with her in the bosom of this night beneath a star-studded sky. Pulling her into the folds of the dunes, and she following him giggling, until they were swallowed up between the tall sand hills that hid them from prying eyes, then he sitting down on the sand and pulling her to him, laying her down on a bed of soft, dark sand, and making love to her with joy and love, enjoying the sight of her submitting to his fluttering, tickling, sure touch, laughing and moaning as he lifts her dress and penetrates her, and she wrapping her legs around him, her head reeling with pleasure, crying out like a vixen as she climaxed.

Those nights were a kind of second honeymoon for Bella too, who had not imagined how much this place would affect her husband by their very detachment from the familiar and being together within this soothing beauty, without commitments to anything except themselves. These moments of joy and spending were the most beautiful in her life, and it was as if they gave her a new insight into the profundity of her relationship with Gershon, and she gave thanks for having felt not only the distress of an abandoned woman, but also the joy of the giving, loved woman, who reaches gratification. She was grateful to him, to Gershon, for bringing her to this point, and her gratitude was clearly evident in her face and behavior.

Their days there were good and peaceful until a telegram cut short their vacation all at once. In it the Hirsch Foundation in Buenos Aires informed Gershon of the sudden passing of Baron Moritz Hirsch. In less than a day they packed all their belongings and returned home in mourning, with the two boys not understanding what had happened, while their parents hastily prepared for the journey to attend the funeral of their patron and benefactor which was to take place in Paris a few days later.

Fifty-one

The death of his patron and friend sent Gershon into a deep depression. He secluded himself in his big library, gradually sinking into the depths of his sadness that was always lurking under the façade of his life of activity.

Bella realized that she must take action. She spoke to the members of the Jewish Colonization Association and decided that on the thirtieth day after the baron's death a reception would be held at the Bergman home, when eulogies would be delivered. Then she summoned Mademoiselle Violette, Isabel, the cook and the maids, and arranged who was to do what. The house must look its best and the dinner would be remembered for years to come, she told them.

Gershon only heard about the affair after she had made all the arrangements. She came into his room not only to obtain his permission for it, but also to inform him that it was going to take place. Gershon listened, his eyes glued to the floor and didn't say a word.

"Now I want you to sit down and compose your speech in Moritz's memory, Gershon. This speech has to be work of art. The best of your writing. Nothing less."

Gershon looked at her, grateful that she had taken the initiative to activate him, compel him to read, think, and to finally write.

He sat down and read the writings of Baron Hirsch while selecting quotations from them. He opened his article on Hirsch's figure and work with quotations from the baron's article, "My Views on Philanthropy" that was published in an American journal and which he sent to all the branches of the JCA. 'Although I am more a man of action than one of the written word,' he wrote, 'I am certainly willing to answer the question of what has motivated my philanthropic work. There is no room for doubt regarding the great duty that wealth imposes on its holder. I am profoundly convinced of this. I must consider myself only as the temporary manager of the wealth I have accumulated, and it is my duty to contribute in my own way to relieving the suffering of those hard pressed in the hands of fate. I fight resolutely against the old system of giving, which only generates even more beggars. The biggest problem of philanthropy is turning individuals who have become mendicants into people capable of working, and thus into productive members of the community.'

While he sat writing his article, Bella sent out invitations to the reception to all the JCA branches throughout the world, including those in Odessa, Kiev, Warsaw, and St. Petersburg. She also informed the ambassadors of Canada and Mexico of the event, knowing full well that in the past the baron had explored the possibility of establishing Jewish colonies in their countries as well; and the Belgian consul, whose country the baron had represented as its ambassador to Constantinople for a certain period. It was important to her to give the event an international flavor.

The only ones she balked at inviting to her home were settler representatives from the baron's colonies, so she drove specially to the Foundation's offices to consult the baron's aide, Wilhelm Lowenthal, about them.

With all the reservations he, like the other Foundation people, had about this woman whose activism often exceeded the bounds of good taste, Lowenthal knew that she and her husband had been well liked by the baron and his wife. He therefore kept his distaste of Bella in check, welcomed her, and even pulled out a chair for her by his desk. She gazed at the portrait of the baron on the wall, a black ribbon attached to its frame, and a tear crept down her cheek.

"He looks so alive," she said.

"It's hard to believe he's no longer with us," Lowenthal concurred.

"The funeral in Paris was so impressive," Bella said.

"And the thirtieth day reception should be no less dignified," Lowenthal said, picking up the thread of her thinking.

"That's why I've come to see you, Wilhelm. My husband is presently not at his best, and there are things I find it hard to talk about with him."

"Please go on," Lowenthal encouraged her with some curiosity.

"I've already invited the people one must invite from among the consuls and government echelons," she told him, "but I find it difficult to make up my mind about the settlers."

"In what sense?" he asked, folding his arms authoritatively.

"I can't seat a Jewish gaucho next to a consul," she replied. "With all due respect to the baron, this is a reception for the elite not the hoi polloi."

"Ah, so that's what's worrying you," he laughed. "Stop worrying. The baron would see it no differently."

"Are you sure?" she asked. "Did he ever speak to you about his attitude toward the settlers?"

"I'll answer you with a letter he wrote me," he smiled, and started looking through some folders on his desk. "Here we are, read it."

'If we seek the success of colonies through an enterprise such as ours, we must at first act without mercy and even almost barbarously', Baron Hirsch had written. 'I make no differentiation between slaves and settlers other than the settlers being forced to work just as hard as slaves, but the fruits of their labors will remain in their hands, while those of the slaves belong to their masters. Tilling the soil is the only way of restoring the nation, but it must be forced upon it whether it likes it or not.'

"He's so right!" Bella said when she finished reading the letter. "When did he write this?"

"When we drew up the contracts signed with the first settlers," he answered. "Before we gave them any land."

"Has anyone else seen it?" she asked.

"Heaven forbid. But its spirit is embodied in the contracts that really angered the first settlers and caused quite a few Jews to disembark in the port, evade us, and go straight to the crowded quarters in the center of the city instead of the settlements."

"I didn't realize that the baron was so clear-headed about them." Bella said, "but perhaps I did. After all, he was of the elite."

"He certainly was," he nodded. "Which is why it seems we can agree on only one representative from each settlement."

"And they must be appropriately dressed," she added quickly, imagining a group of Jewish gauchos arriving at her home in riding breeches, floppy shirts and bandannas around their neck.

"We will provide them with suits here so they won't embarrass either the baron or the hostess," he smiled, stroking his beard. "And how is your husband?"

"He's working on the baron's writings, preparing his eulogy."

They exchanged a few more words, agreed the final details of the evening, and took their leave of one another.

The reception was attended by a large number of people and in great splendor. The street leading to the Bergman estate was decorated with the various national flags, and carriages bearing dignitaries stopped outside their home. Gershon delivered a wonderful eulogy and was so happy at the conclusion of the evening that he fell into his wife's arms to thank her. And she, happy with the great success, gave herself to him and unintentionally became pregnant for the second time.

A short time after the thirtieth day of mourning of the baron's death, Bella received a package from Paris. When she opened it she found a box made of fine wood. Inside, on a bed of red velvet, lay the Giambologna bronze statuette with a letter from the baron's executors. He had bequeathed his art collection to his family, but had instructed that after his death this particular work be sent as a mark of his personal esteem to Madame Bergman.

Fifty-two

Several years elapsed before the song of the ring reached Bella Bergman, which is the nature of songs. A whore stands and extols her friend's ring in a song on the moonlit patio. The song goes by word of mouth from one person to another and musicians play it, once here and once there, until one day they play it at the bar-mitzvah party of twin boys in the heart of the Recoleta neighborhood.

Bella heard the words of the song and stood rooted to the spot. She wasn't sure that she was actually hearing what she was hearing. But once she understood that she was, she spun like a sword in its scabbard.

"Where's that song from?" she asked the three old musicians with a menacing look.

"It's an old song," the elderly bandoneón player replied.

"What do you mean, 'old', who wrote it?"

"What's the matter, Señora Bergman?" the clarinetist asked, taking his instrument from his mouth. "Why are you so upset?"

"Where's that song from?" she repeated, shaking the bandoneón player.

"From the brothels of Argentina," the violinist interrupted, "like all the tango songs in Yiddish. It's from the *shandeyezer*."

"I want to know exactly at which house you first heard that song," she demanded.

The three musicians looked at one another in surprise and didn't know what to say. They played in numerous places – for the aristocrats and the cloth merchants, for The Unclean and the poor. They played at ceremonies in the colonies and at affairs in the Once quarter. That's the nature of playing, they told her, you go wherever you're invited and also to where you're not. We've been playing that song for some years now, and how can we know where it came from?

The bandoneón player's face suddenly lit up. "Of course! It's from Manuel's house."

"Don't talk to me in riddles!" Bella yelled. "What's 'Manuel's house?' Who's Manuel?"

"Manuel Zind, in Calle Junin. It's a song about his whore's ring."

"And why is it about her ring?"

"Because it's special. I saw it once, Señora. It's a heavy ring, special, it changes color."

Bella's heart was filled with tempestuous emotion. At long last she had found what she was looking for. She had found the ring, the ring had found her. She went up to her room and returned a few moments later with a wad of banknotes.

"This is for you," she told the musicians, "you deserve it."

She was already forty-three, the mother of three and a respected member of *Ezrat Nashim* and the Buenos Aires Jewish community. She was admired in government circles and well known in the city. But she was unable to allow herself to do what she wanted most of all – to get into her carriage, be driven to that house, and confront the wanton woman wearing her ring. No, that was not her way. She had to plan, to carefully think it all over. She knew that this time she need not rush. That woman couldn't run away from the house she was in. The ring was in a safe place – either among her possessions or on her finger.

In the days that followed the bar-mitzvah she thought a great deal until she made up her mind.

She summoned the groom who worked in the house, cared for the horses and drove their carriages. His name was Santo, of Indian extraction, average height, and had a strong, sharp-featured face like all the men in whose veins Indian blood flowed. He was young, but a real man. Well-built, powerful, and single.

Santo was very surprised when he was summoned to the Señora's room, but that was nothing compared to her request. She knew that he worked on their estate and was saving his money to marry his beloved, Juliana.

"Go to the Jews' brothel with your money?" he asked in Spanish.

"Go and enjoy yourself," she replied, "there's a woman there who has a ring that belongs to me. I want it back."

"You're sending me to dirty myself for a ring, Señora?"

"No, to have a good time."

"A good time with a whore."

"A good time with the daughter of the man who murdered my husband's parents," she retorted.

"Just a moment – murder? How does the ring…?"

"It's a long story," Bella interrupted. "The most important thing is that the ring returns to me."

After she promised him such a reward that he could not but obey her, he went on his way.

Fifty-three

She knew he couldn't refuse her. After all, he depended on her for his living and he was a man. And like all men he, too, had days when lust rose inside him, when all he wanted was to feel the delicious climax, the soft body. He was shy, but he was a young man.

He went to that brothel.

His legs failed him as he got to the door. Perhaps they were used only to foreign merchants and sailors; perhaps they accepted only Jews, not *porteños*?

He didn't know how they would receive him, but he knew he had to do it.

That evening he owed it to himself, not the Señora, but himself.

That evening Juliana had shrunk from him and not responded to his touch. She came from a very religious family and didn't want to have sex before marriage. But who was talking about marriage? He barely had the money to sustain himself. And to sustain her, with a child or two? Her parents did everything in their power to keep her away from him and she was torn between him and her filial duty. He was working very hard to win her hand, abstaining to preserve her purity. But how long could he go on?

He had to do this for himself, to go into a house where nobody knew him, have a free fuck, and at the same time perform a small service for the Señora. It couldn't do any harm. He was filled with lust and she only let him hold her hand, and on rare occasions kiss her cheek. Nothing more, God forbid. No, no. He wondered about this ring, its hold over the Señora who had given him money to glean information about it.

The Jews had all sorts of things in their head that he didn't understand. They love a different god, eat different food, worship in different places. It's one thing to work for them. It's even good. They've got money. But it's quite another to understand them. And this Jewish ring is something that's impossible to understand.

An elderly woman opened the door for him. She greeted and welcomed him as if he were her long lost son. He found himself returning her smile. The smile is not something that can be controlled.

She led him into a big room that looked like the drawing room of rich people. Various girls, most of them young, were sitting on the couches. They were well dressed. They looked good. The woman told him he could choose. But his eye were already fixed on one, her black hair falling over her shoulders, and her big black eyes were looking at him half invitingly, half gloomily. That's the young woman he wanted. He wanted to sink into those eyes right now.

He motioned at her with his head, and the big woman saw and beckoned the girl to get up and come over.

Miriam did.

She looked even more attractive standing up. The same height as him, her body slim and curvaceous, her black hair cascading down her back. He wanted to touch that hair, stroke it. As she walked in front of him he saw her wide, tempting hips swaying from side to side. He felt his hands sweating. He wanted to grasp that ass. He wanted to be inside her.

A hand was suddenly holding him back. It was the elderly woman. She was asking for the money in advance. The girl halted a few steps in front of him and turned her head to smile at him.

Santo dug into his pocket and fished out a roll of banknotes. He peeled one off and put it into the woman's outstretched hand. She thanked him and motioned them to continue.

They went upstairs to the second floor. There was a row of doors there. With her tiny hand the girl turned the handle of one of them, opened it, and invited him in. She was smiling at him again.

Perhaps she was happy to see him?

The room was neither small nor big. The bed took up most of the space. What happens now? He stood in the doorway, embarrassed.

The girl sat down on the edge of the bed, unbuttoning her dress from behind and letting it drop. Her naked body was revealed to him. Completely naked. She wasn't wearing anything underneath.

He looked at her excitedly, wonderingly, but stood rooted to the spot.

She gave him a little smile, without words, and moved over to him. He could feel his member swelling through the cloth of his trousers. She took it in her hand.

Just like that, through the trousers.

She pulled him to her slowly, moving backward until she reached the bed, sat down, and unbuttoned his fly. His prick was released right into her mouth, her hot, wet mouth.

He was unable to describe the feeling. This was the first time he had experienced it. He suddenly felt tremendous pressure spurting from himself, all at once. She spat his semen into her cupped hand, while with the other she wiped her mouth.

But he was still erect. She saw it, moaned softly, and smiled again. Now her smile was slightly different, he thought.

She motioned him to lie on the bed. She straddled him and then started moving slowly back and forth, in and out, riding him like a horse. She hadn't yet spoken one word to him. But she was moaning, and he was moaning, breathing heavily, until this time they climaxed together with a loud moan. Now he was satiated.

She smiled at him. "Was it good?"

"Very good," he said. "Thank you very much, señorita."

"Miriam," she said, "my name's Miriam."

"I'm Santo."

"I'm pleased to meet you."

"And I'm pleased to meet you."

"Would you like to wash?"

"Yes."

She picked up two carefully folded towels, and with her free hand took his and led him to a wondrous place – a room with running water. A shower.

"Do you want to shower on your own, or would you like me to wash you?"

"With you," he smiled, daring to reach out and touch her hair.

She laughed. "Do you like my hair?"

"Yes, very much."

She turned on the tap while he was still looking at her, bemused. He had never seen anything like this before. She set the water temperature and invited him in. The water cascaded over his head, his shoulders, his back. She took a bar of soap and started soaping him. He stood like a little child and let her touch him. He couldn't understand how she could be so liberated. After all, she didn't know him from Adam. Or maybe it was a kind of game she was playing. He didn't know and was afraid to ask.

Then she started singing. A song about a ring. And then he remembered who had sent him here, and for what.

"What's that song?" he asked.

"A song," she replied. "I wrote it. Do you like it?"

"It's beautiful."

"Thank you," she said.

"Where's the ring from the song?" he asked her.

She quickly turned off the water and wrapped herself in a towel.

"Why do you ask?"

"No special reason," he said embarrassedly following suit, toweling himself and tying the towel around his waist.

"There's no such thing as 'no special reason'," she said. "Why do you ask?"

He tried to wriggle out of it. "If you sing about this ring, that means it's interesting."

"Yes, it is," she said dryly, and strode from the shower.

They dressed in silence and went downstairs to the big room where all the girls were sitting. The big woman came over to him with a smile and asked if he had enjoyed himself.

"Just a minute, Roja-Rosa," the girl interjected, "he was asking about the ring."

"What was that?" a girl asked, getting up from her chair in a dark corner of the room.

"You heard, Esther. He was asking about the ring."

Esther, he thought. That's the name the Señora mentioned. This is the woman she's looking for.

"Who sent you here?" she asked brusquely.

"Nobody," he mumbled.

"Nobody," Miriam repeated. "He said 'nobody'."

"Yes, I heard," Esther said.

He didn't know what she meant, but he was suddenly encircled by tough-looking women beneath whose outward appearance something completely different was hiding. Falling into the company of a gang of women like this was like falling into a hen coop, he recalled his old father saying. But this wasn't a hen coop, it was a den of vixens. He wouldn't be able to get out of here the way he came in.

They questioned and cross-questioned him, wanting every detail. Who he is, who he works for, what exactly has he come here for, who is the woman whose name he refuses to give them, his employer. He didn't mention her name but told them about her summoning him to her room, speaking to him personally for the first time, in secret, after many years of him working there to save money for his wedding. How she had surprised him with her proposal and why he had accepted, and what was he doing there right now. He didn't even want to be there, and now all this questioning.

But they wouldn't leave off, and it was Miriam and Esther who were pressing him the most.

"Who is this woman?" they asked him repeatedly, as if they had something important to discuss with her.

"First show me the ring," the words suddenly came tumbling from his lips.

They exchanged glances.

"Actually, why not?" Esther said. "You'll see it – and you'll never forget seeing it."

She left the room and came back holding a wooden box. Miriam closed the door and drew the heavy curtains. Gloom descended all around. The faces of the girls sitting opposite him became sorrowful and dark. Miriam lit a candle in a candlestick and brought it to the center of the circle in which they sat.

She opened the box.

The object he saw dazzled him.

The ring flickered redly, reflecting the candlelight from its stone, its old, heavy gold. It whispered to him and his head reeled. He couldn't tear his eyes away from it. His consciousness dissipated. His eyes slowly closed. His mouth mumbled meaningless words. He disappeared into himself, into his very being. Now the ring's darkness filled him.

When he came to he found himself on a bench by Plaza de Mayo. He opened his eyes to the blinding noonday sun, to the racket of the carriages around the square. For a long moment he didn't know where he was and what he was doing there. Where he had been earlier. What he had done and what he had seen that had caused this amnesia.

And then, as if by sorcery, the ring surfaced in his memory. A heavy gold ring whose stones flickered in a deep, bewitching crimson, whispering spells of old Jews. And he remembered. He remembered everything. As if it were an illusion, which now was burned into him without him being able to erase it. The ring had taken up residence in his soul, just as it had surely done in the soul of the Señora. And who would save him from it now?

Fifty-four

She had to summon him repeatedly, send one maid after another, until finally she went to the stables herself. She couldn't understand his behavior. Is this how a young man conducts himself after she had given him money to enjoy himself? And what about the information he owed her? She strode purposefully across the lawns separating the house from the stables. She wasn't about to let him off without an answer to her question. She wanted to know what had happened to him in that house.

Santo was sitting deep in thought, his head supported by a hand, his expression glazed as if smitten by something.

"What's the matter with you?" Bella asked.

His hand came up as if trying to make a gesture, and fell back, powerless.

"Nothing," he mumbled heavily, his head still bowed.

"Did you go there?" she demanded.

Santo nodded.

Bella shook him by the shoulder. "What did you find out? I need to know!"

He shook off her hand. "It's better you don't know, Señora."

"Did you see the ring?"

"What does it look like?" he asked, rage rising in him. "What does it look like, Señora? Damn you! Damn you and your ring! Damn those that possess it! Damn all Jews!" His face was completely red by now. He stood there actually yelling at the Señora.

She looked at him surprised. She hadn't expected such an outburst.

"How dare you!" she screamed. "You snake, biting the hand that feeds you!"

"How could you send me to that place, to those witches? Don't you know what that ring is? What a curse it is? Or maybe you do know and that's why you want it!"

Bella did not understand his rage that had made him cross every line and attack her directly. This was the first time she had seen the ring's effect on another person. The first time she had seen how the desire aroused by the ring was turned into wrath.

She asked him to go back to the house with her, sit down and have a drink and tell her what had happened. He told her, leaving nothing out except the intimate details of his sexual encounter. When he finished his story Bella finally realized how much dread was embodied in that ring.

She had heard about objects with power but never imagined that the obsession to find the ring that had gripped her for so many years, come what may, was connected with its nature. She thought it was only pure stubbornness on her part. She had never imagined for a moment that perhaps, many years ago, on that impetuous day in the Danzig synagogue when she had seen the ring on the dead Reine-Chaya's finger, before she had become her daughter-in-law, she had, unbeknownst to her, become yet another of that ring's victims.

A short time afterward Bella was summoned to her sons' school for a meeting with their teacher. She wondered why she had been called for an urgent meeting but when she came out of it she was beside herself.

The teacher, Aurelio Julio, a blond, freckle-faced young man, greeted her amiably but did not dare speak to her himself. He asked her to accompany him to the principal, Señor Ricardo Gustav, a scion of a family of German origin that had emigrated to Buenos Aires many years ago.

The principal's office was designed to strike terror into the hearts of the students summoned there. A large wooden desk divided it, and the heavy curtains allowed in only a small amount of sunlight, leaving the room in a frightening gloom. Señor Gustav, a stocky man, sat at his desk in a chair that had been specially raised for him, very thick glasses and a stern expression on his face.

It was only in the presence of the principal that the teacher had the courage to tell her what the meeting was about. There had recently been several episodes in which her sons, Alejandro and Amado, had been assailed by a sudden detachment from their surroundings. These episodes usually took place in both boys simultaneously, as if there were a kind of dormant fate linking them. It might happen in the schoolyard when they were playing with their classmates, or during a lesson in the classroom. They would suddenly stare at the blackboard with a glazed expression, their only movement being blinking or tiny spasms at the corner of the mouth or in their hands.

"I don't understand," Bella said, "did you go to them? Did you ask them what was happening?"

"Yes, of course," Aurelio replied, "but when it happens they are completely detached. They just don't speak."

"Do they stare straight ahead?" Bella asked.

"Yes, they usually do."

"Aha, they're *golems*," Bella laughed.

"They're what?" Aurelio asked, puzzled.

"*Golems*," she replied. "It's what we call it when a member of the family starts staring into space with a gaze that comes from either daydreaming or over-concentration. It's one of our family games."

"*Golems*?"

"Yes," Bella replied. "Ah, I'm so relieved. You almost had me worried."

"Señora Bergman," Aurelio began with some concern, "I fear that you don't understand the severity of this. It's out of their control. They are simply present-absent."

"They're *golems*," Bella retorted dryly, "my husband does it a lot when he's deep in thought. My sons learned from him to stare into space when they're thinking about something. We're an intellectual family."

"It sometimes continues for half a minute," Aurelio told her.

"I've heard enough. May I go now?"

Aurelio passed his hand through his shock of golden curls, sighed, and fell silent.

"Señora Bergman," Gustav intervened, "Aurelio is the best of my teachers. You should at least consider what he has told you and perhaps take your boys to be examined by a specialist."

"I thank you for your concern, Señor Gustav," Bella told him, "but I'm late for an important appointment."

She got up, bade them farewell and strode from the room. It was only when she was outside in the street, waiting for Santo to collect her in the carriage, that she recalled the story of the ring's healing qualities and which sickness it healed, and she was filled with great anxiety.

From then on she began to pay great attention to the twins, and discreetly asked Mademoiselle Violette and Isabel to keep her informed of any change in the boys' behavior.

Three whole years passed until the boys reached the age of sixteen, when they were simultaneously smitten with a serious epileptic fit.

At the time, Alejandro and Amado were attending the state high school. They were outstanding students, had grown into handsome youngsters, took part in the various sports, and it seemed that their sexual maturity had come upon them earlier than their peers. Since they were sixteen, they had decided to spend the pocket money their father gave them on their first taste of a woman.

While Amado was only a few minutes older than his twin brother, he had become sexually mature much sooner. He was the first to wake up one morning to find his sheet soiled with a thick stain. He quickly wiped it away with an old newspaper he had thrown into the trash can outside, but this thing troubled him until he told his good friend Leandro who affectionately slapped him on the back and told him that he had become a man that night.

The same thing happened to his twin brother Alejandro the next day. Amado laughed and told him it had taken him exactly twenty-four hours to become a man after him.

They started collecting pictures of beautiful women, singers and actresses, that they kept under their mattresses, and looked at them in secret. As they did, they felt something new and unfamiliar filling their body with heat. It was only when Leandro came to stay and slept in their room that they were initiated into the secret of masturbation and began talking about women.

They awoke one morning with the realization that they wanted to visit a whore. They had been surrounded with talk about the brothels since their childhood, but whereas in their home it was mentioned quietly, in the schoolyard the boys would compete with their knowledge of the addresses of these places and with information on how to do it and with what.

That day, when they left the house in the morning, instead of walking toward school as usual, the two brothers walked through the quarter until they came to Calle Junin. They knew that there they would find a few brothels right next door to each other. All they had to do was choose one and go inside.

They were very excited. Embarrassment had prevented them from buying *preservativos*, so they stood at the door without contraceptives but filled with great desire. They both felt that this was a day of celebration especially for them, the day on which they would finally know a woman.

Like many before them they were greeted by Roja-Rosa, who reminded them more of a housekeeper than an elderly whore. She led them into the big room where the girls were waiting, and they stood excited in the doorway. Even among the young women some excitement was evident, for after all, they were so alike, like the spitting image of the same person.

"What are your names?" one girl asked.

"How does your mother tell you apart?" asked another.

"How is it you've come here together?" the girls laughed, encircling them, looking at them as if they were a kind of marvel.

The boys were embarrassed by the commotion they had stirred up, but understood that it provided them with a good opening gambit. A quick glance at the girls around them was enough for them to both point as one man at the same woman, the most beautiful, quietest, who had the strongest expression of them all.

Roja-Rosa was confused. She had never before had identical twins in the house and never been faced with a situation in which two brothers wanted the same woman. They, too, felt some embarrassment because they had planned to each go with a different woman and compare experiences afterward. And now they both wanted the same one.

"You go with her," Amado told his brother, "I'll go with another one."

"No, no," Alejandro replied, "let's go with her together."

Amado looked at his brother wordlessly for he was aware of his shyness.

"When do we pay?" he asked Roja-Rosa.

"You're a good lad," Roja-Rosa replied. "Now."

They took out the money they had readied and gave it to her.

"Are you sure you'll manage together? Are you sure it's a good idea?" she asked with motherly concern.

"Yes, yes," the boys chorused.

With raised eyebrows Roja-Rosa directed the question to the girl they had chosen.

Esther answered with a gesture that for her part it was all right.

She led them to her room, told them to sit on the bed, and stood looking at them. In her eyes they were like children. Their faces still bore a patina of freshness and youthful mischievousness. A closer look revealed the slight differences between them. One looked somewhat chubbier than his brother, and a few golden hairs revealed the first signs of a beard on his soft chin, but the face was exactly the same.

She told them to undress as she slowly took off her dress. They looked at her as if mesmerized while they removed their clothing, leaving only their underpants. They're shy like all the young ones, she told herself. They surely couldn't be shy of one another. She slowly moved over to them, letting them look hungrily at her body. She was standing so close that they could smell her.

At that moment Alejandro and Amado reached out to her and as one man pulled her down onto the bed, falling on her hungrily. The thinner boy, Alejandro, started kissing her wildly, on her mouth and eyes, her nose and ears, while his brother Amado ran his fingers over her thighs as his youthful body covered her legs with its hot touch.

They entered her one after the other, first the thinner one and then his brother, as one watched his brother's actions. Like two halves of a whole, she thought, and that's how they experienced the act. She was happy with them, these two boys, and asked them to visit her again.

They boys giggled and immediately agreed. But they did not manage to dress and finish their easy laughter before they both suddenly fell to the floor, their bodies convulsing as they frothed at the mouth.

Esther gave a terrible scream. Roja-Rosa and the girls rushed up to the top floor. They clustered behind Roja-Rosa who told Esther to help her force open the boys' jaws lest they swallow their tongue.

Esther followed Roja-Rosa's lead and gripped Alejandro's jaw to force it open, but his lower and upper jaws were tightly clenched. Miriam knelt to help her and tried in vain to pull on the boy's chin.

Then she remembered.

She ran to her wardrobe, took out the wooden box, and without a second thought took out the ring and slid it onto the boy's finger.

The brothers opened their eyes as if by magic. As one man.

They looked at each other stunned, breathing heavily, their heads bursting with pain. They suddenly realized that they were lying on the floor half naked, with all the women of the house crowding round them.

"What… what happened?" Amado asked.

"What's this ring?" Alejandro asked, looking at his finger.

"It's nothing, just rest," Esther replied, removing the ring from his finger. "It's nothing. Everything's fine."

She glanced at Miriam and Roja-Rosa and they helped her to sit the boys up and dress them. Roja-Rosa brought them each a glass of water, which they drank reluctantly. They didn't understand what had happened to them but the smell of their urine left no room for doubt. They had fainted and pissed on the floor. Roja-Rosa saw their embarrassment and sent all the girls back downstairs, leaving just her and Esther with the boys.

"Has this ever happened to you before?" she asked.

Alejandro didn't understand the question. "Has what happened to us before?"

"A fit," Roja-Rosa replied gently, "you both had a fit and fell unconscious."

Alejandro and Amado looked at one another.

"Does it happen every time you have sex with a woman?" Amado asked.

"No, no," Roja-Rosa replied, "it's what happens when you've got a very special illness. The saints' sickness. The falling sickness."

"We're not sick with anything," Amado said, buttoning his shirt, "we're fine."

"Yes, fine," his brother repeated.

Holding onto each other, they slowly got up. They didn't understand why they felt so exhausted and didn't remember anything of what had happened to them.

"What are your names?" Roja-Rosa asked. "Where do you live? Perhaps we should send somebody to walk you home?"

"No, not at all," Amado replied, alarmed. "Our parents don't know we're here."

"You can't go home on your own. It's too risky."

"We live in Recoleta," Amado said, "and if our father and mother hear we've been here it'll be more risky for you than us."

Roja-Rosa and Esther exchanged glances.

"What are your parents' names?" Esther asked.

"Bella and Gershon Bergman," Alejandro replied.

Roja-Rosa crossed herself. "*Dios mio*," she said.

"What's wrong?" the boys asked in unison.

"Nothing," Roja-Rosa said, "walk slowly."

The puzzled boys looked at one another and left the house with an odd feeling of heaviness. They were surprisingly fatigued and completely confused. This wasn't how they had imagined their first time with a woman.

Esther and Roja-Rosa were at a loss. The Bergman family groom had told them exactly whose servant he was and all about his employers. Gershon Bergman was one of this city's leading lights, and his wife was well known for her activities against the brothels. From the moment they heard the boys speak her name they knew they were in big trouble.

"You won't do anything about this," Roja-Rosa said as she helped Esther clean up the puddle of urine left by the two youngsters. "You'll go on receiving them as if nothing happened."

"And what if they have another fit?" Esther asked.

"You've got the ring for that."

"Take it out again? In the end they'll realize what's happening."

"No they won't. They don't remember a thing after a fit."

"Perhaps it's an omen that I should return the ring to them," Esther wondered aloud.

"Are you mad?" Roja-Rosa cut her short. "It's the only memory of your mother you've got. And it's also your only insurance."

"I know. But that ring was made to save lives."

"They're two and you're one," Roja-Rosa said forcefully, "and apart from that nobody's proved that it really helps."

"You saw for yourself."

"It's always like that. They always get up after a few minutes or hours."

Esther looked deep into her eyes and then lowered her head. "I'd like to think that, Roja-Rosa," she said slowly, "but that ring really does cure people of the falling sickness. It even cured my mother, at least that's what she wrote to me."

"So let their parents take them to good doctors," Roja-Rosa said. "We don't need that family making trouble for us."

Fifty-five

In the two years that passed since then the boys would regularly leave their home for their Hebrew lesson. At first their mother had tried to dissuade them. Her opposition to separatist nationalist symbols was well known. She wanted them to broaden their knowledge of English or the history of the modern nations in preparation for the law studies she had set out for them at the University of Buenos Aires. But the boys insisted that they should know the Hebrew language, and their father helped them repel their mother's attacks. Bella wondered about this excessive diligence. She also noticed that they attended this lesson in their best clothes. In the end her suspicions led her one day to send Santo to follow them and see where they were really going. But when she heard what he had found out she couldn't believe her ears and decided to look into the matter herself.

For a whole week she lay in ambush until the time of their lesson came round. As they left the house, bathed and reeking of the eau de cologne they filched from their father, Bella was already in her carriage behind drawn blinds, waiting for them to turn the corner of the street. She motioned to Santo and they drove off, staying some distance behind the boys so as not to arouse their suspicion, following them down the wide boulevards and streets of Recoleta, through the northern quarter, the city center, and Once, until they came to a house in Calle Junin and knocked on the door.

"What is that house?" Bella asked Santo.

"It's the one you sent me to," he replied from his seat, the wind taking part of his words. "Manuel's house, the house of the ring."

Bella's rage knew no bounds. The thought that her sons had chosen as their teacher of love the very woman she was searching for pierced her like a dagger.

"You've got to find out what they're doing to them in there!" she told the driver as he whipped up his horses to drive on.

"What did you say?" Santo shouted, trying to hear through the roar of the wind.

"You must go back and see what they're doing!" she shouted.

Santo brought the carriage to a sudden stop and Bella was thrown back into her seat.

"I'm not crazy, Señora! I'm not going into that witches' den again!"

"I'll give you money! I must know what they're doing to my sons!"

"What can they be doing? What they do every time a man comes in!"

Bella fell silent.

When they got home Bella alighted from the carriage without a word to the driver and rushed upstairs to her room. She threw her coat and hat down onto the bed and began pacing back and forth. She thought about her husband Gershon tapping his narrow feet in his study – an intellectual, but too weak to take a stand – and her infant son José, still in diapers and who would grow up like his two elder brothers, and about the twins playing outdoors, growing up in the burning sun, their skin golden and hardening, elastic and honeying, like two sweet biscuits, and now they were defiling themselves with those women and might contract all kinds of awful diseases. So many thoughts weakened her and she fell onto her bed, closed her eyes, and fell asleep.

When she awoke she found that the weakness had permeated her body and she began feeling a stabbing pain behind her eyes, as if pins were being stuck into them from within. She tried to get up but when she realized that she was unable, she called for help.

Isabel rushed in. "What's the matter, Señora?" she asked fearfully.

"Call Gershon. Something's wrong with me," Bella whispered.

The days that passed were precipitate and hurried. What had seemed to be a one-time attack of weakness proved to be a malignant sickness that attacked her organs one after the other. Bella was rushed to various doctors and from one hospital to another, but none of the specialists could find anything. When her face began blistering and her handsome features were destroyed, Gershon rushed her to an eminent specialist in America.

When she returned it was difficult to recognize the noble and assertive woman she had once been. Lesions distorted her face beyond recognition, while she gradually began losing her sight. Everyone around her now knew that what they had thought was only weakness was an illness in which the body attacks itself, and is known by the experts as lupus.

As Bella's condition worsened, her sons' falling sickness also intensified. Now that they were young men they suffered episodes of the sickness both at home and in the street. Each time they fell to the ground foaming at the mouth, their eyes rolled up in their sockets, her entire being quaked. She had never before been in situations over which she had no control, and now she had to experience them twofold. Gershon was concerned about her health. She was worried about her sons' health and was prepared to do anything in the world to cure them of the falling sickness.

Despite her increasing loss of vision she investigated the treatment available for this disease. One specialist told her that the most efficacious was electric shocks to the brain, but she was not prepared to do anything that might impair her sons' intellectual ability. She viewed them as destined for greatness. But for how long could she endure the fact that her two lovely boys, outwardly strong, carried within them that damned epilepsy and were beset by it in the most unpredictable ways and forms and times. She was most alarmed by the possibility that they might swallow their tongue, God forbid, or suffer an attack someplace where no one knew what the sickness was and they would suffocate as they convulsed.

When her disease attacked her other eye she knew that her time was running out, and that she must take action quickly.

She summoned Gershon to her room.

He came to her bedside stunned and concerned. He had never imagined that it would be he who would have to care for his wife in her later years. A strong woman who knew how to run her life and home meticulously was how he saw her, and now she was lying in her bed completely without strength and barely able to see.

Bella heard his footfalls and reached out toward him. "Gershon, are you here?"

"Yes, Bella, yes," he replied, taking her hand.

"You must get the ring."

"Is that what's troubling you at this moment?" he reproved her.

"The boys are sick," she replied, "promise me you'll get the ring."

"That accursed ring!" he burst out. "Forget the ring once and for all!"

"You've got to get hold of the ring!"

"Over my dead body!" he replied so angrily that he even surprised himself.

"If you don't get hold of it, it will be over the dead bodies of all of us," Bella replied.

"All right, all right!" he shouted, and rushed out.

Fifty-six

The fruit seller stood at the corner of Calle Junin in his wooden stall that was roofed with a tarpaulin to protect him from the elements. In winter he would take out a small brazier on which he would roast chestnuts while he warmed himself on it. A chestnut brazier and an urn containing a hot beverage. His customers called him *el frutero de las putas*, the whores' fruit seller.

His name was Emmanuel.

His clothes were faded and threadbare. Each day he would come to work at the same time in the afternoon and remain in his stall almost the whole night through. Like a secret agent of the night he stood there, serving the customers who walked up and down the street with chestnuts and a drink, sugared almonds, all kinds of things he would sell either on thin wooden skewers or in a cone of rolled-up newspaper. He was always there, watching the people passing with his big black eyes, looking up the street as if toward a distant horizon, as if the end of the street promised more than carriages, passersby, and even the rare automobile.

It is impossible to know when Esther caught his eye. He was a young man and she a young woman. But on one of those rare winter mornings when she was allowed to go into town to have a dress repaired and do some shopping, she reached the end of the street loaded with baskets. She stopped to rest by his stall, put her baskets down, not looking at him but up the street, calculating how many more steps it would take until she reached the house.

He came from behind the stall and was suddenly standing beside her.

"I'll help you," he said.

"No, no, really," she said, trying to repel him.

"I'll help you. I want to help you."

She looked into his eyes for the first time. She was tired, but she already knew.

It is no easy thing to have an affair with a fruit seller at the end of the street, especially this street, without anyone knowing. Had it come to light she would be placing her life at risk and possibly his as well.

That is how the Thursday visits began, when she made a habit of shopping in the Once market. His house was in one of the streets close to the market square. Each time they had only two hours. After their assignations he would help her carry her baskets to within a reasonable but safe distance from Calle Junin.

On one occasion they were seen together and Manuel asked her about it.

"He lives near the market and helped me carry the baskets," she replied, "that's all."

It happened, it ended.

It ended when she refused to run away with him.

It ended when I was born.

I was born in 1912. Like all the aunts in our houses, my mother was afraid of becoming pregnant and going through all the anguish awaiting those who did in our houses. But one day she noticed that her period pains were late, and after a week of tense waiting she realized the obvious. She was pregnant and only God knew what she would do.

Left with no choice, she called Roja-Rosa to her room and told her. Roja-Rosa clasped her hands. They both knew how Manuel would react to the news.

Initially my mother went to the Indian woman. She was not young and very experienced in treating our women. She looked into her eyes, felt her pulse, and stroked her belly with her forearm.

"You're pregnant," she said.

"I've got to terminate it," my mother said.

"I'll give you some bitter tea," the Indian woman said, "but it won't help. This is a stubborn pregnancy."

She gave my mother some bay leaf tea and made up a potion that she had to drink every day. The potion embittered her soul but did not bring about my abortion. Much later my mother would say that I'd hung onto her womb by my fingernails, refusing to come out. When she said this she would hug me and add that it was her good luck, really.

But that is not what she thought as her belly swelled and her pregnancy was there for all to see. Manuel flew into a terrible rage and beat her in front of all the other girls. He was no longer young, but was still a very strong man.

"How dare you?" he roared, slapping her with all his might. "How dare you ruin the livelihood of this house!"

"It's not her fault, leave her alone!" said Roja-Rosa, interposing herself between him and my mother, protecting her with her large body.

"Who's the father?" Manuel demanded. "Who's this bastard's father?"

"How can she know? It's one of all the men who come to the house!" Roja-Rosa replied. "The main thing is that she works and rests!"

"Rests?" Manuel yelled. "Nobody rests in this house! In this house we work!"

"She's a whore, not a machine," Roja-Rosa retorted.

"Then get that shit out of her!"

"Like hell!" Roja-Rosa shouted. "Do you want your best whore to go to the grave instead of making money for you?"

Manuel raised his hand to strike Roja-Rosa, but it hung in mid-air, trembling with rage. He knew she was right. Better to swallow the loss of income during the last months of her pregnancy than lose his best whore in the dirty kitchen of some filthy Indian woman. That's how Blanca died a short time after coming to the house, while undergoing curettage.

"All right!" he said angrily. "But I don't want to see the scum she's going have in my house! Do you hear?" he told Esther. "You want to have a baby, then have it. But you're sending it right to an orphanage, understand?"

Esther nodded, her eyes wide in horror. That had been exactly her own fate when her father had forced her mother to hand her over to the Danzig orphanage. She was unable to even imagine a similar fate for her own son or daughter.

But she kept quiet, pale with fear and anger. She knew full well who the father was. Emmanuel, the fruit seller. Only with him had she had unprotected sex, in secret, hastily, on her brief excursions to the market. She had no doubt that he was the father of her unborn baby or babies.

She would go and tell him and ask for his help, she told herself.

The pregnancy rounded her figure, making it even more feminine, and her facial skin glowed with a marvelous light. The rumor that Manuel's best whore was pregnant spread like wildfire, bringing her more clients than ever. They enjoyed coming to her, treating her with exaggerated gentleness, running their hands over her swelling belly in a gesture of sham intimacy.

Emmanuel was overjoyed when she told him about the pregnancy. His face glowed and he hugged and kissed her again and again with great excitement.

"We'll run away from here this week," he said.

"I can't run away," she told him. "There's nowhere in the world I can run to."

"What do you mean? We can go to Brazil, Uruguay, who knows us there?"

"Fate," she said, "and the *rufianes*, they've got friends everywhere."

"There's no such thing as fate," he remonstrated with her, "what are you talking about?"

"Ah, there's no such thing as fate? So tell me, Emmanuel, what do we use for money to run away with? The money from the fruit you sell? And how will we make a living there? Selling fruit or selling my body?"

He bowed his head, pained to the very depths of his soul.

"I didn't mean to hurt you," she said, "but there's no escaping fate."

So she sat down and for the first time told him the story of the whore and the carpenter from Danzig, the story of the ring.

"Sell the ring," he said, a glimmer of hope in his eyes. "That's what'll save us! It's why your mother left it for you!"

"No, Emmanuel," she said, her arms around his thin shoulders, "that's not why she left it. She left it for the memory."

"What memory? What are you talking about? Let's sell the ring and get away from here, I'm begging you."

"Memory," she repeated, "it's what the ring is for. To remember. To learn its lessons. It's my destiny. And I'm not prepared to risk it for anything in the world. Not for freedom, not even to live with you."

Her words were uttered with great gentleness, but still they pierced him like knives.

His reaction was totally unexpected. He detached himself from her and instead of pleading he unleashed a torrent of gall. He could not go on working in this street, he said, knowing that the woman he loved preferred being a whore and giving up their son or daughter to an orphanage. If she was not prepared to sell the ring and escape, he would leave forever and she would never see him again.

The next day the fruit stall disappeared from Calle Junin, and when my mother went to the market with Roja-Rosa, to Emmanuel's house, they found the door barred and the house empty. Emmanuel had vanished without trace.

She never heard from him again.

Joy and excitement mingled with deep sorrow filled her. Sorrow over Emmanuel leaving, and even deeper sorrow with the realization that immediately after the birth she would have to abandon her child as Manuel demanded. This storm of emotion led her to consider approaching *Ezrat Nashim* to help her change her identity and flee. But Roja-Rosa, who knew full well what happened to anyone who tried to escape from our houses, and how slight the chances were of finding refuge in this city or any other, warned her.

"The Association is everywhere," she cautioned her, "and everywhere the Association is they've bought off the police!"

"So where will I have the baby?"

"Here," Roja-Rosa said, "I'll bring a midwife and I'll be at your side."

"Do you promise?" Esther asked, clutching her distended belly.

"I promise."

"Tell him to let me keep the child, please. It will be cruel to take it away from me. It will be cruel to do that to the child."

"All in good time. Rest now and everything will work out."

Roja-Rosa arranged two big pillows beneath Esther's back so she could lie comfortably, and left her to her thoughts. Esther could feel the baby moving inside her. "I won't let them take you away from me," she whispered, stroking her belly. "I won't let them take you away from me like I was taken from my mother."

I was born in this house. They say that the day of my birth was one of great joy. Roja-Rosa brought in a midwife and helped her while she delivered me. Wet and wrinkled I emerged from my mother's belly and as the midwife cleaned Mother, Roja-Rosa whacked my bottom so I would utter my first cry. To their surprise I did not. I lay in her arms turning purple, a tiny, dying lump refusing to come into this world.

Roja-Rosa and the midwife exchanged panicky glances. The midwife took me and smacked my bottom again. Nothing happened. I was not breathing and had no pulse. A stillborn baby.

It was only then that my mother realized that she was not hearing any crying.

"What's wrong?" she called, raising her head from the pillow. "Why isn't she crying?"

"She's not breathing," Roja-Rosa whispered.

"No!" My mother took me and smacked me again and again. "You're alive, do you hear? You've got to live!"

The midwife and Roja-Rosa tried to take me away from her so she wouldn't abuse the dead. But the moment I felt the blow from my mother's hand I suddenly opened my mouth, and with a cry inhaled the air of the world.

"*Dios mio*," the midwife murmured, "nothing like that has happened to me before."

Roja-Rosa placed me onto my mother's chest, who was crying with fright and joy.

"Did you see that?" Roja-Rosa said. "I didn't know what we could do."

"The main thing is she's alive," my mother said between her weeping and laughter. She rocked me in her arms and asked them what she should call me.

"That can wait for a few days," Roja-Rosa told her.

But my mother was insistent. She had to name me there and then.

"I'll call her Leah, after my mother," she said, "but I've got to give her a Spanish name too."

"Esperanza," Roja-Rosa blurted almost involuntarily.

"What?"

"Esperanza, hope."

"Esperanza Leah is a beautiful name," my mother smiled, "but why Esperanza?"

"Because we thought she was dead and here she is, alive," Roja-Rosa said. "This little girl is stubborn. She'll go far."

The midwife nodded her agreement.

"And she was born at a good time," Roja-Rosa said. "General Roca is holding elections next month. Perhaps life here will be better for everybody, and for us too, Esther."

"My sister was killed in the Yrigoyen revolution, in Mendoza," the midwife said, "and here the anarchists and socialists are causing unrest. Maybe elections will calm things down."

"Enough, enough," Roja-Rosa cut her short, "now isn't the time for talk of such things. We must let her rest."

"Esperanza," Esther whispered and stroked my head. "Esperanza Leah."

The two women went out leaving me clasped to my mother's bosom. But not for long.

Manuel couldn't stand my crying, not to mention the fact that his best whore, *la puta mejor*, had suddenly had a baby. It was also the subject of joking among the members of Zwi Migdal. They met frequently, sitting in El Gato Negro or Mamita, at Clarita or other cafés, always elegantly attired and flush with money, to drink and pass the time and plan the Association's future moves.

Unlike Manuel who from the outset had wanted a small house with only ten whores, the others owned large houses. But with them if one of the girls got pregnant they would put her up for sale right away and get her out of the city, to Rosario or one of the suburbs, so she could have her baby there without harming their livelihood. But he was soft-hearted, they told him, following his concierge's advice.

Bald Hershel, Hershel Rosenthal, advised him to arrange an accident for this child. Melech, his brother, nodded. He always agreed with everything his older brother said. This was also the secret of their success. Hershel brought the girls from Poland and the house was managed by both of them.

"Today it's my problem, tomorrow it'll be yours," Manuel replied succinctly. "We've got to think about what's to be done with the bastards born and still to be born."

"Put them deep in the ground," Hershel said, "they're just work accidents."

His brother nodded.

"When was the last time you saw a mother whose daughter was taken away from her?" Manuel asked him. "You'll have such a revolt on your hands that we'll never see the end of it."

318

Hershel was silent. His brother looked at him, confused.

"A Jewish orphanage," Moshe Becker interjected, "that would solve the whole problem."

Manuel pricked up his ears.

After the meeting Manuel went back to his house, summoned Roja-Rosa, and told her what he demanded. Under the conditions rife in the city and in our house, she knew that this arrangement was the fairest possible.

Next day she went upstairs to my mother's room. "You have to make a choice," she told her, "either you give her up to a convent or he will give her to the Association, and then only God will know where she is."

"Give my daughter to a convent?" Esther shouted. "That's exactly what was done to my mother!"

"That's why he thought it up," Roja-Rosa replied, "so thank God he didn't strangle her the day she was born."

Esther burst into tears. Fate was deceiving her, smiting her as if she were living a cruel echo of her dead mother's life.

"Who'll nurse her?"

"They'll find a wet nurse for her."

"In a convent?"

"It's best for both of you. That way at least you'll know where she is."

"But I won't be with her and she won't be with me," Esther sobbed.

"That's life, Esther, that's life."

"The life of a stinking dog," Esther blurted bitterly. "First they kidnap us, sell us, force us to go with virgin boys and old men, married men, single men, religious men, perverts, and when we get pregnant they take our children. The life of a stinking dog."

Fifty-seven

Bella Bergman's incurable disease attacked her from within, devastating her organs. Darkness gradually overtook her, striking terror into her heart. But more than she feared blindness she was afraid of losing her sons, and in its urgency this fear became a malignant necessity: to find the ring, the ring that healed falling sickness, and restore it to her, come what may.

One day when Gershon was out of the house and the boys at school, she summoned Santo to her room and asked him to ready the carriage.

"Where are we going?" he asked, avoiding looking at her face deformed by the disease.

"You'll see."

While Santo readied the carriage, Bella asked Eva to help her put on black clothing, the black-veiled hat, her funeral hat, and help her down the stairs. When Eva tried to dissuade from going out she curtly dismissed her protestations. Santo was accompanying her, she had an urgent matter requiring her attention and would be back before noon. Gershon did not know that she was out of the house.

After seating her in the carriage, Santo asked her where she wanted to go.

"The house in Calle Junin," she replied dryly.

"What have you got to do there?"

"You know very well what I've got to do there," she said, arranging her scarf around her throat, "now drive."

Santo closed the door and whipped up his horses through the city streets. He and Juliana were already married and she was in the early stages of pregnancy. He knew he must protect his livelihood.

When they reached the house he reined in the horses, jumped down from his seat and opened the carriage door. Bella arranged the black veil over her face, picked up her purse, and extended her hand for him to help her down. She asked him to accompany her as far as the gate. From there, she told him, she would manage.

Santo knocked twice on the iron gate. As always, Roja-Rosa opened it with a welcoming expression, which was immediately replaced by a look of horror when she met Santo's eyes. She realized right away who this woman in black was he had brought with him.

"Good morning," she said fearfully.

"I can't see," said the lady hidden by the black veil, and extended her hand to Roja-Rosa. "I need help to come inside."

Roja-Rosa quickly took the lady's hand.

Bella felt a hand gripping hers and turned to Santo.

"You can wait outside."

Roja-Rosa carefully led her over the threshold and shut the gate behind them. They walked with measured steps across the patio, where light and shadow mingled, and came to the door of the sitting room.

"I'm here to see the orphan girl," Bella said.

Esther was sitting on a bench at the edge of the patio, enjoying the pale sunshine.

"You've got a visitor," Roja-Rosa told her.

Esther raised her head in surprise. "A visitor? Me?"

Roja-Rosa signaled that the visitor couldn't see, and sat Bella down on the bench next to Esther.

"*Esta es la Señora Bergman.*"

Esther gaped, and immediately closed her mouth.

"I'll leave you alone a while," Roja-Rosa said as she withdrew. She pulled over a chair and sat down in the doorway so she could see what was going on between the two women.

"Hello, Esther," Bella Bergman said.

"How do you know my name?" Esther asked.

"I know a great deal," Bella replied, turning up her veil.

Esther recoiled. She had not expected such a sight. Señora Bergman's face was completely disfigured. It bore no trace of her sons' handsomeness.

"My body is devouring itself."

"I'm sorry."

"That's not why I'm here," Bella went on. "I came to talk to you about my sons, and about the ring."

"What ring?"

"I know you've got it."

"I don't know what you're talking about or who your sons are," Esther stammered.

"They've been coming to you for the past two years. Did they have a fit while they were with you too?"

Esther remained silent.

"So you've seen what it's like," Bella said, "the way they lie on the ground with their tongue out, suffocating."

Esther looked helplessly at Roja-Rosa.

"I've wanted the ring all these years because it's my wedding ring. Now I need it for them."

Esther cleared her throat but did not say a word.

"You know that the ring cures attacks of falling sickness. It cured your mother."

"You knew my mother?"

"Yes," Bella replied impatiently. "I met her about the ring too. I want the ring to cure my sons. You're not sick. You don't need it. My sons do."

"Señora..." Esther opened her mouth.

"Don't say anything. I pursued your mother and I've pursued you all the way from Danzig to here just for the ring. I've pursued the ring for a whole lifetime. I don't have long to live. But I want my sons to live. I need the ring."

"Señora Bergman," Esther said quietly, "I haven't got the ring."

Bella froze. "What do you mean?"

"I haven't got it. I sent it to the convent with my daughter."

"Your daughter? A daughter with the ring again?"

"It's what keeps her there."

"I'll give you money. How much do you want?" Bella asked, taking a bundle of banknotes from her purse.

"No, no," Esther said, pushing her hand away.

"Take it. Just return the ring."

"Señora Bergman," Esther said, "the ring is not only surety for my daughter. It's for memory."

322

"What memory? Take the money and get me the ring!"

"It's the only memory I have of my mother. It's the only thing that will remain of me for my daughter."

"A memory of whoring and sickness, of theft and murder."

"You can say what you like."

"Have you no heart? Have you no shame?" Bella shouted.

"Don't tell me what to be ashamed of," Esther retorted sharply.

"If you don't give me back the ring you'll be sorry," Bella said.

"Don't threaten me, Señora Bergman. You'd do better to use your money on a cure for your sons."

"If you won't give it to me none of us will enjoy it," Bella retorted angrily, covering her face with her veil and turning to where she thought the door was.

Roja-Rosa quickly got up from her chair and extended her hand to Señora Bergman, but she shook it off.

"Call my groom," she ordered.

Roja-Rosa went to the gate and called to Santo to come and get his mistress. Esther looked at the retreating back of her troubles. They had not said one word of farewell to each other.

The clouds that had earlier hung over the edges of the sky now darkened it, and a thick, dense gloom descended upon the city. Deep in thought, Esther went upstairs to her room on the second floor. She stood at the window, looking out at the graying houses that were showing their age, at the layers of soot that hid their earlier magnificence. Affrighted, she withdrew into the room, sat at the small table and lit a candle. She shielded it, gazing into the warm light shining between her hands. Her fingers turned golden. The light revealed the many furrows in her palms, the lines of destiny etched in them, the lost wishes.

She felt a shiver rising from within her and intensifying. Be brave, Esther, she whispered to herself. Be brave.

Fifty-eight

Bella Bergman knew that her days were numbered. After her meeting with Esther she went to the *Ezrat Nashim* office, collected a fistful of letters of complaint from mothers regarding their stolen daughters, and took them to Police Station No. 7 to meet Superintendent Julio Alsogaray.

Julio Alsogaray began serving in the police force at fourteen. He worked out of various stations in the city and saw how The Unclean controlled his colleagues by bribery. Kirstein dominated Station No.5, and Cardona, a wealthy merchant who owned several brothels, controlled No. 1. Each time Alsogaray tried to take action against them his colleagues silenced him, kept evidence from him, and sent him on other duties.

Finally Alsogaray was given command of Station No. 7, close to Calle Lavalle and Calle Junin, where the big brothels took up the whole sidewalk for three blocks: Mamita, Norma, Choriso, Clarita, Gato Negro, and others. Their owners, José Bard, Simon Rosemberg, Israel Choras, Moshe Silberstein, and Angel, kept seventy to eighty whores in each house. Due to the great demand they often found themselves short of rooms, so they worked on the roofs too. They set up beds there separated by thin screens, and sent up women and clients.

His work at Station No. 7, which was a less corrupt station than the others, presented Alsogaray with assignments that brought him close to Zwi Migdal. One day he was ordered to bring in a woman named Bruni Spiegler from a house in Calle Uriburo. When he knocked on the door and thundered "Police!" the clients scurried to flee. He broke down the door and went from room to room until he came to a side room where he found the sick Bruni Spiegler. On questioning her he discovered that first she had worked for Manuel Vandeval, who sold her for 500 dollars to a pimp in Calle Colfina. However, since she was sickly she was confined to a side room where the clients would not see her.

Julio Alsogaray conducted a thorough search of the house until he found a *rufiane* hiding in the kitchen. He also discovered Zwi Migdal correspondence in Yiddish that reported on the shutting down of brothels in the provinces, the transfer of women from one location to another, and on financial donations. Thus Alsogaray was first exposed to the sheer size of the Association and he decided to collect evidence against it.

Some time later a besotted client filed a complaint at Station No. 7 regarding the imprisonment of the woman with whom he was in love, Ita Kaiser, at a house in Calle Fuerdon. Alsogaray went to the address only to discover that the owner had been forewarned and had managed to move the woman to an apartment in Calle Azcuénaga. The stubborn superintendent went there as well. He found Ita Kaiser guarded by four women on the orders of her *rufiane*, Victor Semyatin.

Superintendent Alsogaray brought this *rufiane* before a judge, Dr. Lamarque, but the judge, who was a friend of the Association, not only released Semyatin but assured him that he would be able to work undisturbed. The Association's members worked so well that no criminal file was opened in his name.

Julio Alsogaray did not give up. He entered our neighbor Angel's house without a search warrant after a client informed the police of the imprisonment of Beileh Suchka from Lodz. Angel admitted to being a member of the Association, but a few days after the opening of his trial he succumbed to tuberculosis.

News of Julio Alsogaray and his fight against The Unclean reached Bella Bergman before she fell ill, while she was still engaged in voluntary work for *Ezrat Nashim*. But now, when the likelihood of obtaining the ring was nil, she gathered fresh evidence on young women incarcerated in the brothels and took it to the police superintendent. Among the testimonies she conveyed to him was a letter to *Ezrat Nashim* written by Perla Pzedborska from Lodz, in which she wrote: "To the women's assistance organization, I beg you to come and take me from the house of Neumann and Machayevska, Neumann's wife. Come right away and take me away. Perla Pzedborska, 2038 Calle Lavalle."

Alsogaray studied the letter and thanked Bella. Then she told him about the stolen wedding ring that was to be found at the Las Clavas brothel, and requested that he raid it as well.

Next day Alsogaray received Perla's letter from another source, a newspaper editor named Matias Stoliar. That was enough to convince him that the evidence was credible. He led a squad of police officers to Arnoldo Neumann's house to rescue the girl, who was twenty-two when a relative, the *rufiane* Neumann, brought her from Poland. When they burst in he found the young girl in her bed as if she were dead. He took her away, arrested Neumann and his wife on a charge of corruption, but to his chagrin he again discovered how deep Zwi Migdal's connections with the judicial system ran.

The couple were released the following day.

Frustrated by the outcome of the Neumanns' arrest, the superintendent decided to accede to Bella Bergman's request that he raid Manuel's house. Who knows, perhaps there he might find what he needed to convict the Association's members.

One day, without prior warning and at the head of large force of officers, he burst into the house. They didn't ring the bell and wait for the gate to be opened, but broke it down and streamed in shouting and blowing their whistles.

The girls fled screaming to their rooms. The clients scurried through the broken gate like rabbits. Manuel and Roja-Rosa came out and realized that something momentous had happened. The policemen's faces were unlike those they had been on previous occasions, lacking as they did any trace of friendliness, the conspiracy of silence, the mute understanding.

"Are you the owner?" Superintendent Alsogaray asked Manuel.

Manuel nodded.

"And you're the *portera*?" he asked Roja-Rosa.

"There's no *portera* here," Manuel said quickly, "this is my wife."

Roja-Rosa gave him a grateful glance and kept quiet.

"And the other women? Are they your wife too?" Alsogaray inquired derisively.

"Yes," Manuel replied, and from his office brought out a bundle of marriage certificates according to which he had married all the women.

Alsogaray inspected the documents and laughed. "You're like a polygon," he said, "but more like a polygamist," and signaled to his men who immediately surrounded Manuel and handcuffed him tightly.

"Watch it! That hurts!" Manuel yelled.

"That's nothing compared to what they'll do to you in jail, *rufiane*!" replied the policeman who handcuffed him, and spat on the ground.

He and his colleagues roughly shoved Manuel toward the gate.

326

Alsogaray called the other officers who began going from room to room. A half-naked client fled from one of them – a short Jew of about fifty with a small potbelly, wearing a white singlet and holding his trousers to cover his large nether parts.

"Run, Rabbi, run!" the policemen laughed at the sight of the frightened man. He had already forgotten that only moments earlier he had been taking his pleasure on the body of a young girl. All he wanted was to get out of there as quickly as possible. The policemen pushed him outside roughly, ejecting him into the street in his underwear to be seen in flagrante delicto by the crowd of onlookers that had gathered by the gate.

The police then continued to move from room to room, turning them upside down one after the other. In the end they went into Manuel's office, searched it thoroughly, pulling out his desk drawers and emptying them into the big bags they had brought with them. They collected the girls' passports and old identity papers, lists of clients, and what made Superintendent Alsogaray a very happy man – the donation ledger that Manuel kept for the Association that detailed all the donors' names. This ledger's value as evidence in the trial was immediately clear to him.

He went to see Bella Bergman to thank her for her good advice, but told her that regrettably he had been unable to find her stolen wedding ring.

Fifty-nine

On a hot summer day in January an incited mob marched through the city streets. A motley crowd of men, some wearing work clothes and caps, others bare-chested because of the heat, all marching toward the Jewish quarter. There were workers demonstrating for higher pay, and they were joined by anarchists who incited them, saying that it was not the oligarchs but the Jews who had settled in the city and owned the factories who were getting rich from their toil in the sweatshops. They carried sticks, stones, and iron rods. On reaching Avenida Corientes and the back streets leading onto it which housed shops selling cloth and clothing, leather goods and ritual objects, they began overturning carriages and smashing display windows through which they had seen Jews wearing yarmulkes, and dragging them out and beating them mercilessly, and then looting and burning their shops.

Large forces of soldiers were dispatched to the area. The troops took up positions in Once and Calle Junin, set up machineguns in the streets, but did not fire into the mob that wounded and killed Jews throughout that day.

The community's rabbis convened an emergency meeting, wrote obsequious letters of pacification to the Argentinean nation and stuck them onto walls, as if the rioters might stop to read them and weigh the pound of words against the pound of flesh.

People stayed off the streets during the riots, not even going to visit the brothels. The women found themselves both idle and anxious about what might yet happen. The men gathered to discuss what they should do, until in the end they decided to absorb the financial loss and insult, hoping that calm would be restored and everything would be as it was before.

On one of those mornings Esther crossed the street quickly to Angel's house to visit his *portera* and swap stories about the riots and the damage they had caused. Since the establishment of the synagogue Manuel and Angel had forged an alliance and even encouraged closeness between their women.

Esther sat with Angel's *portera* in the sitting room of his splendid house. The windows were closed and red light came from the lamps all around. As they sat chatting, she smelled what seemed to be the smoke of a cigarette that had not been completely stubbed out. Her nostrils quivered but she did not say anything.

The smell intensified and smoke began filling the room. Only then did she ask her friend about the smell. "One of the girls has probably forgotten something on the stove," she replied, but then Esther showed her that smoke was coming inside from under the door. The *portera* got up to see what was happening. She opened the door and a cloud of dense smoke billowed in.

Esther leapt up, went over to her friend and they both looked out into the street: her house was on fire. Huge flames were bursting from it, climbing above the roof, consuming anybody and anything inside. In the windows there were women trapped by the flames, screaming in desperation and throwing themselves from the upper floors to certain death. The street was filled with people and soldiers.

Esther started screaming and ran into the crowd, pushing people aside as she looked for Manuel. She saw him standing in the road, looking in horror at his burning house.

She ran to him and shook him by the shoulder. "Did the anarchists do this?"

He shook his head, panic in his eyes.

All around them excited people were talking. One said that the whores were so hot that they breathed fire. Another said that he had passed the house that morning and seen a young man, an Indian, unloading bundles of hay reeking of kerosene from a cart, and taking them inside. Esther listened to him and was filled with a terrible suspicion.

Rabbi Hirsch suddenly appeared at the scene looking like an old vulture that had swooped down from its mountain eyrie. He went over to Manuel and Esther.

"The sinning body emits consuming fire from within itself," he said, playing with his beard in sham righteousness.

Manuel grasped him by the shoulders and without a second thought began dragging him toward the burning house. Esther shouted at him to stop, but Manuel dragged this sanctimonious Jew along, intending to cast him into the flames.

The dybbuk inside Rabbi Hirsch saw that it would shortly be consumed by the flames, and realized that Manuel's rage was burning within him so that all the openings of his soul were open, and it recalled the instruction of the Maggid of Koznitz. As Manuel threw Rabbi Hirsch into the consuming flames it leaped from his body to the body of another.

Manuel threw the contemptible rabbi into the flames, was momentarily horrified, and then retreated.

The flames quickly caught Rabbi Hirsch's clothing as he ran round the yard, screaming and burning.

Men came out of the adjoining houses with buckets of water and wet sacks, bound wet bandannas around their faces, and ran to the house to try and save anyone from the flames, but in vain. Wrapped in black sacks, Miriam, Roja-Rosa, and the others were carried out, the burned remains of what were once women, and with them the charred body of Rabbi Hirsch.

All the men, including Manuel, gathered round the black sacks wondering what they would do with the remains. They knew there was no point in asking the Jewish community to give the dead women an official plot in La Tablada cemetery, and for them to turn a blind eye to the nature of the women Manuel would have to pay a lot of money at a time when his whole world had gone up in flames.

"We should spread their ashes at sea," Manuel said in a strange voice.

The men were surprised by his words, but brought a horse-drawn cart onto which they loaded the bodies and then drove off to spread the women's ashes on the waters of the river.

Manuel watched the cart as it drew away.

"Very good," he said to Esther in a voice that was not his own, "all the rivers flow to the sea, and the great sea forgets all. The sea doesn't remind us of anything."

Esther looked at him, and without further ado took to her heels and fled.

The following day the newspapers reported that someone had set a fire in a Jewish brothel in the center of Buenos Aires, and the police were investigating. The police went into the houses looking for clues, documents and evidence. Among the witnesses they interviewed there were those who blamed the anarchists, while others said it was law students who were returning from enjoying themselves with the French women and had come to burn the Jewish whores, while the brothel keepers agreed that if someone wanted to search for the murderer they should start at the synagogues, because the murderer was surely a Jew who wanted to cleanse the world of licentiousness. They don't call us The Unclean for nothing, they said.

Only my mother knew the truth: Bella Bergman had taken advantage of the rioting and sent Santo, her groom, to set the fire of her vengeance on the house and its women.

Sixty

I don't remember much about the convent. I was there for seven years, but a seven-year-old child doesn't remember much.

I remember bells ringing for prayers and stern-faced nuns in brown habits with a white stripe. I remember what the nuns taught us to say every night by our beds on our knees, resting our elbows on the rough wool blankets spread on them, reciting the words of St. Francis: "God, grant me the serenity to accept the things I cannot change, Courage to change the things I can, and wisdom to know the difference."

I remember crying a lot from missing my mother, the way she probably cried in the orphanage in Danzig.

I remember the dress I wore there, a brown dress with a white collar, and my hair, smooth and dark brown.

I remember how we got up together. The duty nun would come into our dormitory with a happy voice and open all the windows to let in the sunlight.

I remember the early morning frost. I remember giving thanks to Jesus and the Virgin Mary before meals. I remember my doll, a rag doll my mother brought me, which I guarded zealously. She was called Anastasia. She was made of bits of straw-filled cloth. She was nice and soft to hug. I loved her very much. I'd hug her the way Esther would have hugged me had she been able to.

I remember being sick with a fever and the nuns running around me in a panic until they called the mother superior to my bedside. She came to me, opened my hand, placed something into it, and said, "With the help of this ring you will live, my daughter, you will live," then closed her eyes and prayed.

I made a seemingly miraculous recovery from the fever. The nuns clasped their hands and asked the mother superior who the ring belonged to, and she replied, "Her mother, *la sagrada puta.*"

Throughout those seven years my mother ensured my stay in the convent with the ring she had deposited with the mother superior.

I saw very little of her during those years but I knew she was my mother. That set me apart from the other girls in the convent, most of whom were abandoned or orphans, who either had no parents or didn't know who they were. Why she chose to put me in the hands of the Franciscan sisters I do not know.

A short time after the rioting abated she came to the convent, but instead of asking to see me she asked the nun who let her in to take her directly to the mother superior. The young nun knocked on the heavy wooden door. The mother superior's voice came from within.

"*Si?*"

"*Esta es la madre de la Judia,*" the nun replied from the doorway.

The old mother superior opened the door. She was already totally blind and needed both hands to feel the face of her visitor.

"Come here," she said softly.

Esther went to her so she could touch her face.

"I've been waiting for you," she whispered, "I knew you would come."

"I must thank you," Esther said.

"Give your thanks to the Lord, my child. You lived, thanks to Him."

"Thank you," Esther said, taking the old woman's trembling hand and kissing it. "You have done something wonderful for me."

"You have come to take the child?"

"Yes," Esther replied, "I can look after her now."

"May God protect you both," the old woman murmured.

"Before I go I have to take something else from you," Esther told her.

The mother superior motioned to the young nun to leave them and waited until she heard the door click shut.

"The ring," she said, "you have come to take the ring."

"Yes."

The old woman walked slowly across the room, measuring her steps. After exactly twelve paces she halted and began passing a foot to and fro over the wooden floor. One of the planks suddenly squeaked beneath her foot.

"It's here," she murmured. She knelt slowly, inserted her aged hands beneath the old wood and raised it. Then she reached inside and took out a small box from the space beneath.

She shook the box, which rattled.

"Ah, it's here. It's here now," she said.

They sat facing one another. Esther opened the box carefully. The ring rested there, its light dim like an object that has rested for many days without eyes seeing it. If she only held the ring in her hand she knew it would again glow as it had before.

"You must be careful with it," the mother superior said.

"Yes," Esther replied, "I know."

"It is as hot as fire," the old woman said, "may God protect you both."

Esther placed the box with the ring in the inside pocket of her long coat, thanked the mother superior again, and left the room, striding quickly down the long corridors that opened onto the tiled yard where her excited daughter – me, of course – was waiting.

We passed through the iron gate and into the thronged street. Outside, people were hurrying hither and yon, passing us in carriages, on horseback, and on foot, all wrapped up in coats and woolen scarves protecting them from the freezing cold of a clear winter's day.

I stood there stunned. In one hand I carried a bag in which the nuns had packed my belongings and the other held my mother's hand inside the pocket of her coat. My mother's other hand was inside her left pocket, fingering the box that rested there in silence. I have them both, the child and the ring, she said to herself, and her heart was filled with joy.

Sixty-one

Since the fire that destroyed the house on Calle Junin, Alejandro and Amado Bergman began passing their time with the French women. They were now twenty-seven year-old law students at the height of their powers, and like their student colleagues who were all single and filled with lust, the two handsome brothers spent their free time at the numerous brothels in the city. While the house on Calle Junin was still standing they would go there to the woman they liked most of all. But since the fire they had discovered the places favored by their friends, the brothels of the *frenchutas*, the French whores who were considered the best working in the city at the time.

It was at this time that Alejandro began suffering from psoriasis. He did not know that the disease he had contracted was the consequence of an acute allergy to dust – and the bodily secretions of foreign women. The itching rash would appear on various parts of his body in the form of tiny burning, itching pustules that drove him crazy with the irritation and pain, and then they would vanish without trace until they reappeared somewhere else.

After years of joint recreation with his brother, one day he decided to go by himself to one of the *frenchutas'* brothels. His brother was busy studying, but he was feeling randy. He chose one of the more experienced whores, paid her pimp, and went up to her room.

Since he was on his own he decided to do things he could not have done in his brother's presence. After they had undressed he put his face into her dark cleft and started passionately licking its inside, whose taste was like an anemone burning at night.

The whore felt the vortex of pleasure spreading throughout her body and she began moaning ever louder. Alejandro enjoyed hearing her moans so much that he did not notice his tongue becoming rougher and swelling. The whore climaxed panting, and with such a loud scream that she did not hear his gurgling.

When she finally heard it she thought it was the sound of pleasure. But when it ceased and he stopped breathing and his head fell back, she pushed his body off of her and jumped out of bed in fright.

Then she saw he was dead.

At precisely the same time a rash of virulent pustules appeared on Amado's tongue as he sat poring over his law books in his father's study.

Amado felt a strange taste in his mouth and cleared his throat, but then he felt his tongue distending and how that smell, the strong smell of a woman, was filling him from within. He raised his head from his book, wondering what was happening to him, and as a thought of his brother flashed through his mind his head lolled and his swollen tongue fell back into his throat.

He fell backward with the chair, choking, but no one heard what was happening behind the heavy wooden door of the study. Gasping for air, his body convulsing, he died with a series of death rattles.

A long time afterwards Gershon came home and went to his study. The old father opened the door and saw his son lying before him, his body rigid and his face gray.

Gershon rushed from the room with shouts of anguish and weeping. The maids who rushed to see what had happened started shouting too. Bella, who was lying in her sickbed in her room, immediately realized that something terrible had come to pass. But while the maids were helping her husband and trying to keep the tragedy from her, saying that he had shouted because a heavy jug had fallen onto his foot, an unknown coachman arrived at the house driving an unfamiliar carriage, and in it Alejandro's lifeless body.

After the funeral the last of the mourners filed away. Remaining in the La Tablada cemetery were close friends of the family and the servants, supporting the grieving mother and the father, who looked like a walking corpse. Bella, who was carried in a chair because her illness and grief had sapped all her strength, grasped her youngest son's hand as if this would protect him from all the evils of the world.

As they walked toward the cemetery gate a figure dressed in black appeared. It passed the grieving family without looking at them. But for one moment, just one moment, the aged mother turned to look after it. Only the birds in the sky and the blind mother saw this woman go to the freshly dug graves, stand there for a moment, and then walk on toward the plot of The Unclean at the far end of the cemetery.

During the months that followed Bella Bergman suffered terrible agony. Not only had she lost her sight and was unable to get out of bed, she was assailed by terrible pains in her chest and stomach that could not be alleviated with herbal tea and not even with the medicines prescribed for her.

Numerous doctors were called to the house to examine the noble woman who was being destroyed from within herself. They looked at the scales that covered her face, saw the red-brown color of her urine, and were even present when she was attacked by convulsions. But worst of all were the attacks accompanied by obsessive speech. She would moan with pain in her bed, call to her brother Heinrich to come to her aid, mumble a torrent of incomprehensible words about a ring she must return to her mother-in-law, or burst into silent, heartrending weeping for her two sons.

It was on one of these days, when it seemed that her condition had eased somewhat and her spirits were restored, that she called Gershon to her bedside.

"I want you to bring José to me so I can tell him," Bella said. "Who knows how much time I have left? I have to tell him this story."

"Which story?" Gershon wondered.

"The story of the ring."

"That story? Isn't enough that it tortured your mother and you, two generations, and now he must hear it?"

"Yes, Gershon, yes," Bella whispered, feeling for his aged hand. "He will need that ring. He's got to get hold of it."

"Shhh, Bella," Gershon tried to interrupt her. "Rest, rest now."

"I can't rest. Without the ring I can't rest."

"Bella, please, leave it be," the old man said.

"No!" she shouted excitedly. "He must be told and it must be left for him. He can decide what to do with it."

"All right, Bella, all right," Gershon stroked his dying wife's head.

"He has to know, so that he knows his place in the world."

Gershon withdrew his hand. "Damn the day that ring was made."

"No," she whispered, "that ring was made to save lives, not to take them."

"It would be better if no one remembers it after we're gone."

"You'll get it back whether you want to or not," she groaned in choked anger, barely able to take air into her lungs. "There is no other way for this curse other than constantly trying to bring the ring home."

Her head fell back and she lost consciousness.

From the moment that Bella Bergman died only a few hours elapsed until Gershon's heart betrayed him, as if it knew that its owner could no longer endure life for even one day without his wife. In one day they both died, leaving their youngest son, José Bergman, alone in the world.

The splendid double funeral was held in the La Tablada cemetery. The area at the entrance to the new cemetery hall was filled with somber mourners, all dressed for the cold winter and carrying umbrellas. The rain that fell incessantly from the gray sky accorded a kind of strange, ironic vitality to the shrubbery and trees all around, as if nature was deepening and renewing its hues precisely at the time when two decent, respected people like Gershon and Bella Bergman were being buried, both on the same day, Heaven help us.

José came to the cemetery in a black limousine flanked by Wilhelm Lowenthal and Mademoiselle Violette. They helped him out of the car, swaying in his mourning clothes, to his parents' coffins.

The congregation made way for him and fell silent.

In the large crowd composed of government representatives and people from the colonies, members of the Hirsch Foundation and leaders of the Jewish community, stood a delicate-featured young man, who judging by his attire had come a long way to pay his last respects, and a strange, full-bodied woman whose face was completely veiled by a black scarf.

I'm not to blame, she repeated to herself, I'm not to blame. But what would have happened if I'd returned the ring to her? Would she have saved her sons and not died herself, and her husband not have died on exactly the same day? Nonsense, she told herself. Nobody can determine who will live and who will die. What is to be, will be.

The eulogies were sad and dignified as befitting the departed and the double funeral. Wilhelm Lowenthal eulogized Gershon Bergman, and did not forget his wife. "She was a great woman," he said. "A great and stubborn woman, strong in her way. She always knew how to stand at her husband's side and assist him in his national duties."

The congregation nodded. Clucks of agreement and sorrow were heard from beneath the hats, the headscarves and the sea of umbrellas that covered the entrance to the cemetery. After the eulogies some of the community leaders approached the two coffins and began walking with them before the congregation, leading the departed to their resting place.

Esther moved back, away from the crowd walking along the wide path into the cemetery. She had no feeling of relief. Her bitterest adversary was dead. True. But the ring in her hand was like a terrible scar of guilt.

She turned and left the cemetery quietly, waving to an empty carriage that stopped and took her back into the city.

Sixty-two

The servants and maids quickly made themselves scarce from the house in which death had struck four times. Of all of them, the most hurtful departure was that of Santo the groom. He fled for his life, leaving behind an empty, open, and neglected stable. He took with him the household's two best chestnut horses, whose bodies were lean and curved, and whose dark manes fell over their back like big eyelids. He fled in terror, for he knew that after the fire he had set in the brothel on the Señora's orders there would be people looking for him, and perhaps eyewitnesses would be found who would link him to what had happened. So he galloped to his house in the family's carriage, loaded his wife Juliana, who already had a young baby, and their belongings onto it, and vanished without trace.

Only Eva and Isabel entertained no thought of abandoning José because of the memory of his proud mother who had opened her home, her heart, and her life to them for so many years. They, who had known joy and suffering with her, were left to care for the young orphan, but wondered what fate had in store for them now that all the house's inhabitants had died.

Before the end of the *shiva* mourning period Wilhelm Lowenthal informed José that his father had left his will in his hands. Wilhelm's presence in the Bergman home during the first days after the death of the old man, the final tragedy in the series that this family had endured, was vital in the extreme. José was now on his own in a huge empty villa, which previously had been filled with his brothers' pranks, his sick mother's rages, and his father's silences, and which now echoed with those silences.

At the conclusion of the *shiva*, after they had visited the family burial plot, Wilhelm asked Eva which room they could use undisturbed.

"The whole house is empty," she said sadly, "who is left to disturb you?"

"Still," he said, crumpling the envelope in his jacket pocket, "this should be done in a closed room."

Eva nodded and called José to follow them into his father's study.

The boy was tall and relatively broad-shouldered for his age. But now his face was completely sunken. Wilhelm stroked his head for a moment and they went into the splendid room.

No knowing where to sit, Wilhelm stood by the escritoire. Eva, who sensed his embarrassment, brought over three chairs from in front of the escritoire so that none of them would sit on Señor Bergman's upholstered, empty chair. The three of them sat down, with Eva clasping the hand of the boy, whose head was bowed.

Wilhelm took the envelope from his pocket and began reading. Gershon Bergman briefly reviewed his family's history and bequeathed his estate to his wife and three sons. "In the event of a tragedy, and my dear wife does not live long after me," he wrote, "I hereby request that the Baron Hirsch Foundation headed by Wilhelm Lowenthal be the executors of my estate and the guardians of my three sons until they reach the age of eighteen. Until that time I hereby direct that nothing should be changed in this house, in its way of life and its staff. Special care should be accorded to the Baron's former emissary, Mademoiselle Eva Violette, and the long-serving housekeeper, Isabel".

Eva heard the words and tears filled her eyes. She had not imagined the depth of Señor Bergman's gratitude to her for coming to Danzig and persuading his wife to sail to Buenos Aires with him. José sat there in silence, not daring to raise his eyes to Señor Lowenthal, whose heart was pounding too, almost in gratitude that Gershon Bergman had valued him so much.

"Lift up your head," he said gently to the boy sitting grieving and shy before him.

José looked at him with his dark eyes that were covered with a deep film of sadness.

"Your father was a wise man," Wilhelm said, "and I shall diligently carry out his instructions. You shall grow up in this house with the help of Mademoiselle Violette and the other servants, and with a monthly allowance I shall transfer to them from the estate of the deceased. Together we shall ensure that nothing changes in your way of life until you reach adulthood. Do you understand?"

The boy nodded wordlessly.

"When you reach adulthood you can decide for yourself what to do with your property and your life. Until then all I ask is that every Friday evening you come to dine with me and my wife and children so you can maintain a framework of family, tradition, and of a people."

The boy got up silently and started walking toward the door.

"Just a moment," Wilhelm stopped him and he raised José's head so that he looked him in the eye. "None of us is immune to pain, to death. But I beseech you – if at any time you feel that your grief is unendurable, then come directly to my house. Grief like this can overcome even an adult, and even more so a young man like yourself."

He stroked the boy's head and sent him on his way.

José went to his room, threw himself down onto his bed, buried his face in the pillow, and lay there unmoving for a long time.

Meanwhile Wilhelm was talking to Eva.

"What did Gershon Bergman mean in his letter when he said that you are the baron's emissary?" he asked assertively.

Eva told him. Wilhelm heaved a sigh of relief, walked around the escritoire and sat down almost demonstratively in the dead Gershon's chair, stretching out before the woman who had served this household for so many years.

"According to Señor Bergman's last wishes," he said, "you and the other servants will remain here until José reaches adulthood."

"Thank you, Señor," she said with a curtsey, not knowing how to conduct herself.

"I shall give you a monthly sum for running the household," he went on, "but I shall require full details of the household expenses. Only on receipt of them will you be given the next month's allowance, is that clear?"

"Yes, Señor," she replied, feeling the weight of responsibility suddenly descending on her shoulders as she faced this man behaving so patronizingly.

"And now that the Señor and his wife and their two sons are dead, do your best to reduce the number of servants. We don't need so many."

Eva felt the blood drain from her face.

"I've finished my business here for the moment. And remember, a detailed report," he stressed, picked up his hat and coat and left the room, promising himself that he would return every now and then to inspect the many books that belonged to his dead colleague.

After closing the door behind him, Eva remained where she was. She only turned round when she heard Isabel's voice behind her.

"Well, what did he say?" she called from the kitchen doorway, wiping her hands on her stained apron.

"We're assured of two years," she replied. "The Señor remembered us both."

"Thank God," Isabel said, "finding work at our age isn't easy."

"Now we have to take care of the boy so he gets through this difficult time," Eva said, and hurried upstairs to the boy's room. She tapped gently on the door, and on receiving no reply opened it.

José lay on his bed not moving, his face to the wall.

She sat down on the edge of the bed, reached out and gently touched his shoulder.

"José," she murmured, shaking him gently, "turn round and look at me."

The boy turned round to her, looking at her with grief-filled eyes. His mouth was slightly open but not a sound emerged from it.

"Your mother was my friend," she said, "and my heart is breaking too. But now we must be strong together." The pain in her voice was clearly evident as she comprehended the meaning of her words. The death of her friend, her husband and their two children, a series of deaths at whose end was a will binding her to give up her life entirely, to finally bind her fate together with that of this family, to devote herself to raising this unfortunate boy, not only by virtue of the official will, but by virtue of the dictates of her heart.

"And Isabel will be staying with us," she added, "we're used to her cooking, right?"

The boy blinked at her but did not utter a word.

"Now lay here and rest until I call you for lunch."

José turned his back to her and his anguished face to the wall.

Eva left the room and chivvied Isabel to lay the table for lunch and cook something that would lighten the burden of the day: going to the cemetery, the reading of the will, the unraveling web of life.

Sixty-three

We couldn't stay in the same quarter and community from which my mother had fled. We began wandering. Mother didn't want to remain completely exposed with a child, and day after day looked for a family that needed somebody to work in the house, and which would allow her to live there in return for her work. She went from house to house, street to street, the Villa Crespo and La Paternal neighborhoods, but nobody wanted to rent a room to a woman with a past like Mother's. In the end, the Jewish owner of a pharmacy who lived near the La Chacarita cemetery agreed to rent us a room in return for Mother taking care of his old blind mother.

Mother happily packed up our belongings in the *conventillos* where we were living at the time, and we loaded everything onto a cart she hired.

We lived in that house for a short while. In the middle of the junction was the La Chacarita railway station, a galvanized iron barn covering the entrance to the tunnel, and beneath it rows of wooden stalls selling hot sausages, drinks and roasted sugared peanuts.

Across the road, overlooking the entrance to the cemetery were seven flower shops side by side, narrow stalls in front of which stood the flower seller who looked exactly like her colleagues at the other stalls. The La Chacarita flower sellers were friends, even though they competed for custom. You'd never hear them quarreling, until the day a foreign flower seller arrived, set up a small table in the middle of the area in front of cemetery entrance, and dared to sell paper flowers from it. This upset the calm of the seven flower sellers. Together they left their stalls, walked over to her little table and overturned it with shouts. They drove her away with blows and curses, and quiet was restored.

The cemetery gateway was a big stone structure that lent a sense of splendor to the entire area. It was the only striking building in La Chacarita, a neighborhood of mainly single-story houses with only a few multi-story buildings like ours where working class people lived. It was a dusty neighborhood, whose buildings served as dwellings, garages, vegetable and food shops, and small workers' cafés.

Opposite the railway station and the cemetery was the La Chacarita market. Every day I'd lean out of the window and watch the vendors and their customers at the tiny stalls as they fingered fruit and vegetables, clothing and other merchandise, all amid the clamor of life and the awesome silence of the dead.

At the time I was attending the Shalom Aleichem Jewish school, and I hated it. We had to wear a kind of white pinafore buttoned at the back, with a belt around the waist, and we looked like a flock of stray specters. Yet despite the uniform all the girls in the schoolyard knew who was the daughter of a cloth merchant, who was the daughter of a respected woman, and who was the daughter of a whore.

We stayed in La Chacarita until our landlord's blind mother passed away. When she died we knew it was also the end for us. And in fact, right after the *shiva* he knocked on our door.

I jumped up and flung open the door.

"Where's your mother, child?" he asked, adjusting his yarmulke.

"She's working," I said, "she'll be back soon."

"All right, just tell her I was here," he said, scratching his pate, "tell her I said it's time."

"Time for what?"

"She'll know, she'll know," he said, and turned toward the stairs.

As he went down the narrow staircase he met my mother. She had just walked into the small yard, perspiring from her walk carrying a basket of laundry.

"Ah," he said, trying to get his breath, "there you are. I was just telling your daughter to tell you I'm sorry, but it's time."

Mother dropped the basket of laundry.

"*Lo siento*, I'm sorry," he said as he tried to help my mother with the heavy basket.

My mother stopped him with a forceful gesture.

"What am I to do now?" she asked. "Where can we go?"

"That's not really my business, you know. I agreed to take you in out of pity so you could help me out while my mother was still alive. Only God and you know how hard it was with her."

"And this is the thanks you give me?" my mother said in a hard voice.

"I've got no choice," he said. "I can't keep you in the house without my mother here. People will talk."

"People always talk."

"But I've got the pharmacy. People are my living."

"Then so be it," my mother said, lifting her basket. "Excuse me, you're blocking my way upstairs."

"I'm sorry." He said, moving aside. "How much time do you need?"

"We'll be out in two days."

Mother rented a room for us in Linares, in the house of Señor Baradosevsky, the owner of *La Classica Cesteria del Pantalone Gratis*. He was the first tailor to make a suit with two pairs of trousers. But apart from being a two-trouser tailor he also had a very big heart, or two hearts in his chest. Otherwise I can't understand how he took a whore and her daughter into his house.

Mother was tired from all our wandering and told me that I had to help her make a living for the two of us. I had to go to the houses, collect the laundry and bring it home so we could both wash and earn enough money to eat.

"And don't talk to any strange men," she warned me, "you never know what they want."

I was happy at being given the chance to go out on my own, and even happier that she didn't force me to go back the Shalom Aleichem school with those annoying girls. Shalom to you, I thought. Now I was big and helping my mother. Shalom to you, and I won't be seeing you again.

We lived there until our landlord's wife evicted us, and again we wandered and searched until we came to Calle Tucuman. There, inside a big yard, we found a Jew who agreed to rent us a little wooden room at the top of a staircase at the edge of the yard. It had a kitchen corner and a bed. Under the bed Mother kept a big box with photographs of our house, Las Clavas. Sepia photographs fading with time, and in them the faces of my aunts, as she called them, my mother, Roja-Rosa, and Manuel.

Mother tried to continue working as a washerwoman. She'd go from house to house and collect the Jews' laundry. Some slammed the door in her face. A few consented to let her touch their laundry without fear of her contaminating it. Others gave her washing out of pity. She'd come home carrying sacks of laundry, stand at the concrete sink in the yard, and scrub.

Whenever I was bored she'd tell me to take the cardboard box out from under the bed, look at the photographs, and play with them.

"So you don't forget your aunts, *niña*," she'd say.

On rare occasions, and for the same reason, she'd sit and read from the diaries.

Once or twice a week we'd do the washing in the sink in the yard. In winter, because of the cold, she'd heat water in an iron bucket on the stove in the yard, pour it into the sink and add cold water. She'd chivvy me to undress so she could wash me quickly lest I catch cold, and then wrap me up in a towel and take me upstairs to our room.

To warm me up she'd cook semolina right after washing me. I liked her semolina. She didn't have much money, so she'd use only a little milk and dilute it with water, and add cinnamon and sugar so I wouldn't catch on.

Since then, every time I remember my mother, yearn for her, I make myself that poor man's semolina. A little milk, a lot of water and some cinnamon with sugar to hide the bland taste and the feel of the grains.

There wasn't a toilet in our room. It was in the yard. A wooden cubicle with a plank seat over a pit. At night we used a chamber pot kept under the bed.

After some time the landlord threw us out, and again Mother went looking for another family for us. She found us a place with a Jewish family with seven children. The father owned a shoe firm, but all his children had studied medical professions. The eldest son, who was married and had three children, was a doctor; his three older sisters worked as nurses in the government hospital, and the two younger sisters studied pharmaceutics. Even the youngest son studied medicine in La Plata. The family lived in a three-story house in the Palermo neighborhood, and Mother enrolled me at the high school in Calle Belgrano.

The school in Calle Belgrano was a private-commercial one, and Mother needed a lot of money to pay my fees. There was no chance of her bringing it in from her laundry work, certainly not in a fine neighborhood like Palermo that had no need of the services of a Jewish washerwoman who had previously been a whore. But the family we lived with, especially the younger son, needed services of a different kind.

Juan Yehuda Shlomo, that was his name, was a tall, thin man of twenty-eight. His face was pale, with a thin sickly flush in the cheeks. He was asthmatic and suffered from respiratory problems and allergies at each change of season. Throughout his childhood he had been treated with kid gloves, as they say, and in a family where everybody was engaged in medicine it was quite simple and clear. This youngest son, Juan, was loved by all the family and enjoyed lots of attention. But it was his undoing. He spent most of his childhood wrapped in the cotton wool of maternal concern, lived remote from his peers, so when he came to academe he did not find a single friend of either sex. He would go to the university, study, and come back home as lonely as when he went.

This was of great concern to his parents and family who wanted to see him happy, surrounded by friends, and not shut up in his room all the time with his medical books, anatomy charts, and the notebooks in which he kept his notes on the cadavers he dissected in anatomy lessons. He did not dare to say what he was missing, suppressing his sexuality from himself, masturbating fearfully in the darkness of his room, not even using photographs of naked women in cheap magazines, or alternatively, imagining the body of one of his classmates. He'd just stand in front of the mirror set in the door of his big wardrobe, look at his lax body, stroke his chest on which sparse hair sprouted, and masturbate just to reach a climax. After spraying his semen onto the floor he would quickly wipe it up with a towel that was always folded by his bed, and then dampen it and dry it outside his window to hide what it had cleaned and thus not arouse suspicion.

But the more he tried to conceal his acts and his nature, his old mother felt in her heart that there was something amiss with her youngest son. She knew she would be unable to talk about it with her husband, an honest conservative man, who worshipped at the Libertad synagogue and was a professional respected by the whole community. Therefore, when she heard about my mother and knew exactly who and what she had been, she realized that the time was ripe to effect a change in her son's behavior.

Margarethe, that was her name, who was from a German-Jewish family, summoned my mother for a talk. Her skinny hands were covered with brown spots, the stains of age, and she also had them on her face because in her youth she had over-exposed herself to the sun.

She sat my mother down facing her.

"I've heard about you from the *Ezrat Nashim* organization," she said bluntly.

"Then you know everything," my mother said, embarrassed but feeling a certain relief that she would not have to conceal anything from this woman.

"I know enough," Margarethe said, folding her arms, "and that's precisely the reason I've asked you here."

Mother listened without a word. Her heart was already telling her that in this place she would be required to provide services beyond those that had been required of her in the past.

"This conversation will remain between us for ever," Margarethe said.

"Of course," my mother replied, feeling perspiration breaking out on her brow even though it was a cold winter's day.

"We are a big, respected family," Margarethe said. "My husband established the first men's footwear firm in Buenos Aires, and thank God, we've managed to raise seven children from it."

"Very nice," Mother said, wondering what the old woman was leading up to.

"I understand you have a young daughter," Margarethe went on, "and that you're having difficulty in finding somewhere permanent to live because of your past."

Mother nodded.

"I'm sorry to hear it," Margarethe said dryly, "but now to business. "I have a young son, Juan Yehuda. As you'll see, he's a handsome man but somewhat sickly. He has no wife and no friends."

"I see," Mother said.

"You and your daughter will come and live with us," Margarethe went on. "As far as the family is concerned I shall tell them that you're here to help with the housework, and you really will help me with it. But not a lot. What you must do for me is take care of my son, if you catch my drift."

My mother nodded.

"Because of your past you'll know how to do it properly," Margarethe said. "I don't want to hurt his dignity, I'm just concerned about him."

"I know," Mother said, lowering her eyes.

"I can see you're an intelligent woman. So long as this arrangement works well and nobody knows about it, everything will be fine. But if, God forbid, it comes to light that I've made this arrangement with you, then you and your daughter will leave this house instantly. Understood?"

Mother knew full well what she was getting into, but she had no choice. What could she do? Continue going from door to door to live with me in a cramped room in a *cenventillo* and look for work selling buttons on the street?

She agreed.

Margarethe handed my mother a wad of banknotes. "This is an advance so you can bring the girl and your things here, and buy some food. Now come, and I'll show you your room."

Mother followed her to a spiral staircase. They went down into the cellar and Margarethe opened the door. The room she saw was a total mess. There were piles of firewood, cartons full of children's things, photograph albums, old exercise books, books tied up with string, an old broken fan, and various pieces of furniture.

"It's in a bit of a mess but it's big," Margarethe said, "you'll be able to feel at home here."

"Yes, yes," my mother said quickly, "thank you very much, Señora, thank you very much."

Next day she hired a cart to take us and our few possessions to the house.

The only two windows in the cellar room were long and narrow and set into the wall at the level of the yard floor outside. Even Mother had to stand on a chair to open them now and again. I'd sometimes look up and see the branches of the shrubs in the yard through the strip of narrow window.

Only a little light came in from outside, and the room was lit by a lamp hanging on a wire from the ceiling. With our every movement in the room the lamp cast shadows onto the bare walls and I'd get scared.

It was very hard for me to fall asleep in that room, in the narrow bed, when Mother wasn't there. I heard footfalls from the street and in the pale moonlight the tree branches cast terrifying shadows onto the wall.

One day Mother decided to cure my fear of the shadows. She lit a thick candle and put it on the table at the foot of the bed. Then she got under the blankets with me.

"Would you like to see something pretty?"

I nodded.

Mother raised her hands between the flickering candle flame and the wall.

"Look at the wall," she said. "What do you see?"

"A shadow," I replied, frightened.

"It's the shadow of Mama's hand," she said. She moved her fingers, crossed her thumbs, and opened her hands to both sides. Then she began wiggling her hands in and out, like a pair of wings.

"What can you see now?"

"A butterfly," I laughed.

Mother kissed my forehead and separated her hands. Now she placed her right hand between the flame and the wall, folded her three fingers into her palm leaving only a finger and thumb facing each other, and started moving them like tweezers.

"And now?"

"A bird's beak," I replied.

"Now learn to do it yourself, and every time you see shadows remember that there's nothing to be frightened of. Look at them and see their shapes. The way you look at clouds."

I hugged her, and for the first time in a very long time I was able to sleep peacefully without being frightened by noises from outside and the shadows they brought with them.

I had to get up to pee almost every night. There wasn't a toilet in our room, only a chamber pot and a pile of newspaper that Mother meticulously cut into squares. First thing in the morning she'd take the pot outside and empty it into the cesspit in the yard.

She'd send me off to school in the morning and go out to work. She worked in a textile factory, she said, and now and again she'd bring home scraps of cotton or fine batiste for me to play with. She also brought a needle and thread and taught me to sew one patch to another, so I'd become a lady, so she said. I didn't know that she went out to collect these remnants especially for me so I'd believe that she actually did work in a textile factory, and was not providing services for Juan Yehuda Shlomo.

She kept away from him at first. She made sure he wouldn't think she was looking at him or trying to seduce him. Quite the opposite, she was his mother's servant and did what she was ordered. She cleaned the rooms of the big house, lingering seemingly unintentionally in Juan Yehuda Shlomo's room. She peeked at the papers on his desk, at the journals stacked there, the heavy medical books, most of which were in Latin and only a few in Spanish, and at the anatomy drawings in them.

One day she decided to act. She found out when Juan Yehuda was due home and arranged with Margarethe for the house to be empty. A short time before he was due, she went up to his room, stripped naked, opened the anatomy book on the desk, stood in front of the mirror and made out she was examining her body according to the illustrations in the book.

That is how Juan Yehuda Shlomo found her when he came into his room.

He opened the door and saw her, as naked as the day she was born, a slim woman in the prime of life, standing in front of the mirror that had seen him masturbating, scanning her body and comparing it with the illustrations in his book.

Mother grabbed her clothes, clutching them to her body, trying to hide her groin from him.

"Excuse me," he stammered, moving to the door.

"No, no, stay," Mother called after him.

He turned to her and looked embarrassedly at her nakedness.

"I didn't know you were... here," he said.

"I'm sorry I startled you."

His heart was pounding. "You can get dressed now. I won't look."

"Perhaps you could help me?" Mother asked sweetly. "It seems to me that there's something wrong with me, and I've no money for a doctor."

"I'm not a doctor, just a student," he smiled, his skin tautening over his prominent cheekbones.

"It hurts me here," she said, placing a hand below her ribs, "and I don't know what it is."

"May I?" asked Juan Yehuda.

My mother nodded and moved her clothes away, revealing her body to him.

352

He knelt facing her, his face close to her private parts, excited and trembling, and then palpated her belly with both hands.

"There's no swelling," he said knowledgably.

"But it hurts," my mother groaned. "Maybe if I lie down you'll be able to examine me more easily."

"All right," he replied embarrassedly.

Mother lay down on his bed, her legs straight and her breasts rising toward him. He looked at her in amazement. For the first time in his life he was seeing a naked woman in his bed. He moved to the edge of the bed and began feeling her ribs, her belly, examining her the way he had been taught to discover a distended internal organ.

"There's nothing wrong," he said, his fingers still kneading her body.

Mother moaned and took his hand gently. She led it down, down, to her pudenda, and inserted his fingers into her. Juan Yehuda was beside himself. He submitted to her, feeling the wetness bursting from inside her, exciting him too.

"Like that, like that," Mother whispered. "Now come to me, come."

The house was completely quiet. Juan Yehuda believed that there was no one there but them. He undressed quickly and climbed onto my mother all at once, kissing her face, her lips, her breasts, not knowing what to kiss first in his passion and surprise.

"Not like that," my mother smiled, "slowly, slowly."

He reined in his passion, lay at her side and began caressing her slowly with his big, bony hands. He caressed her breasts, her belly, the curves of her thighs, and then inserted his fingers into her cleft again, moving them back and forth, making her moan passionately.

"Now," Mother moaned.

He didn't wait another moment before he was on top of her, sliding his large member into her. He pumped in and out, enjoying the first sexual pleasure he had known, and then, his eyes shut, he began moving with increasing speed, making her moan, until he ejaculated with a shout.

At that moment I fled from the doorway, unintentionally letting the door bang behind me,

He jumped off her.

"What was that?" he asked in alarm.

"Nothing," my mother smiled, "just the wind."

"What wind?" he asked fearfully. "There's no wind in the house. Everything's closed."

"Perhaps the door just shut itself," my mother said, somewhat timidly getting out of the bed of the young man who had just lost his virginity.

From that day on they saw each other quite often, usually when he was supposed to be at the university, his parents at their shop, and I at school. They thought I didn't know anything, and Mother, who'd seen me out of the corner of her eye on the day I'd peeked at them from the doorway, never brought the subject up.

Juan Yehuda became a different man. Margarethe didn't need to hear the details from my mother to understand that the mission had been successfully accomplished. Under my mother's tutelage that young man, who previously was downcast and sad, had become a thriving man, happy and sure of himself. And although he continued suffering from a permanent head cold and attacks of allergic coughing, it was clearly evident that he felt much better with himself and he also began going out with friends from the faculty.

My naïve mother was very happy and didn't understand that her success in her task would land us in a sorry state of affairs. A few months later Margarethe summoned her and told her that she didn't want her son to get used to her, or that someone in the household would discover what was going on. She gave Mother a little money and summarily dismissed her.

Sixty-four

José Bergman, or "The Orphan" as he was privately called by his teachers, went back to high school looking different. Compared to his late brothers whose pranks were legend, he had always been a quiet, introverted boy, but now he seemed immersed in himself. His silences, which had previously endowed him with the grace of a thinker like his father before him, were now burdened with an eternal sadness that would sink in his young heart only years later.

He would go to school every day, elegantly dressed and his hair carefully combed, and it was clear that he was being well cared for in the house where he remained alone, with a fine inheritance, so they said. But during lessons his mind would be elsewhere and he was frequently detached from the class, his eyes wandering to the windows and the sky outside, the light, the trees.

The tragedy he had experienced made him grow up rapidly, and since he was the first among his peers to sprout a hint of a mustache over his thin lips, it made him captivating in the eyes of the girls his age.

His friends left him alone. Sitting on his own, either in the classroom or on a bench in the schoolyard, he would read one of the books he took from his father's library, seeking to find in the glut of words some solace for his soul. Some say that the inclination to read passes from father to son, but even if this were true beforehand, it now intensified several-fold.

He read a great deal from everything he could lay hands on at the time. In the books he had left, his father had written notations in the margins on things that had affected him, writing his remarks in his distinctive handwriting as if leaving his youngest son a secret map. He also read textbooks with which his father had taken issue by jotting down arcane notations at the foot of the page, and which had later become the seeds of his views. Thus José learned more about his father's mind than he had in his lifetime.

One day he discovered something that dumbfounded him. From one of the books fell a sheaf of papers written in a gentle masculine hand that was different from his father's, a collection of eloquent love letters at the head of which was a Hebrew date and the name Moises Ville, the Jewish colony, and they were all signed by the same man, Shlomo

Azaria. José had no idea who Shlomo Azaria was and to where he had disappeared. But what he read revealed another side of his father. He kept these things to himself, but their discovery pushed him into adopting a more manly mien in his dress and appearance. Although he still retained his gentleness of character and the scar of his pain, he began showing an interest in the ways of men and even surprised the two women who raised him when he began seeking occupation in the garden around the house, and clearing out the abandoned stable in which – so Eva discovered – he made barbells out of iron rods sunk into cement-filled cans, and began weightlifting to develop his muscles.

After a year of hard weight training, when he was almost eighteen, the gaunt young boy became a well built, handsome young man whose features radiated health and his body manliness.

José Bergman overcame his profound grief, completed his schooling and was sent to university where he studied medicine. On his return from his studies he discovered that the economic crisis that beset Argentina had depleted his inheritance which was invested in banks in the city, so he decided to lease his parents' large estate and move into an apartment in Recoleta, which while splendid was within his means.

He donated the Jewish objets d'art he had inherited from his parents and grandfather – who he never knew – to a museum. Most of the furniture that filled the Bergman home he sold to antique dealers. Of all these things he kept his father's escritoire and the Kiddush goblet fashioned by his great-grandfather, until he came to the collection of coins and his mother's brooches, and wondered what he should do with them.

Old Eva was very sorry to see how he was dismantling the house in which he was born and raised, the house that she had been part of since her youth. She found it even more difficult when he summoned her for a consultation in his father's study. She hobbled in on her heavy, tired legs, closing the door behind her so she wouldn't have to hear the noise of the workers taking the house to pieces.

"There's something here I don't know what to do with," José told her, pointing at the carved wood boxes in which Bella Bergman had kept her jewelry collection. He opened them, wanting to show her what they contained.

"I know exactly what's in them," she said, "your mother often showed me."

"I don't know what I'm going to do with them," he said embarrassedly. "Mama certainly would have wanted me to keep them all. But I don't need them. Perhaps you'd like them?"

"God forbid," Eva said, shaking her head. "I've been given everything I needed from this house. I won't lay a finger on your mother's jewelry collection."

"Why not?" José persisted. "As far as I'm concerned you can sell them. The money will go toward keeping you in your old age."

"No, no. I know what's behind this collection. What a price in blood she paid for it. I wouldn't be able to touch it."

It was then that she suddenly recalled an old, old memory, the redemption of the firstborn ceremony for José's dead brothers, when Bella had started to collect these jewels, and that memory was accompanied by the dire warning of Isabel, the only other servant who remained in the house.

"You know," she said after a moment, "on the day you mother began collecting jewelry, Isabel warned her that she had to give the jewels she received at the redemption of the firstborn ceremony for your brothers to the synagogue, otherwise she would be deciding their fate."

José's face contorted in pain.

"I'm sorry, but it's the truth."

José thought for a moment and then opened the door and called Isabel. A few moments later she came in, her face gloomy and hard. Like Eva, she found it difficult to see the house being taken to pieces, emptied of memories and objects.

"You called me?" she asked, straightening her gray hair that was gathered on the top of her head. She came over to the escritoire, looked for a moment at the open jewelry boxes, and then glanced quickly at Eva who returned a warm look.

"I've told José what you said many years ago when the Señora began collecting these jewels," she said.

Isabel nodded sadly. "She didn't listen to me, the Señora, and now look what's happened."

José leaned toward her, offering her a handkerchief.

"*Gracias*," she said as she dried her tears.

"I asked you here to tell me what to do with all this," he said.

"It must go to the place of God," she sighed, "like it should have back then. It's just a pity that it's after everything that's happened."

"The place of God?" Eva asked.

"The synagogue," José interjected. "The Great Synagogue of Libertad. That seems the most suitable place."

"You're a good man," Isabel said, "I always knew it. You'll save the souls of your parents and brothers."

The following day José met with the heads of the Libertad synagogue. He donated his mother's collection of jewelry for them to sell and with the proceeds order new seats for the synagogue, a Torah scroll in his father's name, and a curtain for the Holy Ark on which his mother's name would be embroidered.

Eva and Isabel said not a word to him about the ring. They did not want to rake up old memories and hurt him.

Sixty-five

Yitzhak Gantz, known to all and sundry as Isak, was a man of sixty-eight who had one leg shorter than the other, so he wore one elevated orthopedic shoe. Isak was a widower, the father of four grown children all of whom were married, and he owned a shop that sold household goods, sewing accessories, and ritual objects. In his shop window there was always a confusion of cardboard trays with all kinds of buttons large and small, transparent and colored, copper and bakelite buttons, boxes of pins and needles, embroidery silks in a profusion of colors, gold-embroidered Jerusalem yarmulkes, black yarmulkes, headscarves for religious women, wood and metal mezuzahs, Sabbath candlesticks, menorahs, and around them glasses and goblets, pots and silverware, an odd mixture of ritual and fancy goods which he had managed for almost forty years with his late wife, until he was left on his own, an elderly man but who was still going strong. His children were spread over the globe, one daughter in Uruguay, another in Palestine, one son in America, and another studying agriculture in the provinces.

Yitzhak Gantz lived alone in a big house and worked in his shop all day, into which hardly anyone came to buy because it was so laden with objects and filled with dust. He was looking for a woman who would help him at home and in the shop.

Mother agreed what she agreed with him and we moved into his house. This time we didn't live in the cellar or a wooden room in the yard, but in a big, real house with rooms and a living room and a kitchen and patio.

Mother looked after his house. She cooked, washed, ironed, and when I got back from school there was always a hot meal waiting in the kitchen. While I ate Mother was with Señor Gantz in the shop, arranging the merchandise, airing the shop, somewhat reducing the load of items in the window and adding a vase of flowers, scrubbing the window inside and out, and as she did she managed to persuade him to put up a new wooden sign, "Casa Gantz", in big letters that was hung over the window.

Women passing the shop noticed the change and began going inside. Mother helped him greet them politely and offered them all kinds of things from the stock. Señor Gantz was overjoyed. His face, which previously was sad and tired, now filled with light, my mother's light, as she did her best for him so she could keep us both in dignity.

After I'd gone to bed at night she'd tiptoe out of the room and come back some time later. I don't know how much later. I can only guess what she was doing during that time. I was already old enough to know that it would be better if I didn't peek and see what was happening between her and Señor Gantz. The very thought of my mother in bed with that old man and doing things to him turned my stomach. I tried to turn over and go back to sleep.

But we didn't stay there for long either. My mother met another man, who had a bad marriage, and began an affair with him without Señor Gantz's knowledge. While he was arranging things in the shop in the evening, she would disappear for a few hours and return happy and radiant, something new gleaming in her eyes, something wild. It was the first time I'd seen my mother so happy.

In the end people started talking. Somebody saw Mother getting into a carriage with a tall, slim man, younger than Señor Gantz, and driving with him to the edge of town, and slipped a word to Señor Gantz at the synagogue. Someone else saw her coming back arm in arm with that man, getting off a tram at Once station. It slowly dawned on Señor Gantz that the woman he'd taken into his home was leading a life of her own and putting his honor at risk.

One day Mother was arranging things on the shelves. Isak was sitting at the high wooden counter, watching her nimble hands as she dusted household utensils, her body swaying under her dress, and he smelled the smell of her body rising from her as she worked, until suddenly he was unable to restrain himself any longer.

"A whore is always a whore," he said in Yiddish.

Mother halted in mid-movement but did not turn round.

"*A kurveh is a kurveh*," he repeated, louder this time, coughing into the handkerchief he took from his pocket, not knowing if he was choking with rage or old age.

Mother turned to him. "Do you have something to say to me, Señor Gantz?"

"I've said everything I've got to say."

"What do you want from me?"

"That you decide what you want," the old man said. "Me or the man that people have seen you with at the station."

Mother dropped her feather duster, her eyes spitting fire.

"You made a work contract with me, Señor Gantz," she said forcefully, "not a servitude agreement."

"I didn't say that," the old man mumbled, again coughing into his handkerchief.

"I have my own life," Mother said. "What did you want, that I be yours alone?"

"I don't need people talking about me all over the city," the old man replied, and coughed again. He looked into the handkerchief. There was no mistaking it. He had coughed up a drop of blood into the fabric.

"Look, I've become ill from the shame," he said, showing her the handkerchief.

Mother looked, saw the blood, and grasped his hands.

"Has this happened before, that you've coughed up blood?" she asked.

"No," the old man replied, "it's the first time."

"We've got to get you to the hospital. That's a very bad sign."

"It's all your fault," he said, dropping his hand holding the handkerchief. He sighed and picked up his walking stick. "Come, let's go."

"Where to?" Mother asked. "Hospital Israelita Ezra or the government Hospital Durand?"

"Israelita!" the old man barked. "You think I'm going to let nuns treat me?"

That was a mistake on his part. The nurses at Hospital Durand had far more experience in treating tuberculosis. The Jewish hospital was mainly used for births and common sicknesses and was not well equipped.

Señor Gantz was in the Jewish hospital for several months until he died. During this time the other man left Mother after hearing that the old man she worked for had contracted tuberculosis, and feared – quite rightly – that she might infect him. Mother told this to Señor Gantz, and his heart softened and he proposed marriage, there on his deathbed, so that her daughter, that's me, would not be a bastard.

"But what about your own children?" my mother asked. "What will they say?"

"I don't care," the old man groaned, "they haven't visited me here even once. You'll see, they'll come to grab everything they can only after my funeral."

And that's what happened.

Señor Gantz and Mother were married in the hospital. He asked the doctors to bring a rabbi and they found one who was prepared to marry a dying old man and a former whore.

I was there at that strange wedding. Señor Gantz lay in bed, breathing heavily. Mother held his hand, and a few doctors and nurses dressed in white held an improvised wedding canopy made of a sheet. They brought the glass of wine to the old man's lips for the Four Blessings, and wondered what was to be done with the ceremonial breaking of the glass.

"You break it for me," the old man told the rabbi, who stroked his beard and nodded. His raised hi foot, stamped on the glass, and everyone broke into shouts of "Mazal Tov! Mazal Tov!"

"Now the groom may kiss the bride," the rabbi said.

My mother brought her face to Señor Gantz's. He motioned her to wait, took a deep breath, and then fluttered a kiss onto her lips. As he did he started coughing and my mother recoiled, feeling his saliva entering her mouth.

"Quickly! Wash your mouth out!" one of the doctors ordered.

He directed my mother to the sink where she washed out her mouth thoroughly.

"I'm sorry," the old man groaned.

"It's nothing," the nurses consoled him, looking at mother and the doctor.

We went back home, a daughter and her newly married mother.

The old man passed away in hospital a few days later and was buried in a sparsely attended funeral at the La Tablada cemetery. At the funeral Mother already had that terrible cough that showed she had been infected with the disease.

Throughout the *shiva* mourning period she insisted on staying home. And in the meantime the Jewish community people had informed his children of his passing, and Mother knew that it would not be long before they came to demand their inheritance.

At the end of the *shiva* she ordered a carriage and took me with her to Señor Kaufmann's pawnshop on Calle Cordoba.

The shop was next to other pawnshops and clothing shops. It was nothing special. Its window was darkened, but if you looked closely at the jewelry in it you could see valuable antique pieces that seemed to trap the light inside them. There were pendants, chains, a few silver Kiddush goblets, old watches, odd items of old unpolished silverware on black velvet, obscure, silent objects that did not give away their history to anyone.

Mother asked him why all the items in the window were covered in dust.

"The glint of a precious stone is reflected in the eyes of the thief," he replied smilingly in Yiddish. Mother's eyes smiled back at him. "I've come to you secretly. Nobody knows I'm here."

"The gems keep silent, the walls are silent, and I'm dumb," the old man said as he got up to close the shop door. "There, now we're in complete silence," gesturing at the shop that was now dark and gloomy.

"I've brought you something, something that hardly anybody knows I've got."

"Well," the old man said, "well."

"It's a valuable object. You mustn't sell it," Mother told him, and from her purse took a scrap of silk wrapped around something. She laid the black silk on the table and slowly opened it before him. The old man looked at the object glowing at him from inside the silk, opened and closed his mouth as if struck dumb. I too looked at it in amazement. That was the first time I'd seen it, the ring.

He looked into her eyes as if inquiring whether he might touch it. Mother nodded. He extended a trembling hand to the ring, the trembling of a man who immediately knew the value of the object brought to him, took a large magnifying glass from his desk drawer, brought it to his eyes and began reading the secret verses engraved on the inside of the ring.

"A masterpiece," he murmured, "a genuine masterpiece."

"Yes," Esther replied.

"Would you sell it to me?" he inquired hopefully.

"Heaven forbid. I can't sell this ring. I was given it by my mother. I want you to lend me money for it."

Señor Kaufmann raised his eyes to her.

"Whatever you can give me for it," she went on. "I promise to return the money on time. But you'll keep the ring as a pledge and won't show it to a soul. There are people looking for it."

"Is it yours?" he asked suspiciously.

"It's my mother's wedding ring. But for your own sake, don't show this ring to anyone."

"Agreed," the old man sighed. "At least I'll be able to look at it from time to time." After thinking for a moment he added. "I can give you three thousand pesos for it."

"Thank you," Esther said.

"Do you want the money now?' he asked, taking from the drawer a neatly arranged wad of banknotes.

"There's no need. I'll take it when I need it."

"Don't you want some kind of guarantee?" he asked, puzzled.

"I trust you, and it," she replied.

The old man rewrapped the ring in the piece of silk. "I'll keep it safe for you."

Just before we left the shop, when her hand was already on the door handle, she turned round.

"One more thing," she said. "If anything happens to me, give it only to my daughter. Only she can be given the ring by you in return for the money I've borrowed, plus interest, of course."

The old man stared at me and nodded.

"Only your daughter. Only her," he said.

Mother put her arm around my shoulders and together we left the shop. After we'd started walking away she suddenly halted.

"Esperanza, that ring has sustained me and will sustain you too," she said, as a heavy cough erupted from her throat. "Never forget one thing. Never sell that ring. If you need money then pawn it so you can redeem it later. And always remember to add your own story to the story of the ring."

Back then I did not yet understand that the ring was not only part of my life, but also of the lives of the women who had come before me and of those that would come after me.

A short time after our visit to Señor Kaufmann's pawnshop she began complaining of chest pains. She was weak, suffered the occasional fever, and blemishes appeared on her skin. Again there could be no doubt – the old man had infected her with the cursed disease. She called me to help her out of bed and call for a carriage to take us to Hospital Durand.

At the hospital they isolated her in a small dark room with yellow walls. Mother lay in an iron bed covered with a green hospital sheet. She had difficulty breathing, and now and then was assailed by bouts of coughing, vomiting blood and shouting as she desperately tried to breathe.

The nurse and I would take her arms and lay her down, and then she would gurgle, death gripping her throat like a murderer's thick fingers.

I was only eighteen. "Mama," I wept, "I love you."

"I love you too, *niña*," she whispered in a moment of calm.

The nurse motioned me to follow her outside.

"It's not good for you to see this," she told me, "you're only a child."

"She's my mother," I replied, "and except for her I've nobody else in the world."

She stroked my hair. "It won't be long now. You must be strong."

I hugged her, folding myself into her bosom, weeping into her white uniform.

Then we heard choking coming from inside the room again and we rushed in to support Mother who was fighting for her life, trying to breathe.

"Don't worry, Esperanza," she whispered with difficulty, "you're like a chameleon. You'll manage wherever you are."

"What do you mean?" I asked.

"You can adapt anywhere," she groaned, "learn from me."

"Rest, Mama," I said, stroking her head.

"Know one thing – I did what I had to do to sustain the both of us," my mother said, and her head fell back.

The things my mother told me on her deathbed were like a last testament, a blessing, a punishment. Being like a chameleon meant being rootless, not being connected to any place, being able to wander from city to city and from country to country, to be assimilated into any environment, to reinvent myself each time to become assimilated into a new environment, to protect myself against it, not to be felt in it.

That was my blessing, Flora. It was also my curse.

Mother died in 1930 after a great struggle, in agony, in pain.

After her soul departed her body she lay quiet, her limbs straight on the green sheet. I bent down and kissed her, and closed her eyes and mouth.

The hospital contacted the Jewish burial society to make the funeral arrangements. As soon as they heard who the deceased was they set the funeral for late afternoon when there would be only few visitors in the cemetery, and dug her grave in The Unclean section of La Tablada.

Her funeral took place on a rainy summer's day. The big cemetery's asphalt pathways were completely wet. I arrived with Mother at the cemetery entrance in the burial society hearse, where a few foreign women who Mother knew from the brothels were waiting. They had heard about her death through rumors from the hospital.

From the cemetery office a tall, thin man emerged with a big, black yarmulke on his head. He was followed by several cemetery workers who lifted the stretcher with the body. He stood before them, prayer book in hand, and began reciting verses before Mother's body, gesturing with his head that we follow him. We did so, me and the women I had only just met, Bluma, Rina and Hava, walking along the broad asphalt pathways at whose sides there were beautiful tall trees. Wherever we looked we saw row upon row of beautiful well-tended headstones surrounded by flowerbeds, and each one bore a likeness of the deceased. We carried on walking, turned right toward the cemetery wall, until we came to an area enclosed by a wall.

Inside the burial plot, as if to humiliate our fathers and mothers, stood the cemetery's new toilet facilities. To their left were three of four rows of headstones. Amidst them I saw a pile of fresh soil. I moved closer and saw a cemetery worker standing waiting in the open grave, only his head and shoulders protruding.

The cemetery people approached the grave, lowered the stretcher, and let Mother slide into the grave. The man in it grasped her and laid her on the soil. Then he climbed out, picked up a spade, and very rapidly – because evening was already falling – piled mud and soil onto her.

The tall man looked around, counting the men standing around the grave.

"We are only four," he said. "We need another six for a quorum." He thought for a moment and then quickly left the enclosed plot, searching for mourners in other parts of the cemetery.

366

In the distance he saw a family group concluding a memorial service for their late grandmother. He strode over to them and asked them, briefly, as Jews do in these cases, "Six for a quorum?"

"*Si, claro*," replied the father, a short, potbellied, sparsely-bearded man. He motioned to the other male members of the family, his sons and sons-in-law. They told the women that they would be right back and followed the man toward where we were waiting, happy to help fulfill the quorum precept.

But the closer they came to the plot of The Unclean the men slowed their pace. When they reached the entrance in the stone wall, they looked inside and then looked balefully at the cemetery worker.

"This is where you've brought us?" thundered the head of the family.

"It's a *mitzvah*, a good deed, Señor," he replied, his voice shaking.

"May they all burn in hell," the man cursed, and spat on the ground. His family also spat, turned round, and left.

The tall man came back embarrassed into the plot of The Unclean. He looked at the three gravediggers waiting for him, and his son, and the women standing at the graveside. He did not say a word.

"*Lo siento*," he said finally. "I'm sorry. What will be will be. Let's carry on."

He stood facing the mound of soil that the gravediggers had arranged in the form of a body enshrouded in soil, opened his prayer book, and began reading. Afterwards, as they always do at funerals, he asked for Mother's forgiveness. One of the gravediggers giggled, and the tall man prodded him, demanding silence and restraint.

They hurried to finish their work, fearful of being caught by the night in the plot of The Unclean. As soon as they'd finished and taken the money offered to them by Mother's friends, they lowered their caps in a mark of respect and left.

I stood there for a long time without moving or speaking, looking at the mound of soil beneath which they had laid Mother, not knowing what to think, what to say, what to do now.

"Come," Hava said, taking my arm, "let's get out of here."

"Where to?" I asked.

I had no idea what I was going to do from that moment forth.

"Outside," she said, "and then we'll see."

Sixty-six

On September 6, 1930, army cadets led by General José Félix Uriburu stormed Plaza de Mayo and exiled President Irgoyen to the island of Martin Garcia. A short time later the cold, official voice of the radio announcer broadcast the rebels' manifesto: "Citizens! The army and the fleet have answered the call of the people and the nation and the urgent objectives imposed upon us at this grave time in the destiny of the nation, and have decided to raise their banner to offer those who have betrayed the government, the people's trust, and the Republic, that they immediately relinquish their posts in which they have not acted for the benefit of the people, but for their personal appetites." Military columns were seen on the boulevards, arousing a wild joy in the people's hearts that was mingled with terror and a feeling that something very fundamental was about to change here.

The uprising heralded not only a change of regime, but also the end of Zwi Migdal. In all the unrest, one whore, Raquel Lieberman, managed to escape her tormentors and reach Superintendent Julio Alsogaray in order to testify against the organization.

Raquel Lieberman had come from Poland with her two children eighteen months after her husband. Unlike other husbands, he waited for her in his sister's house in the provinces, but three months after their reunion he died suddenly and she found herself and her children at the mercy of her brother-in-law, who had joined and was active in the organization.

The brother-in-law and his wife took Raquel Lieberman's children and told her that if she wanted to see them again she had to work as a whore in Buenos Aires. She did their bidding, and for several years worked as a whore until she had saved enough money to purchase her children's and her own freedom from her in-laws.

But then she decided to open her mouth and take revenge.

First she accused Felipe Schön, a respected merchant and leading member of the organization, of stealing money and jewelry from her. This stunned everybody, including him. "In our lifestyle people don't accuse each other," he told her when he came to threaten her life. "We don't have to give money to women, they have to give it to us." He added that if she went on working independently, she would be killed.

But Raquel Lieberman was no respecter of the organization's rules. Even though she was frightened she decided to testify against the organization in court, which is why she went to the police superintendent's office.

The moment the organization's members discovered that Raquel Lieberman had made a statement to the police, they realized that something momentous had happened and gathered for an urgent meeting to decide what to do with their businesses and what was going to happen to the organization. Some like Simon Rubinstein openly mocked the powers of the police and the court, and believed that money would resolve everything. Others like Zechariah Sidnitzky argued that it would be better to get out of the city.

At the end of the meeting they sent messages to Sarah Braun, who owned the big brothel in the south, and the owners of the other big brothels in the other cities, to warn them of what they might expect. They smuggled the organization's financial assets to Montevideo, Uruguay. Zechariah Sidnitzky and Mauricio Caro fled to Brazil with everything they had. Others escaped to Rosario, crossing hundreds of kilometers of arid land, where the organization gained a foothold, took over the prostitution, drugs, and gambling, and it became a city of crime.

After taking her first statement, Alsogaray went to the court, to Judge Ocampo, who accepted the credibility of the statement and issued arrest warrants for all the organization's members and their women. But of the four hundred of these, three hundred had managed to flee. Only about a hundred of the brothel owners remained in the city, and immediately at the conclusion of the trial the police raided their establishments.

Two days before the end of the trial, the judges realized that the indictment against the organization's members, harming Argentina, white slavery, was not strong enough to send the organization's members to jail for the rest of their life. They discussed ways of resolving the problem, and found a solution: deportation of the organization's members to neighboring Uruguay under the 1912 Foreigners' Deportation Law, and on the basis of threatening government rule.

All the one hundred and eight members of the organization who had been arrested, men and women, were taken from prison and put on board a ship that took them upriver to Montevideo. It was already clear to all that they would return, not in an organized manner, not in the same set-up, but they would return and try to reestablish their businesses.

The women of *Ezrat Nashim* who realized this collected money from local benefactors to purchase passage to Europe, and tried to persuade as many women as they could to board ship and return to their homeland. Those who refused, due either to guilt or shame, were transferred to Uruguay with papers and a little money to seek their fortune in another country. Thousands of women and children were forcibly removed from the brothels so that the latter could be removed from the public agenda, and as far as possible, from the community's memory as well.

All the furniture, goods and chattels that were in these large brothels, cooking utensils, bed linen, ritual objects, were piled high outside the buildings and set alight. Nobody wanted to touch the belongings of The Unclean. Workers using hammers smashed the glowing neon signs. The houses were taken over by the state, demolished, and dwellings were built on the sites. Nothing was left, no memory of what was once there.

The collapsing walls gave up no secrets. The earth did not cry out. Anyone walking past these places today would never know that once there were Jewish brothels there, houses in which entire lives were lived, destroyed, and rebuilt.

That was the beginning of a profound journey. A journey of erasure from memory, from the memory of a community and its members, as if these places had never existed. As if cries of terror were never heard among these houses, as if the sounds of weeping and moans of pleasure never echoed in them.

In the days that followed the newspapers carried banner headlines. Non-Jewish writers accused the Jewish community of white slavery and called upon the president to limit emigration quotas to Argentina. "It is inconceivable," said one paper, "that our new country should be sullied by waves of Jewish criminal emigrants." Others wrote in the same vein, vying with each other in the volume of venom they poured on the heads of the Jewish community.

All this only served to strengthen the will of the community to eradicate every last vestige of the disgrace.

Sixty-seven

Raquel Lieberman wanted to rescue herself and her friends, but she ultimately brought about the destruction of the only world they knew and in which they knew how to survive. The girls that were released from the brothels were unable to remain in the community that banished them, and they had to seek their fortune in other countries. This is what happened to Mother's friends too, at whose home I was sitting *shiva* when all this upheaval took place.

Each of them followed her own star. Bluma went back to Poland and Rina emigrated to Brazil. Hava crossed the river into Uruguay and suggested that I go with her. I refused. Unlike them, I had something that would enable me to start life anew. I went to Señor Kaufmann's pawnshop where he gave me three thousand pesos for the ring, I rented an apartment near the port and opened my own business.

I was born in Argentina, I am of its fruit like any other woman born here. But I was born Unclean, the daughter of Unclean, and that is how I was destined to grow up, grow old, and die. This fate was not of my choice. I could, of course, have gone to another, strange country to start afresh. But for that I would have had to give up everything: this country, its language, my memories, and the memories that were never mine, the ring swirling like a vortex in my life. But I could not forget or even detach myself from everything I'd known since I was a little girl.

Those were different times, of a conservative government, of dark forces. President Uriburu met the conservatives' demands and announced restrictions on emigration to Argentina and pronounced brothels illegal.

Times changed but needs stayed the same. A man does not change. And every revolution brings its clients with it.

President Uriburu's successor embarked on building roads throughout the country with the help of British firms, which brought in equipment and set up work camps along long routes, from Buenos Aires through Mar del Plata, Mendoza, Cordoba, Rosario. Many men left their homes and went to work in the first road building camps. From morning till night, in the rain, in the summer, they would push barrows of gravel from one place to another, level routes with hoes and spades, boil tar in huge barrels and pour it onto the roadbed. In the evening, after the siesta, they would go back to work, shift after shift, with one shift relieved by another, into the dark of the night, along the wild route illuminated only by circles of flickering orange light, filled with shadows, that was cast by lanterns in the fields at the edge of the mountains.

Along these routes cheap boarding houses were opened that offered these men a warm bed, good food, and sex. Many of the women who had been freed from our brothels moved to the country towns and villages, to these night hotels, two or three women gathering together under the management of a local woman with connections to the mayor and the priest who ran the area, who could then open a small brothel masquerading as a hotel.

In the meantime some of the organization's members returned to the city. Simon Rubinstein was once again seen in the street, dressed as in the past and sure of himself as if nothing had taken place here. Others followed him. Since their houses had been demolished, each of them got hold of a few women, lodged them in rented apartments in the center of the city and forced them to work for him. Whoever had stayed in the city and wanted her freedom, like me, had to work quietly.

In the years that followed the revolution the government intervened in production and made life here difficult. It poured away surplus wine at the Mendoza wineries and limited the cultivation area of the farms. It restricted the growing of beef, wheat, cotton, and wine, and reduced the ability of the workers to live. Teachers were not paid for years, and the managers of the British company that controlled the railway deprived its workers. The men that once came to the big brothels now came in secret, each going to the house of a different woman without causing trouble and without being caught breaking the law.

The apartment I rented was on the top floor of an old building opposite the new port that was then under construction, Puerto Madero. From its windows you could hear the sirens of the big ships entering the port.

In the small apartment there was a long, narrow kitchen, a bedroom, and a living room. The other apartments in the building were occupied by port workers. It wasn't where I wanted to be, but I had no choice. The economic crisis continued after the elections too. The city was flooded with unemployed from the provinces, hungry men with no money to pay for their lust. I had to drop my prices so that I'd have something to eat.

To get hold of clients without getting caught or arousing suspicion that I was breaking the law, I'd get on the underground train at Plaza de Mayo and ride to Once. I'd get off, walk around a bit and then take the train back. I'd get on the train dressed modestly but glamorously, standing out among the tired women going from home to work or back home from the market, the exhausted workers, teachers immersed in newspapers, or students looking alertly at the girls getting onto the train.

Sometimes an exchanged glance was enough to close a deal. It was impossible to actually say anything or make a suspicious movement. I'd sit on the wooden seat in my wide-brimmed hat, looking here and there as if I didn't know the city, and accidentally catch the eye of one man or another. They would understand, lower their gaze to my chest, my thighs, measuring me up with their hungry eyes.

If I was unable to make eye contact with a man, I'd get up and stand in the middle of the car and suddenly stumble, letting my handbag fall from my hands and its contents empty onto the floor. The mascara, the handkerchief, the eyebrow pencil, the lipstick would all fall onto the wooden floor, rolling between the feet of a man who would swiftly bend down to help me gather up the contents of my bag, and be gathered up himself.

I snared quite a few clients on the train, but since they were insufficient I'd go to the cinema in the evenings and buy a ticket for three consecutive films.

I'd go inside and scan the audience. I always sat next to a man sitting on his own with empty seats on either side as if they signified his domain and loneliness. I'd push my way along the whole row, sit down next to him, give him a little smile and immediately look straight ahead. I'd react to what was happening on the screen with excessive excitement, weeping or laughter, and as if unintentionally I'd rub my thigh against the thigh of the man sitting next to me. He'd usually withdraw his leg and give me a fleeting embarrassed glance. Then I'd move my warm thigh against him again, this time unthinkingly raising the hem of my skirt so he could have something to look at. If he was free and filled with lust, that would be enough. If there weren't many people in the audience, he'd try me too, move his hand over my knee and let it rest there for a moment, waiting for my reaction. Then I'd lay my hand on his, and slowly place his hand between my thighs with a soft, seductive movement. That would be enough to drive him mad with desire. In the middle of the first film we were already outside, hurrying from the cinema to my apartment.

As time went by I learned my surroundings and behaved differently. My apartment was in the area of the Italian Mafia. I sought them out and spoke with the right people. Slowly, sailors, tourists, and merchants visiting the city began finding their way to my apartment.

Instead of deluding myself like Bluma, Mother's friend who went back to Poland, whose relatives threw her out when they discovered what had been done to her, I preferred looking the world straight in the eye. I swore not to become a victim of the Jewish community with its clean hands and black heart. Once I'd made enough money I rented another apartment in the same building so I was able to offer my guests somewhere to sleep and eat, cheaper than a hotel, and enjoy themselves at the same time.

Throughout those years I was preoccupied with my life and my fate, rebuilding what had been destroyed. The ring lay safe in Señor Kaufmann's pawnshop and I paid my debt for it in installments. I thought about it only infrequently. I certainly didn't occupy myself with the Bergman family, or who remained of it, José. But the connection made by the ring between our families, generation upon generation, did its work. If not by the ring, then by death. My mother and all his family were buried in the same cemetery, La Tablada, and it was there that our paths eventually crossed.

Sixty-eight

Exactly one year after her death I visited my mother's grave. I already knew that only pimps and their *porteras* were buried in that particular plot in the La Tablada cemetery. The other girls, the ones who died in the brothels at an early age of disease or the complete exhaustion of a body that lay with scores of men every evening, were buried in unmarked graves. My mother only gained the dubious honor of burial in The Unclean plot due to her late marriage to Señor Gantz, and I had a grave I could visit.

I didn't know that since the death of his parents and brothers José had made it his custom to visit their graves on the same day every week, to commune with their memory. That's how it happened that he came to the cemetery on the very day I was visiting my mother's grave, accompanied by Hava who had come specially from Montevideo for the day.

We came out of the plot of The Unclean walking side by side in silence. As we passed the Bergman family plot I suddenly saw a tall, slim man with fine hair standing by the graves, head bowed. I stopped and looked at him from a distance. Hava tried to pull me after her. "What's the matter, Esperanza?"

"Nothing, nothing," I replied. "I'm staying here."

Hava looked at the stranger. "Someone you know?"

"Someone I should have met a long time ago," I replied, motioning her to move away so I could stand and look at him.

But when he heard her footsteps behind him he turned and saw me looking at him, my arms folded.

He walked over to me with measured, polite steps, taking care not to come closer than was befitting for a stranger to approach a lady, and took off his hat.

I inclined my head slightly.

"Have we met, Señorita?"

"Who are you?" I replied with a question, wanting to be sure of his identity.

"I'm José Bergman. And you are?"

"Esperanza," I replied, "Esperanza Gantz."

"I'm pleased to meet you," he said, not yet comprehending why I had stopped at his family's graves. "Did you know my parents? My brothers?"

"It's time we met, José Bergman," I said. "It is I who have the ring."

"The ring?" he asked, puzzled. "What ring?"

At that moment I felt my entire world collapsing around me. Was it possible that this man who my mother had evaded until she died, did not know about the connection between us which had destroyed our families for generations?

"Perhaps I'm mistaken," I said, trying to extricate myself from the embarrassment and shock that gripped me, and turning to leave while wondering if I'd ever see him again.

"Please," he held out his hand. "Wait just a moment."

I halted.

"Come, let's sit down over there," pointing at a wooden bench, one of many standing beside the plot to enable mourners to rest by their dead.

"I'm not sure that we should be seen together," I said, hesitating.

"Why not?' he asked. "We're just going to sit and talk."

His considerate, courteous manner, his warm heart – I don't know which of them made me accept his invitation. We sat on the bench at an appropriate distance from each other.

José pointed at the graves opposite us.

"How beautifully everything is flowering here," he said. "It's hard to believe it's a cemetery."

"It doesn't look like this where my mother's buried," I said brusquely.

"Why not? Where's she buried?"

"By the toilets, in the plot of The Unclean."

His jaw dropped in shock.

"Now you understand why you shouldn't be seen with me," I said.

"If you were standing by my family's graves there must be a good reason for it," he replied.

"Do you know where your brothers died?"

"Yes," he bowed his head. Then he realized and looked at me. "Do you mean to say…?"

"It was our house," I confirmed. "My mother's house. The house where she lived and died."

José was alarmed. "What do you want from me?"

"I don't want anything from you."

"Then what's the connection with what you said, that you have the ring?"

I told him the main points of the story. I could see how he was struggling with it, trying to focus on the scene around us so as not to be drawn into its depths.

"Why are you telling me all this?" he asked in the end.

"They plotted to keep the truth from you, José. They thought that if you didn't know what guided your mother and her life up to her death, they would be making it easier for you," I told him, looking into his eyes.

He sat next to me, his hands clasped, not saying a word.

"It hasn't been made easier for you," I went on, "you grew up like me, in a deep pit of darkness without knowing what was guiding your life and giving you no peace."

"Yes, that's true," he said, digging the toe of his shoe into the soil.

"I ask just one thing of you. Give it up. Cut the connection. Don't go on with this death wish."

"You're like your name, Esperanza, you're a kind of hope," he said in a trembling voice.

"Promise me on the graves of our parents, promise me that we will both put an end to this desire, this madness, this inheritance soaked in memories and blood."

And he promised. He promised that if he had children he would not tell them this story, and I made the same promise.

In my innocence I thought I had triumphed over the curse of the ring.

Sixty-nine

I inherited many things from my mother about which I didn't know back then, among them my sense of smell. Apparently not one of the many men who came to me had ever asked himself what the woman feels when he spills his seed into her, what smells she absorbs. Not one of them imagined that a whore is a creature with a sense of smell. But I never managed to dull my sense of smell so as not to smell the sweat of this one, and the smell of the cheap cologne that another splashed on himself, the smell of fish from one and garlic fumes from another.

But that was precisely the reason why one man didn't gain my bed, because I devoured him in the doorway. His name was Alfred. He was always voracious and passionate, and emitted such a good smell of body simmered in his lust that I always gave myself to his strong hands as he laid me down on the floor at the apartment door – on the inside, of course – where he would fuck me joyfully and longingly.

He'd come to the house every time he returned from his travels, and I swear, Flora, that I knew he was coming by his special, intoxicating smell that was wafted before him. I could smell him coming and when I opened the door and saw him standing there, embarrassed and smiling, I'd fall into his arms because of my desire for his smell. To pass my nose over his neck, his eyes, his face, and smell him. To take his smell into me, to keep it inside me.

He was a tall, muscular, well-built man. His strong face had prominent cheekbones that endowed his head with the look of a cobra. His green eyes changed color with the intensity of the light outside and inside the apartment. Had it not been for his ears which stuck out, he might even have looked frightening.

At first I couldn't put a name to what I felt. It was only after a few visits that I noticed I was waiting for him, on tenterhooks for his arrival, wondering if the ship he was on was already nearing the port. Now and again I even found myself walking on the quays and asking mariners if the ship had already docked or when it was due.

As experienced as I was in sex, I didn't yet know what love was.

It was only when he came to me after a particularly long voyage and I fell into his arms hungrily, with a joy that rose inside like nothing ever before had made me so happy that I realized that he had apparently conquered a place in my heart. And he realized it at the same moment, looking into my eyes with his flashing eyes, stroking my hair, and taking me to him with such great gentleness, stopping my fervor at the door, leading me to the bed, and there caressing me for a long time before he entered me.

You germinated inside me like a seed of love, not of shame, Flora. It's important to me that you know that.

He was an amazing man. Most of the time he was at sea, working as a deckhand on the big freighters that plied the ocean between Argentina and Europe. But each time he returned to the city he'd come to me, to be with me.

We were young and lusted for life. Each time he returned from a voyage we'd go into the city and enjoy ourselves until late. We particularly liked going to an old bar in San Telmo where they played all the old songs every evening. It was built of wood, with long shelves on which there were empty liquor bottles of various shapes and hues. The bar was in the middle, and behind it the kitchen, and around it the guests sat, all talking in loud voices and keeping the owner – a red-cheeked man with thick sideburns – running from one end of the bar to the other. It was great there at night. Women and men sitting laughing together, the music playing, and the fine smell of barbecued meat from the *parilla* that they'd take out into the street, rising and filling the whole area, tempting everyone passing by.

Alfred knew of lot of people in this city. Captains, sailors, stevedores, freight contractors. We'd walk down the street, he in faded jeans and a buttoned shirt, and a black wide-brimmed hat he'd tilt rakishly to give him a manly look, and me in a light summer dress that clung to my body, which back then was full and curvaceous. Almost every minute someone stopped by us, hug and kiss Alfred and shake my hand, look into my eyes so that Alfred wouldn't catch his eyes sliding to the deep cleft between my breasts. After he left Alfred would always spit and say *Hijo de puta*, I saw how he was looking at your breasts, Esperanza. I hope his prick drops off. And I'd laugh and say, Enough, Alfred, enough, it's all yours, just take hold, and so we'd continue down the street to the café. There we'd always join a happy band of young people like us who'd come out late at night to forget the hardships of the day in pleasure, in the city strewn with stars and filled with the special sounds and smell of randiness that can be clearly discerned, which was borne throughout the city.

We'd sit there, celebrating the night like there was no tomorrow, as if Alfred would not eventually have to board a ship that would carry him away for God knows how long, and as if I didn't need to work to keep you and me, at my profession that everyone round the table knew about but preferred to keep silent about. At those moments, when he felt good, Alfred would touch me in all kinds of places, along my thigh and then kiss his hand and smile, and everyone would laugh.

"He's a hot one, your man," a woman would blurt.

"Yes, yes," I'd laugh, feeling my face flush, happy to show them all that I too had a man, a man who was mine and I was his woman, and it didn't matter what I did when he was away.

He was a hot man, your father, a genuinely hot man. I don't know how he came by his name. His mother, he said, was French, and his father Indian. You can imagine who his mother was and what she worked at. But he blocked all my attempts to know more about his past, and I didn't burden him with questions. He had been at sea from a young age, he told me, at first as a cabin boy, then slowly learning and advancing until they started hiring him as a deckhand, and he adopted the rough speech of sailors and learned to drink with them and swear, to boast of his conquests of women that either happened or didn't, the main thing was to impress his elders, to show them that he was no less of a man despite his young age.

One day as we lay in bed, he surprised me.

"Esperanza," he said, "I want to leave something with you until I get back."

"Fine," I replied, surprised. "But what is it?"

"The most precious thing I have," he laughed. "My sperm."

I jumped on him excitedly, almost squashing him in my joy. He laughed and hugged me with his strong arms, and them stroked my hair.

"I love you," he said, brushing aside my hand proffering him a *preservative*, and entering me.

He fucked me wildly, passionately, lovingly, despairingly, with a desire to preserve a memory in me. When he came he lay on top of me, panting, and I beneath him, hardly able to breathe.

"I've fertilized you, Esperanza," he said, "now give me a child."

I gazed at him lovingly, not knowing whether to laugh or cry. After all, in our house, Las Clavas, they called pregnancy 'a work accident'.

"Don't do anything silly," he warned me as if reading my thoughts.

"Like what?" I asked as if not knowing what he meant.

"You know. Nothing that's a sin."

I kissed his forehead.

"But I won't be able to work," I said quietly.

"I don't want to hear about your work," he said. "I'll take care of you."

I tried to pacify him, knowing that this promise was only words, for you can make such a promise but you can't be sure about keeping it.

He left the apartment for a drink with his sailor friends. That night he got into a drunken brawl at a small inn near the port, which turned into a knife fight. Next day I was called to identify his body.

It was only at the funeral, that was attended by his friends, that I discovered what had happened.

Alfred heard a coarse man say to a girl sitting at the bar and who reminded him of me, that she was a whore. She was only trying to solicit him, but the man was drunk and slapped her. When Alfred saw her fall, he didn't see a strange girl but me. In his eyes it was me lying there sobbing with hurt.

He got up without a word and faced up to the stranger, grabbed his head and began squeezing his face that was red with wine. He suddenly felt the stab in his belly and then the warm, wet jet under his shirt, and then he took another stab in the chest, then a third and fourth, and as he fell he heard the women screaming.

Seventy

In the topsy-turvy life I lived you were the fruit of love, not prostitution. The beauty of your moonlike face, the translucency of your skin, your smooth black hair, your big eyes reflecting the sadness in them, were no compensation for his death but were some consolation. I lost him but gained you.

But from your childhood you had this neediness that's never left you. You always needed others, to attract them and then suck out their life for yourself. You wouldn't stop nursing even when my beautiful breasts, my crowning glory, had become two ruined bags. You screamed and chased me until I relented and let you chew at me like a hungry pup. That's how you were, that's how you've stayed. Demanding the full attention of others, not satisfied with the measures of love that would please any other human being.

I didn't want to give you up. At first it didn't even occur to me to do so. I remembered only too well how my own mother had been forced to give me up, I, I told myself, would not be part of this legacy of pain. I decided to find you a nanny. For a long time I searched for a woman who would take you during the morning and after the siesta, for the hours when I had to work. I finally reached Feige, Zipporah, the short, rotund wife of a Jewish watchmaker called Moshe.

Feige and Moshe lived in a side street in the La Paternal neighborhood. The husband would sit for hours at his tiny table, disassembling and assembling tiny screws in delicate mechanisms at which he looked through a large eyeglass that he'd screw into his eye. Most of the time his wife was cleaning and cooking at home. Their three daughters had long since grown up and gone their separate ways, and their house, which was now empty, lay in the gloom of sadness.

For Feige, being given a baby girl was a happy change in her routine. She welcomed us with open arms, with a smile, and with practiced hands showed me how she changed your diaper, how she'd check with her fingertip the temperature of the milk she'd heated for you, and where she'd put you down for a nap after feeding.

Everything seemed fine when I left her standing and waving with one hand, as she held you with the other. But the more I tried to walk away from the house I couldn't but hear your weeping that pursued me down the street, until I turned round and went back.

"What's the matter?" Feige asked.

"I heard her crying. I didn't have the heart to go," I replied, and took you into my arms.

The moment you felt the familiar warmth of my body you stopped crying.

"She's got to get used to it," Feige smiled.

"But I can't," I replied, rocking you until you closed your eyes.

"You're a young woman on her own. You've no choice. You have to work," she said gently. "It's not her, it's you who've got to get used to it." She motioned me to put you into the crib she'd prepared for you, and carefully covered you with a blanket.

I lingered with you for a few more minutes until you fell asleep, and left the house again on tiptoe so you wouldn't wake up and feel that I'd gone again.

When I came back in the afternoon to take you home, I could hear you crying halfway down the street leading to her house. The door was opened by her husband who looked irritable and upset. "A good thing you've come," he said briefly, moving away from the door to let me into the house filled with screams. In the inside room Feige sat helplessly, looking at you as you waved your tiny arms and legs in the air, sobbing with heartrending weeping.

"I'm sorry," I said, quickly picking you up. You stopped crying immediately.

"I've tried everything, believe me," she told me weakly, wiping the sweat from her brow. "Nothing helped. Seeds rattling in a tin, a piece of cloth soaked in sugar water..."

"I know," I said, extending my hand to her pocket with the three pesos we'd agreed on. She pushed my hand away gently.

"There's no need," she said, "find yourself another arrangement."

Carrying you, I hurried out of the house of those two kind, unfortunate Jews to free them of your presence. In the succeeding days I looked after you at home and didn't go out into the street. I preferred waiting at home for a returning client, one I didn't have to hunt for on the train or at the cinema. It caused me losses but at least I knew that you were all right, because you were with me.

A returning client indeed turned up. He was a *porteño* of Indian appearance, about thirty. Ever since I'd seduced him in the Once vegetable market he'd call on me now and again. He was stocky and smiling, well-built and muscular, his black hair gathered into a rubber band, and his tanned skin and fine body were completely hairless.

He knew I'd had a baby but hadn't seen you until that day.

When I opened the door and asked him in, he looked at you in your crib.

"*Una buena niña*," he said, and smiled at me brightly.

I smiled back and invited him into the other room, picking up your crib to bring you inside too so you'd be with me as I worked.

He looked at me bewildered, shock flooding his face.

"I can't if she's watching us, I'm sorry."

"She's only a few months old," I replied, putting the heavy crib down by the bed.

"*Lo siento, Señora*, her eyes are still clean. I can't if she's watching."

I took you back into the hallway and came back inside, leaving the door open so I'd be able to hear you.

"Shall we?"

"*Como no?*" he smiled, taking off his undershirt and unbuttoning his pants.

He looked at me tenderly as I took off my dress and stood in front of him in my underwear.

He kissed my belly and navel, and then put his thick hands into my panties, grasping my buttocks and bringing me to him.

I stroked his head, letting him do as he wanted with me. He undressed me and led me to the bed, throwing me gently down onto it and was already on top of me when a shrill cry burst from the hallway where I'd left you.

Startled, he leapt off me, and I got up quickly to see what was the matter with you. Nothing was, of course. The moment you saw me you fell silent, your face wreathed in an innocent smile as you happily waved your arms and legs at me.

He was leaning against the doorpost. "What's the matter with her?"

"She can't be on her own. Maybe I'll bring her in anyway?"

"All right, let's try," he replied impatiently, his voice choked with passion, and he let me carry your crib into the bedroom. I laid you on your tummy so you wouldn't look at us.

We lay down again, touching each other carefully without making a noise, as if there were a kind of indecency in the sounds of the act of love in the presence of an infant. He was about to enter me when you turned your head, finding the worst possible time to display your rapid development, and looked straight at him with your big eyes.

"She's looking at me," he said.

"She's only a baby," I smiled, catching my breath.

He shook his head. "You've got to decide what you want, a living or a child," he said, dressing quickly and going to the door. Before he left he put two pesos on the table. I tried to dissuade him, but he shook his head again.

"You'll need the money now she won't let you work."

"Thank you," I said, embarrassedly, knowing how right he was.

"But find an arrangement for her, and quickly, otherwise you'll be out of work completely."

That's how you led me to the realization that I had to give you up so I could buy life for both of us.

I took you to the Jewish orphanage.

If you ever wondered where the clothes packages came from while you were there, where the presents that awaited you on your birthday came from, then now you know. It was all bought with the money of the passion ejaculated into your mother.

Every one of the handsome, lonely, unfortunate men that came to me, every one of them was the promise of existence for you, just as I was a mother and wife, or a momentary lover, for them. I often detested them, but I had to remember that thanks to every man on top of me you would gain another day of grace.

You created for yourself a totally different childhood story. At the orphanage you told the girls you weren't really Jewish, only half Jewish, that you were the daughter of an aristocratic family. Your mother was a Jewish Argentinean and your father a Catholic. They lived in a huge castle at the edge of Buenos Aires. You also created a little brother for yourself about whom you related amazing things to the other girls. But you know the truth, even if it was hidden in mist over the years, and intermingled with the stories you invented to create a different, more respected existence for yourself. We both know the truth. And at the end of this book you shall know it fully.

Seventy-one

On Wilhelm Lowenthal's advice José Bergman went to La Plata University to study medicine. Since he did not wish to stand out with his wealth and special status, he leased his parent's estate house to the Embassy of France and moved into a small pension in La Plata. Toward the end of his studies he met Mauricia Feldman, a petite, sensual, golden-haired, green-eyed and pleasant-faced young woman who lived with her older sister since her parents, David and Golda Feldman, found it hard to support their seven children.

But there was another reason for urgently moving Mauricia to live with her sister a year before her graduation from high school. In the face of her parents' opposition she joined "La Junta de la Victoria", a women's organization, and displayed ever-increasing resistance to the acts of President Juan Peron.

One day she came home from an organization activity – packing parcels for the French and British soldiers fighting the Nazi – and on her lapel she proudly wore a cockerel on a golden cross inscribed with the words "Cruz de Lorraine" in the French national colors.

Her father was horrified. "Are you mad? Do you want us all killed because of you?"

"Why so dramatic, Papa?" she asked, and received a resounding slap.

"Take that pin off this minute," her mother ordered.

"Are you with him?" asked the girl, who had hoped for support from her at least. Golda was the daughter of a family of refugees from Russia that had emigrated to Argentina in the wake of the pogroms there even before the outbreak of World War One.

"What did you expect?" the mother replied. She grasped her daughter's arm, took her to her room, and shut the door. "You've lost your mind completely, Mauricia," she said.

"It was given to us by the French ambassador as a mark of gratitude. All the girls who work with me in the organization were given one," Mauricia said.

"Which organization?" the mother demanded, "what the devil are you talking about?"

Throughout the months that Mauricia had gone to help pack parcels for soldiers with food and sweets and adding, like all the other girls, notes in the basic English they had learned at the high school on Calle Belgrano, she had told her parents she was going to do homework with some friends. Now she was left with no choice but to tell the truth, and when she did her mother's face darkened and her eyes revealed her anger.

"You're lucky you haven't told your father and brothers. You'd have gotten a lot worse from them," she said, and ordered her daughter to desist from her political activity immediately.

But the rebellious daughter would not give in so easily. "He supports the Nazis. I can't understand how Jews like you can keep silent at a time like this."

"We've learned to keep silent," her mother replied.

"But you know what they're doing to the Jews over there."

"It's just rumor," her mother said, "there's no evidence that that's what's happening."

"They're murdering Jews and you're going to keep quiet?"

"It's precisely because we're Jews," her mother interrupted. She had inherited the wisdom of the refugee from her parents, the ability to survive anywhere without arousing suspicion by blending into the background, concealing any distinctiveness or out of the ordinary beliefs.

"I think it's contemptible," her daughter spat.

Her mother grabbed her and tore the golden pin from her lapel.

"So long as you're living in this house you'll do as you're told," she said. "You're not going to get us into trouble with this foolishness."

Golda left her daughter's room slamming the door behind her and went into the drawing room, holding out her hand to her husband with the foreign pin, the mark of sin.

"We should keep an eye on her," she said.

They weren't given much time. Only a few days later they were summoned by the principal of the prestigious school their daughter attended. It was a private commercial school that most of their children had attended and so the principal respected them. It was only due to that respect, she told the stunned parents sitting in front of her, that she had not reported their daughter to the authorities when she had refused to sing *El Quatro de Julio* at morning assembly, and instead had organized some of her friends to sing – standing to attention and filled with youthful rebellion – the anthem of the anti-Peronist students.

Señor Feldman was so ashamed he wanted the earth to swallow him. He knew how to deal with superior leather shoes that did not fit the feet of a wealthy customer, putting them onto a last in the depths of his shop, hitting them mercilessly with a hammer, wetting them and hitting, and letting them dry on the last. But he had no idea of how to deal with such an insolent daughter. His wife was also helpless. Then the principal, a close friend of the minister of finance in the Peron government, delivered the coup de grace.

"Your daughter and her friends will have to leave the school," she said. "I cannot permit dissidents like them to poison the other students."

The mother got up, rage suffusing her features, but her husband quickly stood beside her, grasping her arm to silence her.

"*Gracias, señora,*" he said, stepping back and pulling his wife after him.

The principal sat at her desk, not even getting up to see them to the door, her heart swelling with pride. It was with good reason that she was a member of the Peronist women's organization. She had even been present at the ceremony at the Cervantes Theatre at which Evita Peron was elected president of the new women's party, and had seen her close up. She would certainly be completely loyal to her and her husband. She'd show these people what opposing the lady meant, she thought to herself.

The parents returned home bowed in silence. When they didn't say a word to her Mauricia realized that something terrible had happened. They closed all the shutters in the middle of the day. The house was now more like a house of mourning than that of a bourgeois family in the middle of the working day.

Only then they called her to join them for a talk.

Mauricia was a belligerent, stubborn girl, but when her mother had finished telling her what the principal had said, she sat facing them in silence, waiting to hear what her father had to say.

"We've no choice, Mauricia," he said, "we'll have to talk with your older sister Pessia about you moving to live with her in La Plata, and you'll finish high school there."

Mauricia had never imagined the possibility of voluntary exile, of living with her single sister in the small apartment behind her pharmacy.

"You must complete your final year and then go to university," he said. "Which you won't be able to do here."

He looked into his wife's eyes, seeking her approval. Golda nodded. It's the best solution under the circumstances, she told herself.

A few days later they said goodbye to their daughter at the railway station, making her swear that she would not get her big sister into trouble, and sending her on her way.

Mauricia completed her high school studies in La Plata and enrolled for medicine. In her first year at university she met José Bergman who was in his final year, and as a result of his academic achievements had been appointed assistant to a professor. He impressed her with his height and restrained manner which endowed him with the appearance of a doctor even before interning. José was so immersed in his studies that he didn't even notice her, but one of his friends directed his attention to the young first-year student who followed him with her eyes whenever he walked down the corridors.

When he asked her to go to the cinema with him her heart leapt. She said yes right away. She knew how astonished her fastidious sister would be when she introduced him as a student in his final year and a professor's assistant at the faculty. And indeed, her sister welcomed José with open arms, happy for her sister who had found a such a level-headed young man, and she consented to them going to the cinema together. She was particularly pleased when José asked her by what time he should have her sister home, and even brought her home on time.

From that day forward he was a welcome visitor to her apartment. And after hearing his life story she even did some home cooking for him; her heart went out to the young man who had suffered so much pain in his life. Her senses told her that this was an excellent match for her stubborn, impulsive, and to a great extent self-destructive sister. Pessia even reported this development to her parents who immediately made inquiries about the Bergman family to which this young man belonged.

They were not to know that Mauricia had not wasted a single minute and had begun lecturing José on her views condemning Peron and the mass adulation of his wife, Evita. When José mentioned the foundation established by Evita to distribute money and food to the poor, she dismissed it out of hand.

"It's all a big show," Mauricia said. "That woman distributes money stolen by her husband's government to keep him in office."

"Still," José replied in his soft voice, "she helps the poor. Just look at how much she's loved everywhere."

"They love her because she talks about the power of *los descamisados*, the shirtless ones, the humble and the modest. Don't forget she's an actress. She knows how to talk."

Slowly but surely Mauricia succeeded in getting her views over to him, and a few years later when Evita died and the entire nation was in mourning, she tore off the black armband he was wearing and he did not dare protest. That was a mistake because when he got to the university without the armband and a black tie, he was called in to the dean's office. It was made clear to him that if he wanted to steer clear of trouble, then he would do well to replace the armband.

Three years later, when Peron's regime collapsed and he fled the country, Mauricia felt that now she would be able to safely return to the capital she had been forced to leave because of her views. She talked it over with José and suggested they get married and return to Buenos Aires.

"Do you want me?" she asked on seeing the hesitation in his face,

"Of course I do," he mumbled, "but why so fast? What about your studies?"

"One doctor in the family is enough. And I want to begin life itself."

"Your parents won't like it," he said.

"The most important thing for them is that we get married," she replied. She knew her parents well. "If you find work and get settled, especially now they know everything about your family and inheritance, everything will be fine."

A small cloud flitted over José's face.

"What's the matter?"

"Nothing," he replied. "Let's get married."

He didn't like being reminded of his inheritance. He lived modestly, striving for achievement under his own steam and avoiding any display of affluence to his fellow students. And although he was the orphaned son of such a respected family and was a man of means, they never questioned him about it and were all the more happy that he did not patronize them.

Their wedding took place in Buenos Aires. After they were married they decided not to live in an affluent neighborhood so they chose Villa Crespo that was a mixed neighborhood of Jews and other émigrés, including quite a few criminals. José's in-laws expressed surprise at the choice, but their daughter explained that José was a modest man who did not want to stand out with his wealth. Apart from that he had found a position as a doctor at the nearby government hospital, so it would be better if he lived close to his patients.

Mauricia did not go back to her studies. In the first anatomy lesson she had passed out on seeing a dissected cadaver. Additionally, she slowly discovered that dealing with sickness and death horrified her. She preferred being a housewife for her doctor husband who spent long hours at the hospital. It was enough for her.

Quite soon after their wedding she conceived and gave birth to their first daughter, thus bringing great joy to her parents and husband. She only voiced her strong views on Peron incidentally, without thought to the spies lurking everywhere, even in the dry cleaning shop to which she took her husband's clothes, and where they began whispering that she was not a Peronist. One day she muttered a curse against Peron, and Pablo, the shop's owner, was unable to hold back. "Take care, Señora Bergman, because I don't want to do anything."

Mauricia bore José Bergman three daughters, Oliveria, Adela, and Graciela. José had hoped for a son and even planned to name him after his father, but when he asked his wife to name their first daughter after his mother, he encountered fierce opposition. She only softened with the birth of their second daughter, Adela, who was named Adela-Bella, which made him very happy. Her daughters' names, to whose choice she devoted much thought, were intended to reflect man's sublime qualities, she told her husband, not turn them into memorial candles for the dear departed. José did not argue. He was not preoccupied with his past, even though they were sustained by the inheritance that had been prudently invested by the late Wilhelm Lowenthal until it was transferred to him. He was, though, preoccupied by one thing – his ability to do well by his patients, most of whom were either poor or from the petite bourgeoisie, irrespective of religion or gender, worldview or political affiliation.

"We are all orphans," he told Mauricia when she wondered about his dedication to his work. "It doesn't matter who I'm treating, everyone is worthy of shelter under God's wings."

And she looked at him with her warm, flashing eyes that overflowed with love, knowing she had married the right man, a man who was all heart.

It was therefore with good reason that it was said that patients waited in line for hours to see Dr. Bergman. He would seat each patient in front of him, ask him for details about his life, and listen with infinite patience. Only after hearing about all his illnesses, complaints, and real or imagined pains, would he take his stethoscope and listen to his heartbeat, palpate his belly to examine the internal organs, not hurrying to make a diagnosis until he was sure he'd taken everything into consideration, and therefore his diagnoses were almost error-free. Thus he acquired the name of a good, dedicated, and precise doctor, but as slow as a tortoise. These complaints stopped in his waiting room where he employed a receptionist. The patients would grumble to her about the long time they had to wait to see Dr. Bergman, while other doctors worked much faster than he.

"That's how mistakes happen," she would reply smilingly. "Give thanks to God that Dr. Bergman is your doctor."

Dr. Bergman's labors left their mark on him. His hair thinned prematurely, his facial skin became mottled and lax. His eyes, that had been beautiful throughout his youth, were now dulled and tired from studying his medical books, writing prescriptions, and examinations, and when he got home for the siesta he ate but sparingly and fell into a deep sleep, to be awakened to return to work by his wife.

She did not have much help. Her brothers and sisters all had their own children, and her parents were too old to help out. She was therefore very pleased when old Mademoiselle Violette came to visit. She was introduced to the girls as Aunt Eva, which made her very happy. Of all people it was she, who had never had a family of her own and had devoted her whole life to the Bergmans, who in her old age was blessed with José's daughters as if they were her own grandchildren. One day, after the three girls had jumped on her to kiss her on her arrival, she said something about this to Mauricia.

"It's such a pity she didn't get to see the girls," Eva sighed, thinking about her dear friend Bella Bergman.

"You knew her well?" Mauricia asked, straightening the small lace serviette on which she put Eva's cup of *mate*.

"What a question," Eva smiled, "she was like a sister to me."

"What kind of a woman was she?" Mauricia asked. She could only imagine what her in-laws had been like from the ways of her husband who had been raised as an orphan by this woman and her friend, an Indian woman called Isabel.

"She was a strong woman, very strong," Eva began her story, the crows' feet at the corner of her eyes crowding into a smile. She told Bella's young daughter-in-law about the family's life in Danzig and about the big house in Recoleta. And then she began telling her about the ring.

Riveted, Mauricia listened to this colorful story, a sort of mixture of balderdash, superstition, and a kernel of truth. It was certainly fascinating, something she had never heard about. When she mentioned this to Eva, the old woman suddenly fell silent, realizing that she had unintentionally violated the longstanding decision made by herself and Isabel when José was still a boy.

"José doesn't know anything," she said. "After the death of his parents we decided not to tell him about the ring so at least he could be saved from it."

"You did the right thing," Mauricia said quietly. "You can't raise a child on stories like that."

Mauricia poured her some more water into the *mate* cup, and went with her in other directions of conversation. But after saying goodbye to her she remained deep in thought, so much so that even her girls who wanted her attention were unable to shake her out of her musings. In its subtle way, and as it had in the previous generation, the story took hold of the soul of the wife, not the husband, the story's offspring.

The story of the ring preyed on her mind but she made no direct inquiries about it. She kept her promise to Eva not to talk about it with her husband. But one evening she asked him in passing if it was true that his mother owned a jewelry collection, and if so, what had been done with it.

José looked at her, puzzled, and told her that he had donated the collection to the Great Synagogue. Parts of it had certainly found their way to the pawnshops in the city, or to the homes of wealthy women who had purchased from it rings and brooches, bracelets and necklaces at the charity sales held by the community.

Perhaps the ring would have been forgotten in the mists of memory that changed with time had not Graciela, José and Mauricia's youngest daughter, suffered recurring attacks of epilepsy, the falling sickness.

The first attack happened when she was a little girl on a class outing. They climbed to the top of a mountain to look at the view below, a green valley dotted with tiny villages and quilted with golden and green fields from horizon to horizon.

As they got close to the cliff edge, their teacher, Eduardo, warned them not to get too close, for the strong mountain wind could carry them over. All the children lay flat and crawled slowly to the cliff edge. Graciela raised her head to look at the wonderful view – and looked down.

All at once her gaze dropped from the heights to the valley below. The squares of the fields and the villages spread among them dizzied her. She suddenly felt as if a powerful hand was gripping her and commanding her to jump. Her senses became blurred. She stood up, swaying in the wind that battered her face and dimly hearing the teachers' cries as she spread her arms. She would surely have taken the final decisive step from the cliff edge had the teacher not rushed to her and grabbed her arm, throwing her down the slope they had climbed up.

She rolled down, the ground hitting her. She only came to rest at the foot of the slope where she lay silent, her eyes upturned in their sockets and froth coming from her mouth. The teacher immediately saw her tightly clenched jaw.

"Quickly! Bring me a knife or something to open her mouth!" he yelled to the other teachers, who ran to search in their bags.

A moment later, which seemed like an eternity, they came back, one with a sharp knife and another with a heavy spoon with a strong handle. Graciela lay on the ground, her face blue from lack of oxygen, her friends looking on terrified at what was happening.

"Lift her head up," Eduardo shouted to one of the teachers, who knelt and raised Graciela's head.

He grasped the corners of Graciela's mouth with both hands and with all his might tried to prise it open. When a small gap opened between her clenched jaws, he forced the spoon inside and opened her mouth.

"She's swallowed her tongue! Grab it with your fingers!" he ordered the woman teacher who looked at him horrified. "Now!"

She fearfully inserted a finger into Graciela's open, gurgling pharynx. Carefully she felt for the folded-back tongue and pulled it out. The child drew in a lungful of fresh air, then another and another.

"Water! Water!" Eduardo shouted.

One of the children handed him a water bottle with fresh water in it. He bathed her face, wiping the flecks of froth from her lips, and then gave her a sip of water. When she had finished drinking Graciela looked up surprised into the concerned, tense faces of the people around her.

"What happened?" she asked, unaware that anything had befallen her.

"You had either an attack of vertigo or of epilepsy," Eduardo replied bluntly, looking at her with his warm eyes.

"What's epilepsy?" the girl groaned, not understanding why they were all standing around her and why their clothes were wet.

"Falling sickness," Eduardo said tersely. "Is this the first time it's happened to you?"

The girl nodded weakly and tried to stand up, but her strength failed her.

"Rest a while," Eduardo told her, motioning to one of the teachers to follow him.

They moved aside.

"Nobody ever said anything to me," she said quickly.

"Evidently nobody knows," he replied. "Even she doesn't. In any event, we can't let her stay with us. We should get her home as quickly as possible."

She agreed with him wholeheartedly.

The same day the woman teacher took Graciela home on the train, despite her protests. When they knocked on the door of her house late in the evening they frightened José and Mauricia out of their wits, since they had expected her home only two days later. The weeping Graciela went to her room while the teacher told her parents exactly what had happened in complete detail.

When she finished, José Bergman grasped his head in his hands. This was beyond his comprehension and his strength. Although he knew that this sickness was genetic, passing from generation to generation, he had still hoped it would pass over his daughters. He had also repressed its existence so he would not have to repeatedly face the memory of his brothers' deaths on the same day. With all his heart he had hoped and believed that his and Mauricia's life would be different from that of their antecedents, and that the broad education he had acquired would keep tragedy and illness from them. And now this calamity.

"The ring," he whispered, "it's the ring again."

"So you know," Mauricia said.

José nodded.

"What ring?" the teacher asked, not understanding what they were talking about.

"It doesn't matter," Mauricia said quickly. "Thank you for bringing her home. My husband's a doctor, he'll know what to do."

"You're lucky," the teacher said, collecting her bag.

The couple showed her to the door and thanked her for her help. Once they were on their own they moved into the far corner of the room so that the girls would not hear anything.

"I'll take her to the hospital in the morning for some tests," José said.

"Have her tested," she replied, "but you know what really must be done."

"How did you hear about the ring?"

"Eva told me. And you? Where did you hear about it? Eva said they'd decided not to tell you anything about it."

"My mother told me everything before she died, but made me swear not to say anything to my father."

"You can't run away from things like that," Mauricia said, laying a hand on his shoulder. He embraced her, tears flowing down his cheeks and soaking her dress.

"You're crying," she whispered.

"I hoped that it would pass over us at least," he replied.

Mauricia did her best to console him. Her mind was filled with thoughts and worries. How she could find the ring now. How she could search for the only thing that would save her daughter. It was now clear to her, by virtue of a strange certainty in her heart, that the only remedy for her daughter's newly-discovered malady rested solely in the power of the past, the power of the ring.

José had no thought of waiting until the ring was found. He turned immediately to medical research to discover what he could do to save his daughter. He studied medical books old and new until he realized that the best he could do for his daughter was electric shock therapy. It was the only treatment used in hospitals throughout the world, and its proponents held that the electric shock regulated the patient's brainwaves, thus preventing recurrence of the attacks.

Mauricia's protests were to no avail. José was adamant, and so Graciela, contrary to her mother's wishes and under her father's watchful eye, had to present herself at his hospital once a week over several months, be strapped into a chair, and have shock after shock applied through electrodes to her temples. Before the treatment they stuck a plastic cylinder wrapped in a bandage into her mouth so she would be unable to scream and frighten the patients waiting their turn outside the clinic.

Her father was unable to stand the sight of her body convulsing in the chair, her eyes rolling back in their sockets, the involuntary spasms that rocked her back and forth, until she relaxed a long time after the treatment was over.

He waited for her outside. After the awful treatment he would lead his daughter, her legs failing her and her head giddy, to his car. She would sit in silence beside him as he drove carefully home. Mauricia would open the door weeping and take her daughter, still stunned from the treatment, into her arms. Graciela always wanted just to lay down and rest on her bed, disappear from the eyes of the world, feeling how the physical pain of the treatment was replaced by a wave of hostility toward her parents who were causing her so much suffering.

I hope you die, she'd weep in her room. I hope you die and feel once, just once, what I feel in that chair.

Mauricia looked at her daughter, her heart breaking. The illness and the aggressive therapy forced upon her had distorted her features and changed her future. Of the healthy child she had once had only half a daughter remained. Her friends kept their distance from her, due either to repellence or fear. Mauricia felt that she had to stop this torture and restore her daughter to the world of the healthy.

She sent an urgent summons to Mademoiselle Violette.

Eva was already very old. When she heard what Mauricia wanted she shook her head in sorrow.

"That accursed thing will never give you any peace," she murmured. "How can you find it now?"

"I don't know," Mauricia replied, "but I'm going to try."

"Be careful," Eva whispered, "that ring has taken too many lives already."

Next day Mauricia went to the *La Nación* newspaper offices. She asked to see the editor and told him everything she knew about the ring. He sat and listened to her story. "An excellent story," he said, "especially its magical element. I don't know if publishing it will get you what you want, but I will be happy to publish it."

A week later *La Nación* ran the story under the headline, "The Magical Gold Ring of the Whore", and a synopsis of the tale of the ring. It certainly brought Mauricia closer to her objective. Señor Kaufmann, he of the pawnshop at which my mother had pawned the ring, called Mauricia and told her his story.

"Do you know the ring?" he inquired.

"I've never seen it," she replied, "I've only heard about it from my husband and his family."

"Then bring your sick daughter with you," Kaufmann said. "That's the only way we can know if it is the ring you're looking for."

That same day she went with Graciela to the tiny old pawnshop in Calle Cordoba.

The door was opened by a very old man. His white hair fell to his shoulders as if it had never been cut, his face was wrinkled with age, and his back was bent into a permanent hump. Without saying much he showed them into his shop and closed the door behind them. With a careful hand he opened the box and moved it to the Señora. She looked inside and recoiled before the bright light flashed at her all at once by the ring.

"This is it, without a doubt," the old man nodded. "See how it glows. Give me your hand," he said to Graciela, who had no idea of what was going on. She held out her small hand. He carefully took the ring from the box and placed it on her finger.

Graciela felt the ring tightening on her finger as if it had always been there. Strange, secret forces suddenly began coursing through her body, as if lightning was slicing her from side to side, a soft and pleasant precise tremor, a wave of forces whose meaning she did not know and perhaps never would.

She stood up completely revived before the astonished eyes of the old man and her mother.

"Incredible," Mauricia said. "I don't know how to thank you."

"Don't thank me," Señor Kaufmann replied, "it's not for sale."

"What? But it's saving her! Look!"

The old man nodded. "That's why I asked you to come here. To save her, not to give her the ring. I'm unable to do that."

"I'll pay any price you name for it!" Mauricia shouted.

"It's not a matter of money, but of a promise," the old man said regretfully. "I gave an undertaking, and I can't renege on it."

"You gave an undertaking to a whore, a thief," Mauricia hissed.

"You will have to do your own rectification, not me," he answered quietly.

"Where can I find her now?" Mauricia shouted despairingly, while her daughter wondered what had got into her mother to make her shout at the old man like that.

"She had a daughter," he said. "She made me swear to return the ring only to her or her daughter. Find her the way you found me."

Seventy-two

I was the first woman on Avenida Leandro N. Alem to own her own telephone with a number that could be passed from hand to hand.

I had to wait two years for that special instrument, and if I hadn't greased the right palms at the post office it would certainly have taken longer. But I knew that the telephone, which at the time was a luxury item, would change my life.

Clients began asking for my number and passed it from one to another at their places of work. Factory workers all over the city, politically-oriented youngsters who were often organized in underground cells belonging to one party or another, began calling me. They'd spend their days working hard and toward evening put up posters calling for the release of their comrades from jail and writing graffiti condemning the conservative government. Then they'd call and come to me to spend their desire and passion in a woman's body.

My new clients were members of *Confederación General del Trabajo*, intellectual workers, left-wing syndicalists for whom the ideas of Spencer, Diderot and Spinoza were mingled with those of José Ingenieros with regard to the role of young people in respect of themselves and the society in which they lived. They printed *La Nueva Palabra*, distributed it in factories, and did not stop even when they were arrested and incarcerated in the Villa Devoto jail. They actually benefited from their imprisonment, where they taught each other English, history, and communist theory, and on their release were greatly strengthened in their beliefs.

At their meetings these men created the agitation that had bubbled beneath the reality in Argentina and was manifested in recurrent military coups. Many of them had been active in the anti-Franco movement during the Spanish Civil War. They would hold meetings at which they would collect money to help the dictator's opponents, and during World War Two openly opposed the policies of the government that sided with the Nazis, not the Allies.

I remember those days by what was lacking in my everyday life. At first I missed things I liked, like Spanish sardines. But when the World War broke out the shops were short of European products like women's underwear, cosmetics, and so forth. There were times I changed my underwear only twice a week, wearing one pair of panties while I washed the other, or I bought cheap makeup at the Sunday market at San Telmo just so I'd have something to put on my face.

At that time of shortages and social unrest I didn't want the ring with me. In this country, where one revolution follows another, in this profession that burns out the body, I could not know what would happen if it were with me, and it was important for me to know that it was within reach and in safe hands. So I kept it at Señor Kaufmann's pawnshop without redeeming it.

A long time passed until Señor Kaufmann's sons, who were searching for me in various neighborhoods in the city at their father's behest, found me. From then on my life changed radically.

It began with a telephone call. On the line I heard the voice of a young man who asked if I was Esperanza Gantz, and if I was the daughter of Esther Gantz from Las Clavas.

"Who is this?" I asked, afraid that one of my clients or neighbors had informed the police I was working illegally.

"Don't be afraid," the young man replied, "I'm Señor Kaufmann's son."

I heaved a sigh of relief.

"How is your father?" I asked, happy to hear his voice bringing me regards from what my mother had left in his custody.

"Thank God," the young man said, his smile evident in the earpiece. "He asks that you come and see him as soon as possible. He'd like to talk to you."

"Is everything all right?" I asked, seeking a further scrap of information that might hint at what awaited me. After all, a pawnbroker does not call someone who has left an item with him unless he wants to redeem it.

"Yes," he replied, "and your mother's ring is all right too. Still, he'd like you to come."

We arranged that I would come toward evening the following day, and I did. Before calling on them I dressed well. It was important to me that this old man meet me looking my best; that the impression I left on him would erase the memory of the confused child who had accompanied her mother to his shop one morning so long ago, frightened and haunted. I wanted him to see in me the ownership of the ring, my strength as a woman living alone in this city.

One of the sons, evidently the one who had called me, opened the door and showed me into the inner room, a big, dark room that was exactly the way I remembered it. Numerous ornaments were arranged all around, on shelves and big wooden sideboards, among them copper samovars, fine china dinner services, silver Sabbath candlesticks and beautifully fashioned menorahs, decorated Kiddush goblets and all sorts of other items waiting for their owners to come and redeem them.

Old Señor Kaufmann was waiting for me in his semi-darkened room that was illuminated only by a small lamp on his table, and he gestured to a chair beside it.

"Come, sit down," he said in his quiet voice. I approached him, slowly entering the area illuminated by the table lamp. The old man raised his eyes and looked at me.

"You've grown," he whispered. "You've changed."

"Yes, señor," I smiled. "It's what life does."

"How's your mother?" he asked.

I told him what had happened from the day I had come to his shop with Mother until now. He was pained to hear of my mother's death.

"And you?" he asked.

"I'm working," I replied without adding details.

He looked at me for a long time, sighing and stroking his beard. He remained silent for several long minutes and then told me about the visit of Mauricia Bergman and her sick daughter. I sat there in silence. All at once the story of my mother and grandmother resurfaced into my life.

"I can't give up the ring," I said, "just like my mother before me."

"It's saving an endangered life," the old man said.

"It's always saving an endangered life," I replied. "But the ring is a matter of life for me too."

"Then take it back without paying me the remainder of the debt," the old man said. "I don't want to hold on to something that can save the life of one young girl for the future of another."

I tried to protest, but that good, wise old man stopped me, reached into his desk drawer and took out the box with the ring in it.

"Take it," he said. "This way I'll be keeping my word to your mother, but won't be a partner to causing the death of another."

With a heavy heart I took the ring, got up and turned to leave. As I stood in the dark by the door his voice stopped me.

"Tell me, Esperanza," he asked, "why not at least let her bring her daughter to you so she can put the ring on every now and then and perhaps be saved?"

I lowered my head, recalling my conversation with José Bergman at the La Tablada cemetery by his parents' graves, and with it everything I knew about the ring, about everything that had befallen our families, generation after generation.

"Yes," I heard myself saying, "give her my telephone number."

In the darkness it seemed he was smiling.

I emerged from the shop into the cold street, walking quickly from the dark part of Calle Cordoba to the city center where there was more traffic and people walking in the streets, feeling not completely safe with the ring rattling in its box in my coat pocket, holding it in my right hand lest it fall. As I walked I wondered what else the ring might bring, to what degree it would yet dictate the lives of our families.

But even I didn't expect what finally transpired.

Two days later José Bergman called and invited me to their home to meet with him, his wife, their daughters, and Mademoiselle Violette who, so I gathered, was his mother's friend. I told him I wouldn't feel comfortable with that and suggested we meet in a café.

Then José Bergman played his trump card.

"I've got something of your mother's. I don't want to give it to you in a public place."

My heart leapt. I'd barely known my mother. What I remembered was a faded impression of a young woman. There was nothing to which I was more sensitive.

"What is it?" I asked.

"Come and see," he replied. "You won't regret it. And please bring the ring with you so my daughter can wear it during dinner."

"Dinner?"

"My wife insists."

Had I not been adamant that I could get to their house on my own he would have sent a car to collect me and make sure I came. But that was too much for me. Even though I believed that this man, who I remembered as a tall, striking young man, would do me no harm, I still preferred to maintain some degree of independence vis-à-vis him and his wife. I put on elegant but reserved clothes, made up modestly as befitted a lady, and put on high-heeled shoes that made me even taller than my natural height. I wore a rich, multicolored shawl and on my arm I carried a nice leather handbag I kept for special occasions.

I took the underground train from Plaza de Mayo, which was almost empty. Only a few people late going home were in the carriage, and two or three young couples who looked like they were going out. I sat down in an empty seat, clasping my handbag, looking through the window at the dark tunnel that passed at speed. Now and then the dullness of the blank walls was replaced by lit up stations, quiet platforms which earlier had been crowded with people and now seemed like the abandoned roads of an underground ghost town.

It was obvious to me that they would ask for the ring and that I would have to demur. I was never materialistic but even though it was an inheritance of blood, I knew that the ring was the only thing remaining of my family, of the dynasty of women who had worn it before me and kept it for me, for you. Perhaps it had been made for someone else and had come into my grandmother's possession illegally and thus brought down a calamity on the other family. But you can't give up something that no other woman in your family was prepared to give up, and who left it to her successor at any cost. Then why, I asked myself, are you going there when you know what they are going to ask? Why not get off now, at the next station, and go home, have your telephone number changed, and forget the whole thing.

But my heart wouldn't let me do it. This ring had known too many dead and the matter had to be resolved once and for all, I told myself. These deaths could not be continued from generation to generation, for death is no kind of heritage under any circumstances. If it had to be me to put an end to it, perhaps it was happening not for me but for you, so that you would be free of this ring which is bound, generation after generation, to the destiny of two families with no connection other than a cycle of sickness, healing, and death.

I went in with some hesitancy, but Mauricia's welcome, which bore no trace of anger or avarice, won me over immediately. From the moment I set foot in her house she made sure I felt at ease, as if I were a long-lost relative with whom she had been reunited. As if there was nothing separating me from them. Not my occupation, not my status, not the ring.

Their spacious home was lit by numerous wall lamps and a large chandelier suspended over the beautifully appointed dining table. The house was tastefully yet modestly furnished. My attention was caught by the silver candelabrum which seemed to be very old, and a beautiful statuette standing beside it, both bathed in light from the wall lamp above them.

José noticed me looking at them and told me that the candelabrum commemorated his grandfather who was a Judaica master craftsman, and that the statuette was a gift to his late mother from Baron Hirsch himself.

I looked at the others there. Señora Bergman, the three Bergman daughters, and old Mademoiselle Violette who in my honor had dressed as if she was to meet a distant relative. A certain excitement flooded me at the sight of the remnants of the family that had hounded my grandmother and mother, and which was now unreservedly taking me to its heart.

Mademoiselle Violette was the first to speak. After the usual pleasantries she told me everything she knew about the ring, which caused José Bergman and his wife to raise an eyebrow too. The girls were occupied with their own devices and did not listen to the story. José and his wife did not urge me to take the ring out of my handbag. They simply wanted me to tell my own story of the ring and not leave anything out.

It was only after the girls had gone to their room that José Bergman said it was time for each of us to show the others what they had in their possession. He went into his study and returned with an old, shabby leather satchel, which Mademoiselle Violette had given him after his mother's death, and which he had kept for a long time without daring to throw it away. He handed it to me.

"These are your grandmother's and mother's papers from Danzig."

I looked at him in disbelief as I took the satchel. I asked if I could lay the contents out on the couch where I was sitting.

"Of course, of course," Mauricia replied.

I took out the documents, most of which were written in Yiddish and German, which I couldn't read. Together with them were a few discolored photographs whose sepia tint had faded over the years, but the faces of the subjects were still discernible. They showed the face of a proud, tall woman, her hair drawn back, wearing a simple dress that highlighted her curves. She looked straight ahead with her big round eyes from which sprang great sadness and warmth. In front of her she held a well-dressed little girl with a ribbon in her hair. I recognized them right away. They were my grandmother and mother standing against a painted backdrop in a studio, apparently in Danzig, years before my grandmother sent my mother to Argentine as a young girl to work in Jewish homes.

I couldn't stop the tears filling my eyes. Mauricia handed me a handkerchief and I thanked her, drying my tears as I sat facing those three strangers in their big house on an Argentinean autumn evening, not believing that like this, here, this story would come to an end, but emotional at what I was seeing. Scraps of my lost history, the history of my family, of the women because of whom I and you are here.

Mauricia cleared her throat as if about to ask something, but stopped herself. She didn't have to say a word.

"It's here," I confirmed, reaching into my handbag and taking out the small wooden box. Carefully, I put it onto the table. The three of them moved closer, not daring to reach for the ring, waiting for me to do so.

I opened the box but it was empty. The ring was not inside.

They looked at me and then at one another. Mauricia's face was suffused with a terrible rage that replaced the pleasant expression that had inhabited it throughout the evening. José's brow furrowed as if he were trying to understand the trap I had laid for him. Only Mademoiselle Violette sat frozen and didn't say a word.

"You've deceived us!" Mauricia shouted. "Where's the ring?"

"It was here," I whispered, "I swear it was."

I picked up the box and shook it. As I was doing so Mauricia snatched my leather handbag and emptied it onto the floor, while her husband's face flushed with embarrassment. From the bag cascaded a mirror and mascara, lipstick, a cigarette holder and a few pesos. But no ring. I shook the bag and put my hand inside, trying to find the ring that perhaps lay in a hidden fold, but in vain.

"It can't be," I said. "It was in my bag. I swear."

"I don't know what to say," José said, his voice shaking.

"Just a minute," Eva's voice was suddenly heard. "Bring the child in here."

"What's she got to do with it?" Mauricia asked.

"Who is the ring to go to now? Her, right?" the old woman went on, "So bring her here."

"But there's nothing here," José said.

"She's cheated us," Mauricia said sharply. "There's nothing more to say."

"You know nothing about miracles," the old woman smiled, and called out, "Graciela! Graciela!"

The girl's head popped out of the doorway to the next room.

"Yes, Aunt Eva?"

"Come here a moment, my child," the old woman asked gently.

Graciela went over to her shyly.

"Come, come closer," the old woman encouraged her and put her arms round her. "See this box? Pick it up and shake it, but carefully. It's very old."

The girl picked the box up with both hands that covered it.

"Now shake it," the old woman told her.

The child did so.

We all heard the dull rattle from inside the box.

Eva looked first at us and then at the girl. "Now open the box and put on your finger what you find inside, all right?"

Graciela nodded and opened the box in front of us. The ring lay there in all its glory, its color sparkling and agitated as if it had just been born out of the nothingness.

She extended her finger and put the ring on it. It tightened around her finger, and once more Graciela felt the same forces she had felt when she wore the ring in the old man's shop in Calle Cordoba.

"Ah," the ten-year-old girl whispered, "it's that ring."

"*Si, si,*" the old woman smiled. "Come and sit with us with the ring on your finger."

"I've never seen anything like this," José said, totally bewildered as all the truths he had learned at university collapsed before his very eyes. "Now it's here and then it isn't? How can that be?"

Mauricia didn't say a word, she just looked at me, trying to bury herself in shame for the accusations she had hurled at me earlier.

"It's all right," I said. "I didn't know it was like that either. Never."

"You all forgot one thing," Eva said quietly. "This is no ordinary ring. It is intended solely for whoever it was fashioned, for someone suffering from that illness."

"But how was it visible to my mother and Señor Kaufmann?" I asked, looking at her as if she would have the answers to all the questions.

"These things have a logic of their own," Eva replied, "but the main thing is that the ring is here now. The question is what shall we do with it."

"I don't know what to say," I said. "It was always clear to me that I would not give up the ring. It's my only legacy from my mother and my grandmother who I never knew. But until this moment I also didn't know what this ring really is. And if it is only visible to someone with the falling sickness, then I'm completely confused because I have never had an attack."

"You said you've got a daughter," Eva interrupted.

I had not contemplated that possibility.

"She's healthy," I replied, no longer sure of anything, only wanting to get up and flee that house filled with a strange atmosphere of sorcery. The chandelier turned in a draught that suddenly came in from outside even though the windows were closed, and caused flickers of light to be cast from it, a shower of sparks of light thrown onto the walls of the whole room.

"Look," Mauricia whispered.

And indeed, the chandelier was actually dancing above us in a slow movement as if a hidden hand was turning it, casting illusions of magical light all around.

"What has happened here this evening is with good reason," Eva said. "I can feel them around us right now. Bella, your mother. The chandelier is turning for a reason."

"I can't be far away from the ring," I whispered. "It's all I have for my and my daughter's security."

"And where is your daughter?" she asked.

"At the orphanage. I can't raise her at home."

José and Mauricia looked at one another wordlessly.

"Esperanza, I have a proposal for you," José said.

I raised my eyes to him.

"We are well-to-do," he said. "We'll rent an apartment for you and your daughter and pay you a monthly salary. That is if you live near us and our daughter can wear the ring under your supervision."

Mauricia looked at her husband in admiration of his resourcefulness and generosity.

"How can I?" I murmured. "You know who I am and what I do."

"That's none of our business," José interrupted. "Your destiny is your destiny. But our daughter must be saved, your daughter is entitled to a home and an education, and we must put an end to this cycle of blood."

A profound wave of gratitude engulfed me. I suddenly saw you in my mind's eye not as a bitter young girl growing up in an orphanage, but as a happy, well-dressed girl going to high school every day, and later to university. I was filled with great optimism. Now, I told myself, the ring will be beneficial not in the hidden future, but here and now.

They could see my excitement.

"You're a brave and dear woman," Eva said quietly, taking my hand. "God will reward you for it."

"I don't know what to say," I replied, giddy from all the good I could suddenly see, the good I would obtain for you through the ring.

"You don't have to say anything," José said, "and so that you know that my intentions are completely sincere, I will also return the ring to you."

He tried to remove the ring from his daughter's finger.

"What are you doing?" Mauricia asked.

"What must be done," he replied. "It has belonged to all of us for a long time."

With all his might he tried to remove the ring from Graciela's finger but she cried out in pain.

"You need soapy water," Mauricia said, and went into the kitchen to return with a small bowl filled with soapy water. Her daughter dipped her hand into the water, held her finger, removed the ring easily and proffered it to her parents.

"Not to us, to her," her father said gently, gesturing at me. "She owns the ring now."

I returned the damp ring to its box.

"Can I go now?" Graciela asked in a new, revived voice.

"Yes," her father replied, "go and play."

The girl rejoined her sisters in the other room. We were alone once more.

"Thank you very much for your offer," I said. "I'll have to think about it."

"What's to think about?" Mauricia blurted.

"I'm sure you'll find the right thought within you," José said gently.

I thanked them and began replacing the papers in the old satchel.

"No, not that," José said quickly, "first inform us of your decision."

I looked at him, momentarily surprised, and then nodded. His action had aroused my confidence in his proposal and in him. I left their house somewhat light of heart, but thoughtful. I thought about our future, Flora, especially your future.

At the time I could not have predicted what struggles we would have to contend with before the tale of the ring came to an end.

Seventy-three

Life has taught me that people's generosity is always temporary and limited. Although I had accepted their proposal and regained you, I kept the apartment on Avenida Leandro N. Alem for business purposes. That way I was able to completely separate my occupation from my life with you, and you were able to live in a nice neighborhood with youngsters your own age.

A short time after we moved to La Paternal you asked me to register you at the public library. You began going there almost every day, and as you walked slowly home you had already started reading the first of the three books that the librarians allowed you to take out because they were amazed by your passion for reading. You'd spend hours on end reading, not girls' books, but novels by the great authors, poetry, philosophy, building yourself a world in which I had no foothold.

I realized only years later that what had seemed like a wonderful acquisition of knowledge had become a kind of defiance against me.

You had enough years to accept things as they are without thoughts of censuring or despising me, either in private or publicly. You quietly accepted the money I gave you without wondering where it came from. Only I knew that every banknote I gave you, either rolled up or carefully folded, was my profit from hurried sex with strangers. You were young and I had no reason to give you all the details.

It was only much later I understood that you were spinning tales in your silences. What stories your fertile imagination invented about your origins, your parents' origins and their occupations. You yourself believed them and whenever somebody disproved part of them you would immediately repair it with a patch of a different story, trying with all your might to repair the tears in your scraps of fiction, a false version of reality that was rescued from destruction only with the immediate invention of a different story to replace it.

Back then I didn't realize that your tendency toward fabrication was not a gift of God, and that what seemed so enchanting to me, like your ability to fill notebooks with the stories and poems you wrote, was nothing more than the other side of a curse: the curse of a person only capable of living in the worlds of imagination she weaves for herself just because she is incapable of facing up to reality.

It turned out that reality did actually knock on your door in the form of remarks and name-calling by boys and girls at school because you were the only child of an unmarried mother who worked at the far end of the city.

What they needed to verify their suspicions came a bit at a time through rumors, and then they started calling you "the whore's daughter", which was something you never told me and I only learned about years later, when it was already too late to repair the damage it caused you.

Meanwhile you chose another form of defense. You kept yourself completely isolated from contact with men.

I was dumbstruck when I heard about this. But more than I was dumbstruck by it, I was stunned by the way I found out about it.

I came home from another hard day, my feet aching, and I called your name. There was no answer. I was sure you were again immersed in your reading, and in the most natural way possible I went to your room and opened the door to tell you I was home and see how you were.

I found you in bed with a girl I didn't know, a young woman with cropped hair and a tiny rounded body.

For a woman like me anything to do with love is not completely strange. It also wasn't the first time I'd seen two women together. But there'd always been a man there who'd solicited them to perform the act for his sexual gratification. But here there were just the two of you, alone, you and your love that you'd nurtured in secret.

I stood in the doorway feeling my heart being torn apart inside me. You detached yourselves, the strange girl quickly buttoned her shirt, hiding her small breasts from me, and fled.

I didn't say a word. I gave you a hard look, turned round and left the room, went into the kitchen without turning on the light, sat down at the table, and lay my head on my arms.

I was so shocked by what I had seen, wondering if I were to blame for all this and where it had come from, so I didn't hear you leaving the house.

414

Seventy-four

At the end of March 1976 the junta embarked on its dirty war against what it called Jewish subversives, which meant wealthy Jews. A few days later I received an urgent call from José who arranged to meet me at a restaurant in San Telmo.

I got there at 7.30 in the evening. The restaurant was almost empty. A heavily-built man was sitting with two elegant waiters arranging silverware in paper napkins. Another man emerged from the kitchen with a tray piled high with cuts of meat that he lay on the *parilla* where the flames didn't reach so they'd be ready later that evening. The voice of one of the new singers could be heard in the background.

José came in looking like he'd seen a ghost. He was wrapped in a long gray raincoat, his face tragic, alarm in his eyes. Right away I realized that something bad had happened to him. He came over to my table and stood there.

The brawny waiter, dressed in threadbare pants and a white shirt tight against his big belly, got up and came over to us.

"We'll sit upstairs," José told him.

"Upstairs is closed. It's only open at night," the waiter replied.

"Then we'll sit in the back," José said.

The waiter smiled. He must have thought we were having a lovers' assignation. He walked behind us until we sat down at an isolated table, put down two menus and left. I was hungry. I allowed myself to eat out only infrequently. I picked up the menu to see what it offered. I wanted a portion of tender meat like *bife de lomo al punto*, well done.

"Would you like to order?" I asked, offering him the second menu.

"We haven't got time for that," he replied tersely.

"Are you in a hurry?"

"I've come to warn you. They're going into Jews' houses looking for anything that's evidence of social or political activity."

"They're looking for dissidents, not whores," I replied.

"You can never know when it might happen to you," he said. "They were in my clinic this morning."

I grasped his hand. "What do they want from you? You're just a doctor!"

"For them I'm the son of wealthy Jews who chose to live in a poor neighborhood and treat the disadvantaged. For them that sounds suspicious, leftist," he said, and then told me that armed men had burst into his clinic that morning and turned it upside down, going through patients' files, looking for who he'd treated and whether there were suspicious names among them. And they'd promised to return.

"It sounds to me that you're the one who should get out of here, and fast," I said.

"It's too late... they've taken my wife, Mauricia."

"Where have they taken her?" I asked, my voice rising involuntarily.

He silenced me with a gesture.

"No one can hear us," I told him.

"At times like this even the walls have ears," he replied. "They confiscated my telephone book. They'll get to you too. You've got to take your daughter and get away from here!"

"Where to?"

"Montevideo," he replied curtly, picking up his coat and leaving through the back door.

"Would you like to order?" the waiter surprised me a moment later.

"Roasted *morones, bife de lomo al punto*, a carafe of water and one of the house wine," I fired at him.

"And the señor?"

"He had to leave. I'm on my own."

He nodded and went to the kitchen.

Signs of the revolution were apparent on the streets. Troops were posted on every corner, stopping passersby and demanding to see their papers. But they mainly stopped people who looked like they might be likely suspects in subversive activity. Long-haired youngsters, students in jeans or men who were obviously laborers and possibly members of an anti-government trade union. What did they have to do with a Jewish doctor, I asked myself, and would they really come and search my home, and where had they taken his wife and what were they doing to her, and why.

After a while the waiter brought a basket of sliced bread to my table, and a dish of roasted peppers in olive oil and vinegar. I started eating, smacking my lips with the wonderful taste of the *morones*. The waiter came back with my main course, the *bife de lomo al punto*. From the plate rose the fine aroma of cooked meat mingled with the delicate fragrance of spring onions. I bit into the tender meat with gusto as the restaurant gradually filled up with diners. *Porteño* families, couples, and people on their own.

There was a sudden uproar in the front section of the restaurant. All the diners stopped eating and apprehensively looked at what was happening: men in plain clothes and carrying Uzi submachine guns were moving from table to table checking papers.

Three long-haired youngsters, one of them a woman, quickly got up and fled through the back door. A moment later shouts, the sound of blows, and cries were heard. Plain-clothes detectives waiting there loaded them onto a waiting truck to take them to an unknown destination.

The armed men moved into the rear section of the restaurant where I was sitting, intentionally straight-backed to show them I was not afraid, that I had nothing to hide. They went from table to table demanding the diners' papers. Those without papers were dragged outside to the waiting truck. One woman, the mother of one of the three youngsters, started shouting and tried to stop the armed men taking her son. One of them shoved her roughly, throwing her to the ground.

"Be grateful we're only taking your son, señora," he told her, and then turned to me.

"Papers."

I put my hand into my bag with demonstrative slowness. He snatched the bag from my hands and emptied it onto the table among the dirty dishes. From it fell a lipstick, other items of makeup, and a pack of *preservativos*. My identity card also fell onto the table.

The armed man glanced at the items from my bag, looked at me, and smiled.

"Is the señora working?" he asked.

"Only at home," I replied, "here I eat."

My answer apparently amused him. He burst out laughing and moved on to the next table.

I quickly gathered up my things and left. On the paving stones of Calle Bolivar, at the rear entrance to the restaurant, I saw a pool of fresh blood. They had obviously hit someone who had refused to get onto the truck.

I hurried up the street, the smell of danger in my nostrils. The raid had clearly demonstrated José's warning. I wasn't thinking about myself, but about you. I didn't want you to disappear like the youngsters who had been dragged onto the truck.

At that moment I resolved to do what all the women in our family had done before me – to get their daughters away from any danger and distress, whatever that act might cost.

I began thinking about ways of getting you out of Argentina to Israel.

Seventy-five

It was only two weeks later that Mauricia Bergman was sent home. During that fortnight she had been held in a cell at the naval mechanics school, ESMA, at the other end of the city, where she was tortured with burning cigarettes and then electric shocks applied to her private parts.

The name of the *Ficena* was well known as opposing the regime even during Peron's rule, and anyone speaking about it made the junta think she was connected to their regime's opponents.

I remember the day she came home very clearly. It was a wintry day at the end of August. I remember that day because of the cries of José and his daughters when they saw their wife and mother thrown out of a military vehicle at their door, her face battered and her body defiled and wounded. It was then I understood exactly what I had to do.

Two days later I was sitting on a park bench in Palermo in the bright, cold, winter sunshine, wrapped up in my heavy coat.

In the tuff-filled square there were tall margosa trees from whose foliage the twittering of the birds filled the square, while pigeons collected scraps of food from the small red stone houses. Had I not been waiting for a document forger I might have enjoyed the scene.

A man with a fear-inspiring dog came into the square and began walking round it. Two homeless people were sitting on the grass at the other side. And now a man wrapped in a long coat was crossing the road and it seemed like he was walking toward me.

He was quite tall, his hair combed back, and his face expressionless. He approached me, his breath steaming in the freezing air.

"Señora Gantz?"

"Have you got what I asked for?"

He looked around, checking that he hadn't been followed, and from his inside pocket took two faded identity cards.

I opened them and checked them. One bore your photograph and the other mine. They were both stamped with the ministry of the interior stamp and were undamaged.

"They look authentic," I said.

"It's my profession," he replied.

I took out the money I had ready for him. He took it and quickly put it in his coat pocket.

"Aren't you going to count it?" I asked.

"I've got a good eye for people," he smiled. "Get away from here as quickly as you can. The documents are stolen," he added, and walked away rapidly.

I'd got to him on a friend's recommendation. He was the best forger in the city. From the moment I heard that the junta's blacklist had reached Uruguay and Chile it was clear that we would have to cross the river to Montevideo with forged documents so that the Uruguayan authorities would not extradite us.

In Montevideo I put you on a plane for Israel and promised you that I'd follow soon, once I'd wound up my affairs in the city. I never imagined what else would happen here during the junta's rule, and how long it would be before I saw you again.

Seventy-six

When I finally reached Israel I found you changed beyond my expectations. You'd become a tall woman, your hair black and tied back in braids that fell past your shoulders. You were wearing glasses and your eyes seemed smaller because of the crows' feet at their corners. Your face was pale, your thin lips pursed. You already had a small double chin revealing a certain flaccidness, the marks of time. You were wearing an elegant pantsuit and flat-heeled shoes.

You told me that you didn't patronize people with your dress and you only wore jewelry when necessary.

You weren't alone when I met you, you were with your partner. You introduced her as a sculptor who had recently immigrated to Israel from Buenos Aires.

You showed me pictures of her work, bronze sculptures cast in plaster molds, and they were all characterized by the same thing – they were hollow. Both the female and male figures she had sculpted were fashioned in empty loops of bronze that embraced the emptiness, the nothingness. At first, your partner told me on seeing my astonishment at the sculptures that she had tended to sculpt female figures bent into themselves. Then she started tearing lumps of material from inside them to void them of their essence and create recesses of loss within them.

For a long time I looked at her with my old eyes, listening to her unhurried Spanish, refusing to believe what my eyes had seen. In the end I decided to find out if it was only memory and time that were playing tricks on me.

"Was there anything in your childhood associated with a ring?" I asked cautiously.

"What ring?" she asked.

"A healing ring."

You looked at me puzzled, not knowing what I was talking about.

"When I was little my parents used to put a ring on my finger which they said cured me of epilepsy," she said.

"Are you sick, Graciela?" you asked her, surprised.

"No," your partner chuckled, "I had a few attacks when I was a child."

"What do you know about that ring?" I asked, hoping not to shock you both with what was gradually materializing before my eyes. Precisely here in Israel you had found yourselves uniting our two families in a way that none of us could ever have imagined.

"My father never told me anything about it. But after he died a friend of his sent me a letter with the tale of the ring, which according to him was the very ring I had worn as a child."

I asked her to tell me her story.

"My father's friend," she began, "was a ministry of finance official, an obsessive collector of jewelry, most of it antique women's jewelry he'd found in pawnshops and at auctions of antique art works.

"One day, he wrote, he went to a pawnshop on Calle Cordoba that he'd never before visited. On entering the shop, which he said was steeped in the magic of antiquity, his eyes lit on an amazing ring, a sort of total manifestation of beauty and grace, healing and yearning and authority.

"He went over to the owner, a young man who had inherited the shop from his father, and asked its price. The pawnbroker begged his pardon. 'That ring,' he said, 'is not for sale. It's in the window simply to remind its owner to come and redeem it.'

"The collector couldn't tear his eyes away from the ring. He chanced his arm and named a very large sum. But the pawnbroker shook his head.

"'Señor,' he said, 'this ring is a pledge. It must be returned to its owner. I do not have the right to give it to anyone else.'

"My father's friend," Graciela went on, "was so curious about this reply, which was unexpected from the lips of a pawnbroker, that he began questioning him about the ring.

"The pawnbroker told him that a few years earlier, at the time of the junta, his father of blessed memory had been visited by a woman he knew. She was pale and fearful, a little like the quarry of hunters that didn't know for how much longer she would be able to evade them, and had asked his father to re-pawn the ring and a scroll that was attached to it. She didn't name a sum wanted for this item that in the past had been pawned with his father, she took what she was given, gave him the ring, and disappeared. He hadn't seen her again. He didn't know whether or not she'd been murdered by the junta but he waited for her. He was sure that one day she, or someone on her behalf, would return and redeem the pledge. He had promised his father of blessed memory, who had kept the ring before him, that he would do so too.

"The collector begged the pawnbroker to allow him to inspect the ring. The pawnbroker motioned him to follow him into the back room of the shop. He asked him to sit down on the other side of the wooden desk, and passed him the ring and the paper.

"The collector sat in the pawnshop for a long time. Evening fell, the street noises gradually faded. He was totally immersed in reading and did not notice how the pawnbroker's face was slowly vanishing into the darkness, and how his figure was losing its form.

"When he had finished reading he knew that he was in the depths of an unimagined experience: the pawnbroker had disappeared together with the ring and the genealogical record. He found himself sitting in the middle of Buenos Aires on a chilly night, on a park bench, fully aware that he had been in a pawnshop in Calle Cordoba and seen there a most exquisite object whose record cautioned that it would alternately disappear and reappear. But the record had not warned him that the amazing ring possessed not only the ability to disappear and reappear as it wished, but also the ability to make its surroundings disappear too."

Graciela ended her story and smiled at me. I sat there, totally immersed in myself.

"Why did you tell me this story?" I asked, my voice shaking.

"Because you asked me to," she laughed. "But don't take it so badly, Señora Gantz. It's only a piece of fiction, one of those attached to antique objects."

"I don't think so," I said, moderating my reply as much as I was able.

"I presume that my father's friend wove this story while he was at an antique shop, or perhaps a museum of Jewish art," Graciela went on in the clear-minded tone that so characterized her grandmother, Bella Bergman.

She tried to turn this wonderful story into what she did with her works: create them whole and then tear out their insides. What she had related was indeed the whole truth. I am the one who re-pawned the ring with Señor Kaufmann in order to buy you a new life with the proceeds.

With the money I got for it I sent you to Israel.

I suddenly felt a deep sorrow, an old and profound sorrow, engulfing me completely. Sorrow for all of us, for you two, for the ring, which I didn't know if I would ever see again.

"It's all true," I said quietly, "it was me who gave him the ring."

"What?" you asked in amazement. "What are you talking about?"

"It's our story, Flora," I replied, "it's thanks to the ring that you're both alive, you're both here."

"Nonsense," Graciela laughed, "they're just stories."

I raised my eyes to her, scrutinizing her. I realized that she had forgotten our meeting in her childhood, in her parents' home.

"Do you remember a bronze statuette made by some Italian sculptor that was in your parents' house?" I asked her.

Graciela paled. "It's the only thing I took with me when I immigrated to Israel. It's all that remains from my parents' home," she whispered. "It's because of that statuette that I began sculpting."

I started to tell them both the tale of the ring.

The ring I had re-pawned at Señor Kaufmann's pawnshop saved you from the junta and it kept my sanity over all the years I waited until I was able to immigrate to Israel. It was like an anchor of a distant family tradition, a kind of guarantee that the day would come when I would return to you, and on that day it would swallow, like a great eraser, all the years that had passed since we parted. I had hoped that the ring would allow me to live the rest of my life in peace, with you, in a country that is no more mine than it is its children's. But I was wrong. Right after hearing the tale of the ring from me, you resolved to go back to Buenos Aires, reclaim the ring – and with it get married.

Seventy-seven

There are stories that start with good and stories that start with evil. There are stories that make do with little, like in Sedlec, and there are stories with a hunger that cannot be satisfied, and so they swallow up Sedlec and Danzig, and then travel over the sea to other countries and other cities, and after finishing them off too they again go out, by sea or air, until they reach here. That is what happened to this story, which began in Sedlec and ended in Israel, and whose beginning is in a ring.

But this ring possesses a kind of magic that cannot exist here in Israel.

There are different enchantments here. This is a country of small enchantments. Life is stressful, the heat blurs the senses. In air like this great miracles do not grow. Demons need a great darkness in which to evolve. Here, too, there are cities where demons dwell. But here the cities are new and the demons are imported, brought in by Jews from their countries of origin.

When great magic is done here it drives people mad and kills them young. Here you have to disenchant people from all kinds of magic offered to them by the politicians, and get them used to the smaller magic, the signs of the universe embodied in coincidences, new patterns of order beneath the surface of reality.

Even in the Levant there is fiction and illusion, and here too people are longing for a miracle. But the true miracle is found a long way from here. In order to see your story in full you had to travel, to go all the way back. To discover the truth.

When you come back with the ring I will no longer be here. The ring will become the subject of the story of a world that no longer exists, and perhaps never did, because its nature is to be passed on by rumor. It can't be seen, and even if a trace of it can, then it is only a remnant of what was once an entire world.

But things recur, stories that take place generations later are suddenly revealed as the other side of old stories. Fate, which seemed to act randomly, illusively, blindly – reveals is true nature. In the perspective of time one can see that it thrives, orderly and consistent, on foundations laid at the basis of reality, but only the way of visible things is evident. Man's desire, his actions, and the fruit they bear.

Writing this book helped me to observe the ring's nature which in our lifetime created its terrifying dance and left its mark on each of us. The more I wrote, I lost the certainty about the reality of things and their actual existence. I was borne into a black pit together with the subjects of this story, spinning together with them in the open maw of a world, without being able to separate us again. What seemed to be a chronicle of two families became a pleasurable work of fiction whose relationship with the truth is unclear. Who I was and who the two of you are, what was my story and what was yours, what really happened and what never did. These are questions with which you will remain. This book will serve its purpose by giving you a past and the materials of memory, and will illustrate for you from whence you came.

I have tried to live my life as I understood it, and with every fiber of my being I wanted to finish this book and give it to you as a kind of testimony, as a reference map to a forgotten, repressed past that is attacked by the authorities of memory of the community, the people, and this country, who have taken it upon themselves to cleanse memory, to sieve it, and have thus left out of it entire life cycles of joy and pain. But in the end I must admit that there is nothing here but the tale itself, the narrative. And perhaps the tale is the thing, and there is nothing else. In other words, by its very nature reconstruction of the past is doomed to be partial and flawed. As splendid and distinguished though it might be, in the end it will remain a failure. Because you cannot describe the past without its subjects, the people who lived it as a present, and with their passing we were entrusted with creating in this world our brief and cruel dance of life, until we too leave it with only a certain degree of knowledge. Who we were, what we did, for whom, for what.

Sit down, read the tale of the ring, and remember: all is one. One generation follows another. We follow our mothers. The time is the same time and there is no difference between what was and what will be. If you raise your eyes from this book you will be able to see not only Buenos Aires and Danzig, but also the *kleizmers* of Sedlec, one holding his bow and another his flute and another his mouth organ, and they are playing the same sad tune, the tune of every Jew that is composed of the weeping of many generations.

Acknowledgments

My grateful thanks go to my friend Ziva Weinshall who told me the kernel of the tale of the ring; Fabiana Hefetz who told me something of the story of Zwi Migdal; Lior Hayyat of the Embassy of Israel in Buenos Aires for his assistance in organizing the tour; Diego Ginesin who helped me with my research in Buenos Aires; Marcus Kashimosky for translating the research material from Spanish to Hebrew and synopsizing it; Isaac Kremer, Larry Levi, Reuven Plotkin, Albert Nieman, Eliahu Toker, Shlomo Slutzky, José Ginesin, and Jaime Cantor, who gave freely of their vast knowledge of the Buenos Aires Jewish community and of the Zwi Migdal affair; Juan de Nardo and Nestor Talento, Santo and Javier from Lugar Gay, for the home they opened to me in the city; Jerman Weismann who introduced me to the city's gay community; Chef Nelson Witskin whose home and friends were a source of joy for me; Anita and Moshe Koren, Damien Saga of AMIA, and a long line of Israelis of Argentinean extraction who shared their recollections with me, including Sara Turel, Hana Schwartzer, Roxana Levinson, Yehudit Friedkin, Pablo Portnoy, Haya Holtzman, Claudio Kogon, and many more. My thanks to Daniel Galay for the contact with the community in Buenos Aires, and for checking the Yiddish in the book; Florinda Goldberg for the scientific editing of the Hebrew manuscript; Adi Nes and David Hay who shared the anguish of the writing, each in his own way and time; my readers, Aviva Talmor and Michal Nathan, whose valuable comments helped me a great deal, and to Aviva for the Spanish course. Thanks to my friend Mitchell Feigenbaum who was with me loyally and devotedly throughout all the versions and stages of writing this book, and who helped me through every stage of its development; and special thanks to my Hebrew editor, Ronit Weiss-Berkowitz – working with her was a wonderful experience.